# The Wicked Redhead

# The Wicked Redhead

## A Wicked City Novel

## Beatriz Williams

HARPER LUXE

*An Imprint of HarperCollinsPublishers*

HarperCollins books may be purchased for educational, business, or sales promotional use. For information, please e-mail the Special Markets Department at SPsales@harpercollins.com.

FIRST HARPERLUXE EDITION

ISBN: 978-0-06-279151-1

HarperLuxe™ is a trademark of HarperCollins Publishers.

Library of Congress Cataloging-in-Publication Data is available upon request.

19 20 21 22 23   LSC   10 9 8 7 6 5 4 3 2 1

*To the memory of those killed and wounded*
*in the Prohibition wars*

# The Wicked Redhead

## New York City, April 1998

The photograph in Ella's hand was about the size of a small, old-fashioned postcard. It had a matte finish, almost like newsprint, and the edges were soft and frayed, as you might expect from a photograph over seventy years old. From anything over seventy years old, really, but especially a photograph of a naked woman.

And what a woman.

She sloped along a Victorian chaise longue, wearing nothing but black stockings and ribbon garters, face turned upward to receive a fall of light from the sky. Miraculous breasts like large, white, dark-tipped balloons. Everything black and white, in fact, except her hair, which was carefully tinted red. Ella couldn't stop staring at her. Nobody with a heartbeat could stop staring at that woman.

And it wasn't her beauty that so transfixed you, because you couldn't really see her face. It wasn't even her incandescent figure, although that was the point of the photograph, wasn't it? That figure. Ella couldn't put a name to this mesmerizing force, except that it began somewhere beneath the milky skin of the woman herself and never really ended. You had the feeling that if you stared long enough, willed hard enough, she would turn her head toward you and say something fabulous. From the wall behind her hung a giant portrait, in which a painted version of the same woman languished on the same sofa, conveying all that sexual charisma in raw, awestruck, primitive brushstrokes. The title at the bottom said Redhead Beside Herself.

Ella turned on her side and traced the curve of the Redhead's hip. No kidding, she thought. Her fingertips buzzed at the contact, but she was used to that, by now. On the bed beside her, Nellie lifted her head and growled softly, and Ella put out her other hand to soothe the dog's ears.

"Nothing to worry about, honey," she said. "Go back to sleep."

But the dog kept growling at the same low, loose pitch, and the photograph buzzed even harder beneath Ella's fingers, like a dial turning right, until Ella forced herself to look up and saw the hands of the clock on the bedside table.

She rolled to her back and stared at the ceiling.

"Damn," she said. "It's time."

**Before she** headed uptown to the offices of Parkinson Peters to get fired, Ella dressed herself carefully in her best charcoal-gray suit and black calfskin pumps. Mumma used to say you should dress for your worst moments as if they were your best. Dad said to scuttle the ship with flags flying. Probably they meant the same thing.

After a fine, cool Sunday, the weather had turned damp overnight, and the smell of urine and vomit stuck to the air of the Christopher Street subway station. Ella sidestepped a puddle of spilled, milky coffee on her way to her spot—directly across the tracks from a peeling movie advertisement—and tried to breathe through her mouth. The film starred Jeff Bridges, looking even more scruffy than usual, locked in some kind of arabesque with an actress dressed in a gladiator outfit. Ella had spent the last month of mornings trying to decide whether the two of them were bowling or ice skating. The question was driving her slowly insane, and now, as she stared at the distant object in Jeff's hands that might or might not be a bowling ball, she thought, At least I won't have to stare at that fucking movie poster anymore. After this morning, she could stand somewhere else on the platform, instead of the particular spot that would put her on the subway car nearest the exit turnstiles at Fiftieth Street, and stare at some other advertisement.

The rails sang. The train roared softly down the tunnel. Burst like an avalanche into the station a moment later, rippling the coffee puddle, and Ella stepped on board and creased her Wall Street Journal into long, vertical folds that doubled back on each other, just as if this were any kind of regular morning, and she was headed for the office. The electronic bell rang its double tone. The doors thumped shut, found some obstacle, thumped again. The train jerked into motion, and Ella, staring at the blur of words in the newspaper column before her, realized that she had no idea what the name of that movie was. Maybe she never would.

At the Fourteenth Street station, the train filled with Brooklynites transferring from the 2 and 3 trains, and Ella, who was already standing, ended up shoved against one of the center poles, pretending to read her vertically folded Wall Street Journal in the alleyway between two thick male arms, belonging to two men in identical navy suits who were probably not going to get fired this morning.

Fired. Canned. Let go. Laid off, dismissed, discharged. Sacked, if you were British. Query: If Ella were working in the London office of Parkinson Peters, would she be sacked? Or could she demand to get fired instead? She refolded the paper to feign reading the second column and decided she would so demand, damn it. You had the right to get axed on your own terms. The train lurched for no reason. Squealed to a stop in the blackened tunnel between Eighteenth Street and Twenty-Third Street. The lights died. The whir of ventilation vanished, and the sudden stillness was like the end of the world. Nobody moved. The whole car just went on staring at its darkened newspapers, staring at the dermatology advertisements on the train walls, staring at ears and hats and backpacks and necks, staring at anything but someone else's stare. Sweating palms on metal poles, submitting to the close-packed indignity of the New York subway. There was a garbled announcement, something about Penn Station. The car came to life, lights and noise and air, and lurched forward again. Ella fixed her gaze to her knuckles. Next to her, the man with the navy jacket sleeve made a slight movement and slipped his hand further up the pole, away from hers.

The train blew into Twenty-Third Street and stood on its brakes. Pitched Ella into the chest of the navy suit guy, who looked at her in horror.

Five more stops. Thirty city blocks between Ella and unemployment.

And her job was the least of her worries.

**In an** unemployment tribunal, which God forbid, Parkinson Peters and its polished, navy-suited lawyers could probably make a reasonable case against Ella. You could always find actionable cause if you wanted to get rid of somebody, after all, and maybe Ella could have been more careful to make absolutely certain Travis Kemp—the managing partner on the Sterling Bates audit—knew that Ella's husband happened to be employed at Sterling Bates, albeit in a wholly different division. She could have reminded Travis of the information on her disclosure form on file with human resources, instead of assuming he'd reviewed it before assigning her to the project. She could have used that opportunity to affirm that her husband, Patrick Gilbert, had no relationship, formal or otherwise, with the activities of the disgraced Sterling Bates municipal bond department, which Parkinson Peters had been hired to audit, and allowed Travis to decide whether Ella should remain on the team.

But none of those actions would have mattered, in the end. Ella's dismissal had nothing to do with any kind of wrongdoing, at least on her part. She'd known that from the moment she hung up the phone with Travis on Friday evening, brimming with tears, brimming with all the physiological symptoms of shock. She was the kind of person who always paid for the apple she dropped in the supermarket instead of putting it back on the stack, who slipped a tip in the Starbucks box even when the barista wasn't looking. She had tagged the unusual pattern of payments at Sterling Bates not because it was her job, but because it was the right thing to do.

Friday night, she'd shook with rage at the injustice of it all.

Not until later did she realize she had bigger things to worry about.

But she couldn't think about that. She couldn't think about Saturday night and she especially couldn't think about Sunday afternoon, because the subway was really cooking now, congestion cleared up ahead, and by the time Ella had finished pretending to read the left two columns of the Wall Street Journal and started feigning the middle one, she was already crashing into Fiftieth Street, brakes squealing, mosaics blurring past, slowing, stilling. In the instant of silence before the doors opened, Ella nearly gagged on the smell of somebody's sausage sandwich.

And then she was free. She burst out into the sour, damp underground and through the turnstiles, up the stairs, clutching her company laptop bag that contained a laptop scrubbed clean of files, clutching her Wall Street Journal in the other hand. She emerged into a chilly mist and checked her watch—seven thirty-nine, way too early, even for Ella—and ducked into a Starbucks to gather herself. Her hair was already curling into a hopeless cloud; she pulled an emergency scrunchie from the outside pocket of her bag and bound the mess back into a ponytail. Found her security pass and cell phone. Saw that she had missed two calls, one from Patrick and one from Hector, who had each called within a minute of the other. Hector had left a voice mail. Patrick, knowing better, had not.

Her husband and her lover. To be clear, her estranged husband and her brand-new lover, but did that matter in the eyes of God? Maybe it did, but waking up yesterday morning, she hadn't felt a shred of guilt. Had instead felt bathed in something like God's mercy, after six mortifying, agonizing weeks.

Now, as she stood before the pickup counter and accepted a latte she didn't really want, Ella thought that maybe she was wrong. That she had bathed in nothing but sexual afterglow, and God was a vengeful God after all. Like Parkinson Peters, punishing her for a crime that belonged to somebody else.

**By any** absolute measure, Ella had woken on Sunday morning in a state of sin. The waking was Nellie's fault, the sin was all her own. Actually, the waking was probably Ella's fault too, since responsibility for the dog's bladder now belonged to her. She'd set aside Nellie's wriggling, investigating body and squinted her eyes at the clock on the bedside table. Eleven minutes past nine. Also, there was a note.

Nellie lunged forward and licked Ella's nose in frantic little strokes.

"All right, all right," Ella had said. Sat up too fast and wobbled. Set her two hands on either side of her bottom and shook her head. Nellie climbed into her lap and stared beseechingly upward. Nothing more soulful than the round black eyes of a King Charles spaniel who needed to pee.

Across the room, the blinds were down over the windows, but the sunlight streaked fearlessly around the edges and illuminated what seemed like acres of Ella's bare flesh. Full, happy breasts. Flushed, decadent skin. Curling, tumbled hair. Ella hadn't examined her naked body in months, maybe even a year or two; she couldn't even remember the last time she performed that ritual of minute, critical, inch-by-inch dissection of flaws, ending in resolve to eat less, exercise more, use moisturizer, buy another push-up bra, maybe reconsider a long-standing personal prohibition against cosmetic surgery. Back then—happily married—she hadn't cared.

More recently—wronged wife—she hadn't dared.

And now? Right that second? Staring down at breasts and stomach and thighs and calves and feet against the wrinkled, disgraceful white sheets? She'd thought she looked pretty damned beautiful.

Pretty damned beautiful. (That was Hector's voice, echoing in her head.)

Hector. She reached for the note. Nellie barked and spun in a desperate circle.

"All right, all right," Ella said again, retracting her hand, and this time she swung her legs over the edge of the bed and rose. The movement made her head slosh. Made her belly swim. Swamped her with the seasick, full-body hangover sensation of a night without sleep, except that unlike actual hangovers, or those following all-nighters spent at work, this malady represented a small price to pay for what had caused it. If you threatened Ella with a lifetime of such wakings, she wouldn't trade away last night. If you erased her memory of the past twelve hours, she would still know it existed, humming in her bones and skin, shimmering down the long lines of her veins, hovering like a ghost inside her—

"I think I'm going to throw up," she told Nellie, and exactly six seconds later she was leaning over the edge of Hector's toilet bowl while Hector's dog watched anxiously from the door.

After vomiting, she'd felt much better, the way you did. Weak but purged. Purged of what, she wasn't sure. Guilt or sin or something, right? After all, she was married.

Except she didn't feel guilty. She was quite sure of that. Ella knew what guilt felt like, and this wasn't it. This was something more complicated, like when you walked onto an airplane headed to a brand-new country and couldn't turn back, adventures waiting before you, and yet somewhere, in the back of your skull, pounded the certainty that you'd forgotten to pack something important. She found a washcloth on the counter and turned on the faucet and wondered whether her husband had barfed, the first time he cheated on her. Aunt Julie had said that Patrick was a congenital cheater; she could smell it on him, the way you smelled garlic on someone who had eaten forty-clove chicken the night before. He'd probably cheated in kindergarten. Kissing Michelle after telling Jennifer he was going to marry her. He was numb to sin. What was that line from Dangerous Liaisons? It only hurts the first time.

Well, Ella didn't hurt at all, that Sunday morning. She didn't regret a minute of the night before.

Nellie's paws grabbed her knee. Bark ended in a whine.

"All right! All right!" Ella said, for the third time. She set down the washcloth and went back into the bedroom, Hector's bedroom, Hector's bed, Hector's simple wooden furniture. On the chair lay her clothes, neatly folded, nowhere near where she had left them last night. In fact, Ella could have sworn she wore not a single stitch by the time Hector carried her from the living room to his bed, and yet here sat all those stitches, reconstituted, primly stacked, bra and panties on top, just as if they hadn't spent the night strewn all over the living room floor.

This time, Ella didn't bother deciding whether Patrick had or had not ever picked up her clothes from the floor after a night of passion. Didn't think of Patrick at all, in fact, as she dressed herself in the clothes Hector had peeled off her body under a high, bright moon and then gathered together again, in the hour before dawn, while Ella lay absolutely expired under the down comforter. She pulled her hair back in the scrunchie Hector had also recovered from the floorboards. Nearby, Nellie chased her nonexistent tail in a kind of canine delirium. Ella slid on her shoes, tucked Hector's note into her pocket, and called for Nellie to follow her into the living room.

By virtue of being related to the landlord, and also by virtue of his own skill at carpentry, Hector had the entire attic floor to himself: bedroom, bathroom, open living room and kitchen. The Sunday sunshine hurtled through the skylight to land in a scintillating rectangle on the kitchen counter, where Nellie's leash and a plastic produce bag lay together with a bottle of water and a key. By now the dog was dancing on her claws. Yipping and begging. Ella leaned down and clipped the leash on her collar. Grabbed the bag and the water and the key as Nellie dragged her like a sled dog toward the door. Together, they raced along the flights of stairs, and Ella was out the vestibule and leaping down the stoop before she realized she hadn't even looked at her own apartment door on the way down. How crazy was that? When that apartment had changed everything. The Redhead's apartment, now hers.

Ella had to run to keep up with Nellie, who was making for a patch of gravel surrounding a tree near the corner, and her stiff muscles begged for mercy, like

that time Ella's sister Joanie had talked Ella into joining a Pilates class. And maybe she wasn't quite that
stiff this morning, not quite so aware of just how many
muscles the human body could contain; maybe her
soreness today was tempered by that sense of marvelous well-being set off by the joyful firecracker in her
belly, the sensation she still couldn't name.

But something else gnawed at her flesh—even
when Nellie, after some investigation, decided on a
spot and hunched down in relief—and Ella, resting
at last, thought that maybe that gnawing came from
her back pocket, where she'd stuffed Hector's note
as she flew out of Hector's apartment. Moreover, she
decided—shifting her balance, blowing on her fingers in the brisk air—the gnawing wasn't because she
missed him, although she did. She missed him the
way you might miss a bone, if you woke up to find it
missing from your arm or leg or rib cage. She missed
kissing him and laying her hands on him in utter freedom, in the way they had finally done last night, the
dam breaking at last under the pressure of Ella's distress, but that wasn't all; just being with Hector, just
laughing with him and playing piano with him and
lying on the floor staring through the skylight with
him. She could live without the sex long before she
could live without any of that.

She missed him, yes, she missed everything about him.

But the thing was—and Nellie was setting off again, full of purpose, and Ella had to force her legs to move— the thing was, when she woke up this morning, alone in Hector's bed, she was kind of glad he wasn't there.

And the note? Gnawing from the safety of her back pocket? She wasn't in any hurry to read it.

**Hector had** left two other voice mails on Ella's cell phone, one Sunday afternoon around the time he must have landed in Los Angeles, and one in the evening. Both of them untouched, the same as Hector's note, and just like Hector's note the cell phone now went inside the front pocket of Ella's laptop bag. She couldn't listen to Hector's voice right now, any more than she could look at Hector's handwriting. He was probably frantic with worry, and still she couldn't bring herself to hear those words, read those words, return his call and hear him speak more words. Not because she was guilty. Not because she didn't care. Not because she didn't long to hear Hector read the entire fucking Manhattan telephone directory in her ear, in the same way she longed to breathe.

Ella tried the latte. Too hot. She set it down and checked her watch—seven forty-eight—and decided she might as well get it over with. Lifted her laptop bag from the counter stool and walked out the door, forgetting all about the latte left on the counter until she was pushing her way through the glass revolving door of the Parkinson Peters building on Fifty-Second Street and Sixth Avenue and wondered why her right hand was so empty.

**To Ella's** surprise, her security pass still worked. She spilled through the turnstile, in fact, because she'd been expecting it to stay locked. So maybe forgetting that latte was an act of mercy; it would have sloshed right up through the mouth hole and over her suit if she'd been holding it. What a disaster that would have been, right?

Fortunately, the lobby was still empty at this hour, and only the security guy noticed Ella's misstep. Most of the Parkinson Peters staff wandered in around eight thirty, though you were expected to stay as late as it took, and certainly past six o'clock if you wanted a strong review at the end of the year. And that was just when you were on the beach, between assignments, performing rote work in the mother ship. (The cabana, if you didn't want to mix your metaphors.) Ella crossed the marble floor like she owned it—that was the only way to walk, Mumma had taught her—and pressed the elevator button. While she waited, somebody joined her, and for an instant made eye contact in the reflection of the elevator doors. A woman Ella didn't recognize, dressed in a charcoal-gray suit similar to hers. Nice suit, Ella wanted to say, a final act of transgression while she still had the chance. But of course she didn't say it. There was no point. Ella thought she had a finite amount of rebellion inside her, which she had used up considerably on Saturday night, and she didn't want to waste any of the remainder. Unless rebellion was the kind of thing that fed on itself. Unless breaking the minor code of elevator silence—they had boarded the car by now, rushing upward to the thirty-first floor, where Ella was shortly to be made an ex-employee of Parkinson Peters—unless committing that misdemeanor gave her the courage to break other, larger rules, a courage that she was shortly going to need in spades. In which case—

But it was too late. The elevator stopped at the twenty-fourth floor and the woman and her suit departed forever. Ella continued on to the thirty-first floor and unlocked the glass door to the Parkinson Peters offices with her pass. Strode to an empty cubicle, dropped her bag by the chair, went to the kitchen, and poured herself a cup of coffee to replace the one she had left behind at Starbucks. The room was in the center of the building and had no windows. The fluorescent light cast a sickly, anodyne glow, so that even the new granite countertops looked cheap. Ella was stirring in cream when an apologetic voice called her name from the door. She turned swiftly, spilling the coffee on her hand.

"Ella? I'm so sorry." It was Travis's assistant, Rainbow, crisp and corporate in her Ann Taylor suit and cream blouse. Ella always imagined a pair of hippie parents serving her Tofurky at Thanksgiving and wondering where they had gone wrong. "Mr. Kemp asked me to send you to his office as soon as you came in."

Ella turned to reach for a paper towel. "I'll be just a minute, thanks."

She took her time. Cleaned up the spill and washed her hands. Stuck a plastic lid on the coffee cup and took it to her desk, so she could drink it later. Her hand, carrying the coffee, setting it down on the Formica surface, remained steady. The nausea had passed. She unzipped her laptop bag and took out a leather portfolio, a yellow legal pad, and the Cross pen she used for business meetings, the one her father had given her when she first landed the job at Parkinson Peters, and as she walked down the passageway between the cubicles, it seemed to her that she could hear his proud voice as he gave it to her, Ella, his firstborn. Use it for good, he'd said, wagging the box. There's power in this.

She reached Travis's office, which was not on the corner but two offices down—he'd only made partner a few years ago—and knocked on the door.

"It's open," said Travis, in a voice that was neither stern nor angry, and in fact sounded as if he'd just been sharing a joke.

So Ella pushed the door open and discovered she was right. He had been sharing a joke—or at least some pleasant morning banter—with a muscular man sitting confidently in the chair before the desk.

Ella's husband.

Before she even comprehended that it was Patrick, before her eyes connected with her brain and lit the red warning light, he was bounding up from the chair and kissing her cheek. "Well, hello there, Ella," he said, just as if they'd woken up in bed together this morning, as if he still owned the right to her kisses.

"Patrick? What the hell are you doing here?"

There was a brief, nervous pause. Patrick took a step back and laughed awkwardly. Ella looked from him to Travis, Travis looked from her to Patrick. He was jiggling a pen in his left hand, and an artsy, black-and-white photograph of his family smiled over his shoulder. The sight of it, for some reason, maybe its black-and-whiteness, made Ella think of Redhead Beside Herself. She turned back to Patrick and said, Well?

He tried to lay an arm around her shoulders, but she edged to the side.

"I'm here for you, babe," he said. "I heard what happened on Friday."

"How? Who told you?"

He shrugged. He was smiling—Patrick had one of those room-lighting smiles, it was part of his arsenal—and Ella realized he wasn't wearing a suit. Just a pair of chinos and a navy cashmere sweater over a button-down shirt of French blue. He looked like he was off to race yachts or something.

"Just heard from someone at work," he said. "I tried to call you this weekend, but you weren't answering. So I came down here this morning to see my man Kemp and explain."

Travis had turned his attention to some papers on his desk during this exchange, making notes in his quick, tiny handwriting that had always confounded Ella. But she could see that his ears were wide open. His neck was a little flushed above his white collar. He was going to tell his wife all about this tonight.

Ella folded her arms. "Explain what?"

"I quit my job," Patrick said.

"You what?"

"I quit. Tendered my resignation over the weekend."

"This is a joke, right?"

Patrick shook his head. Still smiling. "Nope. I figured if one of us had to take a fall, it should be me. You didn't do anything wrong."

"Neither did you."

"Well, then call me a gentleman."

"Ella," said Travis, looking up from his papers, "I got your husband's email over the weekend and discussed the matter on the partner call this morning, and we've agreed to keep you on at Parkinson Peters. You'll be moved to a different project—"

"No," she said.

If she'd taken a pistol from her pocket and fired a bullet through the window, the two men would probably have been less startled. The pen dropped from Travis's hand and smacked on the desk.

"No, what? No, you want to stay on the Sterling Bates audit? I'm afraid—"

"I mean, no, I don't want to stay at all." Ella opened up her leather portfolio and removed a sheet of paper. Set it on the desk in front of her, edges exactly straight. "My resignation letter."

"Jesus," said Patrick.

Travis stared at the letter and said, Well.

Ella snapped the portfolio shut. "So that's that. I'll stop by HR with a copy for them—"

"Can I ask where you're going?" Travis said, looking up from the letter. He gathered up the pen and started clicking the end. His eyes were bright and narrow. "Who's recruited you? Deloitte?"

"No one."

"You're not moving somewhere else?"

"No."

Travis sat back in his chair, still clicking the pen. He bounced a few times, causing the chair to squeak. His window faced east, and the gray sun balanced at the back of his head. Between the buildings, where Queens should be, there was nothing but cloud. His lips stretched into a smile.

"Can I ask what you're planning to do?" he said, in a tone of absolute pity.

Ella returned her portfolio under her arm and smiled back. "Nope," she said, and walked out the door, right past her dumbstruck husband.

**But Patrick** never stayed dumbstruck. He always had something to say. He chased her down the corridor of cubicles and caught up when she reached the one she'd claimed with her suit jacket.

"Ella," he said, "wait."

"I have nothing to say to you."

"Did you get my flowers?"

She turned. "First of all, how did you get my address? From my family?"

"No." He hesitated. "From Kemp."

"Oh my God. How illegal is that?"

"We're still married, Ella. I have the right to know where you're living."

"And I have the right to get a restraining order, if I need to."

He took her elbow and spoke in a low, heartfelt voice. "Don't. It doesn't need to be like this. Come home, Ella, please. I mean, seriously. You left our place for some shithole in the Village?"

"I left you because you were cheating on me, and it's not a shithole. It's—" She stopped herself before she said magical. "It's a special building."

"It's a dump. You can't live there. It doesn't even look safe."

Ella removed his hand from her elbow and reached for her suit jacket. "It's the safest place I've ever lived, and I'm not moving anywhere, especially not with you."

"For God's sake, Ella. I just quit my job for you! Managing director at Sterling Bates, and I threw it all away just to prove to you—"

"Look. I don't know the real reason you quit the bank, Patrick, but I'm pretty sure I wasn't it. This conversation is over. You'll be hearing from my lawyer pretty soon. As they say." She dodged his reaching hands and slung her laptop bag over her shoulder. Headed for the elevators, followed by every pair of eyes on the floor, and she didn't care! Maybe a little, but not really. Didn't care, for once, that everyone in the office had just heard the soap opera that was Ella Gilbert's life. That her husband had cheated on her—too bad she had no time to rehash for them the full story, the visceral details, the grunting-sweating-banging of an orange-skinned hooker in the stairwell of their own apartment building—and that, as a result, Ella was divorcing him. Omigod, poor Ella, did you hear? She passed Rainbow, whose awed eyes followed her all the way to the glass doors, while Patrick followed, saying something, some blur of words.

As she found the door handle, Patrick reached out to cover her hand.

"Ella, you can't just cut me out of your life," he said in her ear.

She stared at Patrick's hand, his left hand. The gold wedding band that circled his ring finger, engraved on the inside (she knew this because she had ordered it herself, picked out the Roman lettering as both traditional and masculine) EVD TO PJG, 6*13*96. He had nearly lost it on their honeymoon. Nearly lost it while they were swimming together off some beach in Capri, because a ring was such a new, unfamiliar object to him, and he kept jiggling it on his finger like a toy hoop. Off it came. He was distraught. Dove for it, again and again, even though Ella begged him to stop because each time he plunged under the water and the seconds ticked by, panic took hold of her stomach. Then he came up at last, triumphant, brandishing the plain gold band between his thumb and forefinger like he'd recovered some pirate's diamond from the seabed. Salt water dripping from his skin. He handed Ella the ring and made her put it back on his finger, right there in the chest-deep water, and she did as he asked, wiggling it all the way down to his knuckle. He'd snaked his arms around her waist. "That's the last time," he said, when he was done kissing her, which took some time. "It's never coming off again. You'll have to bury me with that ring on my finger."

And now, here they were. Ella stared down at the shining band that reflected the fluorescent office lights, at his big hand covering hers, and she remembered thinking, in the sunlit moment while she kissed Patrick on that beach, how lucky she was. How lucky she was to have found a man who loved her so much.

With her own left hand, which contained neither engagement ring nor wedding band, she plucked Patrick's fingers away.

"Honestly, Patrick?" she said softly. "I don't think we have anything left to say to each other."

**A quarter** of an hour later, Ella pondered this lie as she sat on a Starbucks stool, drinking a fresh latte to replace the one she'd left behind earlier. Her phone buzzed from her laptop bag. She waited for the buzzing to stop, waited for another minute or two after that, and then she tilted the bag toward her and plucked the phone free. Hector again. She put her fingers to her temple and stared at the screen, Hector's name—just that single word, Hector, formed of tiny green LED lights, followed by his phone number—until it blinked out. Until her ribs ached. Until the joints of her fingers turned white, she was gripping the phone so hard.

She put it back in her bag and took out the note.

You have to face him sometime, Dommerich, she told herself. (She was now addressing herself by her maiden name again—that was something, right?) If she couldn't yet trust herself to listen to his recorded voice, to God forbid speak to him, she could at least do him the courtesy of reading the note he'd left behind for her, when he slipped out yesterday before dawn and caught his flight to L.A. The flight he'd already rescheduled in order to spend Saturday night in bed with her.

Ella. *Think I'm supposed to wake you up and say good-bye right now, but it might kill me.* [There was a clumsy drawing of an arrow and a heart, with *you* written next to the arrow, and *me* written next to the heart.] *Stay here, sleep in my bed, drink all my booze, play my piano, listen to my band watching over you. Think of everything we have left to do. Don't be afraid. Back soon. H.*

Back soon.

Today was Monday; Hector would return to New York on Saturday. On Saturday morning he was going to come bounding through the door, he was going to call her name anxiously, he was going to scoop her up and demand to know why she hadn't returned his calls, hadn't picked up the phone, hadn't let him know she was okay, that she loved his apartment, she loved Saturday night, she loved him like he loved her.

What was she going to say?

Don't be afraid, he wrote. My band watching over you.

But Hector had it wrong. She was afraid, yes, but she wasn't afraid of the band playing inside the apartment building on Christopher Street. They had kept her company Sunday night, when she had buried herself under the covers of Hector's bed and wrapped her arms around her stomach and cried. The clarinet had played her something beautiful and comforting, until she loved that clarinet almost as much as she loved Hector himself. Then, as now, she had taken out the photograph of Redhead Beside Herself and stared at that image, that naked, wicked woman who had inhabited those walls over seventy years ago, and the sight of her—just as it did now—dried up Ella's eyes and her despair.

Don't be a ninny, the Redhead told her. I got no time for ninnies. You got yourself in trouble, you go out there and figure out how to fix it. You go figure out what to do with yourself. Just go out there and live, sister. Live.

Ella slipped the note and the photograph back into her laptop bag. Gathered herself up and walked out of Starbucks to start looking for her.

For the Redhead, whoever she was.

Wherever she was.

# ACT I

# We Fly South for the Winter

## *(better late than never)*

**Cocoa Beach, Florida**
**April 1924**

# 1

The schooner cruising before me looks innocent enough. I am no expert on maritime matters, having been reared up inside the walls of a mountain holler, yet still I can admire the beauty of her lines, can't I? Lubber though I am, I can appreciate the sky's pungent blue against the cluster of milk-white sails, and the way the dark-painted sides reflect the shimmer of the surrounding water.

As we draw near, the ship grows larger, until the sight of her fills my gaze like the screen at a picture house. I am wholly absorbed in her, and she in me. She bobs and rolls, and I bob and roll in sympathy. The boards of her deck articulate into view, and it seems I see every detail at once: the seams sealed in tar, the coils of perfect rope, the black paint of the deckhouse, the wooden crates in stacks at the stern and the middle, each stamped with a pair of letters: FH.

We come to board her, my companion and I, and I can't say why I'm not alarmed by her lack of crew. Not a single man hails us as we pass over the railing; not the faintest rustle of movement disturbs the dead calm of the deck. I do understand she's a rumrunner, this vessel, carrying liquor to America's teetotal shore from some ambitious island, and it seems reasonable that the fellows on board might have gone into hiding at our approach. Why, even now they might crouch unseen behind those silent objects fixed to the deck, or wait speechless at the hatchways for some kind of signal. My friend hovers watchfully behind me, pistol drawn in case of ambush, but I don't feel the smallest grain of fear. Anticipation alone drives the quick pulse of my blood. Something I desire lies below those decks, I believe, and I will shortly see it for myself.

At what instant my anticipation transforms into dread, I don't rightly notice. Maybe it's the sight of the dark, irregular stain on a section of deck near the bow hatchway; maybe it's the unnatural blackness that rears up from below as my companion tugs away the cover of the hatch itself. My breath turns stiff in my chest as I commence to descend those stairs, and I have gone no farther than the first two steps when my foot slips on some kind of wetness, and I tumble downward to land like a carcass on the deck below.

The impact shocks my bones back into wakefulness, but in the nick of space before my eyelids open to the clean, sunwashed Florida ceiling above me, I catch glimpse of what lies in the hold of that silent, innocent ship.

The piles of mutilated men, and a pair of beloved eyes staring at me without sight.

# 2

Now, for a redheaded Appalachia hillbilly bred up in the far western corner of Maryland, I do reckon I've seen a fair measure of this grand country of ours. New York City, mostly—well, don't snicker, you meet a lot of everybody atop that pile of concrete and wickedness they call Manhattan Island—to say nothing of the splendid estates of Long Island. And the long, rain-soaked corridors of Pennsylvania: you can't forget those. And Baltimore and all points in between, as seen from the window of a third-class carriage along the Pennsylvania Railroad, hurtling passage across slum and swamp into the belly of Pennsylvania Station.

But Florida. The state of Florida is something else. Like you have been plucked from the gray mire and dropped into a land of warm, green abundance.

For a moment, I can't quite recollect where I am, and why I should be swathed in such divine warmth, and what angel did dress the room around me in the clean, white colors of heaven, when—but an instant ago—I was staring into the face of death. I consider I might have died.

Then I remember it's not heaven, it's Florida. We have arrived here to this place of safety during the night, my beloved and my baby sister and me, and every nightmare is now behind us. My pulse can surely settle, my breath can lengthen into calm. We are free. The long, hellish ride is over.

At this memory—sister, beloved, hellish ride—I bolt straight up. White counterpane falls from my chest. I cast my eyes about the room, which contains but the one double bed and no other person, inside bed or out of it, for we have come to a respectable house, the three of us, in which unmarried persons must sleep without the comfort of a nearby human body. Why, he and I parted company before we even climbed the staircase to the bedrooms upstairs, and I confess I made no protest at this separation. Did not even question the identity of the woman who led me to this chamber. Me, Ginger Kelly, who never did shy away from asking somebody a question or two, when she needed to know the answers! I guess I was plumb worn out, and so should you be, had you spent the past three days driving a Model T Ford south down the endless Dixie Highway, driving and driving, past pines and palmettos and salt marsh the color of chewing gum, to arrive at this house in the hour before dawn, to meet its astonished owners and collapse into its astonished spare bed. There is just about no question in the world that can't wait, when you are so worn out as that.

But you can't help to dream, can you? A dream so real as that, so alive in every aspect, how can you possibly set it aside?

And where is the fellow whose lifeless eyes terrified you most of all?

The fellow is now gone. Nothing remains of him, not a single one of those details I have memorized over the course of the past days. Not a hollowed-out pillow, not clothes nor hat nor wristwatch wound up on the bedside table. Not a trace of warmth on the white linen sheets. Not the faint, familiar scent of his skin, weather and soap and perspiration and something else, sharp and medicinal, belonging to those bandages on his chest that I cleaned and changed by my own hands, twice every day. As if he's been swallowed up and carried away during the night, and maybe that's the reason for this dream of mine, when I have never set foot on such a ship as that, have never had a thing to do with rum-runners until I first met Oliver Anson Marshall in a Greenwich Village speakeasy two months ago.

This light, quiet room, absent of any danger. This innocent bed. Is this the reason I dreamt of Anson's death? Because he lies not here beside me, not safe inside my refuge, but elsewhere? Surely I am not so weak as that.

After all, I don't worry for my baby sister, Patsy, though she occupies some other bedroom nearby. Why, I figure she has probably charmed half of Florida while I lay asleep, so marvelous is her beauty and her sweetness.

You see, Ginger? There is nothing more to fear.

# 3

We have brought no luggage to speak of, but a dressing gown hangs thoughtfully from a curving silver hook on the door. I wear neither nightgown nor pajamas, only the most ancient and serviceable of underthings, obtained from a dry goods in Virginia somewhere, last supplied in the previous century. My clothes—likewise ancient, likewise Virginian—lie slung over the back of a nearby chair. I can't stand the sight of them. I drape myself in the dressing gown instead, which is made of some kind of expensive silk, as fine as gossamer, trimmed in satin piping and no lace whatsoever. I tidy my hair with the silver-backed brush lying on the dressing table, and as I do these elegant things, I consider that our hosts—whoever they are—are likely well-stocked in the lettuce drawer, if you know what I mean.

And just as I'm giving this point the full weight of my concentration, some noise drifts in from the window, the screaming of happy children, and I lift the window sash and stick my head out into the hot afternoon sky. Underneath it, two girls and a boy tear apart the oncoming foam of a most blue ocean, supervised by a tanned, long-limbed, gravid woman wearing a shocking pink bathing costume that does nothing whatsoever to disguise the girth of her expectant belly. One of the girls in the surf is my Patsy, shrieking her head right off as a crest-fallen wave swirls about her knees. The damn boy holds her hand solicitously. (As well he might.) The woman, perhaps hearing the slide of the window sash in its casing, cranes her head to meet mine. Waves. Calls out with cupped hand. Motions me down to the white, sunlit beach. Her head's wrapped up in a matching pink scarf, and she's so gorgeously happy, so free of every care, I want to fly right out through the window and into her arms, where my own sorrows might dissolve by the heat of her joy.

## 4

Instead, I take the stairs, which lead downward to a series of bright rooms arranged around some kind of courtyard, smelling of lemon and eucalyptus, and go out through the front door and across the beaten lane to the beach on the other side. The woman awaits me patiently, wearing a calm, beatific smile beneath a pair of strict cheekbones, and a wary tilt to her dark, straight eyebrows. The Florida sun has washed her fair skin in shades of delicate apricot, which become her extremely. Under the cold sky of a New York City winter, she might be nothing more than handsome.

"I hope you slept well, Miss Kelly," she says, by way of greeting, in a voice that speaks of private schooling and a dignified upbringing. I want to reply, Sure looks that way, don't it, by the late angle of that afternoon sun, but I can be civil when civility is called for. My own vowels were shaped by a cadre of disciplined nuns, you know, though they do have a tendency to revert to their original form when left unattended.

"Very well, thank you," I reply, in my best Bryn Mawr accent, though I did attend that fine institution but a single year. "I appreciate your taking us in like that, right in the middle of the night like a pair of thieves. I hope we didn't scare you."

She laughs pleasantly. "Well, you gave us a shock, that's for certain. But Ollie's an old friend, a dear old friend, and he's welcome in our house anytime. Even at three o'clock in the morning."

"I see Patsy's making herself at home. I hope she hasn't been any trouble."

"Oh, not at all! She's a darling. She's your sister, Ollie said?"

"My baby sister. Five last year." I shade my eyes and watch the small fry gambol about, soaking themselves in the kind of abandon we older, wiser ones have long since discarded. We haven't yet told my baby sister that she is an orphan, that her daddy has joined our mama under the wet soil of River Junction, Maryland, and that the brother she adored—the brother who all but reared her up himself—now basks in the everlasting peace of the Lord Almighty. She imagines, I guess, we've taken her on a surprise vacation to a southern paradise, and as I watch her play, I have no desire to disabuse her of this illusion. The sun grows hot on my hair and my shoulders, the milky skin of my redhead's neck. The salt air fills my chest. The pungent sky makes my heart race in recollection of my dream, and I clench my fist to quell the memory. "She must be over the moon. I don't know that she's ever seen the ocean beach before."

"She's taking to it wonderfully. Sammy and Evelyn practically grew up in the water. They've been looking out for her."

"So I see. You have beautiful children, Mrs.—" I cut up short and turn to her. "Ah! I apologize. Ollie never did tell me your name, and I was about dead last night by the time—"

"Oh, look at me. Chattering on like this, and I haven't even introduced myself! Fitzwilliam. Virginia Fitzwilliam." She holds out her hand. "And my husband, Simon, who's gone off with your Ollie right now, I'm afraid."

I clasp her hot, firm hand and tilt my head back to the house. More like a villa, I perceive, the kind of Mediterranean building you see in pictures of Italy or the south of France, an impromptu eruption of yellow walls and red tiles and round arches. I consider the words your Ollie, carelessly uttered, and my stomach grows a pair of energetic hummingbirds. "In there?" I ask.

"No, no. In town. To our offices. I understand they meant to talk business." Her expression turns a little blank, enough to send an electric signal shimmering across the surface of my brain, which—as you perceive—is something of a suspicious organ to begin with.

"Business?" I inquire.

"Now, Miss Kelly. I imagine you can tell me far more about all this than I can tell you."

"But you're too polite to ask."

Mrs. Fitzwilliam places her two hands on the underside of her enormous belly, as if the infant has begun to weigh upon her insides and wants support. Turns her head and looks back out to sea, where her children play. "For what it's worth, Miss Kelly, my husband left the rum-running business some time ago. He wasn't cut out for it."

"A rumrunner, was he?"

"We own a shipping company," she says simply, and I guess she doesn't need to say more. After all, any fool with a seaworthy boat and a sober pilot can get his start in the rum-running trade off the coast of the eastern United States, and a lucrative trade it is, too. A fellow with the foresight or the luck to own a fleet of such craft? Why, he might clear a fortune, in short order. He ought to clear a fortune, if he's got a lick of mortal sense. Nothing extraordinary about that.

"I see. And I suppose that shipping company brought you to Anson's notice?"

"Anson? Do you mean Ollie?"

"I beg your pardon. Anson's his middle name. He took what I guess you'd call a nom de guerre for a time, which is when I met him. And you know how it is with names."

She smiles. "They have a way of sticking to people."

"Yes. But to you he's Oliver Marshall. Reckon I shall have to get used to that."

We have both returned our attention to the children splashing in the surf, but when I say these words Mrs. Fitzwilliam glances back at me. "No, don't do that. Keep him by the name you knew him first. The name you fell in love with."

"Who says we're in love?"

She laughs. "Nobody needs to say it, Miss Kelly. My goodness. I have eyes in my head, even at three o'clock in the morning."

"Then you might consider an appointment with an oculist, Mrs. Fitzwilliam."

Instead of replying, Mrs. Fitzwilliam calls out to the boy, who—together with his sister—has begun to swing Patsy between them. "Sammy! Put her down, now. She's not used to the ocean."

"Oh, she'll be all right," I say, but Sammy and his sister obediently lower Patsy back to her feet. Patsy makes an imperious squeal and tugs at their hands, yet they will not be moved by her. I start forward to settle the matter, until Mrs. Fitzwilliam takes my arm.

"No," she says. "Let them be. Sammy's got a way with him. He knows how to handle the younger ones."

"Lucky for you, I guess. With another one on the way."

"Yes." She releases my arm and nods to my sling. "Simon tells me you took some bruising."

"Did he, now?"

"Well, he didn't need to. For one thing, there's a nasty swelling right there on your left cheekbone. And Ollie told us a little of your story, while Simon was changing his bandage."

"Oh? And just what did Ollie tell you?"

"That the two of you had been through a fight. Beaten about by a criminal of some kind." Her voice is kind, full of sympathy and all that, but not over-spilling. I don't believe Mrs. Fitzwilliam is the over-spilling sort of person, which is a trait I prize, and one you rarely find in women. Why, most females about smother you with sympathy for your troubles, and then expect you to smother them in turn, until the two of you can hardly breathe for the wetness of your mutual commiseration. Whereas I prefer the wetness of a nice dry martini, myself.

I tell her: "I guess that's true. But we survived, I guess. I'll do just fine, as I'm sure your husband told you."

"No doubt." Mrs. Fitzwilliam speaks so soft, the words be swallowed right up by that purring ocean nearby. "But the truth is, Ollie's worried sick about you. And I don't know what happened back there, among those bootleggers of yours. I'm not sure I want to know. God knows I've seen enough evil to make me grateful for my present peace. But whatever it is, whatever you've endured, believe me. That man would rather die than see you come to further hurt."

I wrap one hand about my stiff elbow and stare at the round, bald spine of a rising wave. The heavy pause as it commences to overturn into the foam. Because what can I say to this woman? Can I tell her how my insides ache like murder from the battering of my stepfather, who did punish me for my betrayal of him? Can I tell her about my arm he nearly broke in two, about my belly into which he drove his meat fist? Can I tell her about the sight of my brother's neck, broken like a rag doll, or how it feels to witness a man being struck in the jaw with a set of brass knuckles, such that you will never forget the sight, you will witness it evermore you close your eyes?

She's but a stranger, after all, and my hurts belong only to me.

Mrs. Fitzwilliam touches my shoulder. "I have an idea. Let's drive into town and meet them, shall we?"

# 5

Town is Cocoa, a collection of mostly wooden buildings sprawled along the edge of what Mrs. Fitzwilliam calls the Indian River, and is really some kind of inlet from the ocean itself. Maybe a river feeds it, I don't know. Anyway, you reach this squirt of a town by means of a pair of long, flat bridges directly west from the barrier strip of Cocoa Beach, leapfrogging an island they call Merritt, which I confess I have no recollection of crossing the night before.

"You were likely asleep," Mrs. Fitzwilliam says. "I've never seen such an exhausted pair as the two of you last night. Not since the war, anyway."

"The war? Did you nurse?"

"No. I drove an ambulance on the Western Front. Well, a number of ambulances. They had a tendency to break down often."

She tosses this off gaily, like she's describing some kind of picnic expedition. Shifts the automobile into another gear—it's a fine blue Packard roadster, immaculate cloth seats, a real nice piece of tin—while the draft loosens her scarf from its moorings to spread out behind us like a white flag of surrender. Air smells of salt and muck and burning oil. I narrow my eyes against the afternoon sun and say, "I guess that explains the way you drive."

"Oh? Just how do I drive?"

"Like you mean it."

She laughs and steers us into Cocoa, pulling up outside a large brick building that proclaims itself home of the Phantom Shipping Company.

"Who's the phantom?" I ask.

She sets the brake and leaps free of the seat with breathtaking agility for a woman with so much baby inside her.

"Me," she says.

# 6

The men have gone out for a sail, says a receptionist in a neat navy suit, and if we hurry we might just catch them. I tell Mrs. Fitzwilliam I don't especially enjoy messing about in boats. She tells me don't be silly and takes my arm. The Phantom Shipping Company warehouses and dock lie but a pair of blocks away, she explains, and so we stride down the broiling sidewalk so fast as we are able, one of us recently beaten up to blazes and the other one set to whelp any minute, sweating and puffing, and lucky enough the ship is still moored, though a tall, bull-shouldered man stands beside her, unwinding a rope from a bollard.

Now, while I have spent the past three days and nights in Anson's company, while I have lain in his bed and wept in his lap, while I have woken in the dark to the sound of his breath, have dressed his wounds and whispered to him things I have never before whispered to another living person, while we have eaten together and drunk together and driven together and slept together, still my cheeks burn as I make my way up the dock, and the shape of his brown, clipped head becomes clear against the green edge of mangrove lying along the opposite bank of the river. Mrs. Fitzwilliam calls out. Anson straightens and turns, stiff as some kind of machine, lit by the high, white sun.

Another man appears at the boat's edge and, spotting us, calls something back, her name I think, crammed with delight, and leaps to the dock. Mrs. Fitzwilliam surges forward, and I envy the quick, eager way she hurries across the boards toward her husband's open arms. My own feet have turned to sand. Anson spares not the least regard for Mrs. Fitzwilliam, propelling her great belly toward the man presumably responsible for it. Just stands there, tethered to the boat by the coil of rope in his left hand, and watches me approach. He's not smiling, either. I have the idea that he's making out the state of my injuries. The degree of strength returned to me by my night's rest.

As for me, I walk forward measuredly, because I am yet incapable of swift movement. Because I am yet incapable of saying a word. What do you say to this man, when you have lived by his side for three days, and now find everything has changed between you, in the space of a morning's separation? Now that the horror's over. Now that you're safe by the sea in Florida, under a tranquil sun, under the care and protection of a doctor and his wife. Now that you're in paradise, the two of you, when a moment ago you were trudging through hell. How do you turn yourself into an ordinary, happy couple, like the one embracing next to you?

On the other hand. Here stands Anson, my Anson, wearing a white shirt and an ill-fitting suit of pale linen, too tight about the shoulders, his olive skin soaking up the light and his golden-brown hair bristling unfashionably; his navy eyes as grave as they ever were, his lips as thick; every detail, every bruise and scar so blessedly familiar in this strange new world, this Florida. I find myself smiling.

"Good afternoon," I say.

"Good afternoon. Sleep well?"

"Had no choice, did I? It was either sleep or die." I lift my hand and touch the bruise purpling his jaw, and I guess it says something for the both of us that he doesn't flinch. "You?"

"About the same. Where's Patsy?"

"She's having the time of her life playing with the Fitzwilliam fry. Housekeeper's minding them." I nod my head toward the boat, which is some kind of sailing vessel, maybe twenty feet long, single mast, pulling eagerly at the rope in Anson's hand. "Where are you headed?"

"Just for a cruise offshore."

"For what purpose?"

His eyes slip away to inspect the rigging. "No purpose."

"Liar. You're going out to see the rum ships, aren't you?"

"I guess we might happen to catch sight of a few. You can't avoid them, after all."

"Oh, naturally. You weren't going to pull up alongside some old ship, some rum warehouse anchored just outside United States waters, and maybe flap your gums for a bit? Maybe tease a little knowledge out of somebody?"

He lifts the hand that holds the rope and rubs his chin with one thumb.

"Anson. You look guilty as my brother Johnnie used to look, when he was caught skimming off blueberries that were meant for a pie."

"There's no danger, Gin."

"I thought you were done with this business. I thought we were on the lam. Fugitives. Price on our heads, probably."

"I wasn't planning on giving anybody my name."

"It'll never work. You've got fishy written all over that beaten-up mug of yours, in case you didn't know. Anyway, what am I supposed to do if something happens to you out there?"

"Nothing's going to happen to me out there."

"Oh? Good. Then I guess you won't mind that I come along." I start for the edge of the dock, and Anson makes a noise of objection and takes my elbow.

"See here. What's going on with you two?" booms Dr. Fitzwilliam.

"Why, your wife and I are coming with you, that's all. Aren't we, Mrs. Fitzwilliam?"

She frowns and puts her hand on her belly. "Oh, I shouldn't. I stopped sailing months ago. But you go on ahead, Simon."

Now, this Dr. Fitzwilliam of hers is a handsome fellow, I'll give him that, though his hair has turned to silver and the skin of his face has toughened under the sun. His eyes are hazel and terribly sincere, and his smile is too cheerful for my taste, exposing a vast amount of perfect dentistry. I guess Mrs. Fitzwilliam likes it well enough. He exchanges this speculative look with Anson, who is scowling fit to thunder, and turns to me. Speaks in a profoundly correct English accent, not softened at all by the Florida climate. "Can you sail, Miss Kelly?" he asks.

"I can learn."

"In other words, she can't tell a sheet from a sail," Anson says, "aside from the fact that her right arm's almost certainly sprained. Anyway, Gin, you can't just leave Virginia onshore by herself, in her condition."

"That's all true," says Mrs. Fitzwilliam. "So why don't Ollie and Miss Kelly take the motor launch by themselves, Simon? You could keep me company onshore."

"But—"

And Mrs. Fitzwilliam lowers her chin and sends some kind of telegraphic message in her husband's direction, some kind of Morse marital code I can't quite comprehend, and I'll be damned if the good doctor doesn't just cut his sentence short and lose himself in translation of those blue eyes.

"I think that sounds like an excellent idea," I say, just to move things along.

Dr. Fitzwilliam runs a hand through his hair and casts a look at Anson that puts me in mind of a hound dog in the act of apologizing.

"I don't see why not," he says.

"Now, hold on a minute, Doc. I thought you were supposed to examine her first, before any kind of strenuous—"

"Oh, she seems about as healthy as you do, in my professional judgment," the doctor says airily, "and in any case, Marshall, I was just thinking you might be better off in a motor launch yourself, in your bruised condition."

"My condition's just fine. It's hers I'm thinking about."

"Why, then! It's settled, isn't it?" Dr. Fitzwilliam takes his wife's arm. "Come along. The launch is moored directly to the warehouse, there."

# 7

Something I should tell you about, before I step on that motor launch with Anson. Head out to God knows where on the skin of the Atlantic, the two of us together.

On the second day of our journey south from Maryland, we woke at dawn. Or rather, Anson woke at dawn and roused me by the mere act of whispering my name—Ginger—against my ear.

The sleep had done me no good, I'm afraid. My arm had stiffened in the night, and the rest of me just hurt. We lay as a pair of spoons on our left sides, because of the injuries to our respective rights, attached by the

exact same intimacy in which we had fallen asleep six
hours before, and for a minute or two, or maybe more,
neither of us moved a muscle. Maybe we couldn't. As
bad as Duke had beat me, he had done Anson worse:
hung him by his arms inside a wet, frigid building
made of mountain stone, while his earlier wounds
gaped untended, in such a way as Christ Himself must
have suffered upon His holy cross. So I guessed Anson's
limbs ached too, his muscles lay stiff alongside mine,
his head drummed an old, fatigued beat. Above our
heads, our left hands clasped. I felt the slow thud of
his heart passing through his shirt and mine, to enter
into my shoulder and spread along my bones like
some kind of uncanny medicine. I said, We're alive, at
least, and he said, Yes, thank God. Didn't ask me how
I felt, how I was doing, any of that rote, empty talk.
Didn't mention my brother, who had died for our
sakes, nor his brother, who had nearly died for mine
alone. Didn't tell me about love nor lust nor devotion,
not pity for my present misery nor awe for our mutual
survival. Just lay with me while the sun did creep up
the edge of the sky outside our walls, and those words
we didn't utter lay there too, like smoke against our
skin, like incense filling our lungs, like a benediction
laid upon us.

The air began to take on light, and Patsy stirred in the cot beside us. Anson kissed my hair and ear and cheek and said it was time to go, we had rested enough. Go where? I whispered, because I had plumb forgotten where we were supposed to be headed, and he said, Florida, and I guess I might could then have asked him what waited for us in Florida, what lay at the end of our road, what was the nature of this life to which we were fleeing together.

But I did not. Maybe I was scared to ask, maybe I was too numb to care. I helped him clumsily with his coat and shoes, and he helped me clumsily with mine. We woke Patsy and carried her out through the drizzle to the waiting automobile, and I settled us both inside while Anson returned the key to the motor inn's office. Started the engine and the automatic wipers and rolled back onto the black highway, and we never did stop for the night again. Just drove on, by sun and by moon, catching food and sleep by the side of the road, until the clouds parted and the air commenced to dry out and warm, and sometime in the middle of the third night we came to rest on a stretch of beach they call Cocoa, for no reason that I can properly tell.

And I don't recount all this history to you now in order to illuminate some measure of what we endured together, Anson and I, before arriving at this earthly paradise. I don't hold with wallowing in past afflictions; I like to walk into my future looking square ahead. Just to point out, so delicately as I can, that we have yet no actual future to speak of. No covenants between us, no vows of any kind, no physical sacrament to reunite us in the wake of that horrifying rupture at my step-daddy's hands. Only a blind trust in that thing—that smoke and incense, that benediction, whatever you care to call it—that has taken form in the darkness around us.

Such that whatever lies upon this road along which we presently hurtle, it is surely made from this unknown substance. We ourselves are built of it. For better or worse.

# 8

Now, I have taken to the seas but one other time in my life—if you don't count the Hudson River ferries, which I don't—and in that instance, as in this one, Oliver Anson Marshall himself was my pilot.

Then, we traveled in a racing motorboat, and the speed of that craft near enough flattened my chest forever into the fashionable silhouette. And if that boat was your naughty little sister, sleek and fast and amoral, why, this one's your mama's lazy uncle. Old and slow and overfed, kind of prone to fits and starts of his engine, if you know what I mean. Still, we're free, aren't we, the two of us. Making a white trail toward the ocean, while the sun heats our skin and the draft cools it right back down, and the other craft go about their business, large and small, without paying us any mind. We might be waterbugs on a pond so great as the universe. Free.

As you might expect, Anson's not best pleased with me for my overturning of his usual neat plans. Gives me a dose of what they call the silent treatment as we head off down the Indian River, disturbing the peaceable green water with all the noise and energy of our sturdy motor. The draft rattles the brim of my hat until at last I remove the damned thing and toss it on a bench, and the sudden freeing of hair is like plunging from a cliff. Exhilarating and messy. "I remember the last time the two of us went on a boat ride together," I call out, over the noise of the engine. "Was it only last week?"

"Didn't end so well, as I recall."

"Oh? I thought it ended pretty well, indeed. Best ride I ever took."

A slow blush climbs over the top of Anson's collar and up his neck.

"Now I guess you might have been referring to the fact that somebody shot you," I continue. "But if that bullet hadn't grazed you, and the good doctor hadn't prescribed you a brandy cure for the pain, why, the whole evening might have been ruined."

He says something I can't quite make out over the wind and the engine. But he isn't smiling, so I don't press him. Maybe he wasn't talking about getting shot at all; maybe he was thinking about what came after, caught in Duke's trap, and that none of that horror might have come about if we hadn't ventured out on the waters of New York Harbor in a high-powered speedboat that evening, hadn't passed through the Narrows and into the wide ocean, hadn't afterward spent the night in pleasure as we did.

"I guess we paid for it, all right," I say, mostly to myself, but Anson has got the ears of a cat, I guess, because he replies, Paid for what? and I say boldly, Joy.

He doesn't say anything to that. Maybe I was expecting the sound of this word—joy—might cause him to shut off the engine and seize me in his arms and deliver some kind of physical comfort to daub the wounds inside us both, but all I detect is a fresh whiteness at the joints of his fingers that hold the wheel and adjust the throttle. The boat pursues its long, clean course down the Indian River, mangrove passing to the left and the buildings and wharves of Cocoa slipping away to the right. Then the buildings thin out and disappear altogether, and Anson speaks up over the deep, angry throat of the engine.

"I telephoned my parents from Fitzwilliam's office. Asked how Billy was doing."

"And? Have they put his poor jaw back together again?"

"Yes." He pauses. "Seems he hasn't yet woken up. May be some injury to the brain itself, because of the force of the blow."

I grip the edge of the seat with my good hand. Feel a little sick. "Poor Billy."

"Yes."

"Can't they do anything? Some kind of operation?"

"I don't know. It was a bad connection; I couldn't hear half of what she was saying."

"You mother, you mean?"

"Yes."

I stare down at the ugly blue serge covering my knees, against which an image of Mrs. Marshall takes shape, as I last saw her. She stands in the moonlight beside a Southampton swimming pool, consuming a cigarette in swift, fierce drags, and she tells me about her sons. She wears a long, shimmering dressing gown, trimmed in down, and an aspect of fascinating beauty, made of delicate, high-pitched bones and preserved skin. In the tension of her face, I perceive a universe of keen emotion, which might be love but also fear. I swallow back a cup of misery and ask, "How's she taking it?"

Anson lifts his hand from the throttle and works the brim of the flat newsboy's cap atop his head. His profile is terribly grim. "How's she taking it? Her son's lying in a hospital bed with a broken head. I guess she's taking it as well as the next woman. Considering she's already lost another son to the war."

"I hope you're not blaming yourself. It's my fault, if anything."

"It's Kelly's fault, Ginger. And mine, for bringing you into this, first, and then dragging my brother into it because of you."

I rise from the seat and grasp his elbow. "Don't you say that. Don't you even think it. You didn't mean for that to happen. You were doing your job, that's all."

"But Billy wasn't. Billy had nothing to do with this."

"No, he got into this mess because of me, and I'll never forgive myself for that. I should never have taken up with him. A sweet wee cub like that."

"He wasn't so naïve as that."

"No, but he was fallen in love with me, and I let him fall, because I was vain and shallow and flattered by him. Because I needed a little solace. Because I hadn't met you yet."

Anson makes a noise in his throat, but nothing else.

"Anyway," I say, "how was I supposed to know poor Billy was serious about me? Men make all kinds of promises. They'll say anything. Maybe they even mean it at the time; I don't know. Every man wants to run away with you, until suddenly he doesn't."

"Well, I knew," he says. "I knew he was serious about you."

"See here. You have nothing to be guilty for, do you hear me? If I'd known you were brothers, the two of you—"

"I knew we were brothers."

"And you didn't touch me, did you? I was the one who came to your bed, that night we went out on the ocean. I was the one who gave you that brandy and climbed in beside you."

"I let you in."

"You were an innocent before me, Anson. Don't think I didn't know."

"Maybe so," he says, "but I wasn't so innocent I didn't know what we were doing together. Wasn't so drunk I didn't mean what I did. I knew I was breaking my brother's heart, and I did it anyway, because . . ."

"Because why? Because you're such a mean, selfish, awful bastard and wanted me for yourself?"

His hand yanks down the throttle, smacking the engine back down to size, cutting our speed to a mere crawl. He turns to me, left hand gripping the wheel, and his face sort of shocks me, bruised and brutal, lit to blazes by the afternoon sun. "All right. Have it your way. You seduced me. I'm just some poor, innocent rube who fell in love with the wrong girl and stuck himself with nothing but trouble."

"If you want out—"

"Want out? Out of what? Out of loving you? Out of waking up and thanking God you're still alive, I haven't killed you with this life of mine, this job of mine—"

"Oh, if that's what's bothering you—"

"There is only one thing that bothers me, Ginger. I might ache for my brother, I might burn for my part in what was done to him, but there's only one thing that makes me so sick I can't sleep, I can't think straight, I can't see reason, and that's the thought I might lose you. Might not ever again kiss you or lie with you."

"You can't lose a thing that doesn't ever mean to be lost, Anson. You can't lose a thing that belongs to you. A girl that was made for you, the same as you were made for her, like a handle for a bucket, like a pillowcase for a pillow. A hearth for a fire."

And I say this brave thing, and I sit back on my heels and wait, gazing at his battered face with my heart right there in my eyes, in such a way that I have never yet looked upon a man, stripped and raw, and still he doesn't seize me in his arms. Still he doesn't touch my skin nor kiss my mouth. His stare is that of a man condemned to death. His left hand grips that wheel as if some frightful hurricane be bearing down upon us.

"What's the matter?" I ask.

"There's another thing."

"So tell me."

"Something your stepfather said, back there in the springhouse."

"He said a lot of things."

"You know what I mean, Ginger. I didn't say anything before. I figured we had enough to do, making it safely down here to Florida. Making sure you weren't hurt any worse than I feared. And I know Duke said a lot of things, and most of them didn't have any truth to them. But if there's any chance, Ginger, any chance at all . . ."

He cuts himself off and looks away, blinking back something in his eyes, and how can I blame him? A question like that. And I know why he's asking it. Not because he actually supposes he might have started a child in me; not even so much as a week has passed since we lay together in the cold, black Southampton night, reckless as two young thieves, while this same ocean spoke outside our window, and though Anson might have lost his wits entirely during the sweet course of those hours, he is yet sensible enough to understand the limits of nature's bounty. No, indeed. A far more complicated possibility has risen up before him, and my step-daddy is to blame for that, as for most of our troubles.

So I forgive him for the indelicacy of his question. I feel his torment like an ache in my own breast. I take one step toward him and lift his right hand with my left hand, the one that isn't near to broken by one of Duke's various methods of torture.

"Do not," I say, "for God's sake, do not give that man the power to haunt you still. You just forget every word Duke Kelly said in that springhouse, do you hear me? Every word. It was the devil that spoke through his mouth that terrible morning, and the devil never did speak a word of truth to mortal men."

He curls his fingers tight around mine and stares out across the boat's bow. "Speak plain, Ginger. Just tell me. I know it's a private matter, it's your own business, but I'll go nuts if—"

"I'm not carrying any man's child, Anson. Not Billy's and not yours."

The faint, high scream of a steam whistle carries across the water. I take another step to stand but a breath away from his shoulder, and it seems to me that the tension in that coil of muscle is fixing to burst right through his shirt and his ill-fitting Florida jacket.

"You're certain?" he says.

"As certain as a woman can possibly be."

He just turns his head, that's all, turns his head and lets his forehead fall against mine, and the tension in his big shoulder sort of dissolves in our blood. And that's when I realize I've been feeling it all this time, down along the road from Maryland, thinking this wound-up tautness was just his ordinary pitch, his shoulder was just built that way, and it turns out his shoulder is more like a cushion than a rock, more like a cradle than a coil of tarred rope, and it fits the curve of my head like they were made for each other.

# 9

Now I wasn't lying when I told Mrs. Fitzwilliam that I don't relish this business of messing about in boats. I wasn't bred up to it, for one thing, and for another I can't help but think of what happened last time I took ship with Oliver Anson Marshall. You know what I mean. The rough chop of that speedboat across the water, and the rat-a-tat-a-tat of a Thompson submachine gun searching out your flesh. The whisht-thud of a bullet whisking past you in the night air to find purchase in some nearby object, and the sickness of death that clung to you like the smell of blood.

So I try to close my eyes, but that only brings on nausea and the usual visions of broken necks and brass knuckles and blood creeping across a black-and-white floor, so I stand up instead and share the journey with my beloved. The water changes color from deep, tranquil green to an eager blue, and the shore thins out into sand. We don't say much, just trade observations on the scenery. I wonder if he's thinking the same things I am, if he's thinking about all the death and hurt we have left in our wake, but that's not a question you can ask a man like Anson in the golden light of a Florida afternoon. You ask him in bed, in the dark, when your skin lies against his skin, and he tells you the truth. Here and now, you ask him about the ships that lie ahead. Those smugglers' warehouses floating atop the skin of the Atlantic, three miles out to sea. Why three miles? Because three miles marks the limit of United States territorial waters, that's why. The sum total of the Coast Guard's jurisdiction.

"I don't know what you think you're going to learn," I tell him, just exactly as if I know his business as well as he does. "Surely the Florida racket's got nothing to do with the northern rackets."

"But they both have the Bureau and the Coast Guard to deal with. Any kind of news spreads fast, believe me." He pauses. "I used to be assigned down here, remember? They sent me down to help break up one of the big family gangs. That's how I met Fitzwilliam."

"Aren't you afraid they're going to recognize you?"

He shrugs. "It's a chance, I guess. I'll just tell them I've left the Bureau. Out on the water with my girl, looking for a little refreshment."

"Oh, they'll believe that, will they? Mister Law and Order's gone all wet suddenly?"

"Nothing corrupts a fellow like falling in with the wrong kind of dame."

"You mean some kind of wicked red-haired floozy who drinks her own weight in gin and falls into bed with any old meathead Prohibition agent who strikes her fancy? That kind of dame?"

"She sounds just about perfect to me."

"I see. And how are you going to explain our busted appearance? Don't you think it might make a smuggler nervous, all these bruises and slings?"

"Don't you remember? There was a fight at the Palm last night. I was defending your honor, as I often do, and you pitched in to help, as you often do."

"Oliver Anson Marshall. You disgraceful liar."

He smiles a little.

"Why, you're enjoying all this, aren't you? You relish a little adventure."

"It's what I do, that's all."

"What you used to do, you mean."

"Yes. What I used to do."

I guess I ought to ask him the obvious question. Ought to ask him why we're out here on this boat, heading into a little adventure, when he's no longer employed by anybody to do such things, when he's found himself a nice place of refuge with a floozy who adores him. But what's the point? When a man's trying to get back his honor, prove to the world and the Prohibition bureau that he's nothing but an honest, straightforward fellow caught up in some scoundrel's game, he'll keep hunting and hunting until he dies, won't he? He's not going to stop trying to find the man who has cast him into purgatory.

So instead of wasting everybody's time, I just ask, "And me? You don't mind dragging your dame into this nest of smugglers?"

"Ginger, these Rum Row skippers, they aren't the kind of fellows you need to be afraid of. They're just businessmen. Sometimes not even that, sometimes just fellows trying to make a few dollars, who wouldn't put their necks at risk."

"Then exactly whom should we be afraid of?"

"Pirates, for one."

"Pirates! You don't say. You mean like Bluebeard? Wooden legs and eyepatches? Chests full of gold doubloons?"

"Chests full of Scotch whiskey is more like it. They don't usually attack the big storage ships on Rum Row. But they'll stop the boats ferrying liquor to shore, or else the schooners out of Nassau or Havana hauling in more stock. Not small potatoes like us—we're not worth the trouble—and mostly at night, when the rackets from shore are doing their dirty work."

"And the men running the rackets? What about them?"

"Pretty ruthless fellows, by and large. You'll want to give them a wide berth."

"Thanks for the tip."

"Why, you're not anxious, are you, Ginger?"

"Of course I'm not anxious. The idea."

"Because if you're anxious, I'll turn this boat around and take you back to shore. Can't have a nervy partner out there. They'll smell it on you."

"Thought you said they weren't dangerous."

"They're not exactly sissies, either."

By now we have cleared the inlet entirely, and there's nothing but blue sea ahead and yellow sand behind. The Atlantic wind drenches us clean. I savor the word partner on the back of my tongue. Glance across at Anson's thick neck, pinkened by all that wind and excitement, and his eyes narrowed gleefully at the encounter ahead.

"Why, then, Mr. Marshall," I say, folding my arms across my chest, "if that's the case, I guess you're going to need my help."

# 10

They lie anchored in a line from north to south, at intervals so regular it's practically unnerving, if you're that breed of person who misplaces his nerves from time to time. From three miles out you can still see the shore, verdant and kind of mysterious, but it might as well be another universe for all the good it does you. The boat bobs nervously under your feet, the ship looms large and black-sided, sails folded neat against masts and spars. I turn toward Anson and open my mouth to tell him about my dream, about the schooner that looked exactly like this one, only packed to the hatches with dead men. But he's concentrating on bringing the motor launch alongside, on some exchange of hails with the sailors on deck.

I take his arm. "Are you sure about this? You know what you're doing?"

He gives me this amazed look. "Why, what's wrong?"

"I just got a feeling, that's all. Chill down my spine."

Anson examines my eyelashes, slings his arm about my neck, and pulls me in for the kind of long, soft kiss that draws forth a chorus of whooping from above. I am surely too shocked to resist. When he's done, he touches his forehead to mine and whispers, "You're safe. Trust me."

I want to scream back that it's not my safety giving me the chills, it's his, but somebody's calling down words of some kind—afraid I'm still too discombobulated by the kissing to hear them properly—and then a rope ladder falls at our feet, and the time for turning back has long past. Tick tock. Just swallow back your terror and climb that rope, I guess, doing your best to hold on with your one good hand.

# 11

Turns out they know each other, Anson and this captain of his, I haven't yet caught his name. He thinks it's a great joke that Special Agent Marshall is no longer agent of anything to speak of. Pours him a bumper of Scotch whiskey to celebrate, and to my amazement Anson slings it right back. Yes, he does! Slings it right back, sets the glass on the table, and delivers me a slow wink that sets my insides to bubbling.

"For you, madam?" asks the captain.

"I'll have what he's having."

I sip my whiskey with considerably more reserve than Anson does. I figure one of us should remain sober. The captain—turns out his name is Logan or something—pours out another for Anson and another for himself, and Anson asks Logan how's business since he's been away.

"Business is booming, Marshall. Business is booming. I can't keep my vintage champagne in stock. Fellows come all the way from Palm Beach for champagne."

"Can't they get champagne in Miami?"

Logan makes a noise of disgust. "These boys out of Nassau, they got plenty of British liquor but they don't get no French ships no more. So I have a fellow from up north who supplies me."

"From where? Saint Pierre?"

"That's the place. Ever been there?"

"Haven't had the pleasure."

Logan laughs and tops everybody off from a bottle of what claims to be a fifteen-year-old single malt from Ayrshire, though I have my doubts. In case you're wondering, we're sitting in the captain's own cabin, which isn't so grand as it sounds. Cramped, damp, dark, smells of fish and piss and wood soaked in brine, all of it baked together like some kind of stew in the oven of a Florida afternoon. There's a bunk built into the wall, a green sofa—on which I'm presently sitting next to Anson—and an armchair for Logan the color of mustard, everything built of sticks and horsehair cushions and scraps of old upholstery. You'd think they were smuggling milk instead of a commodity so lucrative as rum.

"Neither have I," Logan says, setting down the bottle, "but I heard it ain't much. Just some wet rock off the coast of Newfoundland with a port that don't ice over in winter."

"I guess that's useful, in your line of work," I say.

"Oh, it's useful, all right. But the real kicker is it's French."

"French? But doesn't Newfoundland belong to Canada?"

"Thrown around between the two of them for centuries. England and France, I mean. The point is, Saint Pierre ended up French, which makes it a gift from God direct to champagne vineyards and Scotch distilleries. And the Canadians, too, by God. Especially the Canadians."

Possibly my face betrays some confusion. I take in a little more Scotch whiskey and watch Logan as he pulls out a cigarette and lights it with a match kept in this special jar with a lid. I guess sailors worry about such things. Anyway, he watches me watching him and offers me a cigarette, which I accept because a low-down wicked dame like me ought to take a cigarette when it's stuck in her direction, oughtn't she? The better to corrupt her menfolk with. And I pick up a little courage with the familiar smell of burning tobacco, so I say, "Why does that make any difference? Being French?"

"Why, because of taxes, Miss Kelly."

Anson lays his arm across my shoulders and speaks in this low, gravelly voice. "In the first place, Saint Pierre's import duties amount to maybe a tenth of what they charge in Nassau, which is pure profit for suppliers."

"And the French don't even pay that," says Logan, "so they don't send no more bottles by way of Nassau. Why should they? You could about bathe in champagne, on the island of Saint Pierre."

Anson smiles. "And second, the Canadian distillers don't have to pay duty on export bottles, so the government refunds the tax once the company provides proof it's been imported into another country. That's where the good men of Saint Pierre oblige. Unload the liquor, hand the captain a stack of stamped import certificates. Distiller gets his tax bond back from the Canadian government and sells the cargo to whatever racket's waiting there in the harbor for some merchandise."

"Or else ships it direct to the Row," Logan says.

"Now every man, woman, child, and dog in Saint Pierre keeps busy from dawn to dusk in the liquor trade."

"I bet they never had it so good." I wave my cigarette to indicate the ship around us. "The liquor trade beats the fishing trade, any day. In price and in general atmosphere, if you know what I mean."

Logan leans forward. "Listen to this, Miss Kelly. Listen good. I spent seventeen years fishing the coast around here, and I never cleared more than a thousand dollars in a single year. Just enough to get by. Keep my wife and my three kids. Now? I clear more than that in a month. Sometimes a week. I make so much dough, I got a wife and a girl down in Port Saint Lucie." He roars his joy and slaps Anson's knee. "Now that's what I call prosperity!"

"I guess your wife's over the moon," I say.

"Aw, she don't care. Why, she's sitting in her nice new house right now, wearing a nice new dress." He inspects the uninspired neck of my own serge frock. "You could use some more dough yourself, Marshall, now that you're out of the enforcement business. You need to set this doll of yours up like she deserves."

I suck on my cigarette and say I couldn't agree more.

"You see, Marshall? A beauty like this, she likes a fellow with a little bread in his pocket. If she don't get it from you, she'll be looking elsewhere fast."

Anson shrugs his big shoulders. Fingers draw a circle or two on my upper arm, through the thick material of the dress. "I might have a plan or two up my sleeve. You never know."

"Well, you better not wait too long, brother. You better not. I hear there's some talk of a new treaty. Move the line out another ten miles or more."

"Is that so?"

"You mean the boundary for United States waters?" I ask.

"That's what I mean." Logan points out the nearby porthole. "You can just about see the shore from here, when the haze don't set in too bad. From ten or twenty miles out, you might as well be in the middle of the ocean, for all you can catch glimpse of the United States. And some fellow carrying a few bottles from ship to shore, why, he's got a lot of water to cover. Lot of salt water for the Coast Guard to catch him in."

From the gathering tension in the muscles of Anson's arm along my shoulders, I figure this piece of information interests him. But his fingers continue that delicious circling at exactly the same pace. His voice continues in the same gravelly drawl. He reaches out the other long arm and gathers up his glass of whiskey, and I guess I'm the only one who feels him wince. Those poor abused ribs of his. "Lot of water," he agrees.

"Sitting ducks," says Logan. "Sitting fucking ducks. Forgive my language, Miss Kelly, but it ain't going to be pretty, if such a thing comes to pass."

"Stinking Coast Guard," I say.

"It ain't the law I'm thinking of, Miss Kelly. The law plays fair, most days, and they got a job to do, I understand that, and if you want to break that law you might get arrested and your booze took away. But the pirates." He shakes his head. Waves away the gathering smoke. "Pirates just as soon kill you. And when a fellow's taking a few bottles from ship to shore, and he's got ten or twenty miles of lonely ocean to cover, who do you think is going to find him? Coast Guard with a few little boats and a stingy Congress behind 'em, or a fellow with no conscience and a nice profit dangling in front of his nose? Why, already they're getting greedier." He turns to Anson. "That gang you was taking down the year before last, the Wilson boys. They was killed in ambush a few months ago, and what do you think happened? Do you think the trade went away? Got any softer?"

"I'll guess it didn't," says Anson.

"No, it did not. Got worse. You can't cough out here at night without some pirate hears you and flies on in with his machine guns. Sometimes mounted right there on his boat, like the Coast Guard itself. And he ain't there to arrest you. Oh no. He ain't worried about your constitutional rights. Why, we brought in a crate full of guns just last week, armed every man on board. Had no choice. Some ship got boarded a few miles south, and they killed everybody, everybody, dumped the crew over the rail, and left behind nothing but the captain's head. Just his head, Marshall, just his head sitting there on the deck by the wheel. Now what kind of fellow does that?"

"Who was it? Which ship?"

"Aw, it was some new outfit, I never knew him. Maybe he was muscling in on somebody else's neighborhood, I don't know. But the whole thing shook us up. Put everybody on edge, up and down the Row. Sometimes you can hear the gunshots at night, and I don't know whether it's—"

Pop-pop-pop-a-pop-a-pop, comes a noise from outside, like somebody is making popcorn, like somebody is setting off some distant fireworks.

# 12

Now I am already gone cold, already froze up and sick at the image of that dead captain's head standing guard by his wheel, so what do I do at the sound of those fireworks but shriek. Shriek and startle and spill my whiskey all over the floor, the deck as they call it, while Anson lifts his arm away from my shoulder and puts his hand inside his jacket. Draws out a revolver. Logan jumps to his feet and swears. Heads right out the cabin door, and Anson turns to me.

"Stay here, for God's sake!"

"You know I won't."

Anson is not a man who speaks profane, not the kind of man who takes the name of his Lord in vain, but he does now. Swears good and loud, better and louder than the captain himself, and hands me the revolver.

"You keep under cover at least, all right? You do as I tell you. And if you need to shoot, you just shoot. God knows you can fire a gun straighter than any man here."

I stare down at the revolver in my palm, and then I look back up at Anson. Blazing, bruised face full of trust.

"Jesus God, how I love you," I say.

He snatches my hand and commences to bolt straight out that door, pulling me behind, and I move my legs after him so fast as I can, because I will not be left behind to discover Anson's blank face staring sightless, no sir. No more than I will be left behind to die in some dank cabin.

# 13

B road daylight, and the deck of this Rum Row schooner reminds me of nothing so much as a good old church picnic brawl back in River Junction, except that nobody is drunk. You can chew on that irony if you like. I got more vital things to do.

Anson is all business, you understand. He has done this kind of thing before. He waves me back to the stern, behind some tall stacks of wooden crates, and because I did swear to follow his commands in this fight, I dive right into place, fixing myself a station by which I can watch the deck and fire that gun if I need to. The fear has fallen away from my skin, like it does in a set-to when your blood turns hot and your mind sharp, and only later do you start to shake and cry, only later do your insides curdle up and go cold. Now you're just nothing but an animal, just a creature bent on keeping alive.

Seems the attack comes from the starboard side. Sound of bullets firing from my right, sound of bullets whizzing dead ahead. Some of them catch a mast or something, and the splinters go flying. Not twenty yards away, a man cries out and goes down, clutching his side. Idiot standing there in plain sight, no wonder.

Anson's ducked under the starboard rail, holding a rifle. Jumps up, aims, fires, ducks back down, all in the space of a second or two. His flat newsboy's cap remains on his head, good solid plaid wool. I stare at that cap and pray.

But aside from Anson, nobody seems to possess the least idea what he's doing. How to defend against a surprise attack from a shipful of what has got to be pirates, seeking to hijack Mr. Logan's valuable cargo. Anson shouts out to a couple of Logan's crew—Take cover! Wait and aim, goddamn it!—and they drop down and clutch their guns, but I can see they don't know what to do with them. Me, now. I was reared up inside a mountain holler alongside three sturdy brothers, and I can shoot an acorn off a squirrel's paws if I need. I can shoot a worm from a robin's beak. I cradle that revolver in my palm like a diamond. Bring it to the level of my eyes and lift the safety latch, while Anson rises and fires again, rifle aimed at a more acute angle now, like to a boat drawing so close you might could count the noses of the men inside. He turns his head over his shoulder and calls out, and this time those two nearby men are paying proper attention. The deck is full of noise, guns firing and men shouting. I don't know how you stay calm in a circus like that. He counts off on his fingers—one, two, three—and they rise together and aim down and fire, and maybe they hit a few men, I don't know, because in the next second a small black ball flies over the railing and wobbles across the deck.

I don't understand how it doesn't hit anybody, but it doesn't. Just wobbles there like an egg while the men carry on, while no one sees it except me, and I scream Anson's name, scream, Grenade! so loud my throat seems to split, but I can't even hear myself in that din.

So I run out from behind my crates toward that thing, that black ball fixing to murder us all, and now Anson sees me, now Anson sees what I'm after.

He shouts and motions the men back, dives forward and grabs that thing and tosses it over the side, and I'll be damned if it doesn't explode a half second later in an almighty boom, right there in midair, smacking everybody backward, even me, straight on my backside on that hard wooden deck.

I crawl forward, calling Anson's name, but he's already picking himself up from the deck, staggering a little, while a pair of hands appears over the side and then a man, skinny and blood-streaked. Anson's lost his rifle—anyway, you can't fire a rifle when a man's that close—so he grabs the fellow by the shirt and hauls him back over the side into the water, and I yell with relief, except I can't hear anything now, ears all stuffed up with cotton wool.

Yet already there are more men climbing over, five or six at a time from some rope ladders hooked over the rail, and I lose sight of Anson in the jungle of slinging arms and tangled bodies. Pick myself up and reel back to my crates and look for my gun to fire, but it's gone. Clean gone.

Cold wave washes over me. No gun, Gin. Nothing between you and some pirate fixing to murder you, nothing between you and some pirate fixing to murder your beloved. I catch glimpse of Logan, punching at some fellow while another one comes up behind, lifting a knife, and the world just kind of tunnels around me while I hunt for Anson among all those fighting men, all those flying bodies. Start to climb up those crates so I can see the deck better, and that's when I spot him, some kind of dervish, hauling men back over the side as soon as they pop over the ladders, and so great is his strength, so immense is the animal momentum in those arms and shoulders, the attack starts to falter. I don't know how to describe the way everything changes. Just that these men are falling back, the center of gravity rolls toward the rail, the attack just thins and starves without new flesh to feed it. Anson's cap is lost, his hair flashes in the sun. His skin seems to blur into his clothes, and I realize it's my own eyes blurring. Blink blink. Perspiration stinging the corners. Perspiration slick on my palms. It's over, it's over. Men groaning on the decks. Smell of blood. Anson pausing, casting about, chest heaving for air. Picks up a rifle.

And I am so drenched with relief, so weakened by it, I don't even notice the fellow who comes up behind Anson, not until the blade of his knife catches fire from the sun.

# 14

I clutch the edge of a wooden crate. Throat too dry to scream. Each muscle frozen against its ligament. Gun, where is the gun? Anson whips around last second. Grabs wrist. Somebody help. Help for God's sake. Nobody helps, nobody sees, fists still swinging all over the place, and there comes over me this strange sensation like I am looking upon this scene from somewhere else, I can't possibly be living inside this present moment, clinging with my one good hand to these wooden crates, standing here on this damned ship on this damned ocean while a pirate fights Anson with a knife.

When a couple of hours ago I drove across a sunlit bridge in a Packard roadster, laughing a little.

My fingers slip against the crate and down I go, crash bump crash, sliding along wood, stumbling to the deck. Gun, where is the gun? Anson struggling. Someone in the way, can't see. Knife flashes. Big hand grabs my shoulder and whips me around, some mad, grinning, red-faced meaty demon, I go down on my back behind the crates.

The impact knocks away my breath. The man comes down on top of me, fumbling, tearing cloth. God no no no. Gun, where is the gun? Hot stinking breath on my face. Hand forcing my leg. You can't fight a beast like that on strength alone. You can't just pitch your feminine muscle against his masculine one. Nature favors the conqueror in these matters; Nature wants the strong to populate the earth. You have but one chance, and that's what he don't expect. I force myself limp, gather myself together. Bring my knee up hard and dig my teeth into his neck, I mean I tear his flesh like I am tearing meat from a sparerib, and he screams and falls away, screams a fisher cat scream. I roll the other way, toward the crates, spitting out blood and skin, and there in the crack between two stacks of booze lies the barrel of a Colt revolver.

Snatch it up.

Brace myself and heave up to my feet.

Wheel around the corner of that stack of crates.

Gun in my left hand. Raise it. Find that silver flash, find Anson's white shirt, still struggling, knife surging toward his throat.

Fire.

# 15

There are two men dead of bullet wounds and another four injured. Anson piles them into the motor launch with the help of the first mate, who jumps in, too. Logan's left arm and leg are badly slashed, but he insists on staying with the ship. Thanks us profoundly. Tells me I am a damn good shot. I stick the revolver in the pocket of my dress and acknowledge the truth of this compliment.

I don't believe Anson and I exchange a single word the entire journey back to shore. The first mate has brought a bottle of whiskey, and he and I take turns. Settle our nerves. Anson just pilots the boat and refuses the bottle. I nudge him with the neck of it. "Come on. Not even your nerves are made of that kind of steel."

"I'm all right."

"You threw back two full glasses on the ship. Watched you do it."

Without so much as a blink, he says, "We're back inside United States waters now."

And all at once, I am filled with fury. I fling that bottle into the water. Take him by the arm and strike my good left fist against his chest, over and over, while the boat makes this crazy lurch and the first mate dives for the wheel.

"Why? Why? We were safe, Anson, we were safe at last, and you head out to some ship and near enough get us killed!"

He pulls me right up against his chest while I keep screaming.

"Was it worth it? Was it? That fellow nearly killed you, and for what? What the hell did we learn that was so important as that?"

"We learned that the game's about to change, Ginger. Learned that more people are going to get killed. More blood's going to spill."

I have nothing to say to that. Just fall back into my seat. The engine's roaring, the boat lurches across the water. Blue sea jumps and spins before me. I think I might vomit. I turn my head over the side and I do vomit, heave the sparse contents of my stomach over and over into the horizontal draft. When I'm finished, when I'm collapsed on my seat, Anson's hand lands gently on my back.

"All right?" he says.

"I'll live. You?"

He pats my back once more. Caresses my hair swiftly. Returns his hand to the wheel and says, "So long as you'll live, I'll live."

# 16

The sun's long set by the time we arrive back at the villa in the blue Packard, and for an instant I'm bemused to see a small figure running from the shadow of the house, calling my name.

Patsy. I plumb forgot my baby sister.

I sink on my knees in the gravel and take her sobbing body against mine. Tell her it's all right, I'm here, everything's fine, what's the matter?

"She wouldn't go to bed until you came home," says Mrs. Fitzwilliam, who stands nearby in a pale dressing gown like a ghost, doing her best not to sound reproachful.

I don't dare look up at her face. The one pressed against mine is bad enough, cheeks all wet and hot, breath coming in tiny, desperate pants. She sticks to me like a burr, like a marsupial, like I am a kangaroo and she is my kangaroo baby enclosed to my chest and belly by some invisible pouch. Her small back shudders under my hand. I keep saying I'm here, I'm fine, I would never leave her, but my words ring hollow, don't they? Not once did the thought of Patsy enter my head as I took off across the dangerous blue sea with Anson. Not once did I think of her left behind. Not once did I imagine some kindly person telling Patsy that her sister has been split clean apart by a Rum Row pirate, and she has no kin remaining to cherish her.

"W-where w-were you?" she hiccups out.

"I was with Mr. Marshall. Out in a boat."

"Why didn't you take me with you?"

"Because . . ." Because I forgot all about you, cherub. Because it was too dangerous, anyway. Because there is no sister in the world so bad as I am, nobody in the world less capable of looking after you, poor baby, poor darling, I'm so sorry.

I start to pull away from her, because I can't stand the weight of her terror, and also I'm starting to cry myself, tears leaking out the corners of my eyes at this terrible, terrible day that started out in such peace. My arm hurts, my back hurts. Maybe every bone in my body hurts, every tendon and joint, every fingernail. A weight falls next to my left shoulder. Anson, crouching beside us in the gravel.

"Patsy," he says quietly, "do you know what your sister did today?"

She peers out over my arm.

"Your sister saved my life."

"She did?"

"She saved my life, and her own life, and the lives of a shipful of men. In fact"—he takes his finger and carefully parts her damp hair from her face, one side and then the other, so he can look in her eyes—"I think your sister's about the bravest person I know."

"That so?"

"That's so. Ginny's the kind of sister who will do anything to keep you safe."

I let my arm fall away, so Patsy leans against me, turned toward Anson.

"But who's going to keep Ginny safe?" she asks, terribly small.

"Well, I guess that's my job, isn't it? As best I can." He holds out his arms. "And now I think it's time you went to bed, sweetheart. You and Ginny, you need your sleep."

Patsy goes so willingly into his embrace, I think my heart stops. Lays her head on his shoulder while he lifts her up with one thick, exhausted arm and takes my hand with the other. By the time we reach the stairs, her eyes are already half-closed, and her wet eyelashes stick together at the tips, and I can't help recollecting the way we entered this house not twenty-four hours before. Just like this, except we have fresh, new bruises and hurts atop the old ones, and though the house is exactly the same, pale and peaceful, and our hosts make identical noises of relief and welcome, I am overcome by this swift, terrible vision that we are stuck on a wheel, the three of us, a nightmare Ferris wheel that turns over and over and never lets us off.

# 17

I stay with Patsy until she falls asleep in her bed in the room she shares with Evelyn. The wee Fitzwilliam sprig doesn't even stir throughout this disturbance, just lies there under her white counterpane, sweet cheek turned to the moonlight. I stroke

Patsy's hair and count the beats of her breathing. The house around us has gone still; even the slight, worried murmuring of the doctor and his wife has died into silence.

My own room is the one next door. I slip inside and climb under the covers, which smell drowsily of lavender. The window's cracked open, releasing all the heat of the day, and for some time I listen to the strange, wild music of the Atlantic Ocean and recollect the night I spent in Southampton, when that same water beat against my shore in exactly the same key. Isn't this supposed to lull you to sleep? Lavender sheets and the ocean noise? Well, it doesn't. I turn on one side and the other. Stare at the blank ceiling and see visions of violent death, of lifeless faces, though I tell myself I'm safe and sound, safe and sound, nothing to fear.

Start to get angry.

I'm the lucky one, aren't I? Survived all this trouble to find myself lying in a soft bed by the sea. I ought to be happy. Ought to be sleeping the sleep of the fortunate.

I sit upright. Stare at the billowing curtains. Throw off the counterpane, slide from the bed, and take my dressing gown from the hook on the door.

# 18

However deeply I am attached to Oliver Anson Marshall, I am not bound to him by anything so respectable as marriage. He sleeps virtuously, therefore, on the other side of the villa, in some kind of guest quarters that exist on the other side of the courtyard.

You might be in Italy as you steal through the French doors from the dining room and across the paving stones of that courtyard, breathing in some exotic scent of citrus and spice while a stone fountain rattles happily in the moonlight. The air is soft and still warm, blowing in from offshore, and I can taste the wholesome salt on the back of my tongue.

There is just enough glow to guide me to Anson's door, which opens directly into this enchantment, and—to my vast surprise—the handle turns easily. Wouldn't a fellow like Anson lock his door as a matter of course? Then he says my name as I enter the room, and I understand the oversight. I shed my dressing gown but not my nightdress and climb into the bed. Lie on my side, facing him, while he gathers me close. His skin is so hot as a fever. I press my forehead into his collar. "I can't do this anymore," I say.

"Do what?"

"Can't go out into danger with you. Can't keep watching people get killed."

"I'm sorry."

"Don't be sorry. Just stop. Give up." I bring my good left hand up to cover his jaw and his ear. "Just stay with us, where we're safe. A nice, quiet life."

"Is that what you want? A quiet life? You, Ginger?"

"I'm done. I'm done."

"Shh. It's all right. You're shaking."

"Of course I'm shaking, you damn fool. Nearly died out there, the two of us, out there on the ocean. What's my sister going to do, if we're killed?"

"It's over, it's done. We're safe. Won't happen again, I promise."

"Won't it?"

He is silent for some time, resting his left hand upon my hip, his right hand up around my head, inside my hair. He's bathed and shaved, I can smell the soap of him, and also the faint reek of antiseptic. I guess the doctor saw to him. Clean and dry and warm, bursting with bone and muscle and adventure. Pitching villains into the ocean one minute, carrying my baby sister tenderly in his arms the next.

"Just let me clear my name," he says. "That's all I want."

"Why? Why does it matter?"

"It just does. So we can live honestly. No shadows behind us."

"I've got news for you, bub. It's too late for that. Why do you think I came down here tonight?"

"I don't know. Why?"

I start to answer him, but my throat hurts when I try to make words. So I just breathe, breathe him in, breathe his soap, breathe the faint note of antiseptic and the particular scent of a warm bed and a warm man inside, like no other smell in the world. My heart slows. "I had this dream," I whisper.

"What kind of dream?"

"Last night. Just before I woke. Dreamt I was trying to find you, and you were on a ship. A ghost ship, nobody on board until I went below decks. And then I found you, and you were dead. Everybody was dead."

He sighs. "I see. Is that what all this is about? Some dream?"

"Wasn't just a dream. Too real for that. Back home, we would have called it a vision."

"A vision? You mean like a premonition?"

"I mean a vision, Anson, a glimpse of some future scene. A prophecy."

"You don't really believe that?"

"Don't I?"

"Ginger, it's a dream, it's nothing more. You've never believed in that kind of thing. It's a figment of your imagination, that's all."

"Why, you think I'm neurotic, don't you?"

"No, I don't. I think you're exhausted, you're—you're full of nerves. Look at you, you're shaking. It's because of what happened in Maryland. Naturally you're having nightmares. God knows I am. But it's not real. There's no such thing as visions, second sight, all that magical nonsense."

"Isn't there? Those men liketa murdered us tonight, out there on that damned ship, and you think it's just a coincidence?"

"But we weren't murdered. I'm alive, and so are you."

"So maybe we got lucky. Maybe it's a warning, I don't know. What I do know is someone's trying to tell me something. Someone's trying to make me listen up."

"Who, exactly?"

"Doesn't matter."

"Well, what, then? You want me to hide forever, just because of some foreboding?"

"Yes!"

"Ginger." He shakes his head. Strokes my hip. "Ginger."

I lift my face, so our lips nearly touch as I move them. "You're going to keep going out there, aren't you, and I can't go with you. I'm done. I can't follow you anymore. I've got my sister to rear up. I've got to love her and keep her safe."

"Don't say I, Ginger. Say we. We will love her and keep her safe."

"We? There is no we, Anson. Not so long as your heart is out there on that ocean, out there on those highways at night. This fight, it's in your blood, like Patsy and I could never be."

"That's not true. You're in my blood. You are my blood. Heart and bone and everything else. You have no idea, Ginger, no idea how much I—"

I lay my hand quick over his mouth. "Don't say it."

Anson reaches up and picks my fingers away. Holds them inside his palm. "Tell me what you want."

"You tell me first."

"I want you. That's all."

"Really? What about the rest of it? Family, kids, house in the country? Dog lying on the hearthstone?"

"Is that what you want? No more city life?"

"Doesn't matter what I want. I want what's best for Patsy, I guess. She shouldn't have to lie scared in her bed at night, waiting for me to come home."

"I shouldn't have taken you with me."

"And if you hadn't, you'd be dead. We neither of us should have gone out on that water."

"Maybe not."

"Maybe's not enough, Anson. Not anymore. You need to decide what the future's going to look like. You need to decide what you can take or not take, when it comes to me and Patsy."

"I will take whatever comes with you, Ginger. Whatever comes."

I lower my face back to the pillow and close my eyes. Listen to some faint, slow drum that I realize is not the ocean but Anson's heart. Drop one hand to rest against this organ, and the slight movement of its contraction contains more soporific power than all the lavender, all the waves, all the salt breeze in the world.

"Beats for you," he says softly.

My lips are too tired to move. I move them anyway, because this is important.

"If it stops, I'll kill you."

## New York City, April 1998

It was Hector who brought the matter to her attention, though he didn't realize it at the time.

Long before Saturday night, Ella suspected Hector was a good lover. If she had to pinpoint a moment when she started imagining what her upstairs neighbor was like in bed, fantasizing about jumping into said bed with him, it was probably when they were playing some music together a week or so ago, Hector on the trumpet and Ella on the piano, and he went into some long, gorgeous, aching riff that made her ears warm up, made her fingers tingle, made her stare at the play of muscles in his forearms and the movement of his jaw. The way his eyes closed and his head tilted. When he finished, he lowered the instrument to his chest and stared at the floor for a minute or two, like he was coming back to himself, and Ella thought, I'll bet he is fucking amazing in bed.

Well, it turned out, he was. He took his time. He paid attention to everything. At one point, during a sleepy interlude, he had bent his head to touch her nipple delicately with his tongue, and when she shivered he said to her, in an awed voice, "You have the most sensitive breasts."

She remembered thinking drowsily that he was wrong. Her breasts were no more tender than normal, at least so far as she understood from the sisterhood. "Not that sensitive," she told him, so he started to suckle, very gently, and she jumped and cried out.

"You see?" he said.

"You just surprised me."

"Keep going?"

"Sure," she said, and this time she was expecting the tug of his mouth and didn't jump, but he was right, it almost hurt, hurt in a delicious, exciting way but still kind of, well, hurt. Like there were a million more nerve endings bristling under his tongue than had ever bristled under Patrick's tongue, even in the early days, and maybe that was just because Hector did it better, or maybe because she had already come so many times tonight, she was like a live, hot wire. Whatever the reason, something had changed, her breasts felt swollen and ripe, and the movement of Hector's mouth laid tracks of sensation directly down her belly to her clitoris, tracks unknown until now, and when he took the other nipple between his thumb and forefinger and caressed that too, slid his other hand downward and made just the slightest movement of his finger between her legs, she arched her back and went straight to climax. Hector raised his head and watched her face as she came. When she was finished he kissed her and said that was maybe the most amazing thing he'd ever seen, Ella was the most amazing woman, how did she do that, and she put her arms around his neck and whispered, That was you, you did that, that's never happened before.

Really? he said, kind of pleased.

Really, she said, kind of embarrassed. Kind of puzzled.

But one thing led to another, and she forgot about her puzzlement until the next morning. Until she got back from walking Nellie and took a shower, and while she was washing her skin, that feeling returned to her, the one she'd felt on waking. Dreamy and satisfied, but unsettled, like she had forgotten something, had missed some important appointment. And she was washing herself, running the washcloth over her breasts, thinking about Hector's mouth, thinking her breasts really did look swollen, felt sore, and like a brick falling from the ceiling she remembered just which appointment she'd missed lately.

At which point, her cell phone rang. Her mother, wanting to know how she was feeling.

"I'm feeling fine, Mumma," Ella said. "Why do you ask?"

"Why do I ask? Because you cancelled dinner last night, remember? You were sick?"

"Oh! Right. I mean, yeah. Feeling much better this morning."

"Are you sure? You don't sound well."

"Just tired."

"Well, come and meet us for brunch, then. Eleven o'clock at Sarabeth's."

Ella stood in the middle of Hector's bathroom and stared at her reflection in the mirror. Hair dripping, towel wrapped clumsily around her middle. Hand clasping the phone to her ear. Starting to shake, like when you were coming down with a fever, deep body shakes you couldn't control.

"You know what," she said, "I think I should probably just stay home and rest."

After she hung up the phone, she got dressed and went outside. Walked briskly around the Village for an hour, got a little lost before finding a familiar street and regaining her bearings. Picked up a turkey sandwich on wheat at the deli: mustard mayonnaise lettuce tomato. Turned into the Duane Reade on Sixth Avenue and bought mascara, a bag of cotton balls, and a pregnancy test.

**The night** before Ella discovered her husband screwing a prostitute on the landing between the third and fourth floors of their Tribeca apartment building, they'd had sex, she and Patrick, because they were trying for a baby. Had been trying for a baby for almost a year, in fact, with no luck. Ella had been late a few times, but just before she gathered up her nerve and went out to get a test, her period always came.

"Don't worry," Patrick had said in February, when he found her crying in the bathroom. "It'll happen. Just keep doing what we're doing. It'll happen, I promise."

"No, it won't," she'd bawled. "It's been a year already. It's not just going to happen."

"Then we'll make it happen." Patrick drew her close. "We'll just keep trying."

Trying. Ella hated that word. It made sex sound like some kind of effort, something you could fail at. When she stopped taking the pill, she hadn't even been that excited about making a baby. It was Patrick who begged her, Patrick who wanted to get started on the three or four smiling kids that would complete their Christmas photo. Ella just wanted to make Patrick happy. That, and she was turning thirty. It was time. You had to have kids eventually, or else Social Security was doomed; why not now, while your eggs were still fresh? But the first couple of months, she was secretly relieved when no baby appeared. Babies were a lot of work, almost frightening in the way they took over a couple's lives with their mysterious demands, their vast equipment, their noise and expense. Only after five or six barren months passed did Ella start to wonder if something was wrong—something was wrong with her—and she grew anxious and frustrated, she began to take an interest in the babies passing by in their strollers—babies in their thousands, it seemed, flanked by triumphant parents. She found herself suppressing jealousy of pregnant women, women with babies, women who exuded the smug, Madonna-like joy (or so it seemed to Ella) of having succeeded in creating life.

We'll make it happen, Patrick had said confidently. And apparently, a couple of weeks later, they finally had. Maybe even that final night, their last try, the night before Patrick fucked the hooker and ended their marriage. Who knew? Because when Ella checked her watch Sunday afternoon at three sixteen (having held her bladder for four hours) and went back into Hector's bathroom to examine the pregnancy stick, the line was blue. Not just blue, but a pungent, shameless, cerulean blue, a blue you couldn't mistake for anything else than what it was.

Patrick's baby.

**Of course,** it might come to nothing, Ella reminded herself, as she departed the Starbucks that Monday morning, newly unemployed, in search of the Redhead. She was only a little more than six weeks along. Not much later than those other times, when she ended up getting her period after all: periods that were most likely early miscarriages, failed pregnancies, now that she could recall them objectively.

Was that what she wanted? A miscarriage?

She walked south down Madison Avenue, toward an address she'd looked up in the Yellow Pages. The damp was strengthening into drizzle, and she hadn't brought a raincoat. She, Ella Gilbert, who always brought rain gear when rain was a possibility! She'd just . . . forgotten. Well, the truth was, she'd stopped by her apartment early that morning for a suit to wear to work, and the sight of Patrick's flowers had brought her up short. Dozens of bouquets, a dazzle of color, roses and stargazer lilies and hyacinths, producing a scent so rich and so expensive she just stood there, sort of drunk, holding on to the doorknob to keep herself upright. Like Kew Gardens, Hector had warned her. The lyin', cheatin' flowers, Hector had called them on Friday evening, right before he kissed her and told her he was falling in love with her, he was crazy about her, and maybe he couldn't afford flowers like that—Hector composed music, not investment banking deals— but he could give her himself, and she'd forgotten all about the existence of Patrick's latest peace offering until that second.

So, yeah. She'd lunged forward to the closet, grabbed her charcoal suit and calfskin pumps, and left the rain-coat behind.

On the other hand, she didn't need the suit any-more, did she? She'd just resigned her secure, well-compensated position at a conservative accounting firm. The drizzle could fall where it damn well pleased. Frizzing her hair, disfiguring her wool. Who cared? The shop was about five more blocks down Madison, in the genteel, downtrodden Twenties before you reached the Flatiron. The pavement darkened, the cracks grew wider. She passed a Blimpie, a liquor store. Madison Square Park opened up to her right. Inside a Starbucks, people huddled over their books and laptops, and Ella found herself wondering who they were. Who were these people, who didn't have to report to an office during the day? Were they unemployed? Actors or musicians, maybe? She could join them, if she wanted. For the first time in her life, Ella could walk into a Starbucks—any kind of coffee shop, really—and nurse a latte while she read a novel or tapped away at her computer. Except she didn't have a computer anymore. When she'd stopped by human resources and submitted her resignation letter, she'd turned over her company laptop, too.

The smell of wet pavement rose from the sidewalk. Ella's skin was slick with drizzle. She crossed Twenty-Third Street and started looking in storefronts: a pharmacy, a bodega, an apartment vestibule.

And there it was, next to a deli, just as the Yellow Pages promised. Peeling gold letters in a plate glass window. Ionia Antique Maps & Prints.

**The fellow** behind the counter was about forty years old and thought he was sixty. He had thick, black-rimmed glasses, not to follow some trend but because they were old. He wore a tweed suit jacket over a burgundy sweater vest, thoroughly pilled, and a felt hat hung on the wall behind him. His hair was stiff and shiny, brown peppered with gray. He stared disapprovingly at her wet shoulders as the door jangled shut.

"Hello," she said. "I'm Ella Gilbert. I left a message on your machine yesterday?"

The disapproval lifted away. "The one with the Redhead card?"

"That's me."

He stepped out eagerly from behind the counter and held out his hand. "Fergus Smith. So glad you could stop by. Can I—can I take your jacket?"

"No, thanks. I'll just let it dry on me." Ella released his hand and let out a weak laugh. The place smelled of oldness, of newsprint and must and maybe a hint of the beeswax polish Ella recognized from Aunt Vivian's beach house in the Hamptons, which dated back about a century. The wooden cabinets lining the walls contained a few shelves—filled with books—but mostly drawers. Rows and rows of drawers, all shut tight.

Fergus was already moving to a glass-topped display table in the center of the room. Reaching for something in a drawer underneath, which turned out to be a pair of felt gloves. He put them on reverently, one by one, and laid out a black felt cloth on the surface of the table, while Ella extracted the card from her laptop bag. Brushed off a crumb from a blueberry scone. He looked horrified.

"You haven't been keeping it there, have you?"

"I only got it a few days ago. I didn't realize—"

"Redhead cards are extremely collectible, Miss Gilbert. Extremely valuable."

"I had no idea. I just . . ."

Fergus held out his hands. "May I see it?"

Ella handed him the card, which he accepted by the edges and held out carefully in the air before him, framed by his felt-lined fingers. His expression turned puzzled. He set down the card on the black cloth, took off his eyeglasses, and plucked up the card again.

"Redhead Beside Herself," he said softly, and then, without looking up, "Where did you get this?"

"My aunt gave it to me. My great-great-aunt, actually. She lives in the Hamptons."

Fergus switched on the green-shaded lamp at the corner of the display table. He pulled out a small magnifying glass from his jacket pocket, set the card back down on the surface, and bent over it. Ella stared at the upside-down picture of the Redhead's naked figure, her nose bathed in light and tilted to the ceiling, her breasts fuller and more perfectly round than Ella's pregnant ones. The juncture of her thighs, coyly hidden, which now suffered the minute inspection of Fergus's right eye. Ella shifted her feet awkwardly. Somewhere in her laptop bag, her cell phone buzzed. She reached inside and turned it off.

Fergus raised his head. "Excuse me for a moment, please."

"Okeydokey."

He set down the magnifying glass and went to the shelves behind the counter. Ran his fingers along the spines. His movements were jerky, full of excess energy. Ella's hand was still inside her laptop bag, rubbing the curve of her silent cell phone. Fergus made a noise in his throat and pulled out a volume from the shelf at the top, a catalog of some kind, shiny and floppy. He opened it as he walked back to the display table. Flipped through pages, wetting his finger every so often.

"Here!" He thrust the book forward.

Ella, taken by surprise, took it gingerly. The page before her looked like an encyclopedia entry, illustrated with sepia cards, all of them depicting the Redhead in various poses, various scenes. She was naked or mostly naked in each one, her miraculous chest in clear, adoring focus, her face either disguised or turned away, her hair the only patch of color. Redhead Goes to Bat. Redhead Takes the Cake. Redhead Dreaming. Bon Voyage, Redhead.

"They sold in their thousands when they came out," Fergus said. "But very few survive to the present day. Maybe a dozen or so examples of each. Lost or thrown out by wives and lovers, probably."

"When were they made?"

"The first one was issued in 1922. The last one in 1924. A new photograph came out every month or two, and its arrival would have been much anticipated among the gentlemen of Manhattan."

"I'll bet. But it's not exactly pornography, is it? It's something else."

"Actually, the photographer was a minor artist. A fellow who went by the name of Anatole, although his legal name was Andrew Green. Andy Green. You can see the skill in composition, the way he poses her, the way he lights the scene."

"He was in love with her."

"Probably. We don't know anything about the model herself, unfortunately. Not even her name."

Ella looked up from the catalogue. "Seriously? Nobody knows her name?"

Fergus shook his head. "Nothing at all. She's like a ghost. Appeared in 1922 out of nowhere, disappeared in 1924. No other pictures of her exist, just these. And a series of six or seven paintings by Anatole himself—nobody's exactly sure how many— which were exhibited in early 1922, before the first card was printed. At the time, they were a sensation."

Ella pointed to Redhead Beside Herself. "You mean like that one above that sofa?"

"Yes," Fergus said.

"Where are they now? The paintings?"

"Again, nobody knows. Nobody even knows what they look like. Like the Redhead herself, they disappeared. Not a single one has ever come up for public sale since the original exhibition. We can only speculate how they were executed, based on the descriptions in the reviews at the time. The reviews of the exhibition, I mean. The gallery itself is long gone, of course, and its records and descriptions with it."

"Well, except this one, I guess. We know what that portrait looks like, the one above the sofa."

Fergus looked back down at the card on the table, lying on its cloth of black felt. He picked up the magnifying glass, and his hand was shaking a little. "But that's what's so extraordinary, Miss Gilbert. Has your aunt had this card in her sole possession, all these years?"

"I don't know. I guess so. I think she knew the Redhead, actually. So maybe it was a gift or something."

"She knew the Redhead?"

"I'm pretty sure that's what she said. I don't remember her exact words. I think they used to hang out at the same places, back in the twenties. Speakeasies and that kind of thing. My aunt was a flapper."

Fergus straightened again. Laid down the magnifying glass. Reached for his eyeglasses and set them carefully back on the bridge of his nose. "Is it possible for me to speak to your aunt, Miss Gilbert?" His voice trembled.

"I don't know. She's a very private person. Kind of difficult, to be honest. And she's old, obviously. Ninety-six years old."

"If I could just speak to her. I'd be happy to drive out and meet her in person—"

"But why?" Ella demanded. "What's so extraordinary about this card?"

Fergus took a deep breath and knit his fingers across his ribs, almost like he was readying himself to pray. "Because Redhead Beside Herself never actually made it to sale. It was the last of the series. Printing was halted and the cards themselves disappeared. Presumed destroyed, all these years. And nobody has ever seen one, until now."

By the time Ella returned to Hector's apartment, it was almost lunchtime, and she was both ravenous and nauseous at the same time. That was a bad sign, wasn't it? She opened the fridge. For a guy, Hector kept a fair amount of fresh groceries on hand. There were apples and carrots in the fruit drawer, eggs and cheese, a tub of hummus, milk and juice and pickles— pickles, dear God!—and three different kinds of mustard. None of it appealed to Ella. She shut the fridge and went to the fruit bowl and started to un- peel a banana, but the smell made her gag. She set it down again and poured a glass of milk, which she sipped slowly, sitting at the counter. Staring at the open shelves of glasses and thinking about how much bourbon she had drunk here, how much wine. Not every day, never enough to get drunk, but still. She put her head down on the counter, on top of her folded arms. She should be drinking orange juice, right? She'd heard something about the importance of folic acid.

On the other hand, what did it matter? She might still lose this one, like the others. And even if she didn't . . .

She lifted her head and reached for the laptop bag, before the thought could take hold. Before the word, even, could sound itself out in her head. Unzipped the main compartment and pulled out the ziplock bag con- taining the felt sack that now contained the Redhead.

Fergus hadn't wanted to part with her. Asked Ella if she realized just how much this card was worth, if she realized that some of the world's wealthiest men were Redhead collectors. He could pick up that phone, he said (pointing to the telephone on the sales counter, next to the tarnished brass cash register with the pop-up numbers), and get her a dozen six-figure offers for Redhead Beside Herself, not including museums, not including universities.

No dice, Ella had said. Sentimental value. The Redhead belonged to her.

Think it over, said Fergus. And in the meantime, maybe he could speak to her aunt? Drive out to the Hamptons and meet her?

Sorry, Ella said. Aunt Julie's sick.

That was a lie, her first lie. The second lie was more in the nature of an omission. She thought about telling Fergus what she knew, as he wrapped up Redhead Beside Herself in her swaddling. His long, manicured fingers caressed the photograph; at each painstaking step in this process—wiping the card clean, slipping it inside the felt sack, folding the sides of the sack so it encased the card exactly—he let out aggrieved sighs. Possibly he was contemplating murdering Ella and taking the Redhead for himself; possibly he was calculating the odds that he could get away with it. The necessary logistics for such a crime, in a city like New York. When he finished, he presented the ziplock to Ella with both hands, still covered by their felt gloves.

Let me know if you change your mind, he said.

Ella grasped the sides of the plastic bag and said she would.

And as they stood there in the center of the shop, the glass display case between them, each holding a piece of the Redhead, she thought maybe she should go ahead and tell him the Redhead's name.

But she didn't.

**Ella took** the milk and the ziplock bag and her cell phone into the bedroom, Hector's bedroom, and lay down in the middle of the bed. Nellie jumped up behind her and settled near the warm part of Ella's waist, turning around three times before curling into a tight, silken ball. Nellie didn't go to sleep, though. She kept her round eyes open, fixed anxiously on Ella's face.

Ella had been right about Hector. He was a fantastic lover, and the most amazing thing about Saturday night—the telling thing, in Ella's view—was this: he had only come once. He spent the entire night running up to the brink of orgasm and drawing back. They made love on the bed, on the sofa, on the piano; sitting up and lying down; they had made love with their mouths and hands; they had made love with words and deeds. But Ella was the one who climaxed, over and over, while Hector just paused and bided his time. What about you? she asked breathlessly, at one point, and he kissed her and said he was just enjoying the journey, not to worry, they had all night. Ella was mystified. With Patrick it was all about the orgasm, it was all about the finish line. During one twenty-four-hour period on their honeymoon, he came five times and called it his PB. His personal best. The last one took forever, but he refused to quit until he got there. Ella was so sore the next day, she couldn't wear her swimsuit.

Hector, on the other hand. Whereas Patrick turned inward during sex, concentrated on his own pleasure, actually rated each climax on a scale of 1 to 10, Hector went outward. He was fascinated by Ella, transfixed by Ella's responses and by the arc of Ella's sexual experience. Only at the end of the night did he let himself go. Ella lay on her back on the edge of the bed, and Hector was thrusting luxuriously, holding her hips, and for some reason—some surge of reckless trust—she opened her eyes, and there was Hector, eyes also open, watching her watching him in the literal act of making love. Ella thought, This is the sexiest thing I've ever done. She reached up and touched his cheek, and the next second his hands tightened, his shudders passed through his body and into hers, on and on, and she was so happy she thought she might pass out. His joy was her joy. At the end, he sank quietly atop her, and she loved his weight, his tranquility, his silence. When he lifted himself away and took care of the condom, she rolled on her side and watched him. His rangy, unashamed limbs, his olive skin. Nellie came up to him as he emerged from the bathroom, and he bent down and caressed her ears. Ella held out her arms and said, Let's go to sleep now.

So they slept.

But this was Monday afternoon, not Saturday night, and though Ella was lying in the same spot in the middle of the bed, the same dog curled into her waist, she couldn't gather back that peace. Just couldn't find the sense of that moment, the proximity of Hector, the way it felt to drift to sleep to the rhythm of Hector's breathing. She put her hand on her stomach and thought, If only you were Hector's baby. This would be so simple if you belonged to Hector. If, in some alternate universe, she had discovered Patrick's seedy habits a month earlier, and Hector hadn't been so careful with the condoms. And for an instant she pictured telling Hector he was going to be a father, what he would say. The strangeness of making a baby with someone you had only known for a month, the rightness of its being Hector. She felt sure that Hector would be happy. Dazed, maybe, but happy. He would be into the idea of fatherhood. He would find her pregnancy sexy. Six weeks. Six stupid weeks, and this would be Hector's baby, and it would be complicated but it would be okay.

Poor baby. Not your fault. You can't choose your daddy, can you?

That's mommy's job.

And mommy kind of screwed up. Not on purpose. Actually, it was daddy's screwup, but mommy should have known, she should have realized long before what daddy was up to. Should have realized that daddy and mommy were inhabiting two completely different marriages. Just like Aunt Julie had realized and known.

Ella sat up and drank the rest of the milk. Unwrapped the ziplock bag and the felt until Redhead Beside Herself rested on Ella's lap, her skin bathed in ethereal light. Geneva, Ella thought. That was her name, the name Aunt Julie had called her. A woman named Geneva Kelly, who had lived right here in this building and then disappeared. Was that the reason for all those sympathetic clarinets echoing about the walls? The jazz band drifting through the cinder-block wall in the basement, the speakeasy laughter interrupted, from time to time, by a gunshot and a scream? Who knew, maybe the Redhead had also gotten herself knocked up by the wrong fellow. Or maybe that was the least of her troubles. A woman like that, she could get into any kind of trouble she wanted.

Ella flipped open her cell and scrolled through the memory list until she found Aunt Julie's number at Maidstone Meadows. The phone rang and rang. Aunt Julie had her own apartment at the Meadows—Tombstone Meadows, as the residents blithely called it—and her own private line, but she never had turned on the voice mail function. Also, she only picked up the receiver when she felt like it. If you really wanted to speak to Aunt Julie, you had to drive out to the Hamptons and find her.

After the fourteenth ring (Ella counted), she hung up. Sat with the phone in her lap and stared not at the Redhead, but at Nellie. The wonderful thing about dogs; you could gaze at each other without embarrassment, without the naked intimacy that she'd shared with Hector Saturday night. With Nellie, there was no intensity, no nakedness. Just a frank exchange of opinion. You should call him, Nellie told her. It's the right thing to do. The poor man is worried sick, and it's not his fault. He did everything right.

But I can't tell him now. Not over the damned telephone. Not before I've even told Patrick.

You don't have to tell him that. Just tell him you're alive.

Ella flipped the phone back open and dialed Hector's cell number. Prayed it would go to voice mail, but he picked up on the second ring.

"Ella! Are you all right?"

Deep breath.

"I'm fine. I'm fine. I'm so sorry. I should have called you before. I just—I just . . ." I just found out I'm pregnant with my husband's baby. "It was just so much."

There was the slightest pause. "Okay," he said slowly, and then, "Hold on a sec." (She heard him talking to someone, faintly.) "Give me a minute, okay? Yeah, I'll catch up. Go ahead, I'll get a taxi." (Then his voice again, low and urgent.) "Ella?"

"Right here."

"Where are you now? How did everything go at work?"

"I resigned, actually. Handed in my letter. It turned out they weren't going to fire me after all, but I resigned anyway."

"Happy?"

"Yeah. I think so. Still a little dazed. How about you? How's everything with the movie?"

"It's great. It's great. I played them my stuff. They were excited. Going to watch the rough cut now. Ella, seriously. Are we good? You're okay? You didn't answer my question. Where are you?"

She smiled. "I'm sitting on your bed right now, okay? Thinking about you. Nellie's here with me. She misses you. Says hello."

There was an audible release of breath on the mouthpiece. "You have no idea—"

"I know, I know. I just—the sound of your voice—I couldn't even read your note at first. I missed you too much. It hurt too much. It hurts to hear your voice right now."

"Ella, you have no idea, no idea how much it hurt to walk out of that apartment Sunday morning. The sun wasn't even up. Everything dark. Felt like I'd ripped myself open and left my guts behind with you."

"Eww."

He laughed. "Sorry. What I mean is that I hated that, I hated walking away from you without saying good-bye or anything. Then the radio silence. So I basically went from miserable to worried. Then frantic worried. First I thought you'd freaked out because I came on too strong, and then I thought—well, I thought the opposite, like maybe I didn't make myself clear enough."

"No. I mean, neither one of those things."

"Because, just to be clear, Ella, crystal clear, that was it for me. Saturday night was it. Being with you, that was the best night of my life, on every level, does that make sense? You know what I mean, right? Don't be afraid. Don't think you need to hold back."

"Okay," she whispered. "I won't."

"Ella. You're okay?"

"Yes. Sorry. You're just making me cry, that's all. Saying all that—and your voice—I've always loved your voice."

"Well, you had me going last night in my big lonely hotel room when I hadn't heard back, so fair's fair."

"I am so, so sorry for that. I was a total jerk. I was just scared, I guess."

"That's what I figured. That's what I hoped. I mean, not that I wanted you to be scared, but—"

"I know. I'm not. I mean, I'm not scared about—it's not what you think. It's not you."

"As in, it's not you, it's me?"

"No! I mean, yes. I mean . . ."

She faltered and went helplessly silent. Turned to Nellie, who laid her head on her paws and looked worried. The door to the living room stood open, and she could just see the black tip of the piano around the corner, surrounded by the gloom of a rainy Manhattan afternoon, and her breath stopped in her throat.

Hector said, "Phones suck, don't they?"

"Yes."

"So I have an idea. I'm taking the red-eye back Friday night. Let's not talk until then. We'll say it all on Saturday. Whatever needs saying. How does that sound?"

"Sounds like you're going to miss your taxi."

"Fuck the taxi. Saturday morning. Do we have a date?"

Ella closed her eyes. "I'll make the coffee," she said.

"Good. Great. Perfect. Love coffee. I will be thinking about nothing else."

"Me neither."

"Okay, then. Agreed. No more words. Hanging up now."

"Hanging up."

"I love you," he said, and clicked off.

# ACT II

# We Are Cleft in Twain
## *(sic transit gloria mundi)*

**Cocoa Beach, Florida**
**April 1924**

# 1

A thing you may not know about me: I am a bastard. I was born a full two years before my mama married my step-daddy, and I never did know the man who sired me. Some New York swell, whose identity I have never discovered. He must have been a devil, however, if he left my mama and me to the tender protection of Duke Kelly.

So Patsy and I are but half sisters, and I reckon—sired as we were by these two different devils, out of the same cursed mother—Duke must have represented the lesser evil after all, for my Patsy is as sweet as a barrel of warm cider, as innocent as a new hound puppy. She has tempted even so grave a fellow as Oliver Anson Marshall into a tea party with the Fitzwilliam fry and a trio of bored teddy bears, right there at the dining room table, not quite a week after our arrival here in Florida, and the sight brings me up so short, my heart liketa crash upon my ribs.

"Patricia Ruth Kelly," I say, "what in the name of the good Lord do you think you're doing?"

"It's a tea party!" She gestures down the row of teddy bears. "And you're awful late. You may sit next to Hansel."

"Which one is Hansel?"

"The one with the missing ear, I believe," says Anson.

I attempt to fold my arms. With no success, I'm afraid, on account of the new sling Simon has fashioned for me—Simon is Dr. Fitzwilliam's Christian name, you recollect—with strict instructions not to lose it this time. "I will do no such thing, Patsypet. You've bamboozled poor Mrs. Fitzwilliam long enough."

"Oh, she's no trouble!" trills Virginia—that's Mrs. Fitzwilliam's Christian name, don't you know—who sits on Anson's left. "We're having a grand time. A new house needs a good tea party to warm things up."

"We baked a cake!" says little Evelyn, jiggling in her chair.

Simon circles around me to admire the tableau. "You baked a cake! What kind of cake?"

"Ginger cake with orange icing! See, Daddy?"

He claps his hand to his heart. "My favorite! May I have a slice?"

"Your place is right there." Patsy points her finger to the opposite end of the table.

He takes his seat obediently. "I hope you've saved me some tea. I'm jolly parched."

I throw up my one good arm and sit down next to Hansel, who leans attentively in my direction, perhaps because of his bad ear. Patsy rises from her chair to fill my cup from a blue-and-white porcelain teapot of alarming fragility, while little Evelyn Fitzwilliam cuts me a clumsy slice of ginger cake. I devote my concentration to this succession of offerings, in order to avoid Anson's electromagnetic gaze across the table as it seeks to connect circuits with mine. But I can't avoid the effect on my redhead's skin, it seems. Evelyn tells me I'm blushing.

"Evelyn!" her mother says sharply. "It's not polite to make personal remarks to our guests."

"That's all right, sweetie. It's just the heat, is all. I'm not yet accustomed. Up north, it's still bone cold."

"Your hair is red," Evelyn adds solemnly.

"Evelyn!"

"Well, it is, Mama."

"Evelyn, my dear," I say, "you've hit the nail right on the head. There's no getting around the awful truth. My hair's the color of a bunch of new carrots, crossed with a handful of pennies, and it's an affliction I shall carry to my grave. And do you want to know why?"

"Why?" the three children ask, in unison. (Even Sammy, down the other end of Teddy Row, who must be nine or ten, and whose expression throughout these proceedings I'll describe charitably as one of bemused tolerance.)

"Because I'm wicked." And I take the entire slice of ginger cake into my mouth at once, in a snap of my sinful teeth.

The kids erupt into a jazz chorus of squealing. Anson finishes his tea, folds his napkin, and asks if he might speak to me privately.

# 2

When we are done kissing—and this takes some time, you understand—Anson leans his head back against the sand and stares gravely at the sky. I ask him what's wrong.

"Nothing's wrong."

"Too peaceful for you? Six days in paradise and you're already bored?"

"Not at all."

I inspect his face, which wears an expression of almost pain. Like me, he's wearing a bathing suit, which lays bare most of the splendors of his physique. You might prefer your fellows more elegant, of course, but I've grown to appreciate these bull-like shoulders and barrel chest and thick legs. Grown to envy the way his olive skin absorbs the sun the way my redhead's dermis—shielded now by a long linen towel—does not. I run my fingernail along the line of his jaw, from ear to chin. "You don't say. You're maybe discovering there's a little more excitement in this world than chasing the demon rum from our shores?"

"Ginger," he says, "I might suffer from a lot of things in your company, but a lack of excitement's not one of them."

"Is that so?"

"That's so."

"Suffer from what, then?"

My finger, by now, has wandered up to his lips, which have blistered a little in all the sun. A small patch of vulnerability. There is something about this coast that beckons you forever outside, even when it comes on to rain in some tropical habit. You might play in the surf or the sand, comb the beach for shells and such things, watch the manic antics of the sea birds while the sun warms your blood and the salt water cleanses your ankles. And though Anson and I frolic mostly with Patsy and the Fitzwilliams, we do sometimes steal off by ourselves, down the long line of beach, where we found this spot a few days ago, a little notch where the land thins almost to nothing and the mangrove turns into common marsh grass, and you can sit without anybody seeing you until they're just about on top of you. But nobody ever comes. Just the two of us. Lying under the hot sky. And I expect there must be some kind of tonic in the air, some kind of vaporous love potion, because I cannot look at this man without desiring to touch him, without desiring to worship inside the temple of his arms, his chest, his knee, his neck, his toes. I am punch drunk, I am dead gone, I am a thousand times more enamored than I was a week ago, like this love of mine is feeding on its own enchantment. Enough to make mamas cluck their tongues and grannies smile. Enough to make the Lord Almighty weep for Anson's suffering while I taste the skin of his shoulder.

He's grinning now, grinning right up at that sky of ours, fixing to electrify the heavens or something. He snatches my wandering fingers and kisses them, by way of answering my question I guess, and then he leaps up and runs for the ocean.

I rise on my elbows and enjoy the sight of him. Legs like giant pistons, throwing up sand, and then the brilliant arc of his body as he plunges into the water. Surf's as gentle today as I've ever seen it, God's own bath, and he finds little trouble slicing his way through the feeble breakers and into the calm. He swims in long, clean strokes, out to sea and back again, and when he has worked off the weight of his suffering he returns to shore and holds out his wet hand to me. Still grinning.

"Oh no," I say. "You can keep your ocean to yourself."

"Come on. It's as calm as a millpond out there. Nothing to be afraid of."

"I'm not afraid."

"I won't leave your side for a second. Come on." He reaches down and finds my hand and hauls me to my feet. "You can't let a bad dream keep you from an ocean like that, Ginger."

"It's got nothing to do with my dreams," I say, which is partly true but not entirely, and even that truthful part isn't so true as it was yesterday.

He just swoops me up into his arms. "Look at that horizon. Not a ship in sight," he tells me, as he carries me down to the drink.

"Nothing to do with ships."

"Then what's the matter? Can't you swim, after all?"

"I can swim, all right."

Anson's reached the water right now, and it doesn't slow him down a bit. Just marches on, so I am forced, forced, to sling my arms around his neck as the surf washes around his ankles, his knees, the rim of his navy-blue bathing suit. Wave starts to build up before us, and I scream at him to hold on, don't let go, and what does he do but turn his back before this thing, this growing monster. Turns his back and lets it crash over us, but he doesn't let go, keeps strict hold of me until we emerge, floating, and then one arm drops free so he can propel us out beyond that line where the waves rise up.

"All right?" he says.

"Water's cold."

"It's not cold. It's a lot warmer than up north, that's for sure. It's April, that's all. You'll get used to it in a second or two."

He's still got one firm arm around my waist while we tread in place. Water rises and falls gently against our shoulders. I open my eyes and find his face next to mine, droplets all down his browning skin, eyes bluer than I have ever seen them. Lashes black and wet. Solid, primeval bones. The cold panic in my blood starts to warm back up. Must be the sun, I reckon.

"You can let go now," I say.

His arm slides away, and I'm swimming, just like I used to do in the fishing hole back home in River Junction, except for the all-powerful atmosphere of salt that surrounds my head and invades the cavities within. And this new, unnatural buoyancy that the fresh mountain water cannot lend you. I turn back my head and allow my feet to rise. Examine my toes peeking out of the water. Anson's fingers touch my head and part the hair in delicate strokes, the way he did with Patsy when we returned home from Rum Row in the dark of night.

"You are the most beautiful woman in the world," he says.

"Applesauce."

"Like a naiad. A water nymph. We had this picture book when I was a kid—"

"Now, don't start to tell me about all your complexes, Anson."

He just laughs. Takes his hand away and starts to float alongside me. "I always knew you were out there. Growing up somewhere, reading your own picture books. I just never figured you'd be a redhead."

I flip back upright and deliver him a shove.

"Like a—what was it? Handful of new pennies—"

I sling my arm around his chest and dunk him under, and when we come up we are somehow kissing each other. You know how it is. Covered with water and salt, kissing each other like the world might could end in a minute or two, staying afloat by the sure stroke of Anson's legs. His hands about my waist. Waves pop against us, dislodging our embrace from time to time, but that just adds to the fever between us, the heat of his skin against mine, the sweet struggle as he pulls down each strap of my bathing suit, one then the other, and I help him do it, God save me, wriggling each arm in turn, until I am half-naked before him, milk-white breasts open to the sun, gathering freckles on the slopes of them. And Anson does sink before this sight, both arms around my waist lifting me high in the water, the better to feast on me, and I think, this is nothing like how we came together two weeks ago, this is something else. This is making love to a different man entirely, a man I thought I knew well enough, but it turns out I only knew a piece of him, and now I have discovered more pieces, each one more intricate than the last, and his hot mouth suckling the tip of my breast is just about all I can bear.

And I can't say anything more about it, because a series of waves commences to jostle us, the wake of some passing ship or something, and we are broke apart, gasping, treading water, regarding each other in shock.

When the water calms again, Anson swims back to me. Helps arrange my bathing suit back into place. Gathers me with one arm so we float together, held up by the tranquil movement of legs and arms and longing.

"We can't stay here forever," I say.

"I know."

"Houseguests are like milk. After a week or two, they start to turn sour on you."

"Where did you hear that?"

"My mama."

He laughs. How he has laughed this past week, more than all the laughter that ever came before. And what a laugh. Warm and loose and rumbly, like you could curl up next to it and warm yourself. Chest rattles us both.

"So what do we do next?" I ask. "I mean, if we aim to stay together in this. You and me and Patsy."

He doesn't speak. We bob together, and I realize his toes are touching the sand, that the water isn't so deep as I imagined. Sun burns the top of my head. I think,

Should probably get out of the water now. Find some shade before I burn. I start to pull away, and he bends his head to my neck.

"You tell me," he says.

# 3

Now, to be clear, I never did want to get married. There is this photograph of my mama and Duke on their wedding day, my only glimpse of her before she took to my stepfather's bed, and I look upon that picture as I would upon a funeral. Here lies the old mama, about to be buried six feet under the earth of Duke Kelly, may she rest in peace. So I had this idea, when I fled River Junction at the gentle age of nineteen and threw myself into the beating heart of New York City, that I was never going to bury myself under six feet of any man. I was going to live. And how. I chose my own work and I chose my own drink; I chose my own friends and I chose my own lovers. And I always did wonder why my mama didn't do the same. Why she returned to River Junction from the great big hustle and bustle, the island of brash female independence that is Manhattan, and sunk herself beneath Duke Kelly for the rest of her livelong days.

Now I understand. The answer is me. Some darling young creature entrusted to her care.

Mind you, I still think my mama made a mistake. I think the two of us might have been better off without Duke, even living alone in some New York slum. But maybe we wouldn't. Maybe my mama was fleeing some worse devil than the one she wound up marrying. I guess I never will know the facts of that story. But I understand the why of it. I do. I know why she made her bargain with that Mephistopheles I called my step-daddy.

And there's another thing I understand, down inside the marrow of my bones, down inside the innermost chambers of my heart: Oliver Anson Marshall is no such devil.

# 4

Wait, there's more.

I admit I have spent my Florida nights in Anson's bed, every one, stealing there when the household is quiet and rising again with the first glimpse of sun. And I have spent hours lying with him on the sand, sitting with him in the courtyard, walking with him in the paths cut through the mangrove, swatting at mosquitoes.

But we have not been intimate, not in the manner of husbands and wives, not once. Maybe you noticed. We have kissed and touched and held ourselves in check, and that is perhaps mostly for a private reason of my own, but not entirely. And that additional constraint maybe arises from Billy, or from Anson's sense of virtue, or from respect for our hosts, or some combination of all those things. I don't know exactly. Possibly Anson could tell you why, though he doesn't talk much, and certainly not to strangers. One thing's certain. We do not lack desire for copulation. Lies right there in the bed between us, in the infinitesimal space between my skin and his skin, in the overheated air between my gaze and his gaze. In the sun and the haze and the sea and the food and the furniture. Just about everywhere you look, and especially when you close your eyes.

So maybe it's no surprise, after all. No surprise that after a week in this fevered, fertile paradise, caring for my Patsy, cavorting with my beloved, I've made my peace with that little word marriage. Maybe even discovered something tantalizing about it. Carries a certain promise, doesn't it, the promise of consummation. All constraint gone. With my body I thee worship. Maybe even sacred, as the vowels and consonants swirl around us like some kind of insect, thirsty for blood, while we tread the ocean water together, legs tangling up, arms clasping waists, Anson's lips resting on my neck. So sweet and heavy is this word, so ripe its temptation, so explosive its power, we have not dared to speak it. Not dared to imagine it. Might shatter everything.

But now. You tell me, he says, holding me in his arms. You tell me what we are to do next, you and me and Patsy.

I open my mouth to speak.

"Marshall!" Like a dog barking. "Marshall! That you?"

We jump high as a pair of guilty dolphins, Anson and I. Break apart and turn to shore, where Simon Fitzwilliam stands in white shirtsleeves and a Panama hat, hands cupped around his mouth.

"Telephone message! It's New York!"

# 5

Back on dry land, dripping and shameful, our feet crusted with sand. Not daring to touch. Simon avoids my face. Hands Anson a folded piece of yellow paper.

"Billy?" I say hoarsely. (For I have sinned, haven't I, and must be punished.)

Anson looks up and shakes his head. Trades some kind of glance with Simon.

"You can use the telephone in my office," says the good doctor.

# 6

You know, it's funny. You can lie there on a riverbank, a mere stripling, newly come into your womanhood, while a man holds you down and tries to take from you something that's not his. You can stand there, years later, in the cold, wet air while that same man rains blows upon you, shoves his fist in your belly and wrenches your arm behind your back. Strips you naked and shames you before a pair of brothers who have each lain with you and loved you, in their turn, and somehow you survive those ordeals, and all the others in between, large and small, that knock against your flesh and the soul beneath.

You can shoot a man stone dead for the crime of holding a knife to the throat of your beloved.

And having endured these things, you think that you are therefore toughened, that you have grown a kind of callus over yourself, and nothing can hurt you again. You have come at last to a place of safety. You have outrun all your nightmares. You have swum in the salt ocean and lain in your lover's arms.

And then somebody tells you he's leaving.

# 7

I guess my face must register some kind of shock, because Anson gives my hand a tender squeeze, and the skin around his eyes turns soft. "I'll be back, of course," he says. "As soon as I can. But I can't stay here. I have to go to New York."

I yank my hand away. We are sitting in the courtyard, surrounded by lemon and eucalyptus, while the children finish dinner on the other side of those French doors over there. "New York? What are you, nuts? The entire United States Bureau of Prohibition's going to be hunting you down, to say nothing of the fellow who arranged your disgrace to begin with. Whoever he is. You're an outlaw, as far as they're concerned."

Anson steps back and leans his shoulders against the eucalyptus, which looks far too slender to bear such a large, square burden. On the other hand, as I well know, the man's capable of shaping all that raw bulk to no more than a whisper of pressure, as the occasion demands. The sun has now dropped behind the ridgepole, leaving his face in shadow. He folds his arms across his chest and says, "Not anymore, I'm not."

"I don't understand."

"It seems the Bureau's had a change of heart. Reinstating me to my previous position."

Well. I don't know what I was expecting him to tell me. I guess I was expecting news of some kind, a decision. The raw material of a plan to navigate this complicated future of ours. But I never imagined that future might prove singular instead of plural. Never imagined the Prohibition bureau might claim Anson back from me, after tossing him over the walls for such crooked reasons of its own. In my ignorance, I figured only the Marshall family had that kind of power over him.

"You can't be serious," I say, sort of choked.

"I am. Reinstated to the Bureau, to be awarded some kind of a medal at a public ceremony. Then assigned, I think it's safe to predict, to some plum, quiet location far from New York City. Possibly even a desk job."

His voice has taken on this hard, ironic quality that raises the hair on my arms. I step forward and detach his hands from the crooks of his elbows. "Who told you all this?" I ask him, even though I suspect I already know the answer. There was, after all, another person by my side, another person involved in all this derring-do, as I bore down on River Junction ten days ago like an army of salvation.

"Luella did," he says.

"Luella. Of course. It was dear Luella who telephoned you today, wasn't it? She's known where we are, all along."

"Yes. I told her where I was taking you, before she left with Billy for the hospital."

"I see. And I reckon she might have had something to do with all those miracles flying your way? Reinstatement and medals and promotions?"

"I suspect she had something to do with it. I expect she made her official report in such a way that they couldn't very well keep me in disgrace, having helped her take down your stepfather . . ."

"Helped her? You took him down all by yourself! I was there, remember? And dear old Luella came in well after the fatal blow was struck, as I recollect."

"But she was the one who fetched you there from New York. And without you in that springhouse, I'd be dead. And so would Billy. And Duke Kelly would still be alive, running moonshine up and down the coast."

"So maybe they should award me a medal."

"Maybe they should," he said, "but it's me they want back under their watch, Ginger, instead of out in the wild, tracking down the fellow who was protecting Kelly's racket. Me they want to throw off the scent, by pretending everything's just fine."

"So don't go back. Don't take the bribe." My good left hand, which had been holding his fingers, down there somewhere at the waist of his gray trousers, traveled up his jacket sleeve to land on his shoulder. "Stay here with me."

"Ginger. This isn't a request. It's more in the nature of a summons."

"Nuts to that. This is the United States of America, remember? Home of the free, land of the brave."

"It's the other way around, actually. Land of the free."

"Don't be fresh. You know what I mean. If a man can't tell the government where to stick its stinking medals and its desk jobs and its low-life partners . . ."

"Luella isn't my partner anymore, and she's certainly no lowlife. Be fair."

"An alley cat's got more native discrimination than that blonde."

"I'm beginning to think you're jealous."

"If I thought you had the poor taste to sniff around after some vamp who possesses no color whatsoever in that limp, pale mane of hers—"

"My God. You're jealous of her."

"—then I wouldn't have fallen in love with you in the first place."

Anson shuts his eyes and presses his hands to the small of my back. I step forward a little unwilling, but once I'm there, smelling his fresh-washed skin, my cheek can't help but come to rest against his shoulder. One of his palms rises to cup the curve of my head. Hold me in place, I guess, as if I had any present plans to move.

"This is my favorite kind of hair," he says.

"Don't go."

"No choice, Ginger."

"You're making a mistake, Anson. You surely know that."

"I know what I'm getting into, if that's what you're asking."

"And they know that you know. They'll be counting on it. I don't give myself above fifty-fifty odds I'll see you again in this lifetime."

His fingers commence to stroking my hair. The panic in my mouth tastes like blood. I swallow it back and continue speaking, so calm as I am able.

"So going to play that game for them, are you? Be their stooge, their monkey on a stage. I can't see you up there, in front of the cameras and the reporters."

"It's not what I want. But I'm going to play along, anyway."

"Why?" I lift my head and step back, breaking his hold. "Lord Almighty, Anson. Duke's dead. You've got what you wanted. He's dead, he's gone—"

"But the gang's still there, Ginger. They're still in business. The stills are still there, the men are still there. They're not going to stop just because Kelly's dead. They'll keep going, probably with the help of Kelly's protector, the one who got me canned from the agency to begin with."

"And why do you care? Let them do it! People are going to drink, Anson, they're going to get stinking drunk, they're going to get pie-eyed any chance they get, and if it ain't River Junction's moonshine they'll get it somewhere else. They'll run it in from Canada, they'll run it in from Nassau, they'll run it in from Saint Pierre. You're just sticking your finger into the crack of an almighty dam. There's nothing you can do. It's an ambush; even I can tell that. You'll just get yourself killed, and where will we be, Patsy and me?"

"I am not going to get killed, Ginger. Do you think I would do that, leave the two of you alone?"

"That's what you're doing right now, so near as I can tell. Leaving the two of us without so much as a good-bye kiss—"

So he kisses me, soft and deep. I taste the Pepsodent on his mouth, the same as the soap on his skin, all cleaned up and ready to depart on the very next train. I put my hands on his neck and kiss harder, like I can kiss all this readiness away, like I can hold him right here by the act of kissing him. Like I never mean to stop. Neither does he, but he stops anyway. Turns his lips to my cheek and jaw and ear, and sighs against my hair, and that's when I know it's over. This kiss of ours was the good-bye kind of kiss. He's going to New York, and I'm staying behind in Florida to wait for news of him. Me, Ginger Kelly, who waits for no man! I make a noise of frustration and bite him in the collarbone. Not hard. Certainly not so hard as he deserves. He doesn't flinch. I lick the tenderness at the base of his throat and allow the salt of his skin to settle on my tongue. Say to myself, what if I never get the chance to taste him again? What if that single Southampton night is all I ever learn of the Anson beneath those austere, snug-buttoned garments?

"Just let me go, Ginger. Let me do this."

"Are you saying I could stop you?"

There is so much physical breadth to this man. So much girth and substance. His arms are of a terrible thickness, enough to snap the bones of a Yale fullback like you might snap a turkey's wishbone on Thanksgiving Day—a task I'm told he performed admirably, during his years on the Princeton grid-iron, not so long ago—and yet the weight of them against my body is that of air. Even the burden of his own mass, he takes upon himself. Gazes down at me without answering my question. Without speaking at all. Bony face and sleek hair, eyes as hard as bottle glass. My head commences to spin, because I recognize that stare, I recognize this man, and he's not the fellow who dragged me into the sea this afternoon. Not the fellow who lay beside me in his bathing suit and smiled up at the sky.

I lift my head and lay my thumb against the side of his cheek. "Well, then. I guess that's all I needed to know."

# 8

Anson's first letter arrives five days after he departed from the Fitzwilliam parlor, and it's almost as brief as the telegram that preceded it three days earlier, to assure me of his safe arrival in New York City. Anson never was one to wax poetic, as some men do. Still, it's something.

I carry it down to the beach, where the children swim bravely in a determined surf, and read it under an umbrella that shields my fair skin from the sunshine.

*Dear Ginger,*

*Forgive me for not writing sooner, but events have moved swiftly since my arrival. I enclose a clipping from the* New York Tribune, *regarding the ceremony last Tuesday, so you can see for yourself I am alive and well.*

*Before I inform you of my present assignment, remember you are not to worry. I write this note from a small cabin in the Coast Guard cutter* Watchful *(out of Sandy Hook), to which I have been attached since my reinstatement to the Bureau. Our mission, as you can guess, is to intercept the supply of liquor from the rumrunners offshore, and mine in particular is to observe and advise the captain in his work, from the advantage of my experience.*

*Let me reassure you, however, that I am not going to join in the boarding and searching of vessels. I am here in an advisory capacity only, and you are not to make yourself anxious for my safety. At this moment, I am mostly concerned that this particular assignment—more than just about any other—prevents me from conducting any investigation of my own. I guess, in retrospect, we should have expected it.*

*I will not write often, as I do not wish to draw any attention by our correspondence. You remain constant, however, in my thoughts and prayers.*

*Yours,*
*O.A.M.*

# 9

When I reach the words Coast Guard, my brain turns a little numb, as if some doctor has injected me with a modern anesthetic for my pain. I sit there for some time and run my eyes over the words, trying to jolt myself back into comprehension. The children scream, the sun beats down on the umbrella above me. I set the letter in the sand and weigh it down with a seashell. Unfold the newspaper clipping, which smells strongly of ink.

The column is naturally effusive, and the photograph's blurred. Anson stands on a platform next to somebody who might be the mayor, and on his other side stands a smiling Luella, her hair altogether white in the sunshine, her figure trim in a fashionable dark dress. So far as I can tell, she is gazing not at the beaming mayor but at Anson's profile.

I look up from the clipping to find the blue sky facing me down over the top of a foaming wave. The image of a ship flashes behind my eyes, bobbing and dipping on the ocean's eternal surface. My heart's beating so hard, it might jump straight up my throat and out my mouth. I swallow it down and shove the clipping under the blanket with Anson's letter, and I leap across the sand and into the sea, until a wave crashes over me and for an instant I am drowned, overcome by a rush of heavy brine that stings my face with salt and sand, and still I can't wash that picture away. Can't wash away the sight of that trim ship, of the stain on the deck, the human flesh stacked in the hold, the frightful dull eyes regarding me.

I emerge gasping and choking, and the children laugh, thinking I mean to play.

# 10

Now, Anson does strive for truth in word and deed, and though I reply faithfully to his letter as soon as I'm able, in sentences considerably more daring than his, no further envelope arrives at the Fitzwilliam villa bearing my name in his firm, black handwriting. No word arrives from his family, either. No newspaper, no telegram, though I do swan I hear the rattle of every engine on the nearby road, the crunch of every wheel on the gravel drive. The days pass, and the sun climbs higher and stronger in the sky, and there is no word of him, not one almighty word.

It's as if he has vanished into the ocean, the same ocean that beats outside my window, by day and by night.

# 11

Because I never did like to lie about idle, Mrs. Virginia Fitzwilliam is teaching me to drive. I have the feeling Dr. Simon Fitzwilliam would disapprove of these lessons, did he know about them, but he doesn't. He's in town, attending to business of some kind. The two of them, they own a citrus plantation inland, and while the shipping company seems to belong to his sisters, he contributes to its management. A busy fellow, I suggest to my companion.

She agrees. "He can't sit still, really. And he's so anxious about the baby, he needs the distraction."

"Anxious? Why? You're as fit as one of those Kentucky broodmares, it seems to me."

"It's just his nature to worry. Now pay attention. The Model T's got its own way of getting about. That pedal on the left, that's forward. The middle one's reverse."

"What about the brake?"

"On the right. But it's only a transmission brake, not a wheel brake, so use it tenderly. Your throttle's that lever on the right of the steering wheel, and the spark retard's on the left, and that floor lever to your left—"

"Am I trying to drive an automobile or fly to the moon?"

"It's only the most reliable, versatile motorcar ever invented, my dear."

"And you would know, I guess?"

"I drove a Ford Model T ambulance over the battlefields of Europe for over a year, Ginger, and she never once let me down. And she won't let you down, either, if you treat her well. Now start the engine. And be grateful you've got an electric starter, which is more than I ever had in France. I nearly broke my arm a dozen times on that crank."

She says all this in her calm, ladylike voice, much at odds with the heroism suggested by the words themselves. I now count ten days since the headlights faded away from the Fitzwilliams' parlor window, bearing Oliver Anson Marshall with them, and Virginia's silhouette has grown to extravagant proportions, though she assures me the baby inside is still a couple of weeks from harvest. The woman bears more resemblance to one of those ancient stone goddesses dug from the earth than to a dashing driver of wartime ambulances. "I'll take your word for it," I tell her, and I follow her instructions as to choke and ignition and so on. The engine putters and sneezes and rouses itself to a screaming growl.

"Now set the spark retard," she advises, over the din.

I pull back the lever in question. The pistons relax. I rather like the way they obey me without question, the way this wonderful machine bends itself to my every command. You don't have to argue with a Model T, do you? Carries you along, turns right and left, speeds and slows and generally serves you to the best of its abilities. In return, you change its oil and mend its tires and fill its tank with gasoline. It's a fine arrangement, really. A set of simple transactions for mutual benefit. As I release the floor lever to my left and nudge the throttle beneath the steering wheel, sending the flivver rolling down the dirt track before us, I start to feel as if we understand each other, Mr. Ford and me.

The day is hot, the air throbbing quiet. The ground thirsts for rain. A savage sun beats down upon our necks and the crowns of our hats, such that I welcome the draft that washes over us, laden though it is with a fine, light grit. We drive north along the road that tracks the ocean, while said ocean heaves to our right, and as we approach the highway that makes east for the bridge, I see a long band of dust rising above the mangrove. I slow the car. "Why, that's not Simon, is it?"

Virginia cranes her head above the dirty windshield. "Shouldn't be. Said he wasn't coming home until later, so he could finish up work."

"Expecting anyone else?"

"No."

I think of the children left behind with the housekeeper. Glance sideways to assess Virginia's state of worry, but she's maintaining her usual calm facade, the one that bears no windows into her soul.

"Should I turn back?"

"No," she says. "Just carry on. Likely someone from town, out for a picnic. Or an investor looking for property."

She says that last bit with a touch of disgust. There is some kind of land rush gathering a little speed in Florida at present, I understand, and the deeds for beachfront lots have begun to take on the weight of gold. Already they're staking out property lines along the empty territory to the north, and Simon has begun to grumble about selling up, before they turn this stretch of marvelous sand into another Miami Beach. Virginia just teases him. Why, what's wrong with Miami Beach? It's heaps of fun! she'll say, and he grumbles back, Everything. Anyway, for the past three days they've been packing up the villa to return to their plantation inland—Virginia wants the baby born there, though the house itself is but half-finished after a terrible fire—and I do wonder if privacy's got something to do with this decision. Grubby land agents aside, there's something rather dangerous about a vast, teeming ocean right outside your window, isn't there? You never know who's plying its byways. You never know when it might be fixing to throw some kind of tantrum. Not the most reliable of neighbors, the mad Atlantic.

On the other hand. The human kind of neighbor isn't much better, I reckon, and as we approach the intersection of northbound and eastbound, I keep a careful watch on that line of approaching dust, matching our relative speeds, until the mangrove opens up and an automobile appears, a long, open-top roadster, deep yellow, driven by a woman wearing a blue cloche hat.

I ease the Ford to a crawl. "Look familiar?"

"No."

"Should I stop and say hello?"

She doesn't answer. The roadster stops to let us by, like some kind of large, lugubrious lion allowing a zebra to pass unmolested, and once we're gone it commences a massive turn to the right. Southward, in the direction of the Fitzwilliams' house.

I turn my head toward Virginia, and that's when I notice her right hand shoved up against the small of her back, and her mouth drawn tight against her teeth.

"Jumping Jehosaphat!" I exclaim. I turn the wheel so fast, the poor woman liketa whelp right there in the front seat of my old friend Carl Green's Model T Ford, driven to this coast by sun and by moon, all the way from River Junction, Maryland.

# 12

My mama did not die in childbed, but the birthing of babes did surely kill her. I lay that crime at Duke Kelly's doorstep, along with all the others, though I do sometimes wonder if he deserves it entirely. Maybe her native fecundity was just a fatal match for his native virility. Maybe they never did hear of rubbers in River Junction, let alone how to get your hands on a box of them. Maybe there was nothing else to do in the dark of night—there inside the holler betwixt two mountains, in the far western corner of Maryland—except to hump each other to kingdom come.

Now, I wasn't present when that final, unnamed child did slide from her womb, sending her into fever and decline and a harrowing, prolonged death. But I did attend her passing, which came on the first morning of February. I lay by her side while she burnt to ashes, and as I held her dying, papery hand in mine, I remembered the thirty-eight hours she labored to bring forth ten slippery pounds of my brother Johnnie into this world. I remembered the mess of Angus's delivery, and how she nearly died of it, and I remember all the miscarriages afterward, until I went off to the convent for my education, by her orders. From then on, I remained at a merciful remove from the tragic rhythm of her life. I did sometimes wonder how she bore it. What were her thoughts, as her husband ground yet again between her thighs in the dark of night, a-grunting and sweating, sowing the possibility of death in her womb? Resentment or resignation? Did she ever love him? Did she ever love the act of love? Why did she not push him off, push him away, demand for herself some freedom from this deadly tyranny?

I believe I would have. But I'm not Mama. And we can't judge others for not being ourselves, can we?

Well, anyway. When I first came to New York, fleeing the selfsame tyranny my mama hadn't the strength to fight, I knew one thing for certain: I never meant to endure the bearing of children. And though I did soon fall in love with the usual unworthy object and succumb to nature's imperative—which runs high in my blood, you understand—I read diligent pamphlets and listened to the talk of the other girls in the typing pool, and I discovered that while an unmarried lady had little hope of obtaining such female devices as I knew existed, any fellow could now walk into any drugstore and obtain a state-of-the-art glass-dipped rubber condom—so long as he bought this thing solely for the prevention of disease, of course—thanks to the legalistic persistence of Mrs. Sanger.

Now, I explained all this to Billy Marshall last December, when our first kiss led to another, and he began to journey each day from Princeton, New Jersey, to Greenwich Village, Manhattan, in order to court me. Dear Billy. One night, about two weeks after we made acquaintance, Billy met me at this jazz joint for dinner and dancing, and as we frolicked before the orchestra, his expression curved into a kind of seriousness. We left not long after that. Slipped outside to the frosty street and set to kissing with such fervor—I had not kept a beau in many months, had not experienced the joys of consummation since the long-past summer—that he pulled away right in the middle of it and took my face in his hands and begged me to marry him. I'm afraid I laughed. Told him I wasn't the kind of girl he should marry, and he insisted I was, insisted he couldn't live without me, I occupied his every thought, waking and sleeping. And he's a handsome fellow, that Billy-boy, and he knew how to kiss a girl, let me tell you, and the night was cold and his body was terribly warm, terribly strong, smelling deliciously of soap and cigarettes and juniper. The cashmere wool of his overcoat smooth under my fingers. My young skin sparkling with needfulness. I looked into Billy's eyes and told him about the drugstore around the corner on Bedford Street, and how to find the rear courtyard of my boardinghouse on Christopher Street, and his comely face lit up with marvelous gratitude. He kissed my hands and dashed off, and a half hour later there came a tapping on my window. In slithered Billy. I unwrapped his coat and jacket and shirt and trousers, one by one, and he unwrapped my blue silk kimono. His eyes grew soft. He pulled me down to the narrow bed and set to work, so eager and expeditious that I ran my hand in his silky hair and whispered him a reminder of the present from the drugstore.

Now, as I recollect, at that instant Billy happened to be kissing a trail down the center of my belly (or some such thing) and seemed not to notice, so I reminded him again, adding a little mustard, and he looked up all groggy and said, Darling, don't worry, I'll take care of you, and I said, I don't want you to take care of me later, Billy-boy, I want you to wear a rubber now, and he said, Don't you trust me, Gin? and I explained a few words about my mother—she was still just alive, last

December—and how I never, ever intended to let such a thing happen to me.

He said, Never?

I sat up and looked him square and said, Never, ever.

So Billy rose and fetched the box from his overcoat pocket, and I helped him roll the thing on, and in the end I reckon this exercise proved just as well for him. The fellow scarcely did last a minute, even sheathed to the hilt in vulcanized rubber.

# 13

Still, the earth must be populated, and I thank the Lord Almighty who, in His infinite bounty, created women such as Virginia Fitzwilliam, who were brave or foolish enough to do my share of it.

As we hurry back down the road toward the villa, I ask her just how long she's been having these pains, and she says about an hour or two.

"An hour or two! Good Lord above! Why didn't you say something?"

"I wasn't sure. Thought it might be false labor at first."

The pain has passed, and Virginia speaks as calm as you please. As if no baby whatsoever presses hard against her bones, begging for admittance into the vast, green world. I reckon I'd be screaming in terror by now, and I tell her so.

She laughs. "Oh, it's not so bad as that. Not yet, anyway. You'll hear me screaming later."

"I'd be happy to take the children into town for ice cream, when that time comes."

"Now, what kind of talk is that? You might as well stay and learn. God knows I wish I'd known what was coming, when I had my first."

"I'm afraid I don't intend there to be a first. Or a second or third. Anyway, I've seen enough of child-birth already, believe me."

She starts to reply, but the words sort of clip in her throat, and her hand grips the side of the doorframe. I put my hand to the throttle but she gasps out, "No! Slow down!" and I obey. When a woman in the throes of travail tells you what to do, why, you just fix yourself to do that thing.

Another mile to the villa, and by the time we swing left into the drive, the pain has passed away, and Virginia seems to have forgotten my statement of maternal intentions. Just as well, for we now have other troubles to occupy our attention.

In the driveway rests an enormous open-top roadster, the color of new-burst dandelions.

# 14

I pull back the throttle to a gentle rumble. "I thought you weren't expecting anyone."

"I wasn't."

A blue cloche hat comes into focus above the driver's seat. The owner's hands still rest on the steering wheel, clad in white gloves. She turns her head as we draw close, and Virginia makes a wee gasp that sounds an awful lot like recognition.

But I don't have time to ponder the nature of Virginia's reaction, because I recognize that impeccable profile, too. That sharp, neat nose; that jaw perhaps a touch too strong. That careful white skin, that beautifully drawn eye. Long, pale neck like a marsh egret. And her hair, curling from beneath the bottom of her hat, the exact golden-brown color as that growing from the thick skull of her son Oliver.

"I'll be damned," I say, bringing the flivver to a stop at her side, and by the expression on Mrs. Marshall's white face, turned toward mine, I'm probably right.

# 15

"Good morning, my dears." Mrs. Marshall swings her elegant, long body from the embrace of her yellow automobile. "I thought I recognized you on the road."

Virginia opens her own door and swivels her body into position. "Mrs. Marshall. Welcome to Cocoa. What a lovely surprise."

Mrs. Marshall's beautiful eyes go pop. "My goodness! When are you expecting?"

I hurry around the hood of the Model T to haul Virginia from her seat. "In about an hour or two, from the look of things. Would you mind giving me a hand?"

I expect the woman would rather kill me first, but the thing about Mrs. Marshall, she keeps a time and a season for everything under the sun, as the Bible commands. A time to kill, a time to be born, a time to help another woman give birth. She lays aside her steel-rimmed expression and steps forward to take Virginia's other arm.

"For goodness' sake," Virginia says, exasperated, "I can get out of a damned car by myself!"

It's the first time I've heard such a word from her lips, and I reckon it means there must be another pain coming on strong. I motion to Mrs. Marshall, who curls an arm around Virginia's back, and together we ease her upward to stand on the gravel. She takes a step or two and then sort of curls her shoulders and her knees together, makes a ball of herself, and Mrs. Marshall says, Keep breathing, darling, that's it, my goodness, aren't you brave, let's walk on a bit, just to the house, and Virginia seems to obey her, breathing and walking, right through the front door where her body sags in sudden relief.

"That was a stiff one, wasn't it?" says Mrs. Marshall.

"Rather," Virginia replies, in a dry tone mimicking her husband's.

"Do you have a doctor somewhere nearby?"

"My husband's in town. He's going to deliver the baby. He's a doctor," she adds quickly, to Mrs. Marshall's look of utter amazement.

"Oh! Thank goodness. You gave me a real fright. A doctor, you say? I'd ring him up right away, if you've got a telephone. Miss Kelly, perhaps you might perform this service while I settle Mrs. Fitzwilliam in her bedroom?"

She lifts both eyebrows in such a way that you can't refuse, especially if you happen to be languishing in her moral debt, as I am. Besides, the terror is coursing right down the channels of my body at this moment, acid and instinctive, laden with terrible recollection, and I could no more argue with Mrs. Marshall's authority than I could argue with the moon. I turn tail and make for the alcove off the parlor in which the telephone nestles, largely ignored on ordinary days. From the courtyard comes the sound of the children playing. I lift the receiver and hold it to my ear, and when the operator comes on I lean forward and say, very clearly, Phantom Shipping Company offices, please.

Please hold the line while I connect you, the operator instructs.

I turn my head while my heart pounds and pounds. I can see the children playing through the glass of the French doors, some kind of hopscotch, chalk squares scribbled over the paving stones while the sun beats down on the small, silvery eucalyptus leaves above their heads. The housekeeper watches benevolently from the bench in the corner. Same bench where I sat kissing Anson in the hours before he left for New York. Feel as if my gut is made of sorrow. Made of some kind of bitter jelly that wants to rise up my throat and fill my mouth, except I keep swallowing it back, swallowing it back, until the tears start up in my eyes at this gargantuan effort.

Loud click in my ear. "Hello? Hello? Virginia?"

"It's not Virginia, it's Ginger—"

"What's happened?"

"It's all right. She's started her labor, that's all—"

"Where is she? How far apart?"

"About a couple of minutes, I guess. Mrs. Marshall's taken her up to her bedroom—"

"Mrs. Marshall?"

"Anson's mother. She's just arrived from New York. She—"

"Never mind. I'm on my way. Keep her moving, if you can. Get some water on the boil, get the towels ready. I'll swing past the hospital to pick up the nurse." Each word is sound British staccato, a machinelike rattle of commands across the hollow static of the telephone wire. I recollect that Captain Simon Fitzwilliam served on the Western Front, operating on terrible wounds that likely came to him in huge, bloody waves, one after another, and the delivery of a single baby presents no particular crisis for him. Except that it's his baby, of course. I expect that makes a difference. Wouldn't you think?

"Right-ho," I say, hanging up the receiver.

A mere twenty minutes later, the doctor slides his green Packard roadster into the driveway and leaps for the front door, tearing off his hat as he goes. "How is she?" he demands.

"The baby's still on the inside, if that's what you mean. Where's the nurse?"

"God knows. She wasn't at the hospital. My secretary's trying to track her down. I suppose she wasn't expecting the call so soon."

"Well, Mrs. Marshall seems to know what she's about. I heard them laughing a minute ago."

We've reached the bottom of the stairs, where I plant my feet as Simon bounds upward. He stops halfway and turns, hand on banister.

You know, there's something about his gaze. I don't know what. I haven't had to do with many doctors; we kept but one in the county where I grew up, and nobody trusted him much. For one thing, he was a drunk, and for another thing, the women swore he enjoyed certain aspects of his work a little too much, if you know what I mean. Most doctoring as I knew occurred inside the shelter of a school infirmary, first at the convent at which I boarded when I was a girl, and then during my single year at college, and those doctors were the stern, elderly kind, convinced of my original sin and not terribly concerned with my mortal welfare. Anyway, for all my faults, I'm no fool in the judging of men, and as I study the lines of care in this fellow's face, I confess to a pang of envy for Mrs. Fitz-william, who finds herself in such thorough, capable hands, under the watchfulness of such steady eyes.

"Aren't you coming?" he asks.

"Too many cooks. You need someone to manage the downstairs, anyway."

He makes a noise of impatience or something and continues up the stairway at a run. I hear his urgent footsteps, the noise of running water—he's washing his hands first, like a good doctor—and then the sound of voices. I fall into the chair in the hallway. Let out a long zephyr of a breath. Didn't realize I was holding down quite so much oxygen.

Nice and easy, now, Gin. Doctor's here. Clever, competent Simon. He's spent the last few months consulting with the brand-new maternity wing at the hospital in Cocoa, just to keep himself up-to-date on the latest advances in obstetrical medicine, and the missing nurse is herself a veteran of said maternity wing, who's agreed to take on this private assignment in exchange for a handsome payday. No doubt she'll be along shortly, and Mrs. Marshall and I can sit down on the parlor sofa and pour ourselves a pair of well-earned gin and tonics while they get down to business upstairs. Or a pair of pairs. Maybe even more, as needed. As the day bleeds into the night.

A shriek drifts down the stairs. Not of laughter.

I jump from the chair and bolt for the parlor, where a well-stocked liquor cabinet reposes in the corner, Simon having cleverly bought up a cellarful of the essentials, in those months between ratification of the Eighteenth Amendment and the solemn anniversary in January, nineteen hundred and twenty. Rattle, rattle. Clink, clink. Tall highboy glass. Bottle of gin, siphon of tonic. No ice nearby, but I'm the kind of girl who can do without luxury in a moment of crisis. Just as I lift the glass for sweet relief, Patsy comes running into the room and flings herself into the folds of my skirt.

"What's that noise, Ginny? I'm scared!"

I set down the glass on the cabinet and bend to my sister.

"Why, that's just Mrs. Fitzwilliam having her baby, that's all," I tell her, and her exquisite little face crumples into red distress. "Oh, but it's fine, darling, just fine! Dr. Fitzwilliam's with her. Everything will be just fine!"

Patsy fills my skirt with wet tears, and I kneel right down on the rug, just inches from the exact spot where Anson took his leave of me, and I gather her against my breast. "What's wrong, darling?"

"Is—she—g-going—t-to—die?" sobs my baby sister.

"Of course not."

At that instant, a long, keening, banshee wail pierces the plasterwork and vibrates the warm Florida atmosphere, and Patsy makes this scream like she is snakebit. I squeeze her hard and press my lips to the parting of her gold hair, and I think, my God, I'm not alone after all. My poor baby sister burns right here in this purgatory with me.

"Don't cry, darling. Don't you be one bit afeared, do you hear me? The good Lord would never take so fine a woman as Mrs. Fitzwilliam, not when she has her babies and her husband to love her."

"The—L-Lord—t-took—M-Mama!"

"But Mama wasn't strong, darling, not near so strong as Mrs. Fitzwilliam. And she had no proper doctor to look after her, like Dr. Fitzwilliam is. He won't let her die. Why, he loves her so, she can't help but live forever. He'll get that baby out of her in a jiffy, and won't we be happy, Patsy-pet, won't it be wonderful to clap eyes on that baby's face, and see the doctor and Mrs. Fitzwilliam so happy?"

"S-she—be—s-screaming! B-be—screaming—l-loud!"

"Well, it does hurt, sweetie, of course it does. Pushing a baby out, that's hard work. But she is strong enough, I promise. Most women scarce even recollect the hurt, once the baby's born. Mama, she was just unlucky, that's all. But I do reckon she looks down upon us now. She keeps watch upon us both. She won't let anything hurt us again, now that she be safe in heaven and full of joy."

I don't know that I believe those words, even as I say them. I'm only trying to comfort Patsy. Only trying to still that sobbing, that terrible rumpus in her little heart, which I never did suspect until now. But of course it existed. You can't protect a child from something so big and so fearsome as the death of her mama, and how it came about. Like me, she will carry it inside her chest like a cyst, like a boil, all swole up with white, bitter fear, crowding out whatever is supposed to thrive there instead. You can't lance a wound like that. You can't heal it. You just learn to live with it. You hold your baby sister close and stroke her hair, until the sobs die down in her throat, and her small body turns calm in your arms.

You think, maybe I had better leave the rest of that drink for another time.

# 16

Neither of us can stand the shrieking as Virginia brings forth this new soul into the world, so I gather up the other children from the courtyard and take everyone to play on the beach. The housekeeper brings out a pair of striped umbrellas against the sun. Pails and shovels for the building of castles. The air is still and packed with heat. We are just somberly commencing to mold a turret or two when a female figure emerges from the villa, clothed in blue. She pauses to slip off her shoes. Makes her way gracefully among the dunes toward us. I rise and dust the sand from my hands. My nerves set to shaking. I can scarce move my mouth to ask her the fatal question; thank goodness the dame speaks first.

"All done. A beautiful baby girl. Fat and feisty. I expect she'll be a great deal of trouble, but then most girls are."

"Virginia?" I say hoarsely.

She waves her hand. She smells a little of antiseptic. "So easy, it's almost indecent. She's already nursed the little thing and is presently making up the bassinet."

"She's out of bed?"

"The doctor's one of those intolerable fellows who believes in the virtue of physical exercise. Had her up and walking almost to the last moment. I'd have smacked him, myself, but for some reason Mrs. Fitzwilliam seems to think the sun rises from his shoulders. In any case, I'm here to fetch the children. The doctor wishes them to meet their new sister." She claps her hands. "Children! Follow me. On the double, please. There's a little visitor waiting for you inside."

# 17

Of course Patsy goes with them. I remain downstairs and finish my drink, which is now flat and warm but still wet. A fan rotates drowsily above my head. As I set the glass on the cabinet and contemplate pouring another, a pair of footsteps beats down the staircase and into the parlor.

"There you are. Not interested in babies?"

"Not especially. Anyway, I'm not family, am I?" I turn my head to address Mrs. Marshall, who stands impeccably near the door, not a stain nor a crease on her blue linen dress. She nods to the cabinet.

"I don't suppose I could trouble you?"

"Gin and tonic?"

"With pleasure."

"There's no ice."

"Then we shall have to make do without, shan't we?"

I open the cabinet and pour a pair of drinks into fresh highball glasses. Hand one of them to Mrs. Marshall, who takes it from me without any kind of thanks or toast or even ceremonial clinking of rims. We swallow in tandem. I think she looks a little pale, but maybe that's her ordinary color. Two smudges of lavender support her eyes, which are brown and beautifully shaped and fringed by thick lashes, like Anson's, only smaller. Also, his are blue. Dark, solid blue, the color of the center of the ocean.

"How is he?" I ask.

"Kind of you to ask. He's awake, at least." She pauses. "Oh, I suppose you mean Ollie."

"Both of them."

She turns and makes her way to the front window, overlooking the beach. "They gave him a splendid ceremony. I suppose you've seen the press clippings. An American hero, with a medal to prove it."

"His wound? It's healed?"

"Why, haven't you heard from him yourself?"

"Yes. But you know he'd never write about a thing like that."

"That's true. Well, he's all healed up, as near as I can tell. Blood never did stick long on Ollie. He's simply invincible. Billy, on the other hand." She drinks and turns her chin over her shoulder. "I don't suppose you have a cigarette?"

I point to the enamel case on a nearby shelf. She lopes after it. Opens the lid and selects a cigarette. Lifts her eyebrow in my direction, and after an instant's hesitation, I nod.

"Billy, on the other hand," she continues, handing me a lit cigarette and then starting her own, "is a terrible mess. Three surgeries already, and his face will never be the same. The scars on his jaw. They actually took some bone from his hip, you know, in order to repair it. A new procedure those clever surgeons developed during the war. Dreadful ordeal."

"But he will get better."

"Oh, will he? How reassuring. Thank you, Miss Kelly."

"I'm sorry. I didn't mean—"

"Of course you didn't." She folds her left arm beneath her right, dangling her drink from one and her cigarette from the other. "You're suffering, too. Ollie's suffering, poor thing, though he won't say a thing about it. We're all suffering. My husband's a broken man, I believe. Sits in his chair all day, in his study, drinking and smoking his damned cigars. Leaves everything to me. Well, he always did."

I toss back the rest of my drink, the way you might smother a fire with water, except the fire only burns more. "I wish . . ."

"Wish what, my dear?"

"Wish I could do something."

"Do you, indeed? What a strange coincidence. Because I was just now—just this second, in fact—thinking that you've done enough already."

"What's that supposed to mean?"

"I mean you've been something of a plague on our house, haven't you, my dear? Not that you meant any harm. But the fact remains, I wish most ardently that neither of my boys had ever laid eyes on you, Miss Kelly."

"Is that so? What if I tell you I feel likewise, Mrs. Marshall?"

She wagged her finger. "Not true. You've fallen in love with my Ollie, and no woman ever regrets when she's fallen in love. Even if it leads her into disaster. Believe me, I know."

"I'm sure you do."

"Don't think that I blame you, now. I'm well aware it was Billy who tumbled headfirst into your lap, poor lamb, and Ollie who dragged you into this damned bootlegging circus. A thing I could just about murder him for, if I weren't afraid someone else would do it for me." She finishes her drink and heads for the liquor cabinet to pour another. Unscrews the lid in a supple twist of her fingers. "No, it's not your fault."

"Well, my goodness. I appreciate that."

Mrs. Marshall pauses in her work to cast me some kind of look over her shoulder. "Gracious me," she drawls, turning back to the bottle, "what a mouth you've got. You're not afraid of your betters, are you?"

"I don't necessarily consider that I do have any betters, Mrs. Marshall, with the possible exception of the Lord Himself. And if I do, you're not one of them. I suspect you've ruined far more men than I have, or ever will."

She slams down the highball glass and turns to face me. "You don't know a thing, Miss Kelly, not a thing. You're just a tart from the hills who thinks she's a woman, thinks she's the smartest trick in Manhattan. How old are you? Twenty-two, maybe? You haven't got the first idea about men, believe me. You haven't got the first idea about me."

A flush has overcome her cheekbones; her eyes have gone all brilliant and hard, like a pair of Byzantine agates. Her fingers still enclose the top of the highball glass, and from the white strain along the knuckles and the delicate nailbeds, she might shatter it to smithereens, a terrible great waste of good gin.

"Maybe I don't," I say softly, "but I do know this: I never meant Billy any harm. What my stepfather did to him near enough broke my heart. The sight of his poor face will stain my dying day."

"Good." She turns her head away. Not, however, before I detect a tiny glitter between the black lines of her eyelashes. She lifts the glass, though she hasn't yet added the tonic, and drinks down all the gin inside. "Then maybe you won't object to my little proposition."

At the word proposition, the hairs commence to tingling along the lengths of my arms. The nape of my bare neck. I head for the ashtray next to the lamp and make a great show of stubbing out the cigarette. "In my observation, there's no such thing as a little proposition."

Her laugh is just the kind you might find tinkling in a Manhattan drawing room, brief and bell-like and insincere. You can almost hear the crimson of her lipstick in it. "Well, I guess you're right about that, anyway. Maybe restitution is a better word? And we'll leave out the little, for the sake of honesty."

"Restitution for what, exactly?"

"Why, for allowing my sweet Billy to fall in love with you in the first place. And don't tell me you couldn't help that, Miss Kelly. You might seem as irresistible as an ice cream sundae to my boys, but I have no doubt whatsoever that you're perfectly capable of resisting them."

"I don't know about that. Anson drives a pretty hard bargain, for a Princeton boy. I don't recollect that I had much choice in the matter, in fact."

"Ah, but you did choose Billy, Miss Kelly. Didn't you? You might have told him to—what's the phrase?—to get lost. You might have told him to get lost, like any number of your admirers, but you didn't. You took him to bed, and you let him believe any number of pleasant things. You led him to believe you were in love with him."

"That's not true. I never said any such thing."

Mrs. Marshall opens the cigarette case and lights herself another, and those fingers of hers, they're shaking a little, trembling, and for some reason I'm drawn into study of them: long and elegant, sure, but to such a degree that they might also belong to a cadaver, whose unhappy white flesh lies sparse against her bones. She smokes solemnly and turns to gaze out the window, toward the pulsing ocean. "Of course I don't know what you said or didn't say. I know it's possible to promise a great many things in the middle of the night, which you don't necessarily remember in the morning."

"Not in this case, Mrs. Marshall, I assure you. I told Billy exactly where he stood with me, the last time I saw him. I told him we were through. He asked me to marry him, and I told him I couldn't do it. I made myself about as clear as I could, in fact."

"How peculiar," she says. "Because when Billy finally woke up from that last operation, when they stuck the bone from his hip into the hole in his jaw, the first thing he said—the very first words he spoke aloud, through the wire cage holding his face in place—had to do with you."

"How flattering. What did he say?"

"Why, he wanted to know how you were, Miss Kelly. Isn't that good of him? He wanted to know where you were. He told me you were engaged, the two of you, and that you were already expecting his child."

# 18

Babies. They all look alike, if you ask me. Bald and squashed and red-faced, like your dyspeptic old uncle, or else crowned by a ruff of strange dark hair that makes you think of a newborn skunk. Loud as the devil himself, smashing apart the brimstone down below.

The new Fitzwilliam pup is no different, I'm afraid, though her beaming parents seem to find her perfectly exquisite. She is of the bald variety, long and scrawny; though perhaps she only suffers from comparison to Duke's babies, which emerged from my mother's womb at a monstrous size. My half brother Johnnie was fully ten pounds, and I believe Angus weighed even more; this one can't be more than seven. Her lips move restlessly as she sleeps in her father's warm arms, as if searching for milk. "Her name is Alice," Simon says fondly, not to me but to wee Alice herself, who nestles in the crook of his elbow as if the Lord had fashioned that particular joint just for her shape.

"She's beautiful," I lie, venturing out a polite finger to tickle the swaddling at her midsection. Alice's lashless new eyes fly open, and she commences to squall like a demented seagull.

"Dear me," says Mrs. Marshall. "It seems you need a little practice at this, Miss Kelly."

"I've had all the practice I'll ever want, I assure you." I take a step backward from the bawling bundle and turn to Virginia, who sits cheerfully in bed, looking no more than windblown, pink of cheek and disheveled of hair, stretching out her arms toward those awful cries. Simon bends down and transfers the creature into her embrace, in such a delicate, symphonic maneuver—a kind of pas de deux—that my cheeks commence to toast, and I cast my gaze hastily to the window. "Well, then. I guess I had better see how the children are getting on downstairs."

But of course I do no such thing. I pass right by the dining room, where the housekeeper is giving the small fry their tea, and I head out into the hot, panting beach and I walk and walk, northward, dangling my shoes and stockings from my left hand. The late sun strikes my cheek; the air is thick with salt. I want to walk this shore all the way to New York, all the way back to the city I know, the mad, anonymous life I had before. But as far as I walk, as many footprints as I lay on that slick, golden sand, as much as my muscles ache and my throat strains and my eyes sting, I cannot, I cannot get back to the place I once lived.

# 19

She's waiting for me when I return. A woman like her doesn't give up easily. She stands against the

hood of her beautiful yellow car, ankles gathered together in the sand, and the late afternoon sun makes a
nimbus around her head and shoulders. "Let's go for
a drive, shall we? Clear our heads?"

"My head's already clear."

Mrs. Marshall straightens and opens the passenger
door. "I haven't much time, Miss Kelly. I really must
be back in New York. My family needs me, you see.
They're a terrible burden, families."

What can I say to that? I climb into the passenger
seat and Mrs. Marshall slams the door shut. Settles
into the driver's seat beside me and starts the mighty
engine. We roll forth through the sand and the gravel
onto the main road, turn north, and drive silently for
some minutes while the sun lays its burning hand upon
my left cheek. We pass the road into Cocoa without
pause, and Mrs. Marshall speaks at last.

"You're quite certain you're not expecting?"

"Yes."

"How certain?"

"Do you want the particulars?"

"I believe you understand me."

"In the first place, Mrs. Marshall, I have a habit
of insisting my suitors arrive properly dressed, if you
know what I mean, and Billy was no exception."

"Hardly an iron-clad assurance, Miss Kelly."

"In the second place, on the very morning of our arrival in Florida, I received a familiar visitor, who informed me in no uncertain terms of my childless state. Is that iron-clad enough for you, or do you require to view the evidence for yourself?"

Her gloved hands slip down a few inches on the steering wheel. "That won't be necessary."

"So you can just run back to New York, Mrs. Marshall, and give Billy my best wishes for his speedy recovery, and tell him he needn't worry any longer about becoming a father at such a tender young age. He's in the clear."

She makes a considering noise, sort of like hmnh, except turned up a little at the end, like a question. I turn my head toward the ocean, which passes by in dizzy gulps of surf. Deep blue rimmed by hungry white, devouring the yellow sand. Hazy pale sky pressing the horizon. To the north, Cape Canaveral sticks its green, mangrove finger into the sea.

"The thing is," Mrs. Marshall says, raising her voice above the racket, "I don't believe that news would lift his spirits at all. The opposite, in fact."

"He'll get over it, I'm sure. Sweet hearts heal fastest. They don't have so much trouble finding someone new to love."

"What's that?"

I turn my head back to her. "He'll find someone else!"

She barks out a bitter laugh. "Oh, that's rich. From his hospital bed, perhaps? Wooing some pretty nurse with his face like Frankenstein's monster?"

"Once he heals, I mean."

"My dear girl, he's not going to heal. Haven't I made myself clear? It's not just that his dear face is ruined, you know. It's his head. Some kind of injury to the brain, the doctors think. He'll never be quite the same."

Her profile is blurred and radiant against the sun, hurting my eyes. I turn to stare through the dusty windshield at the road ahead. A skift of sand covers the new asphalt; the dunes to the left disappear into the dense, exotic tangle of the mangrove swamp that rims the Indian River and separates us from the rest of the country.

"He can't speak properly, for one thing," Mrs. Marshall continues. "Not just because of his jaw; it's the words themselves. All jumbled up, the wrong ones mixed in. And he can't move properly, either. Jerks and spasms. The left side, especially. No, it's going to take a special girl indeed to take on the task of loving him now."

"I'm sorry. I can't tell you how sorry I am."

"Still, he contrives to make himself clear, at least about one thing. He loves you, Miss Kelly, for whatever damned reason. And he's quite certain you're carrying his child."

"I've already told you—"

"In fact, you might say it's the only thing that gives him hope, just now. The only thing that animates him at all, in the face of his misery. Where's Ginger? he asks. Is she safe? Is the baby safe? He wants to see you."

"Well, I'd like to see him, too. Help him get better. But it's impossible."

"Impossible? Why?"

"You know why."

"Because Ollie's told you to stay here in Florida? You hardly strike me as the kind of girl that any man can command to stay put."

"It's not because Ollie told me to stay here. It's because, between the two of us, we've murdered the man who's built a poor, ramshackle town into a seat of illicit prosperity, and where I come from, townsfolk don't take kindly to that sort of disloyalty. I don't dare show my head back home, Mrs. Marshall, not if I want to keep it whole."

"And here I thought there was nothing you wouldn't dare, Miss Kelly. Nothing to scare you. Certainly nothing to make you run to ground and hide like an animal."

"Well, some may call me daring, I guess, but I'm not stupid, either. I was reared up alongside those boys in River Junction, and believe me, there's nothing they can't track down, no scent on this great earth but they can trace it." Mrs. Marshall starts to interrupt, but I continue, in a loud voice, rising well above the thunderous draft of ocean air, "Oh, I know what you're getting at, all right. I know you want me to come home and nurse poor Billy back to health. Make him think I'm going to marry him, pretend we've got a baby and a future together, so he's got something to live for. And I want to help him, I really do. I ache all over for what's been done to him, for what my stepfather did to him. I shall carry that guilt with me to the end of my days. But I won't lie to him, Mrs. Marshall, not even to help him. That would be the cruelest thing of all. Because I never did love Billy, not the way I love his brother, not the thousandth part of the love I bear for that other son of yours, the one whose well-being you seem to have forgotten in all this. And I won't break faith with Anson, not after all we've endured together. Not in a million years, not everhow you seek to persuade me. Mrs. Marshall."

I end this speech nearly shouting, nearly rising out of my seat, so that the dust flies into my mouth and scratches the back of my throat. I start to coughing, and Mrs. Marshall hits the brake. Pitches us to a stop, smack in the middle of the road, where the sun can properly roast us against the smooth, elegant cloth of the roadster's interior, and reaches across my legs for the glove compartment. She produces a flask, which she offers me. I wave my hand, but she insists, unscrews the lid for me, and what can I do but allow myself a swig? To my surprise, it's just water. My throat clears, the coughing subsides.

"That's better," she says. "Now, let's get down to business."

# 20

But before Mrs. Marshall and I get down to business, let me first assure you—in case you may possess any doubt—that I have spoken nothing but the truth to her, driving up that hot, sandswept Florida road. During the night before we arrived at the Fitzwilliam villa, I honest-to-God experienced a familiar cramping in my midsection, which grew so severe that I had to bite down on my lip and squeeze my fingernails into my palms to hold back the groans.

But for all the misery, I did welcome those pains. I felt relief at the sight of my underthings when I woke up the next morning, for although I said nothing to Anson, nothing to any living soul, my stepfather's words had awakened a terrible fear inside me. I knew he must be lying—I told him he was lying—but when he proclaimed in front of Billy and Anson, chained together against the wall of a stone springhouse as the waters of a great flood rose around us, that I had the look of a woman with child, I realized he might be right. That, in all the tumult of the previous weeks, I had lost count of a certain ordinary rhythm, and I spent that entire journey south along the Dixie Highway in a dudgeon of high anxiety for the state of my womb.

So while I told Anson the truth, while I told his mother nothing but the truth when I insisted I carried no bud of life inside me, I couldn't say for certain that Duke hadn't perceived some nascent truth, at that particular moment near the end of his life. Inside the springhouse, a few weeks ago, it's not altogether impossible I might have been carrying Billy's child, by some failure of method or material, and I don't know whether Duke's fist struck away that possibility, or whether Nature took her own course, or whether there was nothing there to begin with. Hardly matters now, does it? The end result remains the same.

Barren I be, and I swan I shall take care to remain so.

# 21

"There is no business between you and me," I tell Mrs. Marshall, as we sit in that open oven of a roadster, broiling like a pair of fresh-plucked hens.

"Isn't there?"

"Not a bit. I'm all through with that kind of thing. Turned a leaf, you might say. My business these days is nothing more than to wait right here in Florida for my fellow to return to me, and then to live together with my baby sister as quiet as church mice, honest as paupers."

She starts to laugh. "You, Miss Kelly? A church mouse?"

"You bet."

"No pining for the old white lights? A little excitement?"

"I've had my fill, believe me."

"What about in a year or two? You don't think you might find yourself just a little bit bored?"

"As those nuns used to tell me, Mrs. Marshall, only boring people ever get bored."

"Everyone has a price, Miss Kelly. Even you."

"No amount of money in the world—"

"I'm not talking about money."

Her right hand slips into the pocket of her square linen jacket, and such is the state of my nerves that I actually flinch. Reach for the door handle and make some kind of stupid gasp at the top of my mouth.

But Mrs. Marshall only laughs and holds up a piece of folded paper, the thick, expensive kind, creamy white in the middle and yellowed at the edges.

"You really ought to be more careful with your correspondence, my dear," she says.

I snatch. She lifts the note just out of reach and wags a forefinger at me. "Now, now. Don't be greedy."

"Give me that letter!"

She tsks. "Such elegant manners. Didn't that hillbilly mother of yours teach you the word please?"

I hold out my hand, palm up. She sighs and places the letter in the exact center, and I close my fingers around it, taking care not to crumple the edges, and set it in my lap. Mrs. Marshall returns her hands to the steering wheel.

"The rest of them are in my apartment in New York. I'm afraid you'll have to fetch them yourself."

"I'll be damned if I do."

She shrugs. "Very well. If you don't want the old things, then I suppose I'll simply have to destroy them."

"You wouldn't."

"Why not? I haven't got any use for a stack of old letters. Particularly when honor forbids that I peek inside and find out what they're all about."

"Haven't you read them already?"

"I couldn't possibly. Well, except the first few lines of that one, which you left so carelessly on the bedside table of my pool house last month." She makes an elegant gesture in the direction of my lap. "But as soon as I understood that I wasn't the intended recipient, I naturally folded up the passionate little thing and gathered it together with its companions."

"I don't believe you for a second."

"Believe what you like, Miss Kelly, but a lady doesn't read another person's private letters." (She puts a little unnecessary emphasis on the word lady.)

"You kept them, however."

"Oh, old letters can be useful things, even if you don't know what's in them. After all, they represent some kind of value to somebody, or no one would have taken the trouble to preserve them."

I turn my gaze down to the letter in my lap, folded twice into a square, by such firm, sharp creases that the paper's already begun to fray along those edges. Might start to fall apart, so long ago are the days in which it was written. I can't recollect all the words inside, but I remember the sense of them. The long, flowery phrases by which my father (the Lord Almighty forever damn his faithless soul) declared his devotion to my mother.

"Well?" she says. "You're not even going to allow me a hint? I must confess, I'm awfully curious. I could see by the salutation that it's a love letter. And by the age of the paper, and the manner in which you treasure it, I suspect this little collection once belonged to someone dear. Am I right?"

"That's none of your business."

"Isn't it? Ah, well. I don't suppose you're going to tell me, and I don't suppose it really matters what's written inside. To me, I mean. To you, on the other hand—"

"I don't care a bit. Burn them all, if you like. He's nobody dear to me, that's for certain."

"Really? You could have fooled me, the way you snatched that letter away, a moment ago."

"It's personal, that's all."

"I see. Then I imagine you wouldn't want the contents spread about? In some sort of public manner?"

"I thought you said you hadn't read them."

"I haven't. But I might, if I have to."

Beneath the snug straw hat, my head is starting to ache. A dull pain spreads up from my ears and around my temples, while the perspiration's trickling the opposite direction, down along the edge of my hair and into my collar, funneling through the slight gap between my breasts to dampen my belly. Hot and sticky and aching all over, fit to burst, while this letter rests here atop my thighs, balanced on the skirt of fine, cream-colored linen that I bought in town last week from the money Anson left me. I've got no money of my own here in Florida. My little sum, husbanded over the course of three years' labor in the wicked city, sleeps safe inside the portals of the First National Bank of New York, a thousand miles away. Before all this happened—the springhouse, Florida—I had some idea of withdrawing that money and picking up Patsy in the dead of night and escaping with her to some quiet place where Duke might never find us, where we might safely build our bright, new, untainted lives. A fresh start, as they call it. And now that fresh start has been thrust upon me anyway, and I've grasped it with both hands, and somehow it doesn't feel the same as I thought. Not so empty of care. Just hot and sticky and worrisome, one set of burdens exchanged for another, wondering when we get to the good part at last. When, if we wait like good girls, do as we are told, clean and patient by the side of the ocean, Anson will come back to us and make us happy. Right?

"You know, they're a lovely family, the Fitzwilliams," says Mrs. Marshall. "I once knew Virginia a little, back when she lived in New York, and I'm glad to see her settled so well. A husband who dotes on her, a pair of beautiful children, beautiful home, new baby daughter. I'd say it's terribly kind of them to take the two of you in, at such an inconvenient time."

"Oh, they're kind, all right."

"Of course, you can't stay with them forever."

"I don't mean to stay with them forever. Just until . . ."

"Until Ollie comes back for you?"

I turn my head to the ocean, which is calmer than usual today, almost tranquil, waves rolling drunkenly to shore as if the heat's getting to them, too.

"That might be some time, of course," she continues. "He adores you, that's plain, but his first love is his work. I expect it always will be. And you! You don't strike me as the kind of girl who sits around waiting for any man to come home at night. Knitting baby booties and that sort of thing."

"That's not the kind of girl he wants, anyway."

"Maybe not, but it's going to be dreary, coming in second all the time. Like now, for example. He chose the Bureau over you—ran away as soon as he could— and it won't be any different as you go on. However much he loves you, my dear, his duty will always have the first claim on his attention. Whereas, if you returned to New York with me—"

"Oh, no—"

"—returned to New York with me, why, you'd have all the freedom you want. You can do whatever you like. If you'd like to set up some kind of business, we'd give you whatever you needed. If you want to enjoy yourself, we'd send you off in style, every night. Introduce you everywhere. As Billy's fiancée, you'd—"

"I wouldn't marry Billy!"

"I didn't say you would, did I? If there's no baby, there's no need to marry. Just play along. Make him happy. Once he's got his strength back, why, we'll manage something, between the two of us. Break the terrible news about the baby, and then—"

"Break his poor heart, you mean."

"Of course not. I mean find some other girl to turn his head. Shouldn't be too difficult, by then. Billy's a dear, but his imagination's easily captured, if you know what I mean, and plenty of girls don't mind a few scars and tremors in exchange for . . . well."

"Oh? Then why not find this accommodating girl now?"

"Because I haven't got that kind of time. Because, for the moment, you're all he wants. You and that imaginary baby. You consume him."

The ocean grows blurry before my eyes. "I can't do it. I've done enough hurt to that poor boy."

In response, she takes her hands from the wheel and finds her pocketbook on the seat between us. Rummages around and discovers the cigarette case. She lights one for me, which I accept, and then one for herself. The smoke hangs in the still, hot air, not going anywhere. Just building into a tobacco fog. She waves it away from her mouth and speaks in an intimate voice. "If only you could see him, Ginger. One moment sick and melancholy, the next raving. He won't rest. Keeps wanting to rise up from his bed and find you. Believe me, I wouldn't have come to you if I weren't frightened to death for him. I know you think I'm some kind of monster, but I'm only a mother, Ginger, only a mother who's terribly scared for her youngest boy, the one who always needed a little more care. Ollie, he's got strength for ten men. He always did. But Billy . . ."

Her voice drifts and expires. We sit there smoking, staring at sand, at nothing at all. A gull dives for the surf, howling angrily, and all at once the air is full of birds, wrestling over I don't know what. Some poor crab.

Mrs. Marshall pipes over them. "Ollie told me something interesting, when we were at the hospital the other day, getting ready to move Billy home. I asked him who your people were, and at first he wouldn't say, just that this bootlegger fellow in Maryland wasn't your real father. But I kept pressing him and pressing him, until he allowed that your father was some New York gentleman, though he wouldn't give me any names. Couldn't give me any names, I surmised. And I thought, here's a pretty mystery."

"Do me a favor, Mrs. Marshall. Don't think so much."

"Well, I can't help it, can I? This busy brain of mine. I've always been clever at putting two and two together, Ginger. I suspect those love letters—the ones on the elegant old notepaper, the ones you carelessly left in my pool house last month—might have something to do with this mysterious gentlemanly parent of yours. Don't they?"

I crush out my cigarette on the dashboard and toss the stub into the sand. Mrs. Marshall reaches out to put her hand around my arm, just above the elbow. "Listen to me," she says fiercely, "I can find him for you. If you want to meet him, to force him to own you, to claim your rightful share of him, I'll see to it. If you want revenge, my God, he'll rue the day."

I start to pull my arm away, but she holds on tenaciously.

"And don't tell me you don't care. I can see how much. I can see how your fingers are shaking, how your skin's gone pale. You want this badly, Ginger, and I can give it to you. Your father. A home, where you'll be safe and loved at last. All the money you need. I'll manage everything. God knows I know how to manage these things. And in the end—say, by the end of summer— you'll have everything you want. Think of that. This terrible guilt you're feeling will be all atoned for. You can start fresh. A new woman."

This time, when I yank my arm, she lets go. I turn the door handle and free myself from the interior of Mrs. Marshall's yellow roadster—I wonder, did she ship the thing with her on the train, or did she hire one right here in Cocoa?—and stumble down to the edge of the water. The gulls tear off southward, still screaming. Behind me, a door bangs, and a moment later Mrs. Marshall comes up on my right side.

"You're trapped, Ginger, trapped here in a lovely tropical cage. And I can set you free."

"Or just trap me in a different kind of cage."

"Not at all. I understand, you see. I know how dangerous it is, to try to lock up a girl like you. The terrible consequences."

I consider asking her how she knows all this, what terrible consequences must arise from the caging of high-spirited women, but the answer's obvious, isn't it? The answer's standing right next to me, elegantly clad in a dress of pale blue linen, smelling of some kind of rare perfume, trailing a diminished cigarette from the first two fingers of her right hand.

"Patsy." My throat's scratchy. I swallow hard and say it again, more clearly, clutching the note between my fingers. "My sister, Patsy. We're a package deal."

Mrs. Marshall takes a last draft of her cigarette and tosses the stub into the salient of an incoming wave.

"I have a young daughter of my own. She's in need of a playmate. I'm sure they'll get on famously."

## Cumberland Island, Georgia, April 1998

Granny Annabelle and Stefan were waiting for Ella at the ferry dock. Granny waved with both arms; Stefan just stood, his hand on the small of Granny's back, and smiled. He wasn't really Ella's grandfather—he and Granny had lived together since the sixties, after Grandad died, although they'd never married—but he couldn't have loved Ella more if he were Daddy's own father. Actually, Stefan was the only grandfather Ella had ever known, because Mumma's father died of a heart attack when Ella was only four years old.

As usual, he waited for Granny to hug her first, and then he stepped forward and gathered her up, exactly as if she were a little girl again, without saying anything. His arms were still strong, and he smelled of horses and shaving soap and Granny, like he always did. Ella nearly lost it, right there.

"We brought your bicycle," Granny said.

**There were** no cars allowed on Cumberland Island, which was one of the reasons Ella loved it there. They pedaled the old bicycles to the house without saying anything, just two and a half miles of sweet, sea-scented silence. She and Granny rode side by side, while Stefan followed. He had done that as long as Ella could remember; he always said he liked to keep an eye on them, his best girls. Ella inhaled the familiar smells of salt and marsh grass, the tanginess that meant she was home. Well, not home exactly. Cumberland was her summer home, her refuge. Better than home, without all the baggage that came with parents and siblings and schools and work and marriage. When Ella was in college, she used to show up unannounced, to call them up from the pay phone at the St. Marys ferry terminal and ask if she could stay the night, the weekend. Stefan always answered; Granny hated telephones, because they sometimes brought bad news. "Of course you are welcome, my love," he would say, in his courtly German accent. "You have always a place here. Let me find your bicycle." There were fourteen grandchildren altogether, but Ella knew she was Stefan's favorite. His first. The one who always came back, every summer.

When they reached the house, Granny made coffee while Stefan put away the bicycles and fed the horses. It was morning; Ella had driven all Monday afternoon and night in Aunt Vivian's ten-year-old Mercedes station wagon. The air was still damp and fresh, the sunlight luminous. They brought the coffee to the porch and sat there, drinking quietly. "It looks different in spring," Ella said. "Greener. More tender."

"I love all the seasons here," said Granny. "We used to have a place in Cocoa Beach, but we sold up when it got too crowded."

"I remember that house. It had a courtyard. With lemon trees."

"I raised your father there. That's where he fell in love with your mother, you know. I found the glamorous Pepper Schuyler down in Palm Beach, all alone and friendless—"

"And you took her under your wing. I always thought there was something more to that story."

"There's always more to any story, darling. You just have to ask the right questions. More coffee?"

"Let me get it."

But Granny was already rising from her wicker chair. She moved more slowly now, which Ella hated. Her skin, always luminous, was turning transparent; her hair was silver. She was eighty-two: a young, healthy eighty-two. But eighty-two. Stefan was even older; Ella wasn't sure exactly how old. Maybe eighty-five, though you wouldn't know it by the way he walked and talked. They kept busy with the horses, with the house, with each other. Ella followed her into the kitchen, where Granny topped off Ella's mug and then her own. Added milk and sugar before Ella could reach forward to do it herself. (Granny was like that, she had to take care of everybody.) A few years ago, the grandkids had given Granny and Stefan a fancy European machine for Christmas, because Granny and Stefan—who had both lived in Europe before the war—used to complain about the insipidity of American coffee. She was about to ask Granny about Mumma and Daddy and the house in Cocoa Beach, but Granny, leading them back to the porch and its old, familiar chairs of white wicker, spoke first. "Tell me about this terrible husband of yours."

"He's terrible."

"Your mother said he was sleeping around."

"You might say that." Ella curled back in her chair and sipped her coffee. "Personally, I don't think there was much sleeping involved."

"To tell you the truth, I wasn't surprised when I heard the news."

"Oh, you too? You and everybody else. Was I the only one who didn't see through him?"

Granny shrugged. "Darling, that's just you. You always see the best in people. You can't imagine sin because you haven't got any inside you. What's that Bible verse? To the pure, all things are pure."

"You realize what that verse is about, right? It's all about Jews."

Granny startled. "Is it?"

"Yes. But to them that are defiled is nothing pure, or something like that. By defiled, they mean Jews."

"Oh," she said. "I never realized. Well, if you leave the Jews out of it, the principle still holds."

Stefan came up the steps from the lawn and stamped his boots on the mat. "Leave the Jews out of what?"

"Out of the Bible verse, darling."

"But why the devil?" he said, bewildered, and Ella remembered that Stefan was Jewish, that he had fought in the Resistance or something during the war, though he refused to talk about it with anyone, except probably Granny.

Granny laughed and said never mind and turned back to Ella. "My point is that you believed he was good and faithful, because you are good and faithful. Don't blame yourself for Patrick's wickedness. That's his own sin, not yours."

"Patrick," Stefan said darkly, hanging his jacket on the hook. "I want to shoot that fellow with my own pistol. Right in the balls, where he needs it."

"Don't be a hypocrite," said Granny. "Remember, you weren't so different when you were a young husband, were you?"

"That was in the days before Annabelle, when I was very stupid."

Granny said, blushing a little, "Anyway, if anyone gets to shoot Patrick, it should be Florian. It should be your father."

"How about me?" Ella said. "Why don't I get to shoot him? He's my fucking husband."

Granny reached out and covered her hand. "Because you're too good, darling. It would lie on your conscience."

**The house** was small and old, though Stefan had built an addition when Granny came to live with him, Granny and her teeming flock of children and stepchildren and grandchildren. Then, as the family multiplied, he scratched his head and built a bunkhouse next to the barn, where the teenagers could brood and play music without agitating the adults. Stefan was a great intellectual—the house was full of books in various languages—but he also liked to work with his hands. He liked to build things. He built this bed in the guest room, the one where Ella went to take a nap, on Granny's insistence. "You look terrible," Granny had said, taking away the coffee cup and herding her toward the stairs. "You're getting far too old to be driving all night."

"I'm only thirty," Ella protested, though she actually felt worse than a hangover; she felt like she had the flu, only without a fever.

"By the time I was thirty, I had three children and six stepchildren, and I was touring the world with my cello," Granny said. "And I was tired all the time, and I should have slept more."

So Ella allowed herself to be shooed up the stairs to the guest bedroom and the bed that Stefan made with his own hands. Everybody obeyed Granny Annabelle, including Stefan. If she had asked Stefan to fly to South America and pick the beans for her morning coffee himself, he would have done it, and as Ella lay drowsily under the quilt she listened to their voices through the floorboards, Granny soft and lyrical, Stefan rumbling and warm. They were talking about her, probably. No, forget probably. Certainly they were talking about her. Ella could tell by the hushed way they spoke. They were worried about her; of course they were. And they didn't even know the half of it.

She didn't know why she'd come to Cumberland Island. When she borrowed Aunt Vivian's car, she'd said she was going out to visit Great Aunt Julie in the Hamptons, and that was the plan, in fact. Drive out to see Aunt Julie and ask her about Geneva Kelly and the Redhead photographs, spend the day out there on Long Island, maybe stop by Aunt Viv and Uncle Paul's old beach place in East Hampton and hang out on the dunes for a bit. Get her head together in the middle of some good salt air.

But when she pulled out of the garage on East Twenty-First Street, she failed to turn right on Park Avenue and head uptown to the Queens-Midtown Tunnel. She kept going west. Turned south and headed into the Holland Tunnel instead, and then she was flying down the New Jersey Turnpike like a bird heading south, without any more idea than a bird why she was doing it. Just instinct. A craving for some particular geography, a point on a map that meant refuge.

Now she was here, her refuge, her place of childhood memory, and Stefan's and Granny's voices murmured below, and the quilt made a cocoon around her body that had held up bravely all night, all the way down the Eastern Seaboard, without rest. Her body that had also betrayed her, nourishing life when it was supposed to lie barren. Fallen in love when it was supposed to remain chaste. Her woman's body, the cause of all this trouble.

She must have fallen asleep, because some time later she heard someone rustling in the room, and when she opened her eyes she saw Granny putting something in the chest of drawers.

"Granny?" she said.

Granny turned. "Oh, I'm sorry. I didn't mean to wake you. I was just putting a fresh nightgown in the drawer, in case you forgot. How are you feeling?"

"Fine."

"You don't look fine."

Granny's large brown eyes managed to seem both soft and sharp at once, as Ella propped herself on her elbows, trying not to throw up, while her grandmother gazed down at her. For a condition called morning sickness, this thing had an inconvenient habit of striking at any time of day. Or maybe it was just hunger, or stress, or fatigue, or the quantity of coffee she'd consumed. (Was she allowed to drink coffee? Probably not. God, she was doing this all wrong, she was a total failure at everything now, and she had once been so competent.) She lay back down and stared at the slanting roof. "You're right," she said. "I'm not fine. I'm pregnant, actually."

"Oh!" Granny sat suddenly on the bed, next to Ella's feet. "Oh. I see."

"It's Patrick's, obviously. We were trying for a baby, before the thing happened. Finally got there, looks like. Just a little late for popping open the champagne. Or whatever it is you do."

"Have you been to see a doctor?"

"Not yet. I just figured it out a day or two ago."

"But you haven't told Patrick."

"I haven't told anyone. Not even Mumma. You're the first."

"Oh, Ella." Granny laid her hand on Ella's leg. "Oh, Ella. What a fix."

"A fix. A fix. Yes, Granny. I'm in a real fix, aren't I? And it's worse than you think. Aside from the fact that I just quit my job, because I couldn't stand dealing with the Patricks of the world any longer—"

"Well, I don't blame you for that," Granny said.

"But that's not the worst thing."

"What's the worst thing, darling?"

"The worst thing is . . ." Ella sat up again and drew up her knees. Granny's face was tilted at a sympathetic angle. She wore a buttoned shirt the color of fresh limes, untucked over a pair of navy blue pixie pants. For as long as Ella could remember, Granny had exuded an effortless chic, even living out here on Cumberland with nobody to dress for except Stefan. Her silver hair simply curled about her ears without complaint. Around her wrist she wore a single gold bracelet, which she never took off. Ella knew without being told that Stefan had given her this bracelet, that it had some meaning between the two of them, and as she stared at Granny's wrist, the delicate metal against the delicate bones, she felt a tug between her ribs. She wrapped her arms around her legs and said, "I met someone. This guy in my new building. Hector."

There was a deep sigh from the end of the bed. "I see. You've fallen in love with this Hector?"

"I've only known him a month, Granny. I just left my husband."

"That has nothing to do with it. Are you in love with him?"

"I think so." Ella knit her fingers together and closed her eyes against the sight of the bracelet. She thought of Hector pulling down the blinds in the living room, standing naked under the skylight, covered in silver, picking up her two hands in his two hands and kissing each one. "Yes. I do."

"The same way you loved Patrick?"

"No! Totally different. This is—I don't know—it's in my gut, it's in my skin. It's like he's always been there. Every time I see him, it's like, Oh, it's you."

"Ah," Granny said. "Ah."

"I'm starting to question everything. I'm starting to think that maybe I never really loved Patrick to begin with. Does that sound crazy? Never even really knew him at all. Like I was just going through the motions of love, playing house with Patrick, because—because he was so charming and smart and, I don't know, ticked the boxes. And when I found Hector, I started to see how wrong I'd been, all the signs I'd missed, the pretending I did. Everything Hector has that just fits into something in me—damn, that came out the wrong way. I mean—"

"I know what you mean, darling. I understand perfectly. This Hector of yours, I think I'd like him very much. More than I liked that Patrick."

Ella lifted her head and opened her eyes. "You know, if all of you were sitting around agreeing that Patrick was such an asshole, why didn't you bother to tell me before I married him?"

"Because you don't do that. You can't tell a grown woman these things. She has to decide for herself what she wants."

"Wonderful. Thanks. Because it's that easy."

"It isn't that easy. It's terribly hard."

"Not for you. You had Granddad, and then after he died you had Stefan. You found two good men who loved you. Look at you, you're so serene, and I'm a mess. I thought I had this all figured out, and it's a mess."

Granny put her hands in her lap and looked out the window. "Oh, Ella. It wasn't that simple, believe me. I was a mess once, believe me, a dreadful mess, worse than this. Imagine you're in love, and Europe is about to go to war, and you have a terrible choice to make, and whatever you do, there will be grief. Life is not composed of perfect little scenarios. Life is a mess. There is only love, dear. Love for each other, and forgiveness. Especially forgiveness, I think."

The afternoon light shone on Granny's face, flattening out the lines. Ella thought she looked like a painting of a Madonna, ageless. She stared through the glass with such tenderness that Ella turned too, and there was Stefan, pushing a handcart full of hay out to the horses. He wore a faded plaid shirt and trousers and work boots, and an old tweed cap covered his white hair.

"He shouldn't work so hard," Granny said softly.

"I don't know. I think it keeps him strong. You keep him strong."

"He is my earth," said Granny. "He is my gravity."

Outside the window, Stefan reached the gate and opened it. Pushed the handcart through, and Ella lost sight of him. The grass was growing taller under the spring sun. A breeze rippled across the green tips, like it might ripple across the ocean.

"Mumma told me you knew each other back in Europe," Ella said. "Before the war, before you and Granddad came to America."

Granny was still gazing out the window. "Yes."

"So what's the story? You weren't having an affair or something, were you?"

Granny turned at last, and Ella was startled by the color under her skin.

"It is Stefan's story to tell," she said. "You should ask Stefan."

**After dinner** Ella found Stefan leaning on a fence rail, watching the horses against the darkening horizon to the east. The island was famous for its wild herds, descendants of the Conquistadors' horses or else the livestock brought by English settlers, depending on whom you asked. Stefan had begun looking after them during a bad freeze some winter, back in the fifties or sixties, and never stopped. He was like a caretaker or a gamekeeper. Built them a lean-to for shelter, brought food during the barren months, watched out for the mares in foal. But he never encroached on their wildness, never tried to tame them or ride them, even though Granny once said he could ride expertly. As Ella approached, a few of them made restless movements, lifting their large, scruffy heads and stamping their feet. But they stayed, snatching at the grass, swiveling their ears in Ella's direction to make sure she kept her place.

Ella handed him a mug of coffee and nodded her head over her shoulder. "The sunset's that way, you know."

"I know. I like the ocean better. You can just see it, over the slope." He wrapped his large, bony hands around the mug. "Annabelle tells me you are going to have a baby."

"Maybe I am and maybe I'm not."

"Which is it?"

"Well, I'm knocked up, as they say. Knocked up by my no-good husband. Let's leave it at that."

"All right," Stefan said agreeably, and he drank his coffee. Ella drank, too. A beautiful silence settled between them. Stefan was good at silence; he was the only person Ella knew who could make you feel better without saying anything at all, except maybe Hector. Hector could do that. As she was pondering this, Stefan spoke again.

"I was just thinking about when you were born."

"That was a while ago."

"Thirty years. But I remember it very clearly, you know. You came a little early, and there was some excitement, because nothing was quite ready yet, nobody was expecting you."

"I was only a week early. Geez."

"But first babies are always late, you see. Your grandmother was very steadfast on that point. It was gratifying to see her proved wrong for once."

Ella laughed. "I'll bet."

"So we all hurried to the hospital in New York, because your mother was staying with her parents, and there you were, so tiny and beautiful. When I walked in, your father was holding you, wearing this face of intolerable joy, and I thought my heart would stop, I was so happy. Finally they let me hold you." He stopped and threw back more coffee.

"And then what?" Ella asked.

"Nothing," Stefan said, in a rough voice, and he put his arm around her. "I fell in love, that's all."

"I thought you were already in love with Granny."

"Well, there is that. But it seems the heart has a limitless capacity for such things."

Ella leaned into his warm chest. "Granny said you have a story to tell me."

"What kind of story?"

"About you and her. How you fell in love."

"She said I was to tell you this?"

"Mmm-hmm."

Stefan heaved a giant sigh under her cheek and set down his mug on the fence rail. "Okay. As Annabelle commands. How I fell in love with your grandmother is this. I was shot by the Gestapo, and your grandmother walked into this boathouse where I was bleeding to death, and I looked up and I saw her, and I thought to myself, what a terrible shame I am dying, because I am going to love this woman into eternity."

"Oh please."

"It's true. I was a scoundrel, you know, a handsome devil back then. I was not faithful. I thought life was a great game, but really it was a desert to me, I was like a desert at night. And I lay there bleeding to death, and your grandmother came in like the sun, like the rain to nourish me, and I came to life. She was nineteen," he added, after a slight pause.

"But what about Granddad? Wasn't she married to Granddad?"

"Well. That is, I suppose, the interesting part of the story. We had a beautiful time together, we were sun and earth to each other, and then God parted us. Annabelle married your grandfather instead."

"I don't understand. Why would she marry Granddad if she was in love with—oh my God."

"Yes."

"Oh. My. God."

"My dear, dear girl," Stefan said.

**When Ella** first brought Patrick to stay at Cumberland, the first June after they met, the little house was already full for the summer. Daddy and Mumma were staying in one guest room, and Aunt Else and Uncle Clark in the other, and the cousins all stayed in the bunkhouse, which did not amuse Patrick because you couldn't sleep with your girlfriend in a bunkhouse. You had to sneak in for sex during the middle of the day, which was tricky and not very convenient. Anyway, they had a big barbecue dinner the first night, and Ella and Patrick stole off for a walk afterward to debrief and make out. The sun was only just setting, and the heat stuck to their skin, smelling of rot from the salt marsh.

"Why do you call your grandfather Stefan?" Patrick asked. "Is that some kind of pet name?"

So Ella explained that Stefan wasn't actually her grandfather, that Granddad had died before she was born and Granny had—well, not remarried. Settled down with Stefan a year or two later.

"That's weird," Patrick said.

"Why?"

"Because when I met him, I was like, wow, you can really see the resemblance. Like, he and your dad are so alike. Your grandfather must've looked a lot like Stefan."

"No," Ella said, "I think Granddad was blond, actually. Like, super blond. Dad has Granny's hair and eyes."

"Seriously? Recessive genes, I guess."

"What's recessive?"

"Blond's recessive, right? Hides out waiting for a match. That's how you got your blue eyes, Blue Eyes," said Patrick, pulling her into the grass, and Ella happily tumbled with him and forgot about the resemblance between Stefan and Daddy. After all, they were just Stefan and Daddy. She'd known them all her life.

Sometimes it took new eyes to see something that had existed right in front of you, all along.

**Now their** coffee mugs rested next to each other on the split rail. Hers was plain, Stefan's was lurid blue and said WORLD'S GREATEST GRANDPA in rainbow bubble letters, a gag gift from one of the cousins some Christmas. He had laughed, but Ella, who knew him best, thought his eyes looked wet when he put it away in the cupboard. Stefan's arm was warm and strong, his plaid shirt soft. Over the slope of the hill before them, the sunset echoed pink.

"Does Daddy know?" Ella whispered.

"If he does, he hasn't said so."

"Why didn't you tell him?"

"We discussed it, your grandmother and I. She thinks he should know the truth. I am not so sure."

"But why not? He has the right to know!"

"Maybe so. But does he need this knowledge? Will it make him happier? Or will it only disturb his memory of the man who raised him, a man for whom I have—I admit—great jealousy, but also gratitude. For me, it is enough that Florian and I have each other now. That I am permitted to share some part of his life."

"Oh, Stefan." Ella turned her face into his chest, and his other arm came around her, and at last she was crying, mighty sobs, while the mugs toppled from the rail and spilled in the grass.

**"You must** tell Patrick about this," Stefan said, as they walked back to the house.

"About you and Daddy?"

"You know what I mean."

"I will. Once I decide whether—you know."

Stefan stopped and turned to face her. "No. You must tell him, either way. He is not some nameless fellow you met for a night. He is your husband."

"Was my husband."

Stefan's face was stern. "I know you have fallen in love with this other fellow, this Hector—"

"Oh my God, did Granny tell you everything?"

"Yes, she tells me everything. And I know also that Patrick is a bastard. But still he should know about this child of his, regardless of what you decide."

Ella looked down at her sneakers, because it was too awkward to be talking about sex and pregnancy with Stefan, with her grandfather, for God's sake. He was eighty-whatever, he slept with Granny; he made a baby with her, long ago. A baby who was somehow Daddy. "I don't—it's not his business—not unless I decide to keep it."

"Maybe not. But it would be a kindness to him, one he maybe does not deserve, but one which you, Ella, have the power to give him. It is man's burden, you see, to send his seed into the world, and sometimes never to know how it grows."

"Some burden," Ella said bitterly.

Stefan put his finger under her chin and lifted it to meet his gaze. "And it is woman's burden to have life thrust upon her, whether or not she wills it, and this is by far the greater burden. So perhaps it would have been better if I shot your husband in the balls with my pistol, after all."

His expression was still grim, like he meant it. Ella slung her arms around his neck and started to laugh. "You would've been too late," she said, and she was still laughing, holding Stefan's hand, when they returned to the house, where Granny was waiting for them on the porch.

**The evening** air had turned chilly, so Stefan built a fire inside the stone fireplace in the living room. Ella and Granny sat on the sofa; Stefan poured out the cocoa and sat in the armchair. "What is this about quitting your job?" he asked, sipping his cocoa, in a voice of ominous grandfatherly concern.

"Long story. The short version is that I was doing this audit of an investment bank where Patrick happened to work, except in a different division. And I flagged this weird transaction I found, a monthly payment to some investment fund in Boston, shop I'd never heard of before, and the next thing I know, the partner's calling me up and saying I never told them I had a family member working at this bank—although I did—and they were going to fire me on Monday."

Granny waved her hand. "This sounds very tedious, darling."

Stefan, who was more interested in strategic operations, leaned forward. "So you think they wanted to eliminate you, because you found something interesting?"

"Pretty much. I spent the first part of the weekend freaking out, and then I talked it over with—with a friend—"

"With Hector?" Granny smiled.

"With Hector. And it just kind of hit me the next morning, that it was all bullshit. Excuse me. It was just, you know, nonsense that I was working for a company that would do that to me. I mean, life's too short to work with assholes, right? Also, it's a small world, really— finance, I mean—and I was just going to keep running into the same people, people like Patrick, Patrick himself. That whole overpaid attitude. The entitle- ment, oh my God, the stories I could tell you. And I got up in the middle of Sunday night and typed up a resignation letter on my laptop and printed it out at Kinko's before I left for work. And it turned out they weren't going to fire me after all, but I still resigned anyway. I was done."

"That's my girl," Stefan said.

"Why didn't they fire you after all, though?" asked Granny.

Ella blew on the film atop her cocoa. "Um, because of Patrick, actually. He sort of—well, he heard about the whole thing, somehow, and quit his own job at Sterling Bates. Went over to Parkinson Peters and convinced them to keep me."

"My goodness," said Granny.

"Clever fellow," said Stefan. "But you did not take this lure of his, did you?"

"I did not, Stefan." Ella smiled at him, and he smiled back from his handsome, lined face, and she thought, in awe, He's my grandfather, my actual grandfather, and the warmth in her chest was like cinder. She'd never known Granddad, bore him no loyalty except in the abstract—how could you adore a man in a photograph, a man you only heard about in stories? But she had always adored Stefan. When she was small, he used to carry her on his shoulders to watch the horses, and hold her hand when she went to meet the waves beating on the ocean side of the island. He taught her to play chess and never, ever let her win, so that when she finally did beat him, sometime in college, she knew she'd earned it, and also that Stefan was even more delighted than she was. At her wedding she danced with him, and nobody outside the family imagined that he wasn't her real grandfather. Except that he was.

For Daddy, it would be different. He approved of

Stefan, liked him; he had maybe even grown to love him over the years, for Granny's sake and also because Stefan was a good and fascinating man. But he'd worshipped Granddad. What would Daddy say, if he knew this shattering fact? What would he think of poor Granny?

Granny was speaking now, in her sweet, firm voice with its slight accent. Granny's mother was American, but her father had been some kind of French nobleman, and she'd spent most of her childhood overseas until the war came. "But what about this investment firm?" she said. "The bad one? Who's going to hold them to account, if you've left?"

"I still have my notes. I took them away with me. I was going to do some digging, now that I'm on my own."

"Which firm is it?" Stefan asked idly, poking the fire.

"Something called FH Holdings. A small shop, probably. Based in Cambridge, Massachusetts. Never even heard of it until I was looking at the Sterling Bates municipal banking spreadsheet, which is kind of strange, because—"

Granny startled on the sofa beside Ella. "Did you say Massachusetts?"

Ella turned to her. "You've heard of them?"

Granny looked at Stefan, who gazed back at her, and Ella had the feeling that some kind of communication was passing between them. "Hey, what's up?" she said. "Enough with the eye contact already."

Granny went back to her cocoa. "Nothing," she said, very firm, just as Stefan, looking devilish, said, "The name is not unknown around here."

"Are you serious? You've heard of them?"

"It's a family trust," Stefan said.

"Your family?"

"It's probably not even the same firm," said Granny. "Such a stupid, common name. And it was a very long time ago."

"What was a long time ago?"

"The house in Cocoa Beach." Granny drew a claw-like thumb along the rim of the mug. "Johann and I—Granddad, I mean—we bought the house from a firm of that name."

"Trust, though, wasn't it? FH Trust," Stefan said. "I saw the papers."

"Yes, that was it. Back in 1939, after the land boom was over and the Depression had made things even worse, and Florida beach houses were going for nothing. That's all. I'm sure it's only a coincidence."

"Oh." Ella settled back on the sofa cushion and sipped her cocoa. The thrill inside her stomach—that

fluttering she always got, whenever the numbers starting leading her somewhere interesting—fizzled away.
"Yeah, probably. I doubt this outfit was around back
then, let alone investing in Florida real estate. Boston
firms are usually super conservative. Old money."

"You never know," Stefan said, in his devilish voice,
and Ella could have sworn he winked at Granny from
the side of his face she couldn't quite see. "If I were
you, I might keep digging."

**Ella left** early the next morning, on the very first
ferry, carrying hot coffee inside a thermos and Granny's
famous walnut loaf inside her tote bag. Stefan and
Granny both bicycled to the dock to see her off. She
waited to board until they began to throw off the
ropes. Granny was crying. Granny always cried when
people left.

"I don't know why you can't stay another day or
two," she said. "You're still exhausted from the drive
down."

"I promised Aunt Viv I'd get her car back to her
ASAP. Don't worry, I'll come back again soon." Ella
hugged Granny's slight form, the bones that felt like a
bird's skeleton. Inhaled the lemony scent of her soap.
"I mean, I'm unemployed now, right? Nothing but
time on my hands."

Granny whispered in her ear. "Talk to your Mumma. She understands more than you realize."

"Okay," Ella said, just to please her. She turned to Stefan, lurched into his chest, and squeezed with all her might.

"Remember what I said to you," he said sternly, too sternly, which meant he felt something exactly the opposite. The horn blew. He said, more softly, next to her ear, "If you need us to help you raise some damn baby, we will do that."

Ella kissed his cheek. "Love you," she said. Pulled away and picked up her tote. "Love you both."

She walked up the ramp and found a seat on the outside, even though the morning was chilly, so she could watch them standing there together on the dock, holding hands, until the ferry drew too far away and they disappeared.

# ACT III

# We Pass Like Ships
# in the Night

## *(blow me down)*

**New York City
April 1924**

# 1

Now, I don't quite recollect when Anson told me about his own baby sister. We have had so few opportunities to talk about such matters, with bootleggers and bribery to demand our attention. I do recall thinking how uncanny it was that a man of twenty-five or six (he never did say exactly) should have a sibling of less than two years, but then Nature will have her way, won't she? And a husband will certainly have his.

Anyway, two days after I formed that reluctant alliance with Mrs. Marshall on a hot Florida beach, the evidence of Nature's headstrong method stands wobble-legged before me, in the shape of a striking young girl. I can't say that she takes after either of her two brothers. Her hair is darker than Anson's and right wild, and her eyes reflect a breathtaking shade of aquamarine blue, surrounded by a set of wet-coal eyelashes. Her thick, straight eyebrows astound me. She unsticks her thumb from a pair of wide red lips—

more geranium than rosebud—and tells me her name is Ma-wee.

I climb down from my astonishment and reach for Patsy's hand beside me. "Marie," I say, "this is my sister, Patsy, who's going to be your friend."

I daresay most girls of five or six years long for almost nothing so much as they long for a delicious live doll like Miss Marie Marshall, and Patsy's no exception. She takes Marie's wee hand, wet thumb and all, and guides her to the miniature tea table arranged in the corner of the vast Marshall nursery, where the two of them proceed to feast a menagerie of plush rabbits, bears, dolls, and what have you. Mrs. Marshall makes a noise of fond satisfaction and nods to the uniformed nanny in the rocking chair, who nods back in some kind of code. She then turns to me.

"Well! That's settled nicely. Shall we go visit Billy?"

# 2

Even a modern steam locomotive requires a pair of days to cover the distance between Palm Beach, Florida—where Mrs. Marshall returned the yellow roadster to the fine garage of some friend of hers, who keeps it there for what they call the winter season—and Pennsylvania Station in New York City. The two of us had plenty of time to discuss the question of Billy.

"The most important thing is that you aren't shocked," she told me over breakfast (buttered eggs, bacon, grapefruit, coffee) the second morning. "When you see him, I mean. You mustn't seem appalled or disgusted or in any way"—she paused, sipping her coffee, searching for a word—"distraught."

Click went the cup in its saucer.

"I don't think anything could be so bad as the sight of him when it was done," I replied.

"Are you certain? His head's all bandaged, his jaw's locked tight in a wired cage. Like an animal, like one of those dogs that tends to bite. Except he can't bite at all, poor thing. You have to listen closely when he's talking, because his jaw won't move, and even then you can't understand half of what he says."

I rearranged my eggs with the tines of a delicate fork and told her I was certain. She looked out the window at the landscape of Virginia or Maryland or whatever it was, escaping us in a blur of green pasture and woods, and nothing in her glossed expression offered me a hint of what she was thinking. She didn't hardly eat, just smoked and drank her coffee, moving her lips only enough to imbibe each one in turn, while the new-risen sun turned her eyes gold. I remember thinking, Why, this woman's fixing to be my mother-in-law, isn't she, one son or another. I turned my attention to Patsy, who had finished her breakfast and now played with her doll, murmuring both halves of some kind of dialogue. Just as my head started to move, Mrs. Marshall spoke up.

"Well, I hope so, Ginger. I most sincerely hope so. Because you're going to be acting the greatest part of your life."

At the time, I thought this was all hyperbole—Mrs. Marshall has such a gift for dramatic pronouncements—and I made all the necessary noises of assurance, which she pretended to accept. But as we leave that gilded nursery and proceed down the hallway of the Marshalls' Fifth Avenue apartment, heels sinking silently into a succession of narrow Oriental rugs, I confess I feel a certain stir of anxiety. Not because I haven't before witnessed the horrors of physical disfigurement—there was one poor drunk fellow in River Junction who blew the bottom half of his face clear away with a shotgun, and the good Lord showed not enough mercy to take his life as well—but because Billy near enough died for my sake, believing my heart was his, and now here I be, fixing to deceive him anew.

Maybe Mrs. Marshall detects the tremor of my discontent, the way scientists measure the buzz of atoms in the ether. She snatches my arm as we prepare to descend the staircase and forces us both to stop. Takes in the sincerity of my expression with narrowed eyes.

"You're certain?" she demands.

I remove her hand from my arm and say I'm certain.

"Not just serene, Ginger, but loving. Delighted to see him. You can't wait to marry him, can't wait to bear his child. Just as soon as he's healed up and able to stand at the altar."

"May the good Lord forgive me."

"Never mind the good Lord. If you fail, I won't forgive you."

She stands aside and motions me down the stairs, which separate the nursery and the maids' rooms from the grander rooms below. The Marshalls own what they call a duplex apartment, most of one floor and part of the one above, a thing as natural as breathing to Billy, who was reared up here. He now inhabits the bedroom of his childhood, to which Mrs. Marshall removed him as soon as they could load him safely into an ambulance after his last operation. Nobody ever gets better in hospitals, she said. He'll heal faster in his own bed.

Well. I don't know about that, but you can't deny the sheer marvelousness of the Marshall abode, the airy height of the ceilings and the aggressive cleanliness of the floors, the bright furniture and soft rugs, the scent of new flowers and the sound of a solitary mote of dust as it drifts across the room. It's nothing like the other blueblood apartment I once visited, Julie Schuyler's place, which was large but also shabby, crowded with gramophone music and illustrious, mismatched objects and not awfully hygienic, if you know what I mean. I don't think a germ would dare to raise its head around this joint. Outside all those brilliant windows, Central Park presents a wholesome spring vista of fading blossoms and tender green leaves. Why, I reckon if you stuck around here long enough, you might could grow a whole new limb.

We reach the bottom of the stairs and turn left, strolling past a grand parlor and down a wide hallway, clicking our heels against the glossy parquet, until Mrs. Marshall comes to a stop before a white painted door. Knocks twice, softly. "Bil-ly," she says, singsong voice you might speak to a child, "I've brought a vis-itor!"

She doesn't wait for him to reply. Places her hand on the knob and gives it a long-fingered twist, and now

I hear some kind of deep sound from within, blurred words floating through the wood and plaster, and it's too late to turn away, too late to lose courage, the door's open and the sunlight rushes in, and Mrs. Marshall steps through all that brilliance in her dress of delicate lilac chiffon, leaving me no choice but to follow her.

# 3

Gin! Billy cries out, clear as day. I guess it's the kind of word even a steel cage can't muffle. He sits beside the window in a wide, deep wing chair the color of asparagus, wearing a pair of ironed blue pajamas and moccasin slippers. His hair's trimmed short beneath a ring of white bandages, and I'll bet you a dollar his teeth are brushed too, at exquisite trouble through the gaps in the wire mesh. His eyes, squinting from within a cushion of aging yellow-green bruises, are light and hopeful. His right arm's in a sling. The left hand stretches toward me. What else can I do? I hurry forth and take it.

"Dear Billy. You look awful," I tell him.

"Don't I, though?" he says, though the words come out all smashed and murky, so that I have to pick through the sounds and put them back together again in my head.

"How are you feeling?"

"Pretty well."

"Does it hurt awfully? Are they giving you something for the pain?"

He makes this noncommittal noise, which must signal assent to both questions.

"Thank goodness you've got the best doctors Mama can buy. How long before they take this old thing off?" I touch my finger to the cage—that's the only word I can think of, this contraption of chicken wire and screws and gauze, holding Billy's mandible in place—somewhere near what ought to be his chin.

"About six weeks," says Mrs. Marshall, so quickly that I almost miss the look of confusion that bends Billy's eyebrows. She ranges up to the window and fingers the creamy curtain. "And then he'll be good as new."

"Shiny as a racecar," I agree. "Handsome as Valentino."

Billy's hand squeezes mine and travels up my arm to my shoulder, up my shoulder to my cheek, where it rests against my own perfectly intact bones, thumb sidling along the ridge of my eye socket. "Beautiful," he says, sort of raspy.

"Aw, you're just sweet-talking me."

He makes a little shake of his head and turns to Mama. "Told you."

"Yes, you were absolutely right, all along," she says. "And wasn't I right, too? Didn't I bring her right back here, where she belongs?"

Now, a fellow takes a hit like Billy took from Duke Kelly, brass knuckles smashing into tender young bone, it has the kind of effect on his face that you really can't ignore, and yet you must, of course. You must look everywhere except at the point of his jaw that took the brunt of those terrible brass ridges; you must think of anything except the moment in which your stepfather drew back his arm and snapped it forward again with the strength of an explosive charge, blood and bone all over the place; you must blink back the tears in your eyes and smile bright and look directly into his warm brown irises, the only things left unchanged on his entire face. Until he turns to his mama and exchanges a look of understanding with her, and you can, for just an instant, allow your gaze to slip—almost unwilling—to all those bandages, and what they hide from the open air. Allow your mind to speculate what remains of Billy's sweet beauty, which he offered up as sacrifice for your redemption, just because he loved you, because he thought you were carrying his child.

You think of the times you have kissed that jaw, that red mouth; of the times you have lain next to him, exchanging the heat of your body for the heat of his, in those days when your chest hurt with craving something you couldn't quite understand, and the closeness of Billy's chest, the friction of his skin against your skin, the sigh he gave out at the end and the sigh you gave out too, seemed to lessen that terrible ache, until someone came along who cured it.

His face returns to mine, and he starts to say something. Makes a noise of frustration and reaches for the round, marble-topped table next to the right-hand side of the chair, where a stack of notepaper and a shiny black fountain pen await his long, elegant hand.

He scribbles something down, practically tearing the paper in his emotion. His blue pajama sleeve wobbles beneath his wrist. He thrusts the note in my hands like a gift and says something like Gin, please, and his eyes are fierce and his lashes are wet.

I look down at the note in my hand, wrinkled at the corner by Billy's enthusiastic thumb.

*HOW IS—BABY!!!*

# 4

One point I made clear to Mrs. Marshall, as we swung up the Eastern Seaboard in our fine Pullman sleeper compartment, eating our buttered eggs soft in the morning and our beefsteak rare in the evening: I was not about to deceive poor Billy in the matter of babies.

We did not agree on this point, I'm sorry to say. Seems Mrs. Marshall longs to be a grandmother, even if the offspring's only imaginary, and she tried all kinds of persuasion in order to change my mind. Still, I wouldn't budge. I told her I wasn't going to make any outright promise of marriage, and I wasn't going to let Billy think he was a father when he wasn't. After all, I do have certain principles of honor, even if I am but mountain bred. Don't never make a promise you ain't aiming to keep, Geneva Rose, old Duke used to tell me, and I will say that the devil hewed faithful to that code all the way to his own bad end.

But something funny does sometimes happen to all your high, cold principles when a man's gaze fixes yours soulfully, and he writes you an urgent note in a lopsided hand, more like a child's than his own.

I commence to stammer, and believe me, I am not by nature the stammering kind of woman.

"Why—why—I suppose—"

"She's feeling just fine, Billy," Mrs. Marshall cuts in, as smooth as you please. (Having practiced this type of deceit on prior occasion, I'll bet.) "Just absolutely fine. Our Geneva possesses the most marvelous constitution. Don't you, my dear?"

"I reckon so," I say weakly.

Beneath that wire cage, Billy's mouth forms a horrid grin. Just a baring of broken teeth, no upward crescent, no sweet, familiar lines crinkling up his face. But you can tell by his eyes that he's smiling. He says a word that sounds like happy.

"Oh, we're delighted, darling," Mrs. Marshall says. "And of course we must have the wedding as soon as possible, under the circumstances. Certainly before Memorial Day, I think."

"Yesh," says Billy. Pressing my hand.

"Everything's healing so well. I think a small, private ceremony, out in Southampton where we can be quiet about it, just as soon as those wires come off so you can say your vows properly. That will be the middle of May. Is that convenient for you, Geneva dear?"

I turn my head to meet her eyes. She's standing a little apart from us, next to the window, arms crossed just under her tiny ribs, wearing her dress of lilac chiffon that softens all those many edges. The color suits her pale skin, though I believe the straight, modern cut isn't her best. Like me, she needs a waist to show off her figure to its proper advantage. Still, she looks fashionable. Her height—again, like mine—lends her enough elegance to pull it off, and as I consider these odd intersections between Mrs. Marshall and me, it occurs to me that it's no great wonder, after all, that two such opposite brothers should come to fix upon the same flame-headed woman. We may not be cut from the same cloth—her of silk, me of homespun—but perhaps the act was performed by the same pair of almighty scissors. In the pleasant, sunlit space now between us, our matched spirits meet and clash to a thunderous draw. Her eyebrows lift, mine narrow. I turn back to Billy.

"Let's just see how you get on, Billy-boy. That's the most important thing."

He shakes his head and says something I can't quite make out.

"What's that? You want to—to pick out a name?"

Billy growls a little and glances at Mama.

"I think what Billy's trying to say," she tells me, "is that your name's the most important thing. The baby should have a name."

"Oh. Of—of course. But he ought to heal first—"

Billy shakes his head hard. "No time. Fancy . . . no!"

"He thinks the two of you should get married right away, I believe," Mrs. Marshall says. "Because of your good name."

"Right away?"

"Please," Billy says. Lifts my fingertips clumsily up to his face, as if to kiss them, except the wire cage sits in the way. I don't know how they feed him; you can't get a spoon through there or anything, and he can't possibly chew while his jaw's shut up like that. Some kind of tube, I guess. Food all strained into soup.

I whisper, "Oh, Billy. You know I don't care about that."

"Take care of you."

"I can take care of myself. Always have. I never did care what other people might say. All I want in the world is for you to get better, Billy, and I won't let you think about anything else until then. Baby or no baby."

He lowers my hand to the table and lays his other palm over it, so my fingers are sandwiched between his, and squeezes me tight. "Take care of you," he repeats, except more urgently, leaning forward a little.

"Now look. I'm here, aren't I? Living under your roof. Under your mama's tender care. We're both here to help you get better, Billy-boy, and so you had better do that thing right quick, is that clear? And once those wires are off your face and you can speak to me properly, we'll talk about the future."

He goes on staring at me, disregarding his mama in her dreamy chiffon, as if my face bears some kind of map that will guide him out of his present predicament. Just as I'm opening my mouth to break the terrible scrutiny, he lifts his topmost hand from mine and reaches into the pocket of his dressing gown. Takes out a small box of night-colored velvet. "Promise," he says, laying the box on the table between us, except he misses his aim a little, it's too close to the edge and falls to the rug below. I bend automatically to pick it up, and when I rise again I'm holding this damn velvet object in my paw, like it was meant to be there all along.

"Promise," Billy says again, more like a question but not quite.

I start to mumble something about waiting a bit, but Billy intends no such thing, and for a man whose physical faculties aren't much to speak of, he manages to snatch that box with surprising dexterity and open its jaw to reveal some kind of starburst inside. Except his hand's shaking so badly, the whole thing pitches overboard once more, and this time I am not so stupid as to fetch it myself.

Although that turns out to be a terrible mistake too, because Billy just laughs and goes clumsily down on one knee and makes it all worse, offering his ring to me in the traditional fashion, offering his love and his life and his eternal faithfulness and all that, grinning his monstrous wire-mouth grin, tears glossing his eyes, and if I might slay that Mrs. Marshall with a single glance, by God, the glance I send her at that instant would surely murder her good.

"Billy, this is all so sudden."

"Promise," he says once more, a word you cannot mistake for anything else.

In order to avoid the appeal of those tears, I allow my gaze to fall upon the velvet box and the ring inside, which is made of a single large diamond surrounded by an array of tiny ones, all set amid tiny gold curlicues and flourishes of a wondrous complexity. Austere it's not. A thought arrives in my head: this isn't the ring Anson would offer me, if he ever meant to offer me a ring. Anson would pick out a simple ring, a solitaire or something, maybe even a plain gold band. His heart would be on it, and that's all. And though I never desired to wear any man's ring, even the one bearing Anson's heart, my ribs start to ache anyway, not because of missing rings but because of missing hearts, missing Anson, the cold stone of worry that has lodged itself in my chest. Don't know where he is. Don't know what he does. And here's poor Billy with tears in his eyes and a ring in a box, a ring that don't belong on my finger, wanting a promise from me that don't belong to him, and I have got to give him some kind of answer that won't crack him in two.

A lilac sleeve intercedes between us.

"Billy, darling." Mrs. Marshall sweeps that ring box clean away. "Geneva's right. You can't possibly get married until those bandages are off."

He barks something unintelligible, Give that back! or such, but she simply clicks the box shut and ruffles his hair.

"Now look. We'll all leave for Southampton tomorrow, and I'll start planning that party for the middle of May, and if you're well enough, darling, and only if you're well enough, we'll surprise our guests with a wedding. How does that sound?"

"I don't know if a party's such a good idea, given the circumstances," I say.

"Oh, only a small one, of course. Thirty or forty guests at the most."

A knock sounds on the door.

"I expect that's the nurse for your pulse and temperature, Billy," says Mrs. Marshall. "We'll discuss the party later, of course. There will be plenty of time for all that, out in the country."

Sure enough the nurse sweeps in, dressed in blue and purpose. Mrs. Marshall leaves but insists I stay, so Billy and I can have a little time together before dinner. The disappearing flash of her figure reminds me of the sun's vanishing. Without her, the room goes gray.

# 5

The nurse checks Billy's temperature and pulse and makes some notes. He submits to these intrusions happily. (As nurses go, she's not without beauty, a fact that must have recommended her to Mrs. Marshall at least as much as her expert discovery of Billy's pulse.) While they get on together, I roam about the room in search of a book.

Mrs. Marshall's perfume lingers delicately in the air, as elegant and manufactured as the woman herself, and when I discover a detective novel in the middle of a stack of magazines on Billy's bedside table, I slide the book free, make for the window and open it a few inches. The nurse casts me a disapproving glare. "Fresh air," I tell her cheerfully, as if it weren't the filthy Manhattan atmosphere drifting under the sash. Prop myself on the sill and thumb through the novel by the strong afternoon light. Some kind of English lord. The nurse finishes up and I offer to read Billy a chapter or two. He agrees. Sits back in his asparagus-green armchair while I open up to chapter one and commence to reading. After a few pages, I take his warm, dry hand into mine. How funny that it should feel so comfortable, reading some detective story to Billy as the sun finds the rooftops of the apartment buildings across the park.

At the end of the first chapter, I tuck my thumb inside the pages and glance at Billy. His eyes are closed. His head rests against one wing of the chair, and I wonder if I should straighten him out.

But his eyes flutter at my silence. Open a little and come to rest upon me, in such a light, confused expression that I imagine he's forgotten why I'm there, or whether I'm some variety of dream. I squeeze his hand, and he starts to speak and makes a frustrated noise.

"It's all right, Billy. You don't need to say anything."

His movements are so sloppy. Every time he reaches for something, he goes too far. He tries to touch the wire contraption around his lower face, and ends up tangling his fingers. I try to help but he turns away, and for a moment we sit there without speaking. I think how ugly bruises are, just at the moment they're healing. The green and yellow somehow more lurid than the swollen, black mess that comes first. What will Billy look like, when that cage comes off, and those bandages beneath? How long before he seems human again, before he can walk down a street or into a party without somebody gasping in shock?

He's murmuring something.

"What's that, sweetie pie?"

His face turns back to mine, and it seems he's thinking the same thing as I am. The tears track down his cheeks and disappear into the white gauze covering his jaw.

He speaks slowly, doing his best to pronounce the words clearly. "Love—still—me?"

I set aside the book and slip to my knees. Crawl to Billy's lap and lay my head upon it. His clumsy hand covers my hair. We sit like that until a maid knocks on the door to summon me to Patsy's bath, because neither of us can properly speak.

# 6

Naturally the Marshall apartment has a service door. You wouldn't want the help entering and leaving across the same sublime checkerboard marble as the family, would you? Your Irish maid is liable to get ideas above her station, and as for your Negro chauffeur—why, it doesn't bear thinking of.

As for the woman you've hired to play the part of your son's devoted fiancée, well, it serves her purposes, too. Mrs. Marshall made some earlier noises about meeting in the dining room—delicate hints as to dress, the promise of meeting the senior Mr. Marshall at last—but as soon as Patsy's tucked into bed, fairy stories dancing in her dreams and all that, I make a right turn instead of a left and descend the back stairs, steal across the kitchen and down the creaking service elevator to the modest door on Sixty-Third Street through which those in uniform enter and exit the building. Walk briskly to Lexington Avenue and catch the IRT downtown, Astor Place station, from which a girl can wander west into her old neighborhood, where the streets are narrower and the minds broader, where the alleyways are dark and silent and the basements bursting with light and noise. Where she can turn a corner she knows well and find a stoop she's climbed a thousand times, fit her key to a sturdy Yale lock and rattle the knob, rattle the knob.

Except the lock's not turning.

I step back and tilt my head upward, where a grid of golden windows ought to signal the presence of ten or fifteen respectable, exhausted working girls, just returned home from the typing pools and stenography desks and department store floors of Manhattan, whipping off long, boxy jackets and high-necked blouses and serviceable wool skirts and replacing them with sequined dresses and nude stockings and crimson lipstick, ready to embark on a night of no good. Or else settling down for the evening with a book and a mug of cocoa, as you sometimes do when you can't take the excitement, or when your monthly visitor comes knocking.

But the windows are dark—all of them—and what's more, the parlor curtains are shut tight. The whole building gives off an aspect of black, silent abandonment. I look down at the key in my palm, unquestionably the key that ought to fit that lock, YALE stamped clearly at the head. Inside my gloves, the skin turns clammy. An electric charge seems to zing in my ears. I curl my fingers around the metal and lift the knocker with my other hand, but I'm not surprised as the seconds tick by and the knock goes unanswered. The stoop remains empty of life and sound, as if some terrible plague has swept from attic to basement, leaving nothing behind.

Just cold, damp dread, of the kind I thought I'd left behind in River Junction.

# 7

For a minute or two, I don't know quite how long, I stare at the knocker, an old brass thing tarnished at the seams. Behind me, an automobile rattles down the street and pauses at the corner in a fine, high squeak of old brakes. Just as the gears grind and the engine roars forward, a hand falls on my shoulder.

I spin hard, thrusting my elbow outward as I turn. Catch a large, beefy fellow right in the soft part of the stomach. He grunts and stumbles backward down the steps to crash on the sidewalk, right smack in that green-black puddle at the bottom, the one that never quite dries out.

"Jesus Mary, Ginger!" he yells.

I rush down the stairs to help him up. "Joe! Lord Almighty, why'd you go sneaking up on a girl like that?"

He rises carefully, one massive leg after the other, and I'm afraid my assistance is all for show: I couldn't lift a single broad, elephant foot of him on my own, let alone the rest of his unholy carcass. Somehow he gathers himself back to a standing position and frowns down, down, down from that airy perch. I once asked him about the weather up there. Never asked again.

"How's your derrière, mon frère?" I ask. "Besides wet."

He jerks his unamused head toward the building next door.

"Christopher says to come inside."

# 8

I never expected to find myself back along this dear, familiar bar, most especially after what happened here the last time. But when Christopher invites you personally inside his eponymous joint, spending the precious efforts of his best goon, why, you don't decline his hospitality. Besides, I have an idea that he's just the man I need to see right now.

Joe's all business. Disappears through a doorway at the back, and soon thereafter a short, burly, baby-faced fellow walks in, wiping his hands on a striped dish-towel, expression of patent surprise. "Gin! What the hell are you doing here?"

"Why, because you invited me. If invitation's the right word for a fellow like Joe."

"You know what I mean. I thought you'd split for good."

I shrug. "Passing through the neighborhood. Thought I'd drop inside and say hello."

He steps behind the bar and tosses the dish towel on some shelf underneath the counter. "You look terrible. Can I pour you a drink?"

"Christopher, my love," I say, laying my pocketbook on the counter, stacking my gloves on top, "there ain't enough hooch in the world."

# 9

We go way back, Christopher and me, even if I don't exactly know his real name. (Nobody does, so far as I can tell.) The joint occupies an ordinary basement on Christopher Street, right next door to the boardinghouse where I used to keep a room, up until that fateful March day when Anson spirited me out the window to a place of temporary safety, and because there never was a name attached to these few plain rooms packed with jazz music and booze and pleasure, everybody just called it Christopher's. The owner naturally became known as Christopher. He never corrected this simple logic, so I reckon he doesn't mind. Serves a purpose, like everything else.

As I accept a squat glass of Old Grand-Dad, no ice—Christopher doesn't serve in teacups like some do, call a spade a spade is his philosophy—I am put in mind of the first time I met the fellow, about three years ago, October of nineteen hundred and twenty. Autumn was just starting to get on, and I'd been living in Mrs. Washington's boardinghouse for maybe a month, returning directly to my little bedroom from the subway, a mere green Appalachia mountain child afeared of metropolitan temptations. Used to lie awake on my narrow bed, listen to the noise of wickedness outside my window, while the leaves turned to gold and my heart beat fast with curiosity. Until one night I just threw back the counterpane and put on my best dress, my stockings, and my buckled shoes, and I walked down the boardinghouse stairs and out the door, thinking someone might stop me, but nobody ever did. I waited until some group of merry city-dwellers gathered outside the basement door and I just slipped right in with them. No password or anything. Made my way to the bar and sat down like I owned the place, like I was fixing to meet some fancy gentleman there, and I asked the burly, baby-faced man behind the bar for a rye whiskey. Pulse knocking to rattle the walls right down.

Christopher gave me this kind look and poured the whiskey. You're the new girl moved in next door, aren't you? he said, and I replied, Yes I be, what of it? And he said, Welcome to the neighborhood, the first drink's on me, and I said that was right kind, and he said I had better lose that mountain accent in a hurry, or some gentleman was liable to think he might take advantage of me. Well, that made me sit straight, you can imagine, and I fixed Christopher a steely one and said I'd like to see some gentleman try it.

I don't know what he thought of that—for all his youthful looks, he doesn't give away much—but he sort of returned my stare for a second or two, a very uncomfortable few seconds on my part, and at the end of it he made this short nod of his head. Asked my name and I told him Geneva Rose, but most folks called me Ginger on account of my hair, and he said, "Well, Ginger. You need anything, anytime, you come right here and ask for me."

Then he turned away and walked down the bar to serve another customer, and I reckon we've been good friends ever since. At least so near to friends as Christopher ever gets.

# 10

Anyhow, we are much more comfortable together now, three and a half years on, like a liquor that takes time to properly age. He puts the bottle back on the shelf and allows me to savor the first sip or two, busying himself with the tidy arrangement of glasses on shelves, until he turns with the instinct of a good bartender and asks if I'd like another.

"Not yet." I raise my glass, hold up one finger, finish off the measure, and then I set the tumbler back on the counter and say, "Now."

He refills the glass and sets his hands on the edge of the bar, settling in. "Feel like telling me where you been?"

"I reckon you might already know."

"I heard Florida."

"You heard right. Which one of them told you? Luella or Anson?"

He shrugs. "Neither one."

"Oh, you've got ears on ears, haven't you? I guess that's fair. Well, I been to hide in Florida until the heat cleared, and now I'm back in the good old city, where I belong. Except I no longer seem welcome at my place of residence."

He makes a movement of his head, pointing next door. "Mrs. Washington sold up, two weeks ago."

"Did she, now?"

"Lock, stock, and barrel."

"But she can't do that! What about my things?"

"I expect she figured you abandoned them. Anyway, the fellow made her an offer she couldn't refuse, is what I hear."

"What fellow? Who?"

He shrugs his answer and starts to wipe down the counter in brisk, unnecessary circles. "What about you, Gin? You all right?"

"What's that supposed to mean? And don't dodge the question. I want a name."

"Can't give you a name," he says, in a flat, final voice that I know well enough to understand there's no point in arguing with it. Might as well kick down a brick wall with your bare toe as get a name out of Christopher. As if to make himself even plainer, he folds his arms and asks me how I liked Florida.

I open my pocketbook and discover a flattened pack of cigarettes. Christopher reaches into his breast pocket for a lighter. "Florida was all right," I say, as he bends the flame over the tip of the cigarette, "but you know how it is with frying pans and fires."

"If you ask me, you shoulda stayed put in the sunshine."

"Well, I didn't ask you, but since you're in the mood to hand out advice, maybe you could explain why Florida's such an attractive proposition just now for a girl like me. The weather, maybe?"

He shrugs and tucks the lighter back in his pocket. "The weather, sure."

"Now, don't you play dumb with me, Christopher. I'm on to you. You know a heap more than you let on, don't you, and I get the feeling your knowledge is the twenty-four carat kind. So cough up the gold."

"Already told you plenty. Told you all you need to know."

"You've told me nothing."

Christopher sets down the dishcloth and puts his fingers back on the edge of the bar, like he is fixing to leap right over and strangle me. "Why do you need to go kicking up a hornet's nest, you dumb broad? This business ain't for you, Gin. You're too nice a girl."

"Oh, that's rich. Me, nice? I'm nobody's nice girl, believe me."

"Believe me, you are. You got a noble soul, Gin, you got a heart of gold, and in this business a girl like you had better stay on that side of the bar, you hear me? You go sticking your nose where it don't belong, you get it chopped clean off."

"You think I care about some damned bootleggers? You think I want to shut down anybody's racket? Let them drown Manhattan in liquor for all I care. What I want is to see Anson safe. I want to know who's behind this fix, who's out to take him down—"

"Take him down? Why, didn't he just get promoted? Some big award, his picture in the papers?"

"Now, how dumb do you think I am? We both know that's no promotion."

Christopher straightens to his full five feet six inches and scowls at me, and while I have seen a multitude of expressions alter the arrangement of that man's smooth skin, spanning the range of emotion from boredom to disinterest and back again, I have never seen him scowl like that. Like some mountain squall builds unseen behind his sweet, pale eyeballs.

"Mr. Marshall," he says, in a deliberate whisper, "can take care of himself, believe me. He knows exactly what he's got himself into, and he ain't going to quit, even though he knows he can't win. You, on the other hand, are about as dumb a bunny as ever walked into my joint, if you think you can outsmart these fellows. You want my advice? You get yourself a taxi, you head back uptown to that nice rich beau of yours and lie about as low—"

"And how do you know where I'm staying? Only just arrived tonight."

The scowl clears. "Wait here a moment, will you?"

"Not going anywhere, am I?"

He disappears into the back, and as I'm waiting for him, sipping at my drink, sucking carefully at my cigarette, observing all the smoky, familiar details of the room, the idea dawns that I'm sitting in the exact same spot where I met Oliver Anson Marshall for the first time, at the tail end of January. He wore a stiff gray suit over a pair of beefy shoulders, and he ordered a glass of sweet milk and waited for me to walk up and introduce myself. I remember thinking he looked like he was jungle-raised beneath those civilized garments. Turns out he only played football at Princeton, which I guess is a kind of jungle in itself. Anyway, I sized him up and he sized me, measuring the color of each other's eyes, the shape of each other's spirit, and I now wonder if I didn't fall in love with him right there, in the space of all that sizing, for how else can you explain what came later? Then Billy broke in and warned his Revenue agent brother away, though—to be fair—he took care not to blow Anson's cover at the time. Not to disclose the fraternal relationship between them.

I stub out my cigarette in an ivory ashtray and consider how things might have turned out if Billy hadn't acted quite so loyal.

Absent the sound of Bruno's jazz orchestra in the corner, and the buzz of voices and laughter, the drab white walls just sit there silently, like they are sleeping, and the unnatural quiet makes my nerves jump. Makes me think of the last few minutes I spent here, holding a dying friend in my arms, right there on that patch of floor behind me, but what can you do? The tiles are scrubbed clean, no sign remains of Carl Green's bloody passing, and unless a floor can retain the soul of a man after he expired upon it—unless a room can echo back the memory of what came before—this pressure of recollection must be a trick of my brain, a hallucination upon my skin. Anson's miles away, God knows where exactly; Carl's body lies beneath the earth somewhere. I am alone in this place.

The door opens; Christopher walks in. He's carrying something in his hand, an envelope, and as he approaches my hunched figure he holds it forth.

"What's this?" I ask.

"Fellow left it for you."

"Who? Anson?"

"What do you think?"

Of course it's not Anson. Anson's out on the Atlantic Ocean somewhere, drinking salt. Still, I snatch the envelope and rip it open, and it says something for my desperation that I feel a sting of disappointment when the handwriting bears no resemblance to that of my lover.

*Dear Geneva,*

*You will not know me, but your welfare lies close to my heart.*

*I should warn you to leave this business alone, but I know you will not take that kind of advice. Instead, may I humbly propose that you and your sister consider the neighboring walls as a place of personal refuge, should such a thing become necessary.*

*Trust the man who bears this letter.*

*Yours,*
*An Admirer*

But it's not the message itself that causes my breath to stick in my throat and the surface of my skin to tingle. It's the object that slipped free from the fold of the paper when I opened it, clinking softly against the polished wood of Christopher's bar, right next to my empty glass of neat rye whiskey: a key, so newly cut you can see a small curl of shaved metal still clinging to one sharp edge.

I pick it up between thumb and forefinger and hold it up to the electric light, right about the level of Christopher's untroubled forehead. "What do you know about this?"

Maybe a little smile tickles the right-hand corner of his mouth. Maybe I'm just imagining things. In another instant, it's gone, swallowed up by a shrug. "I don't know nothing. I just delivered it."

"Sure you did. And I'm the Queen of Sheba." I rise from the stool and gather up my gloves and pocketbook. "I can see myself out."

"Take care of yourself, Gin," he calls softly, as I make my way around all the tables and chairs, which will soon be filling up with men and women and God knows. Jazz music and the smoke of a hundred cigarettes. The hoofbeats of a hundred mad dancers. The pungency of strong grain alcohol, mixed with whatever you please or nothing at all.

At the steps leading upward to the door, I pause and turn my head. He's still standing there, staring after me, not a flicker of a single muscle. If there's an emotion behind that face of his, he's not inclined to share it.

I tell him, "If you hear anything about Agent Marshall, you'll let me know."

He nods and turns away, taking the ashtray and my empty glass with him, so there's not the slightest sign I was ever there.

# 11

Now, here is the thing about a swank uptown apartment building like the Marshalls inhabit: just about anybody can march down that green awning and through the pair of polished wooden doors to the marble-plated foyer beyond, provided she passes muster with the uniformed doorman, but you must have a key to use the service entrance. Not possessing such key, I exit the taxi on Fifth Avenue and proceed like I own the joint, nodding hello to the doorman, speaking briefly to the porter, and nobody challenges me, nobody suggests for a second that I'm not Miss Geneva Kelly, legitimate houseguest of the Marshalls, every right in the world to step into that elegant elevator and proceed to the fourteenth floor. Isn't it funny where a certain kind of coat and hat can take you in this world?

Anyway, I don't count the victory, because I know what lies in wait for me on the other side of the Marshalls' door, smoking a cigarette and drinking something unconstitutional, tapping its expensive toe against the parquet floor. For an instant, as the elevator jumps to a stop, as the attendant opens the door and pulls back the grille, I consider turning back. Then I remember Patsy. I thank the attendant and step forward into the small, paneled vestibule.

There is only one apartment on this floor. Only one entrance. Just turn the knob, Gin. Turn the knob and face the music, which—now that the door is open— floats softly, tinnily on the air, the sound of an orchestra compressed into a tabletop Victrola. It's coming from the direction of what Mrs. Marshall calls the drawing room, which I must pass on my way to either staircase or bedroom. Opposite the front door, an enormous, full-length portrait of Mrs. Marshall stares archly at me, plump of bosom and wasp of waist, dressed in some kind of dreamlike pale gown like they used to wear, back in the days of horse-drawn broughams and

Mrs. Astor's ballroom. She seems to follow my guilty figure as I steal across the checkerboard marble and out the other side, where a short gallery opens out into a room about as big as the entire meetinghouse back in River Junction, grand fireplace anchoring one end and grand piano at the other, light, neat furniture strewn artfully in between.

But it's not the furniture that arrests me as I tear off my gloves and hat and chuck them atop the narrow Oriental table, as I pass the gilt-framed artwork and step into Mrs. Marshall's drawing room. It's the thick chest of Oliver Anson Marshall, storming right back out.

# 12

I put out my hand and grasp his shoulder. "Anson!"

He looks down at me with shocked eyes. Takes a half step back, away from my touch, and his expression transforms into something else, I don't know what. Dislike, almost. Distaste.

"Why, what's the matter?" I exclaim. "What's happened?"

"Nothing." He looks at his wristwatch. "I'm sorry, I've got to leave."

"Leave? Are you kidding me?"

"I only had an hour. Tide's going to turn. They're expecting me back at the dock."

He speaks so coldly, standing there like a slab of mountain rock, so clearly impatient to be away from my person, that I can't seem to find many words. Just: "You're mad at me."

"I'm not mad. I have to leave, that's all. Only stopped for a moment." He looks back over his shoulder, where his mother's just appeared, cool and elegant in a dress of royal blue silk, so rich it's almost purple. "Good night, Mama."

"Good night, darling. Come back as soon as you can."

He looks back at me. "Good night, Ginger."

"Good night?"

He leans down to kiss my cheek—my cheek!—and walks right past me like I'm part of the furniture, some kind of new statuary his mother's installed in the gallery. I spin around and watch him disappear into the foyer, listen to the sound of the opening door, and I'm too stunned to go after him, too electrified to think of something to say. I fumble with a sound or two, and as the door shuts I lunge forward at last, but Mrs. Marshall's hand shoots out to snare my elbow. I try to shake it off, but she's awfully strong for a lady of a certain age. I whip around and take her wrist with my other hand and yank it away.

"Don't bother!" she calls out, as I shoot off down the gallery, and sure enough, when I open the door the elevator's already closed and making its dignified way down the dial toward the lobby.

But while the sight of that departed elevator might deter some horse-faced, Manhattan-raised debutante, it ain't near enough to stop a redheaded hillbilly reared up inside the holler betwixt two Maryland mountains. I study the view from the tiny window. Then I remember the staircase. There must be a staircase, right? In case of fire or electrical disturbance. I cast about until I spot it, plain white door in the corner, and I throw that door open and near enough throw myself down those steps, feet flying eyes blurring, whipping around each landing, trying to count floors until I give up around three or four, until the progression of identical stairs and landings transforms into some kind of rhythm, some kind of slow beat, synchronized with the movement of the arrow on the elevator dial in my mind's eye. Somewhere in the middle of it all I miss a step. Tumble down half a flight of stairs to land on my right side, hip and shoulder, squeezing out an almighty grunt of pain and surprise. Stagger right back up and swing around the post, down the next flight, while my bones ache and my head swims and my lungs saw for breath, and then a white wall appears before me, and a door to my right side, and I open that door and realize I've run all the way down to the damn basement.

Up I go. One flight, landing, second flight. Door that opens into the beautiful lobby, haven of peace, scent of stargazer lilies. The porter starts at the sight of me. I look for the elevator, which stands open, red-suited attendant at the ready.

"Mr. Marshall?" I gasp.

Both porter and attendant point thumbs at the front door.

"Already left, Miss Kelly. About a minute ago," says the porter.

I let out a small, fierce Damn! under my breath and dash for the door, which the alert doorman swings open just in time. "Mr. Marshall! Which way did he go?" I ask.

"Straight down Fifth, Miss Kelly. Shall I catch him for you?"

But I'm already bolting down that smooth Fifth Avenue sidewalk. At this hour of night it's mercifully sparse, just a few dark-suited businessmen heading north, a few taxis pausing at the curb to release their human cargo. I dart between these obstacles, searching for a burly fellow wearing a sharp fedora. The sidewalk clears before me, and he ought to be there, but the next two blocks are empty, empty. I pause in my run and cast about, panting, and my God, there he is, he's crossed the street to walk along the edge of the park instead of the hurly-burly on the eastern slab of sidewalk. Making as if for the Plaza Hotel, which rises up there on the other side of Fifty-Ninth Street. I cry out his name and plunge across the avenue, causing some outraged taxi or another to honk its horn, and Anson turns at the sound, spies me, starts forward and stops. Begins to open his arms, drops them, opens them again when it's clear I mean to hurl myself upon him.

But the embrace only lasts an instant. He puts his hands on my shoulders and sets me back a step or two. "Gin, I can't stop."

"They aren't going to leave without you, are they? Anyway, if you were really in a hurry, you'd have hailed a taxi. So what gives?"

"Nothing gives."

"Your eyes say different."

He brushes his hand across them. "You were supposed to stay in Florida."

"Your mama made me an offer I couldn't refuse."

"You should have refused anyway."

"Well, I couldn't. You're not the only one around here with unfinished business."

He makes this angry little breath, like he's about to give me hell, and I straighten my back and my neck and think, Ha! Now we're getting somewhere. But the seconds tick and nothing comes out. He lifts his wrist and holds it upward, trying to catch a bit of light on the face of his watch, and says, in that voice of godawful calm, "Look, I don't have time to argue. Just try not to get into any more trouble, all right?"

"What's wrong with you?" I take him by the shoulders. "I haven't seen you in weeks, haven't heard from you, didn't know was you dead or was you alive—"

He stiffens. "But I sent you a letter. A telegram."

"Two weeks ago."

"My God. Don't you realize they're watching me, Ginger? Every word I say, every telegram, every letter. I had to pass that note to you through Luella, so they wouldn't find out where you were, and now you've gone and popped up right where—"

"They. They. Who's they? What's going on with you? Have you got something? Something I should maybe know about?"

Anson takes my fingers and removes them from his shoulders. "Just get back to that apartment, all right? Get back to your fiancé—"

"Oh, is that what you're mad about? Billy?"

"Look, you were supposed to stay in Florida. You were supposed to keep out of trouble. And the next thing I know, you've moved right back to New York, moved in with my own mother and brother, gotten engaged—"

"For God's sake, we're not engaged. It's just pretend, it's just until he's better."

"And then what?"

I pause. "Your mama's going to take care of it."

"Sure she will."

"Don't," I whisper. "Please don't. You surely can't think I wanted this mess."

"Then why?" he asks, and though I can't see him so well, the streetlight's too far off, I can hear his voice is full of pain, shorn of calm at last, like somebody tore a strip off the skin of it.

"I didn't know what else to do. I was all alone down there. So full of guilt and worry, and nothing I could do about it. I didn't know where to turn."

"Turn to me."

"You weren't there. You left."

He leans his lips to my forehead. Doesn't kiss me, exactly. Just rests himself there. Pulse strumming between us, a little fast. Heat rising from our skin. Somewhere behind me, the horns blow and the engines roar and the people shout, but I can't seem to hear them so well. We're up against the park wall now, hidden in the shadows. Feels furtive and dirty somehow, like we're meeting here as lovers, snatching a quick one in the midst of the fallen night.

"Listen," he says urgently, lifting his head, lifting his hand, and for an instant my heart makes this wild leap. But he doesn't touch me. Just sets that hand on the wall behind him and says, "Do you still have that list of names?"

"What list?"

"The men you delivered those bribes to, back in February, when you were pretending to work for Duke."

I tap my forehead. "Right here."

"But not written down?"

"I don't need to write them down."

He lifts his other hand to rub the corner of his mouth. Seems to be looking up the avenue, and then down. "Good. Because I have the feeling . . ."

"What? What feeling?"

"Nothing. Just remember those names, all right? Just in case."

"In case something happens to you?"

"Nothing's going to happen to me. But I want that list of men to exist in somebody else's head, too."

"What about Luella's head? You trust her, don't you?" Anson stands there silently, absorbing the weight of this question. Seems to have forgotten all about the big hurry and the importance of tides. I wonder if he can see me better than I can see him. Whether some trick of the streetlamps illuminates my face, while his face remains hidden in the shadow of the trees. That's the trouble, isn't it? You never can see yourself from the perspective of someone else. You never do know how you really look.

"Well?" I say.

He sticks his hands in his pockets. "There's only one person in the world I trust that far, Ginger, one person I trust like I trust myself, and that's you. Now go. Go back to the apartment and stay there, for God's sake."

I stand there breathless for a beat or two, because how am I supposed to breathe when he says a thing like that? Then I catch the anguish inside his eyes and I do like he says, I turn and hurry back the way I came, before I do something stupid, like kiss him. Hurry right back up Fifth Avenue and cross it carefully this time, because I know he's standing there watching me, making sure I travel those three blocks unmolested, until I slip safe into the golden light of the lobby and the scent of stargazer lilies.

# 13

Back on the fourteenth floor, the door stands open for me. I slam it shut with enough strength to rattle the portrait behind me. Turn to face Mrs. Marshall, who waits at the gallery's entrance in her silk dress, a sleek, modern counterpoint to that glorious image of herself a quarter century earlier.

"Everything sorted out?" she asks.

"Wouldn't you like to know. Just what did you say to him?"

"Nothing to your detriment, I assure you. The opposite. Won't you come in? You must be famished, missing dinner like that." She turns around and walks back down the gallery, knowing I'll follow. Haven't any choice, have I? She's got everything I want inside this apartment of hers, one way or another. Inside the palm of her hand.

# 14

S he leads me past the drawing room, past the staircase, past the dining room and library on opposite sides of a grand hallway, past a couple of closed doors and around the corner to the kitchen, where a maid looks up in surprise from a sink full of soap bubbles.

"I'm terribly sorry to disturb you, Mary," Mrs. Marshall says, "but I had a plate set aside for Miss Kelly when she returned from her appointment. Would you please bring it into the dining room?"

"Of course, madam." Mary extracts her arms from the bubbles and wipes her hands on a dishcloth, taking care not to cast any reproachful looks in my direction. She opens up a door on the massive range and brings out a plate piled high with food.

Mrs. Marshall touches my arm. "Miss Kelly. If you don't mind."

In the dining room, a place is already laid for me: not at the head of the table, naturally, but exactly in the middle of one side. The electric chandelier's been switched off, but a pair of wall sconces still shine from either side of a white marble mantel. I turn to face Mrs. Marshall, all ablaze. "I don't want to eat. I want to know what the devil's going on with you. Why didn't you tell me Anson was coming for dinner?"

"Nothing's going on. I didn't know about it myself. Ollie's ship docked unexpectedly in New York this evening—he wouldn't say why—and he came up to see how Billy's doing, right there in the middle of dinner. I told him you were living here. He looked in on your sister and had a bite to eat. He was just leaving when you arrived. I'm afraid he hadn't any more time, you see, before the ship set off again."

"What did you tell him?"

A door opens on the other side of the room, a door you wouldn't even know existed. Just opens right out from the wallpaper and the wainscoting, like somebody cut it there with a saw one day. Mary appears, carrying my plate, and Mrs. Marshall maintains a discreet silence while the maid sets it down amid the cutlery and asks if there will be anything else.

"A glass of water?" I suggest.

"A glass of water for Miss Kelly, Mary," says Mrs. Marshall, and Mary nods and exits. When the door's fully closed again, Mrs. Marshall continues. "I told him why you were here, of course. There was no other way to explain your presence."

"I should have been the one to tell him. You should have given me a chance."

"But you had chosen to leave, Ginger. To sneak out the back way and miss dinner altogether—Billy was awfully worried, let me tell you—and so you weren't here when Ollie arrived. The duty fell to me." She spreads out her innocent hands, palms out.

"He wasn't happy."

"Of course he wasn't happy. His nose was firmly out of joint, but I expect you found a way to put it right, didn't you? And he'll be grateful in the end, when Billy's all better. Here's Mary with your water."

Lord Almighty, the pantomimes that take place in the houses of rich people. Mary sets down the water while the two of us stand, lips compressed, watching her arrange the cutlery and adjust the water until it's the exact right distance from the plate, atop a white linen tablecloth that must take hours to press. Mary straightens and looks at Mrs. Marshall—thank God she doesn't bob a curtsy or anything like that, or I reckon I might scream—and Mrs. Marshall says that will be all, and Mary returns to her soapy sink.

"Eat," Mrs. Marshall says. "I'm going to bed."

"Bed!"

"We keep strict hours around here, Ginger. I'm sure you and your sister will soon come to appreciate the healthful effects of a regular schedule for meals and sleep. Before I retire, however . . ." She walks to the mantel and picks up a small packet, which merged so well with all that whiteness that I didn't notice it until now. She sets the packet next to my plate. "Your letters."

"My letters."

"I am a woman of my word, Ginger. Remember that. Now good night. I suggest you retire soon. We leave for Southampton at nine o'clock tomorrow morning."

"Southampton!"

"Don't you remember? I've got a party to plan."

"There isn't going to be any damn party—"

But she departs the room before I've finished my sentence, and while I have a thousand questions I want to ask her, a thousand recriminations, a thousand words I want to yell in her direction after all this harrowing evening, I'm drawn instead, as if by one of those streetcar cables, to my heaping plate and cutlery and glass of water, and the packet of letters to one side, just touching the folded white napkin. Food of one kind and another, for a lonely stomach and a lonely soul. Just as Mrs. Marshall knew I would, clever woman as she is. I'll bet she had the whole scene planned out.

As I lower myself to the chair, I begin to realize how famished I am, how unsteady and almost sick with hunger. I haven't eaten since noon, almost ten hours ago; I have consumed two glasses of intoxicating liquor instead, and while that kind of ration might just have gotten me started a couple of months ago, I'm all out of practice now. On the plate, there are small, fancy potatoes and creamed peas and buttered carrots cut evenly on the diagonal, arranged around a few slices of green-speckled meat that might be lamb with mint sauce.

Everything's lost its texture in the warming oven—the lamb's gone tough and dry—but I'm not minded to care at the present moment. I begin with the vegetables, shoveling them helter-skelter into my mouth without regard for the mixing of species, and as I grasp my knife for the slicing of meat, my gaze drops inevitably to the packet of letters resting next to the blade, bound together with a black silk ribbon.

Now, the ribbon's not native to the letters. That's Mrs. Marshall's own embellishment, and I guess it adds a certain panache to the whole business. How else do you dress up the sordid truth? Spoiled Manhattan swell seduces showgirl with promises of true love, gets her with child, and sends her back to the hardscrabble hills from whence she came. But swathed in elegant black silk, why, my father's falsehoods take on the tragic mystery of another age, the kind of age in which stars crossed lovers and devotion was eternal. If you didn't know any better, you'd think my parents were Romeo and Juliet.

I do know better, however. I hear Mrs. Marshall's voice—If you want revenge, my God, he'll rue the day—and my heart strikes hard inside my chest, my hands tremble a little around the knife and fork. I set the knife down again and gulp down some water, ice-cold in the glass Mary brought for me, and the swiftness of it makes me cough.

For my own sake, I don't want to know a thing more about this man who sired me. I've always said so, and it's true. I don't give a damn about him. Don't care to know who he is, or what he does, or whether he still thinks of my mama or cares what happened to her.

But for my mama's sake. My sweet mama, who found shelter for us both at the cost of her happiness and her life. Maybe she deserves a little more for her pains.

Or so I tell myself, as I wipe my hand free of the moisture from that sweating glass of ice-cold water and reach for the silk bow holding my father's letters together. A strange, hot breath seems to blow on the back of my neck. My scalp stings, the backs of my arms sting, as if someone's touched the tip of a live wire to my skin and sent a stream of electromagnetic energy along each tiny hair. I pull back one dangling end of the ribbon, maybe a little too fierce, and the bow falls right apart, the letters explode in different directions, onto the tablecloth and the floor. One of them finds my lap, and I leap up from that chair like I am snakebit. Stare down at the mess I've made. White squares scattered over the white linen and the pale rug beneath, each one bearing my mama's Christian name in purpling old ink. I kneel down to gather them up in my hands, and maybe that's when I notice something that turns my blood into vapor.

I don't know how long I sit there on my knees, cradled by the soft rug, staring at this object in my hand while the world forms a tunnel around me, absent of heat and sound. I think, I must rise, I must take some kind of action, but my brain seems to have gone all stiff. Incapable of decision, incapable of directing movement. I just gaze and gaze at my mama's name, until I think I can see someone's hand grasping a fountain pen and shaping the letters, one by one, in his distinct, old-fashioned handwriting.

Somehow I rise. Allow the gathered squares to fall free from my lap and back onto the rug, except for the one I hold in my hand. The twin wall sconces dim slightly and then recover, as if my sudden movement has disturbed the electrical current, though I only register this detail after I've left the dining room and turned right, back down the corridor, past the grand, pale drawing room to the gallery, where—less than an hour ago—I left my gloves and hat and pocketbook on the narrow Oriental table. The recollection stills my hand directly atop the pocketbook's metal clasp, and as I stare at my own knuckles, as I count the delicate bones of my fingers against the dark, plain leather of the pocketbook and consider the uncanny flickering of the Marshall electrics, the clasp itself turns violently hot under my palm.

I cry out in pain and snatch my hand to my mouth, sucking hard against the burn, but instead of calming the pain only worsens. Spreads down to my wrist and up my fingers all the way to the tips, and just as my whole fist catches flame, it winks out like somebody turned off the gas that fed it. Bastard, I mutter. I put my mama's letter into that hand, which is now kind of numb, and use my left to unbuckle the clasp— now so cool and innocent as a baby's silver rattle— and extract the envelope given to me by Christopher that evening.

I hold the two envelopes side by side, my name next to my mama's name, and I'll be damned if they might not have been written inside the very same sentence.

# 15

So there I stand, holding my envelopes, absorbing the meaning of this symmetry, and a hand falls on my shoulder.

I whip around right fast, causing a woman in a dressing gown to stumble backward, clutching her old-fashioned cap above a face I recognize as that of Miss Marshall's nanny.

"I'm sorry, Miss Kelly," she gasps. "Didn't mean to startle you. It's your sister, ma'am. Young Miss Kelly. She's asking for you. I tried to soothe her, but she only wants you."

# 16

Patsy holds out her arms to me. "Ginny!"

"I'm here, sweetie pie. Right here."

"I called and called."

"I'm sorry, Patsy, I'm so sorry. I didn't hear you. This place is so big."

She nestles right up to my chest, resting her cheek upon my breast, and her flannel nightgown is soft against the skin of my arms. The curtains are thick, enclosing the tiny room in an atmosphere of darkness; you would hardly know that outside the window, Manhattan beats and throbs and casts out its glow into the universe. We are a pair of country caterpillars, snuggled together in our tight cocoon.

"I want to go home now," Patsy says.

"Home? You mean back to Florida?"

"No. Home."

The word makes my bones chill. I stroke her hair and try to think of something to say. Patsy starts to cry.

"I want my daddy!"

"Hush, sweetie pie."

"I want my daddy! Where's my daddy?"

"Your daddy's—your daddy's . . ." Dead. Gone. Sucked down into purgatory, where he be stabbed with red-hot pokers for all eternity, or else folded into the scalding embrace of Mephistopheles. But you can't say such things to a child, can you? You can't say such things to a daughter about Duke Kelly, who might have been the devil's own bastard but was also a daddy, her daddy, tickling his moustache in her hair and buying her dolls and smelling of tobacco and whiskey and a safe, warm bed.

And it's nighttime, and little girls must sleep. The truth can wait for the coming of dawn.

"Daddy's got his own business, sweet pea," I tell her. "But he does love you."

"Johnnie loves me, too," she says, and her sobs subside a little.

"Yes, he surely does. Your brother loves you most of all. He always will."

Her voice turns slower. Loses its high, watery pitch. "Mr. Marshall loves me."

"Mr. Marshall?"

"He told me so. Said you would return home soon and come to me."

"Oh, my darling."

"He was just right. Where was you, Ginny?"

"I was—I was—I had to visit an old friend. Eat my supper. If I knew you were still awake—"

"Mr. Marshall came," she says, dreamy now, gathering back the country cadence that had already begun to slip away during our weeks in Florida with the crisp-voweled Fitzwilliam family. "Remember how he carried me out of the rain, that time?"

"I do, Patsy. I remember it well."

"Is you fixing to marry him, Ginny? Cause he might be my big brother, then. If Daddy don't come back."

We are sitting up against the headboard, Patsy and me, and as it's a narrow bed, made for a single person and no more, the conditions are what you might call cozy, even for a pair of slight girls tucked up together. I draw my legs up underneath me and settle Patsy into a more comfortable position. "I don't know, darling. For one thing, he hasn't asked me. For another thing, I don't know that I ever will get married."

"Gin-ny," she says, in the voice of a child explaining a self-evident fact to someone yet younger than herself, "a girl has to get married."

"No, she doesn't, either. There's no law about that."

Patsy chews on this, and for some time there is no more sound in the room than the rustle of her night-gown as she breathes, no more movement than the rise and fall of our ribs together. Air smells of lavender, and it's drugging my brain, making my eyelids heavy. I figure Patsy's fallen asleep, as I myself am fixing to do this second, but just as my head takes on a merciful fog she pipes back up.

"If you and Mr. Marshall does get hitched, you'll take me with you?"

I stretch out my legs and toe my shoes off to the rug below. Thump, thump. Lift up the counterpane with my left hand and tuck us both inside.

"Course I will, Patsy. You're stuck with me now, all right? Any fellow wants to marry me, he has to beg your leave first."

She giggles against my blouse. Drools a little, too, if that spot of wet don't deceive me. I settle my head into the pillow, my sister into the crook of my body. Softest sheets I ever knew, like the sheets they give you in paradise.

"Good," she says. "Then we can be a family again."

# 17

When I wake, Patsy's already up, playing with a dollhouse in the middle of the room. Outside the window, the clouds beshroud the tops of the buildings, so that the world seems made of gray. On the bedside table, someone has placed the bundle of letters I left in the dining room last night, all gathered back up in the black silk ribbon.

I fold my hands under my cheek and watch Patsy in her enormous white nightgown and an air of utmost concentration, adjusting the dolls and furniture while her lips move silently.

"Good morning, sweet pea," I say.

She turns to me. "Ginny! Come play with me."

"In a minute. First, can you do me a wee favor? Bring me a pen and paper from that little desk in the corner."

She rises obediently and brings me the pen and paper, and I chew on the pen's end for a few seconds while I consider what I'm about to do. After all, I'm supposed to stay put, aren't I? Keep myself out of trouble while Anson goes forth on the deck of a Coast Guard cutter and conquers the rum traffic on the high seas. And it's true, I've got Patsy now. All she's got left of a family that crumbled around her. I can't go out at night like I used to, I can't sneak about Manhattan Island trying to untangle the vast tentacles of somebody's liquor racket until I discover the head of it. If something happens to me—liquor rackets being what they are—Patsy's got nobody in the world who loves her.

On the other hand, I never could stay put and do as I was told. When I was but eight years old, my mama sent me to school at a convent and prayed to God that the nuns could straighten me out into a proper respect for authority. And I reckon I did learn how to smooth the rough edges of my disobedience, how to keep my powder dry for the day I might truly have need of it. Learned how to better regulate this restless spirit of mine, so I spent less energy flinging myself upon walls of brick, and instead went looking for some door to the other side.

Now, maybe this brick wall I'm up against hasn't got any door to speak of. Maybe there's no easy passage through. Maybe I shall have to break it down with a sledgehammer or fashion myself a pair of wings to sail over it. One thing's for certain, however: I don't mean to remain quietly on this side of it any longer, waiting for somebody else to demolish those bricks on my behalf. And maybe I can't go forth in search of what I want any longer, on account of Patsy. But neither could Mohamet go off to his mountain, could he?

I set the nib of my pen on the paper and write down five names. Then I set down that pen and blow the ink dry. Fold the paper in half and say to Patsy, "Time for breakfast, now. We're leaving for the ocean."

"Florida!" She bounces to her feet and clasps her hands.

"No, darling. Not Florida. Southampton, New York."

## New York City, April 1998

By the time Ella returned Aunt Viv's car to the garage on East Twenty-First Street and dragged herself home, it was nearly midnight on Wednesday and she was so exhausted, she was almost drugged. She gripped the banister in the stairwell to hold herself upright. Instead of improving, the nausea had turned worse during the course of the drive north. She couldn't keep anything down—not that anything appealed to her anyway, even the walnut loaf—and resorted to barfing in an empty drink cup at a rest stop. Keep hydrated, she reminded herself, but even water turned her stomach.

She reached the fourth floor landing and the door to her own apartment, where she paused. One less flight of stairs to climb, after all, and she was just about done for. But the pipes in there had burst last week, just before Hector left for Los Angeles, and the kitchen and carpets had been ripped out and the water disconnected. That was how she ended up in Hector's apartment to begin with, because her own was pretty much uninhabitable.

One more flight. She could do this. One more flight, or else she was sleeping on a single bed in a room that still reeked of wet wool.

Ella turned her head and regarded the long, steep stretch of stairs to the fifth floor. Her legs wobbled. She put her hand out and leaned against the wall, and into the silence came the low, thin sound of a muted trumpet, wandering upward from the basement.

Ella closed her eyes and listened. A piano joined the trumpet, and then a big-bellied double bass, plucking its way up and down the scale. The familiar tingling began at the base of her spine. She tried to force it away, but it persisted, growing stronger, and she flashed her eyes back open and levered away from the wall and reached for her keys, reached for the doorknob, but the instant her fingers touched metal an electric shock hit the skin on the back of her hand, like the sting of a bee.

"Fuck you," she mumbled, and then Fuck you! She tried again, but the sting dialed up, harder and sharper, making her eyes water, until she whispered a final

Fuck you and slid to the floor. Leaned against the door for a moment, while her spine tingled and her hands stung and the music thrust up from downstairs, like it was pushing her, urging her. All right, she muttered. I'll try.

She left her tote bag on the floor—no way she could carry it—and crawled up the stairs, one by one, until she reached Hector's apartment, alone on the fifth floor. Opened it with the key in her pocket. The air was quiet and dark and full, the moon held back by a thick front of clouds. Nellie rustled sleepily across the floor and sat on her foot. The electricity in her body had gone, leaving behind a buzzing languor, like after sex. Except she was exhausted and thirsty. She stepped to the kitchen and ran a glass of water from the faucet. Sipped a little—not too much—and tottered to the sofa. No way she could make it to the bed. Just the sofa cushion, smelling of dog and of Hector. An afghan slung over the top; she pulled it down to cover her chest. Her head hurt softly. Nellie jumped up and curled into her stomach. She wanted to throw up, but she didn't have the energy. The jazz continued at the same volume as below, not too loud nor too faint, like a lullaby.

**Morning came** a second later. Ella opened her eyes and made it to the toilet just in time. There was nothing to throw up, just bile, and Ella felt triumphant that the water last night had stayed down, at least. She poured another glass in the kitchen and drank in tiny sips. She felt pulverized, battered, headsore. Nellie sat near her feet and looked up, full of anxiety, and Ella thought, How am I going to walk you, babe? I can barely walk myself.

Nellie's ears lifted, and for an instant Ella actually imagined the dog had heard her thoughts, but then she turned her head and galloped to the door and started scrabbling away at the crack, and Ella thought, Oh shit.

The doorknob rattled and opened. Ella dove behind the counter.

"Hey! There you are, cutie pie!" The accent was high and female and slightly Southern. "How's my sweet girl, huh? Ready for your walk?"

Sadie. Ella had asked Hector's sister Sadie—who lived in 4A—to take care of Nellie's needs while she was gone.

"Hold still, honey," Sadie said, laughing her sweet laugh. "Hold still—there, got it. All right. Come on, girl. Let's go."

Ella crouched behind the counter and leaned her back against the smooth wooden side of the cabinet. Squeezed herself into the smallest possible ball, hoping Sadie wouldn't notice the glass of water on the kitchen counter. Just please. She couldn't face Sadie, she couldn't face anybody like this. She needed to shower, she needed to stop puking, she needed to be Ella again.

The doorknob rattled again. Ella's breath started to ease out from between her lips. Her arms loosened around her legs.

"Huh," said Sadie. "That's funny."

Shit, thought Ella. Shit shit shit.

"Ella?" called Sadie. "Ella! You there?"

The sound of her name echoed from the walls, from the windows, filling the apartment, and for some reason this sound made Ella's eyes sting. She dug her teeth into her bottom lip, as if that could stop her from making any sound. As if pain could turn her invisible.

"Ella! You asleep?"

She's going to go into the bedroom, Ella thought.

Nellie whined and scratched at the door. Sadie let out an exasperated sigh.

"All right, all right," she said. "Fine. Let's go."

The door opened and closed, and Ella slumped sideways to the floor. Saltines, she thought. I need a saltine cracker.

By some miracle, there were crackers in the cabinet. Stale but solid. Ella nibbled two of them, nice and slow, alternating with sips of water, and they gave her just enough strength to brush her teeth, take a shower, and dress in the clothes she'd left there Monday. When she was clean, she felt better. Weak, unsettled, but better. She ate another cracker and more water and checked the clock on the microwave. Seven minutes past eight. Sadie would be back any minute with Nellie. She looked for her handbag and remembered that everything was still in her tote, sitting downstairs outside her apartment door where she had left it last night. Except her keys, which were probably still in the pocket of her jeans. She found her jeans in the bedroom, discovered her keys in the pocket, and it wasn't until she hurried back into the living room and made for the front door that she spotted her tote bag.

Sitting next to the sofa, about eighteen inches from where her head had rested last night.

**Patrick sat** at the small, round table in the back corner, drinking coffee from an extra large cup. There was another cup for Ella. When he spotted her, he stood up and smiled—not his usual confident grin, but something smaller and more humble. He took her elbow and kissed her cheek and asked her if she was all right.

She pulled away and sat down. "I'm fine."

"You look a little tired."

"I just got back from Cumberland. Went to see Granny and Stefan."

He glanced at his watch, the way you sometimes checked the time when you actually needed a calendar. "Wait. You flew?"

"No, I drove." She picked up the coffee and set it down again. "What's in here?"

"Latte. You drove? Both ways? In what, three days?"

"I borrowed Aunt Viv's car, so I had to get it back. Excuse me a second." She rose again and went to the counter to order a small decaffeinated tea. She took the teabag out almost as soon as she got it: the weaker, the better.

Patrick raised both eyebrows. "Since when do you drink tea?"

"Since recently."

"You must be wrecked. Are you sure you don't want the coffee?"

"I'm good. I picked up kind of a stomach thing. Don't get too close."

Patrick reached out and covered her hand. "I don't mind your germs. I'm just glad you called. Do you want a scone or something?"

"No, thanks." Ella wrapped her hands around her cup. The tea was too hot to drink, too hot almost to hold, even with the cardboard sleeve. She was avoiding Patrick's gaze, but she couldn't help noticing that he looked at least as tired as she did. His eyes were bruised, his skin loose and sallow. He wore his usual weekend uniform—a cashmere sweater, sky blue, over a button-down shirt and chinos—and a Burberry rain jacket hooked over the chair behind him. His gym-thick shoulders seemed to have wilted. The skin of his hands was red and chapped. Because she was looking down instead of up, she saw a long, half-healed scrape on the side of his left thumb. He caught the look and lifted his hand.

"Burned it trying to cook spaghetti," he said.

"Sorry."

"You see what a wreck I am without you?"

"Patrick, anyone can cook spaghetti. It's not that hard."

"I used to be able to cook spaghetti just fine. Anyway, I don't want to talk about fucking spaghetti. I want you back. I want to make you believe that I—"

"Patrick—"

"That I've changed, I really have. The whole thing about quitting my job?"

"Yeah, about that? You seriously should have talked to me first. I was going to resign anyway, Patrick. You didn't need to do that. I don't need grand gestures from you."

"It's not a gesture. Listen. My therapist—"

"Oh, Jesus."

"No, listen. It's all about habits, right? Habits and environment. And I started to realize that this whole Wall Street thing, the investment banking thing, the big macho entitled whatever, that was all feeding this—you know, this thing I have."

"The thing where you have sex with other women?"

"My sex addiction." He stated it like it was an objective thing, a thing you might own, an Hermès tie, a Ferrari. The guy with the laptop at the nearest table lifted his head and looked their way.

"Oh, that's what it is." Ella snapped her fingers. "A sex addiction. Kind of like alcohol or drugs, right? Except it forces you to break your marriage vows and put your wife in danger of some incurable disease."

"Please, Ella. I know. I feel like—I can't even tell you what it's like, knowing what I was doing to you. What I did to you. What an unbelievable fucking jerk I am." He hung his head over his coffee. "I'm dying here. My life is ruined. I ruined it. No one to blame but me."

Ella stared at the tiny wisp of steam rising from the hole in the lid of her tea, which lasted about an inch before it dissolved into the busy air of the coffee shop. An indie, not a Starbucks. This was the Village, after all. Patrick seemed to be waiting for her to say something. Say what? Blame herself? Oh no, it was me, I should have been a better wife, I should have met all your sexual needs myself, I should have given you head twice a day so you'd never stray. She pressed her lips together. Patrick continued.

"So, anyway. I got to thinking about all this stuff, all this stuff I was learning about myself, and I thought, hell, I'm just going to start over, right? Get away from my old life and start a new one. There's this guy I know from the client side, this company out in Palo Alto that's doing stuff on the Internet—"

"The Internet, Patrick? Are you kidding me? They've been trying to make money off the Internet since, like, 1994. It's not going to happen. People aren't going to pay for this stuff."

"Well, maybe not yet, okay, but he has this idea he's super excited about, he's like a visionary, and I know some people on the VC side. So anyway. Not going to bore you with details. I put the apartment on the market. I hope you don't mind."

"Do whatever you want," Ella said numbly. The room was starting to tilt. The nausea beginning to rise. The Internet. The World Wide Web. She felt a bubble of laughter, of hysteria, making a hollow in her chest. Poor baby, both parents unemployed, losing their shit beyond all recovery. She took a small sip of tea.

"Hey," Patrick said, leaning forward, "are you sure you're okay?"

"I'm fine."

"Because I can delist the apartment again. I just wanted to raise as much cash as I could for this thing, but if you still want it, Ella, if there's anything you want from me—"

She couldn't do this. She couldn't look him in the eye and tell him she was pregnant. She couldn't look anyone in the eye and say anything. She needed the toilet, she needed a nice warm bed. She needed a saltine cracker, she needed to curl up in a ball and die. She needed an abortion, pronto. She needed a baby. She needed Granny's arms, Stefan's arms, Daddy's warm arms, Mumma's brisk voice telling her everything would be just fine, darling.

"I need Hector," she said aloud.

Patrick's face turned bewildered. "What did you say?"

"Nothing." She grabbed her handbag and tea and got up from the chair. "I have to leave, Patrick. I just remembered—brunch with my parents—I'll call you later."

"Brunch? What the hell? It's Friday!"

"I'll call you!" she said, over her shoulder, and she burst out of the coffee shop and down the sidewalk, turning the wrong way, going around the block. Found a garbage can just in time and threw up into it, like a Saturday night drunk.

**When she** got to the apartment building on Christopher Street, she sat on the stoop and finished her tea. Still felt a little lightheaded, but that was just dehydration. Probably she should see a doctor. Yes. She would call her doctor when she got inside. Make an appointment, have this thing confirmed, discuss her options. Options. What a nice, neutral, clinical word, like you were talking about financial instruments. Like you were talking about your employee incentive plan. Mumma, I have all these options, she said, when she got her first stock bonus, and Mumma, who was a judge in a criminal court and never met a thing called a stock option, said, I know, dear, you have so many options. Ella never let her live it down.

The clouds were thinning out, the sun brightening the air. It had rained overnight, and the pavement was still damp, but it was drying, drying, exposing all the stains. Ella took out her phone and turned it on. (She had kept it off during the drive, because of roaming charges, and forgotten to switch it back on when she entered Manhattan again.) A message lit the outside screen: six missed calls, two voice mails. Probably Hector, probably Mumma and Daddy, probably Patrick. The tea was nearly gone. Good. She needed to rehydrate, she needed to feel like herself again. The sun broke out and warmed her head, warmed her shoes.

She flipped open the phone and tapped in Patrick's number. She had taken him off speed dial so she wouldn't call him accidentally, but she remembered his cell without thinking, the way you remembered important things like your husband's cell number, especially when your husband traveled a lot for work. She expected him to pick up right away, but he didn't. The phone rang and rang and went to voice mail. She considered hanging up. Listened to the female voice instructing her how to leave a message for her husband. Or press pound for more options, the woman added helpfully, and then the beep.

Hi, Patrick. It's me. Ella. So . . . thanks for meeting me this morning. Sorry I rushed off. Like I said, I wasn't feeling well. It's not the stomach bug, actually. I'm kind of pregnant. So . . . yeah. I thought you should know. I haven't decided what I'm doing yet. Just wanted to tell you first. Stefan said you should know. Anyway. Talk to you later.

She flipped the phone shut. Did not press pound for more options. Honestly, who ever did?

**Inside the** building, the walls rang with the sound of somebody hammering, but Ella was focused on climbing the stairs and the noise didn't quite reach her perception until it was too late. Until she stood before the open door of her apartment and stared, round eyed, at the sight of Hector and her father installing her new kitchen.

"Dad?" she said.

Daddy looked up and his face relaxed. He picked himself up, removed the nails from his mouth, and dusted off his trousers. "There you are, honey," he said. "We were worried."

Hector rose too, looking more primal than usual in his work clothes, dirty T-shirt and jeans, lean skin coated in California sunshine. Dark hair back to its unkempt glory. Eyes keen, mouth wide. Ella looked back and forth between the two of them, unable to speak.

"You okay, Ella?" said Hector.

"Sure. Just"—she walked into her father's open arms and hugged him—"kind of wasn't expecting—"

"Sorry about that," Daddy said. "Came down here to take you to breakfast, and this fellow here was hard at work. So I picked up a hammer and gave him a hand."

"Of course you did." Ella pulled away and kissed Daddy's cheek. "I appreciate it. I'm in desperate need of a new kitchen, and the handyman was out last week."

"Hey, now," said Hector. "I cleared that with management first."

"Whatever," Ella said. She addressed her father; she couldn't look at Hector. If she looked at him, the jig was up; even a man so oblivious as her father would instantly divine what lay between them. Hector was perspiring a little; his face literally radiated his need to communicate with her. He set down his hammer and leaned his hand on the counter—she saw all this perfectly with her peripheral vision—and such was his natural grace, his easy physical dexterity, Ella had the unnerving sensation that she was being pulled toward his chest by invisible arms. "Kitchen looks good, anyway," she said, half turning to take in the L-shaped devastation.

"Hey," said Hector. "I haven't even started. Wait until you see the cabinets I'm making. I'm using some original boards I found stacked in the basement—"

"Wait, I thought I was getting a new kitchen, not some recycled crap."

"You can't even find American chestnut like this anymore. Not since the trees died."

Now she looked at him. "They died?"

"Yep. Chestnut blight in the early 1900s wiped them out. There used to be billions, all along the northeastern corridor."

"That's terrible."

"And now the elms are dying off," Daddy said. "It's been a tough century for trees."

Hector's face remained fixed on hers. "Anyway, you're going to have a kitchen of genuine American chestnut, handmade by yours truly, so enough whining about the week off. I even flew back from L.A. a day early, just to get started."

"You didn't need to do that."

"It was lying on my conscience. Plus, I knew I was stuck with you upstairs until I got it done, so . . ."

"Sorry about that."

He shrugged. "I've had worse houseguests."

It was Daddy's turn to look back and forth between the two of them. Ella knew her face was flushed, her eyes too bright. She forced herself to return to her father. "I thought you were back home in Arlington by now."

"I was. Granny called me up and said you needed a shoulder to cry on. Everything all right? You're looking tired."

"I am tired. I drove down to see Granny Annabelle on Monday. Drove back up yesterday."

"That's what she said. Crazy girl." He reached out and ruffled her hair. "Don't do that again, all right? You're not in college anymore. Get yourself an airplane ticket instead."

Hector turned around and braced his hands against the remaining countertop, like he was giving them privacy.

"I'm okay, honest," Ella said. "I quit my job on Monday. Thought I'd give myself a little vacation. Check on Granny and Stefan. You know how they love it when somebody visits."

Daddy's eyes narrowed, watching her make this bright little speech. He glanced at Hector and reached for his jacket. "Okay, then. How about breakfast? You look like you could use something to eat."

"Sure," she said.

Hector lifted his hammer. "Don't mind me. I'll just be working on the kitchen."

"Want us to bring you back something?"

"I already ate, thanks. I'll see you when you get back, okay, Ella?"

"Sure thing."

"I mean it. We need to talk countertops, pronto. I'm thinking soapstone, but you're the boss."

"I like the sound of that."

He lifted the hammer, settled the claw on a nailhead, and yanked. "You know I love a girl who takes charge."

———

**"So what** was that about?" Daddy asked, when they were settled in a booth at the ancient diner around the corner.

Ella buried her face behind a menu. "What was what about?"

"You and Hector."

"Me and Hector, what?"

"Ella."

She laid down her menu. "Just dry toast and herbal tea for me."

"What about eggs?"

"What about eggs?"

Daddy reached out and grasped the fingers of her left hand. "One thing I know about my daughter, she likes a good breakfast."

"Well, maybe I would like a good breakfast, but I'd probably just puke it up. Morning sickness is a bitch."

"I see."

"You don't seem surprised. Did Granny tell you the news?"

"No," he said. "Not exactly. But I could tell something was up. Does Mumma know?"

"No," she said, just as the waitress arrived, bored and beautifully supercilious, filling in the time before her next modeling call. "Dry toast and herbal tea, please."

Daddy ordered a bowl of oatmeal with banana and a cup of coffee, even though he usually ate eggs with bacon, and Ella guessed he didn't want to make her jealous. Or make her barf. Daddy was considerate that way. They used to get Saturday breakfast together when she was a kid, just her and him, while Mumma entertained Joanie and Charlie at home. Daughters need their daddies, she said strictly, shooing them out the door, and so Ella and her father strolled a few blocks down to a diner much like this one, though the waitress at that place was no aspiring model. She had four kids and an alcoholic husband who kept getting laid off, and Daddy always left her a tip almost as large as the bill itself. He ordered the exact same thing Ella did, every time. "Make it two," he'd say, whether she asked for chocolate chip pancakes shaped in a Mickey Mouse face, or a bowl of Cap'n Crunch, or Belgian waffles with whipped cream and strawberries, or French toast with peanut butter. Eventually she settled on eggs with bacon, because she knew that was his favorite, and so it went for the rest of her teenage years, before she left for college. Daddy looked at her now, as if remembering those old Saturdays with her, and he stopped the waitress as she turned away.

"Actually," he said, "make it two."

---

**They sat** silently until the toast arrived, and it was not a comfortable silence. Ella pretended to read the advertisements on the paper placemats, Daddy stared at his own linked hands. When she looked up from beneath her brows, she could actually see the struggle in his face as he absorbed this new situation. His daughter was pregnant by her estranged husband. His baby, his precious Ella. She thought about what Stefan had told her, she thought how Stefan and not Granddad was Daddy's father, and now, as she surreptitiously traced his hair and face and eyes and mouth, she was amazed. They were so alike. You just assumed he looked like Granny because they both had brown hair and eyes, but in fact he had Stefan's face, Stefan's features, Stefan's smile and gestures, if Stefan were a younger man.

The tea arrived, followed by the toast. Daddy looked longingly at the pats of cold butter, wrapped in their gold foil, until Ella pushed the dish toward him. "I won't watch," she said.

He snatched a pat and held it between his closed hands, as if in prayer. That was how you softened it, he told Ella, when she was small. "So this baby . . ." he began.

"It's not a baby," she said. "It's an embryo. I might not keep it."

He dropped the butter. "What?"

"I mean I might terminate. I haven't decided."

"Terminate," he repeated. "You mean an abortion?"

"Look. I wanted a clean break from Patrick, I don't want to have to see him again, ever, once the divorce is finalized. A baby is not a clean break, Dad. A baby is forever."

"That's true."

"I mean, how can I bring a baby into the world, when his parents are already broken up? It's completely unfair. Going back and forth between the two of us, and that's the best case scenario. What if Patrick doesn't want anything to do with it, and the kid has no father? Or what if he remarries some bitch who messes the poor kid up every other weekend? I mean, stepparents. Have you ever heard of a happy stepfamily?"

"Yes. Mine."

"Okay, fine. But that's just because Granny's a saint and raised Grandad's kids like her own. In the real world, it's a crapshoot. It's not like Patrick's going to give me veto power over the women he sleeps with. And meanwhile, I have to work and support it, and that means nannies at least, daycare at worst. It's just a—a mess."

"It's not a mess," Daddy said. "It's a baby. It's my grandchild."

"Don't. Please don't. This decision is hard enough without you playing the grandparent card."

"I'm sorry." He picked up the butter and unpeeled the wrapper. "I respect that. I mean, I'm personally against abortion, I'm just an old-fashioned family man, but if you feel differently—"

"I don't know what I feel, Daddy. I honestly don't. Until now, I've had the luxury of assuming I would never have to decide something like this. Abortions were for girls who weren't careful. Which was a stupid way of thinking about it, I know. But so easy to just avoid thinking about the issue." She picked up her toast and nibbled one corner. "Whenever I did think about it, I guess, I was like, how could you possibly get rid of your own baby? I was like, fine, whatever, put it up for adoption instead. But Patrick would have to sign over rights too, and God knows—and I can't—but I can't—" The toast blurred. She set it down and put her fingers on her temples. "I don't know what to do. Either way, it's going to suck, and I have to decide now. Like now."

Inside her jacket pocket, her cell phone buzzed.

"I'm not going to say it wouldn't break my heart," Daddy said. "Because you're not without resources here. You know Mumma and I—"

"I know," she said. The phone kept buzzing, making her skin itch. "I know you would. It's not about that, really. It's just—it's so complicated. Because, you know, Patrick."

"All right. Okay. What does Patrick say? Or does he know?"

The buzzing stopped. Went into voice mail.

"I tried to call him this morning. Left a message."

"And what about Hector?"

Ella swept her tea up to her lips. "Um, what about Hector?"

"Ella. I may be an old-fashioned family man, but it took me about three minutes to realize that boy has the world's biggest crush on you. He couldn't stop asking me about you, even when he tried."

The phone started buzzing again. Angry now, like it knew it was being ignored.

"He's not a boy," Ella said.

"Well? Is there something between you?"

"Shouldn't I be having this discussion with Mumma?"

"No," he said. "You should be having this discussion with me. Mumma can wait her turn. Mumma . . ."

"Mumma what?"

"Listen to me," he said. "There's something I think I need to tell you."

———

**Ella had** known for some time that the math didn't add up. It was Joanie, actually, who pointed it out. Joanie, who was so mischievous and so investigative, who couldn't keep her nose out of anyone's business. It wasn't that she was dishonorable—she had her own code, mysterious and contradictory though it was— but you didn't leave your secret diary or your friends' notes around where Joanie could find them. Which was anywhere. No hiding place existed that Joanie couldn't sniff out. Joanie was two years younger and a lifetime older. Joanie came up to her when she—Ella— was eleven years old and said triumphantly, "I just saw Mumma and Daddy's wedding announcement."

"So?" Ella said.

"So they got married on New Year's Day, and you were born right after Valentine's."

"So?" Ella said again.

"So they had sex for you before they got married!"

Joanie was not quite correct in her phrasing, but she had the logic razor sharp. Ella crept into the study and opened up the scrapbook, and sure enough, the math added up to a six week gestation—seven, if you counted the fact that she famously came a week early—which even Ella allowed was not exactly viable for human beings.

She'd never mentioned her knowledge to Mumma or Daddy, of course. She didn't want to embarrass them. She didn't want to embarrass herself. Hell, she didn't even want to think about it, Mumma and Daddy in bed together, making her, before they were even married. For God's sake. Gross. But her mother was beautiful, and her father was handsome, and she guessed (as she got older) they just had the hots for each other. What could you do?

But it did puzzle her a little. Daddy was such an honorable man, the kindest and most upright person she knew, and he worshipped her mother like a goddess. (Mumma really was that beautiful, a rare and marvelous specimen.)

So why had he waited until New Year's Day to make an honest woman of her? The last minute, almost? Only six weeks before Ella was born.

It just wasn't like him.

**So she** stared at him across the diner booth, as he set down his toast and his knife and took her hands. Told her this was the hardest thing he'd ever done. But Granny said he should tell her now, and Granny was the wisest person he knew. And this was maybe going to shock her, but he wanted her to know that it didn't change anything, had never changed anything, he had always—and always would—love Ella with all his heart.

"What the fuck?" Ella said, in a high, unsteady voice. "What's this supposed to mean?"

"Your mother," he said. "I fell in love with your mother—"

"Yeah, I know, I know. Joanie told me. She was already pregnant with me, okay? I know. You got her pregnant, and that's why you got married, and—and— I'm okay with it, I've known for years, I . . ."

"Darling," he said, shaking his head, "darling Ella."

"Stop." Her eyes were blurring, she was trying to pull her hands away but he wouldn't let her. "Don't say it. Please don't say it."

"You are my daughter. You have always been my daughter. But your mother—when I met her—"

"No, Daddy, no."

He let go of her hands and swung around the end of the table and slid in next to her. She tried to turn away but without much effort, because he had no trouble turning her back and putting his arm around her and drawing her against him.

"She was in trouble, Ella. And I loved her so much, I didn't care. No, I did care. I wanted you maybe more than she did. I proposed to her six times between Thanksgiving and Christmas. She finally said yes. We got married. You were born the next month, and I was the happiest man alive. The proudest father in the world."

Ella lifted her fist and punched him in the shoulder, not hard, not because it mattered, though it did. Because this strange, horrible revelation could not be real. Because she was lost, because she had discovered something beautiful two days ago and it turned out not to be hers after all. Granny and Stefan had lied to her, they had let her believe something that wasn't true. Daddy smelled of butter, his fingers smelled of butter. The scratch of his wool jacket.

"Stefan," she cried.

"Stefan?"

She put her hands against his lapels and pushed him away.

"Ella! Ella, honey. Wait."

She didn't wait. She couldn't wait. She snatched her pocketbook from the table and thrust her arms into the sleeves of her jacket. Climbed over Daddy and ran for the door.

"Ella!" he called.

She turned and looked, just to make sure he was okay, wasn't having a heart attack. Like she was, like she felt like she was, her heart pounding and her head dizzy, the tea and the toast crumbs spinning upward from her belly. In her pocket, the cell phone started to buzz again.

Daddy stood at the edge of the booth, older than he had ever looked. His hair was taking on gray, his face—oh, his face, her handsome Daddy, always smiling, she could see Mumma kissing him on the lips when he came home and his brown eyes crinkling at her, crinkling at all of them—his warm, handsome face now looked like someone had drenched him in ice water.

"Come back," he said, or rather mouthed, because she couldn't hear the words.

She turned and ran out of the diner. Down the sidewalk. Juggled down the stairs of the Christopher Street subway station—Daddy would never think to go there—and leaned back against the dirty wall, right at the bottom of the steps, sucking wind. The buzz of her cell phone made her want to scream. Shouldn't she be out of coverage underground? She pulled the phone out of her pocket and saw that it wasn't Patrick calling, after all.

It was Aunt Julie.

She flipped the phone open.

"Aunt Julie?"

"There you are, darling! My goodness! I had to ring six times."

"You've never heard of voice mail?"

"I don't do voice mail, darling. Whatever that is. Now listen up. I don't suppose you're free for lunch, are you?"

"Lunch? But you're all the way out on Long Island."

"There are trains, you know."

Ella checked her watch. "I could try. Is it important? Don't you have a bridge tournament or something?"

"Do you think I'd drag you out here if it wasn't important? And bridge is for old ladies."

"Aunt Julie, you're ninety-six."

"Look, are you coming or not?"

Ella stared at the gray wall before her, the dirt and grime and damp, April in Manhattan, emerging from winter. Her hands were cold. Her stomach was beginning to revolt against the toast. Daddy. Oh, Daddy. Standing by the diner booth, watching her run away. Daddy, who wasn't really Daddy after all, except he was—of course he was—except . . . oh, God. Who was her father? In the space of a few minutes, a man now existed—had come suddenly to life, somewhere in the world—who had slept with Miss Pepper Schuyler in the late spring of 1966 and made Ella. A man she didn't know, a man who might be anyone, any middle-aged guy walking down the sidewalks of New York, of Washington, of London, of anywhere. A father. But not a father. A sperm donor. But he existed. He'd had sex with Mumma. Mumma knew him, maybe even loved him, had loved him at least enough to go to bed with him. This man, her father, who wasn't Daddy. Who had abandoned her and Mumma.

"Ella? Are you still there?"

"Yes," she whispered.

"If it makes any difference—and it shouldn't, you know, you should gladly rattle on out the length of Long Island if your great-aunt invites you, my God, I'm ninety-six years old, I'm not going to be around much longer—"

"Seriously, Aunt Julie. What's up?"

A long sigh, as of exasperation. "I've got something for you. A little present, I guess, which I maybe ought to have given you before."

"What kind of present?"

"Does it matter?"

"It might."

"In that case. It's about the Redhead, darling. And you'd better come out on the next train, or I might just change my mind."

Aunt Julie's voice was scratchy, the connection poor as it snaked down through the stairwell. Ella had to focus on her words, to review the noise after it passed through her ears. She straightened from the wall and said, "Did you say the Redhead? As in the picture you gave me?"

"Yes, I did. And I know you're interested, because that fellow from the shop on Madison Avenue tracked me down and had the temerity to telephone me yesterday. Tempted? Because I can always just give this thing to him. God knows he'd soil himself with joy."

Ella peered up the stairwell at the clearing sky. Back down at the ticket booth to her right. Her heart quickened against her ribs. "I'll think about it," she said, and hung up the phone. Slid it back into the pocket of her jacket. Stood there a moment, fingering the clasp of her pocketbook, and then she opened it up and dragged out not the picture of Redhead Beside Herself, wrapped up in plastic and felt, but her yellow MetroCard.

Somewhere, she thought. Anywhere.

She banged through the turnstile and came to rest at her old spot, except they had changed the poster on the opposite side. No more Jeff Bridges bowling (or ice skating) with the actress whose name she couldn't remember. Some advertisement for the New School instead.

The train came.

Come back, Daddy said.

My dear, dear girl, said Stefan.

She stepped on the train, which was not crowded at eleven o'clock on a Friday morning. Sat down on the seat to the left of the door. When the subway pulled into Thirty-Third Street, the connection to the Long Island Rail Road, she stood back up and walked through the open doors.

# ACT IV

# We Raise Our Glasses
## *(and cheer)*

**Southampton, New York**
**May 1924**

# 1

A curious transformation comes over Mrs. Marshall once we reach the family digs in Southampton. Doesn't happen all at once; in fact, I don't believe I notice the difference until she summons me into what seems to be an office in the attic of the Big House, a couple of days after our arrival. She's wearing a loose blue-flowered dress and a pair of espadrille sandals without stockings, and in place of her usual hat and coif, she's wound some kind of turban around her head. She looks up from a typewriter and removes a pair of reading specs from the bridge of her nose, and that's when I notice she hasn't got on any lipstick. (At least, not much.)

She holds up a piece of paper. "I don't understand. Who are these men? And why must I invite them to Windermere?"

"That's my business."

"It's my house."

Now, a word about this joint in which we're standing, if you don't mind. For one thing, it's not as big as the name implies. It's got plenty of rooms, all right, each one spacious, each one flowing pleasantly into the next, each one casting out some casually astonishing view of the Atlantic Ocean from a series of tall French windows. The ceilings are white and lofty; the three shingled stories climb effortlessly into the blue Long Island sky. There is a perfume of salt air and old wood that invades every corner and fills your whole head, growing warmer and looser as the sun makes its daily arc over the window glass, and to my mind it smells exactly like summer.

But my stepfather also possessed a mansion, and his could have swallowed this one for a midafternoon snack. He had rooms upon rooms, corridors leading you across the county, chimney stacks and staircases leading you to nowhere at all, and they was mostly all empty, just a-sitting there still and cold like a museum nobody cared to visit. Here, the gentle sprawl of the Big House contains nothing that is not needful for the comfort of family and guests. When you walk down a hallway, you know where you're headed, and the sound of your feet don't echo on the walls and the floors.

Whenever it was the Marshalls first built this place, they was fixing to impress nobody except themselves.

Why, look at Mrs. Marshall, sitting there in her old wicker chair, wearing her old housedress, glaring up at me from beneath that turban wound around her hair. She doesn't give a damn what other people think. She certainly doesn't care what I think, flame-haired mountain tart as I am. Her brown eyes sharp enough to skewer me.

I find the arm of a beaten-up sofa and sit on it. Shrug my shoulders and pick the sleeve of my dress. "Since Mohamet can't go to the mountain, you know . . ."

"You don't mean to say you think one of these men might be your father?"

"I've already told you, I don't waste a single waking thought about my father."

"I don't believe that."

"I don't care what you believe. It's the truth. I've got more important things to worry about, like keeping your son alive."

"Billy?"

"No." I point my thumb at the window, where the ocean beats upon a crisp yellow shore, and a long, polyglot series of watercraft bobs cheerfully against the line of the horizon. "The other one."

Mrs. Marshall frowns and turns her attention to the paper in her hand. "You surely don't mean these fellows are trying to kill Ollie. Bankers and philanthropists."

"Recognize them, do you?"

"A few." She tosses the paper atop a small pile and reaches for the pack of cigarettes at the corner of the desk. "And they're not bootleggers, believe me."

"I didn't say they were. But you can make a lot of dough in the liquor racket without ever touching a bottle, and trust me, these fellows are making it in loaves."

"How do you know that?"

"Because I have personally delivered a neat stack of lettuce to each and every one of them, with compliments of my stepfather. And whoever was protecting Duke Kelly from undue Bureau attention knows he's got to get rid of Anson first thing, the same way a fox knows he's got to lose a hound dog."

"But Ollie was promoted. The Bureau gave him an award."

"Don't be stupid, Mrs. Marshall. You know better than that."

She turns her head to the window and smokes quietly for a moment. One leg crosses languorously over the other, draped by yards of old blue cotton, while some hazy morning light surrounds her profile like an old Dutch painting. (Except for the cigarette, I guess.) She tips ash out the window, which is cracked open a few inches to allow the air inside. "The party's not for weeks," she says. "Not until the wires are off Billy's jaw."

"Then maybe we can arrange something sooner."

"Nobody's out here yet, except us. The houses don't start filling up until the end of May."

I rise from the sofa arm and walk a slow semicircle into her line of vision. She doesn't see me, however. Just stares right through the region of my waist, eyebrows fixed at an angle of deep concentration, while that gentle sunlight bathes her face back into a state of youthfulness. "Mrs. Marshall, you drew me all the way from Florida to keep company with one son. I imagine you'll find a way to attract a few dull bankers from Manhattan in order to help me save the other one."

She casts me a wry look. "And what exactly am I supposed to do with these poor fellows, once they're here? Lock them up in the stables until they confess?"

I reach for the paper on the desk and force it back into her hand. "Don't worry. You can leave that one up to me."

# 2

Billy's doctor recommends fresh air and exercise, and I aim to give Billy plenty. As soon as I've had my word with Mrs. Marshall, I head downstairs to encourage him outside for a walk.

After an early promise of sunshine, the clouds now edge across the sky like a spill of cream. The lawn is made of that brave, wide-bladed grass that doesn't mind a little salt in the air, and Billy and I trudge down its length in the general direction of the two girls, Marie and Patsy, who play at some game near the shrubbery that separates garden from dune. Billy moves with a clumsy, shambling gait, as if he can't quite get his limbs to properly obey him, so I take one arm and pretend he's supporting me. "Doesn't that breeze smell delicious," I say, inhaling deeply to demonstrate.

Billy makes a noise of assent.

"Just imagine your brother out there, sailing across all that water. And those ships lined up, out to sea." I lift my hand and point. "Just outside United States waters, a whole line of them all the way to Florida, filled up with rum. Floating warehouses, waiting for darkness when the customers come. I wonder how much liquor is bobbing about out there, on the horizon."

Billy hazards some guess, which is muffled by the wires.

"Millions of gallons, I'll bet." I sigh. "And poor Anson, trying to capture it. He hasn't got a chance. People are going to drink, aren't they?"

Billy says a word that sounds like Anson?

"Ollie, I mean. You know that's how he introduced himself to me, back at Christopher's last January. Do you remember?"

"Yesh."

"Names stick, I guess."

Without warning, Billy stops and turns toward me. His eyes are soft and gentle, as appealing as a puppy's. He places one hand against my stomach and says, "Name?"

"Oh, Billy." I brush his hand away. "Don't be silly. There's—"

His discarded fingers grasp my elbow. He kind of wobbles a little, standing there, fixed upon me with a look of terror that makes me feel as if I've swallowed poison.

"There's no need to think about names yet. It's so early. Bad luck."

From across the lawn, a girl shrieks—I think it's Patsy—and the sound carries across my ears like the memory of a long-ago childhood.

"We'll talk about it later," I say. "We'll talk about it when you're better. There's no point even thinking about these things now."

Another happy shriek reaches us, and Billy turns his head toward the sound. He says something, and I wish I could understand it. Wish I could pick out the words. It's easier indoors, when there's no ocean and no wind, no music of little girls playing. When we sit together in a quiet room, I can hear him better, and sometimes even make sense of what he says.

# 3

Billy can't smile, not with his mouth, but when we reach Patsy and Marie his whole face tends to brighten. I help him lower himself to the grass and arrange his arms and legs, and Marie climbs happily into them. Grabs the wire around his jaw, making him wince.

I make to pull her hand free, but Billy brushes me away.

"Don't mind," he says mushily.

So I tell Marie to be careful, and the next second she's running off anyway. The nanny sits nearby in a camp chair, darning a short black stocking, and her eyes move swiftly back to her work when I catch her staring at Billy's face.

"She's such a lovely little girl," I say.

"Funny," Billy says.

"Funny?"

He makes some motion to his face. "Ferry."

For a moment, I wonder why he's comparing his baby sister to a boat, and then I realize my mistake. I follow his gaze to Marie, whose thick black hair flies out behind her as she chases Patsy around the shrubbery.

"Oh! I see what you mean. With that round face of hers, and those eyes. My mama would have said she was uncanny."

Billy nods.

"Must have been a real shock, when Mrs. Marshall told you to expect another sibling. Can't imagine what she was thinking, at her age. Youngest already in college. Although maybe it was a surprise to her, too?"

He doesn't reply. His hand, which had slipped into mine, now moves to pluck at the grass. Plucks and misses. Then catches one, but he can't quite grip it hard enough between his thumb and forefinger, so it slides free between them.

"And your father." I chuckle loudly. "He must have been fair proud of his night's work!"

"I certainly was," says a crisp voice behind me, and if I had been sitting on one of those nearby dunes, I guess I would have commenced to bury myself in the sand, right there. Instead, I start like a chicken and spring to my feet.

"You!" I gasp.

He holds out his hand. "You must be Miss Kelly."

Mr. Marshall is much older than his wife. He might be seventy, by the softness at his jaw and the faint brown spots on his skin. All the same, he's a handsome fellow, made of tarnished hair and solid, elegant bones, and I like the passionate blue of his eyes, which remind me of Anson's. I take his hand and manage a reasonable tone of voice. "I am delighted to meet you at last, Mr. Marshall."

He covers our linked hands with a firm, dry palm, and those blue eyes meet mine with perfect sincerity. "No more delighted than I am. Billy?" He turns to his son, who's staring at the shrubbery as if nothing's happened. "Billy?" he says, more loudly, placing his hand on Billy's shoulder.

Billy makes the same start I did, and do you know, it never occurred to me until now that Billy can't hear properly, since my stepfather threw his brass knuckle fist into the side of his face. Never once did I imagine that maybe Billy can't understand me any better than I can understand him.

I bend into the grass and help my Billy-boy to his feet, and my hands are shaking a little, my stomach sick. The air seems to boil on my skin. Not this, too, I think.

Lord Almighty, not this, too.

Before Billy can arrange himself to greet his father, a little voice shrieks Daddy! and a streak of black hair crosses the grass to throw itself against Mr. Marshall's legs. He staggers back a step or two—not entirely in jest—and bends to lift her into his arms.

Why, he might be her grandfather, I think, as I compare her round, satiny cheek to his, made of leather.

And then I take in her black, wild hair, her straight eyebrows, her full lips, the shape of her nose, the strange, pale aquamarine color of her eyes, and I think something else again.

# 4

Here's another thing about the rich: this Prohibition they voted in, all those businessmen and politicians screaming about how America ought to be a godly, sober nation, they didn't really mean it. Not for themselves, anyway.

Now, I don't happen to know whether the Marshalls spoke or spoke not in favor of the Eighteenth Amendment when it came to pass across the land, state by state. Whether they were among those who insisted that liquor was the blight of humanity, and all our ills might be cured by the simple act of commanding your fellow citizens to dry out. What I do know is this. Mr. and Mrs. Marshall never did fix to stop tippling their own tipple, not even when dry words became dry law, not even when their own son swore an oath to defend that law. And they didn't.

The first thing that nice Mr. Marshall does, as the sun begins to tumble downward behind all those clouds and the scent of dinner to waft from the direction of the kitchen, is he offers me a drink, just as if the year were still nineteen hundred and nineteen and nobody ever yet heard of Izzy and Moe. Hospitable fellow, Mr. Marshall. I don't wish to offend him, so I say yes. Gin and tonic all right, he says, or something stronger? I say a gin and tonic is just fine, thank you. He pours one for me and one for him and yet another for Mrs. Marshall, who drifts in from nowhere wearing a silk dress the color of mashed peas and complains about the heat.

Mr. Marshall says it's just muggy, that's all. Unseasonably muggy.

Drink gin and tonic and talk about the weather, that's what rich people do.

Except Billy. Billy sits stiff in his chair wearing a fine black dinner jacket (the women wear silk, the men wear dinner jackets, even out here at the end of Long Island, in a house set upon the beach) and his gold-dark hair brushed sleek from his face. His right hand grips a sweaty gin and tonic, into which his papa has stuck a straw for convenience. I can see he's tired. I rustle over in his direction and brush my knuckles against his temple, the way my mama used to do to me when I felt poorly. His skin burns my fingers, which are chilled from the icy glass. He takes my hand and holds it there, and his eyes turn up at me, all imploring, while Mrs. Marshall's gaze settles upon the back of my neck.

"Awfully close in here," I say. "Might we open a window? The doctor says Billy needs fresh air."

Mr. Marshall rises affably from his armchair—the one in which he's only just settled—but I stop him just as affably and head for the tall French windows myself. There are several to choose from. The room stretches maybe thirty feet west from the center hallway, and nothing but glass separates you from the lawn and beach and ocean. During the middle of the day, a set of bright yellow curtains shields the upholstery and the atmosphere from the sun, but someone's dragged them all open now, and though the wood's swollen from heat it gives way eventually. The damp salt air seeps in. I open the next window too and lean against the frame. The weather today might have been unnaturally warm and muggy, like the summer is shaking itself off for a trial run, but the ocean's still chilly enough to cool the breeze rushing onshore as the evening settles in. To the west, the clouds turn pink above the high gray dock that stretches into the Atlantic, shielded by a jetty of solid rock. The sight of it makes the hair prickle on my arms and my head. Not two months ago, I made landing there with Anson in the middle of the night, and that small white house near the swimming pool? We rested inside until dawn.

"I'm selling Tiptoe," Mrs. Marshall says behind me, in the voice of a grand announcement.

"Tiptoe?"

Mr. Marshall sounds so shocked, I detach myself from the dock and the little white house and turn to the room. Mrs. Marshall's propped against the back of a sofa, gazing out another one of the windows, and her long legs cross at the ankles to bare a section of elegant white calf. The gin and tonic dangles from her finger-tips, by some miracle of physics. The expression on her face I can't describe. Cheeks flushed, eyes half-lidded. Like she's dreaming about something that excites her.

"Yes, Tiptoe," she says. "I find I haven't the time to work her as I should. A mare like that, she's wasted on me. As I am now, anyway."

"But Tiptoe! You can't be serious."

"Of course I'm serious."

Billy makes some noise of concern, and to this Mrs. Marshall turns her head. "It's all for the best, darling. I'm going to have a little party. Ask a few friends over, the ones who've been begging to buy her since I first started showing her. A little friendly competition never hurts the price, I've found."

"That's hardly the point."

"Oh, don't look like that, darling. It's time. Why, I've hardly ridden her at all since Marie was born. You must have been counting the expense of keeping a horse like that, when nobody's making any proper use of her."

"Damn the expense, Theresa. She isn't any more costly than the rest of the stable, is she? And she makes you happy. My God, you adore that animal."

Behind me, a faint, low drone interrupts the soft pulse of the surf. I cant my head toward the water, away from the gentle argument between the Marshalls, and it seems to me that this noise is really a pair of noises, circling around each other. I squint out to sea, searching for some speck of movement, but the flat, fading light absorbs every detail.

"I've outgrown her, really, or maybe she's outgrown me. In any case, sold she must be, and I won't hear any objections. I've made up my mind. We'll have a nice little picnic on Saturday to show her off—"

"Saturday? But that's only a few days away."

"Oh, it's no trouble. I've called Rubin already. He's got plenty of stock. We want the guests sauced, of course; they'll pay more that way. And it won't be a large crowd. Terribly select, just a few fellows I've handpicked . . ."

A thin white wake appears at last, maybe a half mile out to sea, growing steadily from left to right. I clench my hand around the window frame and lean forward, holding my breath still in my chest, while Mrs. Marshall continues in her drawling, beautiful voice.

". . . Charles Schuyler, of course. He's mad for that mare. Your cousin George. And Ben Stone." She pauses and calls out to me. "You might know Mr. Stone, Geneva dear. He's a partner at Sterling Bates."

I snap back to her. "Benjamin Stone?"

"Yes. And Harry Lyme. Perhaps you've heard of him as well?"

"Sounds familiar, I guess."

"Good. You'll have someone to talk to, then." She lifts herself away from the sofa and sets down her glass—now empty—next to a lamp of blue-and-white porcelain. Makes her way toward me, smiling. "I was thinking it might be a lovely way to introduce you to some of our friends. A small, intimate gathering like that. Since you're going to become one of the family, after all."

Her expression is as smooth as milk as she approaches me, her eyes bright and happy. Her arm loops through mine. She smiles earnestly into my suspicious gaze. Behind her, the clouds part, and a brilliant setting sun casts a halo over the top of her head.

"Sure," I say. "Why not?"

"Won't it be lovely, Billy? Oh, Billy. Just look at your Geneva. Isn't she splendid? That marvelous hair, all lit up by the sunset . . ."

Outside the window, the drone amplifies into a roar. I pull my arm away from Mrs. Marshall's grip and turn back toward the sea, where a motorboat now arcs elegantly in the direction of the dock. I climb over the window frame into the grass and commence to run. When the heels of my shoes sink deep and catch on the turf, I pause to kick them off. Mrs. Marshall calls out behind me, but I pay her no more mind than I might pay to a traffic cop. Dress tangles in my legs. I lift up the skirt and go on running, grass to stone terrace to beach, sand flying up my stockings, breath scraping my throat, while the motorboat slings against the dock and a man leaps nimbly onto the beaten wood.

# 5

I do sometimes wonder if I dreamt up that entire night, the night I spent with Oliver Marshall in the little white house set by his mama's Southampton swimming pool. After all, I was near dead from exhaustion and shock; Anson was wounded and also improbably half-drunk, by the legal prescription of the doctor summoned out by Mrs. Marshall. So maybe we only imagined we lay together; maybe it was all fever and delirium and longing, and we woke up sharing a memory that did not exist. And the hours have passed, the days and weeks have passed and we haven't lain together since, we are cut in twain, and now I cannot recollect all the details I once thought I should recollect forever. I can no longer count the number of our kisses, and the peculiar sound of my name in his throat has faded away.

But I do know this for certain, like I know the beat of my own heart: the exact shape of his shoulders against the white pillows of that bed, a sight that burned right through all the layers of my skin and bones and membranes to lay itself upon the matter of my brain, the way a hot iron brands the hide of a steer.

And I know another thing, as this fellow on the Marshalls' dock straightens away from his motorboat, holding a coiled rope in his right hand. I know those shoulders now silhouetted against the dying sun don't belong to the man in my bed that March night, the man for whose sake I have dashed across lawn and sand, for whose sake I might dash across the ocean itself if ever I could.

## 6

I pull up short, maybe ten yards away from the base of the dock. Can't see the man's face, on account of the sunset behind him to the right, but his hair's dark and his figure's lean, and he's wearing some kind of long, light coat over a white shirt.

"Hello there!" he calls out, over the noise of the breaking waves. "Mrs. Marshall send you?"

"You might say that."

He sets to knotting his rope snug about one of the stout pilings holding up the dock. "Everything's here. Nice case-a Dewar's, came in from Nassau last night. There was a shipful of Perrier-Jouët got stopped by the Coast Guard, but my fella gave me his last case when I said you was my favorite customer."

"Oh, I see. You're her liquor man, aren't you?"

"Why, what did you think I was?" He laughs. "Say, you're a sight for sore eyes. Don't suppose you're free later tonight?"

"Sorry, brother. My dance card's all full."

"Give me a hand with this crate?"

"My pleasure."

I make my way up the dock, though I mostly want to hit something so hard I break my fistbone. Want to raise some almighty yell from the bottom of my rib cage, so the pain of it maybe overcomes the pain elsewhere. Fellow's jumped back on his motorboat to lift a wooden box from the back, and I step forward to steady the boat or something, though I don't believe he really needs the help. He just relishes the pleasure of my company, and I guess I can allow him that. You don't see a lot of women when you're running in liquor from Rum Row across miles of open ocean, week in week out, every inch of it crisscrossed by Coast Guard cutters.

"What do you think you're doing, running rum in broad daylight?"

"Well, now," he says, dropping the crate carefully on the dock, "I didn't say I was running rum, did I? Anyways, if I was, and I'm not saying I am, I might happen to prefer sunset and sunrise, myself."

"Why's that?"

"For one thing"—turning back to the boat, discovering another crate—"them Coast Guard boys, they're not expecting a fellow to act so brazen, and he might just as well be a pleasure craft in these waters. Get yourself in hot water, you try to board somebody's yacht around here. Somebody's nice speedboat." Chucks the crate on the dock, to a rattle of heavy glass. "Another thing, nothing blinds them boys like that glare you get, when the sun's right on the horizon."

"I'll bet."

The boat weaves and bobs. Somebody's wake, probably, breaking now upon the open beach in long, curling strokes. The man sticks a hand on the rope, a foot on the dock, and heaves himself back to solid ground. Pulls a pack of cigarettes from his pocket and offers me one. I shake my head. He shrugs his shoulders and starts to light himself up. "Say. What's your story, lady? You don't sound like one of them."

"Them?"

He nods his head to the scene behind me. "Them. Now, don't get me wrong. You got the looks, all right. Nice skin, nice dress. But your mouth is something else. Where'd you come from?"

"You've got a lot of nerve for a rotten bootlegger."

"Who says I'm a bootlegger? Just delivering soda water for a friend, that's what I'm doing."

"Sure you are. You don't happen to have a name of some kind, do you?"

"It's Rubin, ma'am. You?"

"People call me Ginger." He starts to grin, but I cut him off. "How long have you been in business around here, Rubin?"

"What's it to you?"

"Just curious."

He shrugs. "Couple-a years."

"So I reckon you know about Mrs. Marshall's son."

Rubin squints one eye and looks up at the sky. Now that we're closer, his face makes itself better known, and I guess I've seen worse. The sun's got to his skin, turning it the color and texture of seasoned wood, and his dark eyes have sunk deep in their sockets. As he considers my question, he sucks his cheeks and kind of rolls his jaw this way and that, making his long, narrow face resemble that of a horse with a mouthful of oats. A handsome one, mind you, but still equine. "Which one?" he says at last, when he's done thinking.

"Both, I guess. But the older one especially."

"You mean the Prohi."

"That's the one."

Rubin casts his gaze back down at me and takes a long, slow drag on his cigarette. "Good fellow, for a Bureau man. Plays honest. He's out with the Watchful, right?"

"So I hear."

"He mean something to you?"

"Maybe."

"All right." He nods. "All right."

"All right, what?"

"I don't know. Forget I said anything. A nice dame like you, you oughta find yourself a fellow in a better line of work, you know what I mean? Insurance or something."

"I don't happen to be in love with an insurance man. You know what I mean?"

"All right," he says again. Finishes the cigarette, tosses it into the drink. "Does his mama know about you and him?"

"Maybe she does. Why?"

"On account of she's heading our way this minute." He lifts up his arm and waves. "Mrs. Marshall! Nice evening, ain't it?"

I whip around a little too fast, so that the surrounding water renders me dizzy. Put out an arm and find a piling. Lift my other hand against the sun to my left. Mrs. Marshall comes into focus, floating toward us in her green dress, her own hand raised to her brow like a salute.

"Mr. Rubin! What in the devil's name do you think you're doing? Every man in Southampton with a pair of binoculars is watching you right now."

"Yeah, what of it? They're all my customers, ma'am, same as you."

"Well, you can't leave those crates here. You'll have to take them up to the kitchen. I've already sent my chauffeur home for the day."

"Not all the way up there, I'm not. I'll take them up the beach and that's it."

"Very well. Here's your money. Did you find the Perrier-Jouët?"

"Last case in stock." Rubin sticks the bills in his pocket and heaves the crate to his shoulder, making the bottles rattle. "You're lucky I like you so much, Mrs. Marshall."

"The feeling is mutual, Mr. Rubin. Now move those crates before we're arrested." She watches Rubin move down the dock, bearing her champagne on his shoulder, and you wouldn't think she was a bit worried by the possibility of discovery and incarceration. The expression on her face tends to boredom, if anything. She turns to me as if she's forgotten I was there. "Ginger, dear. My goodness. You gave us such a start. What on earth possessed you to take off running like that?"

"I thought it was Anson."

"You mean Rubin?" She laughs. "I ought to have warned you he was coming. It's a nice little arrangement. He takes care of all our needs around here. Calls on everybody."

"It's funny, though."

"What's funny?"

"Isn't he the very kind of fellow Anson's trying to catch?"

Mrs. Marshall turns up her chin and laughs gently to the sky. Takes me by the arm and leads me back down the dock toward the house, which is now alight, each window golden against the gathering dusk, except for the rooms of the children upstairs. Patsy and Marie are already tucked in their beds, sleeping away the day's sunshine. We pass by Rubin on his way back down for the other crate, and he nods affably, even touching the brim of his cap. Possibly his eyes meet mine; I can't quite say for certain. By the time we reach the main house, Billy and his father are standing by their chairs in the dining room, and the maid's laying the first course upon the table. Cream of asparagus soup, carefully pureed so that Billy can drink it through a straw.

7

After dinner, while Mrs. Marshall takes Billy upstairs to bed, I slip into Patsy's room on the third floor and listen to the sound of her breathing.

She's lying on her back, sprawled out like a starfish, with the blankets tangled up around her ankles. I straighten everything out and tuck her back in. Open up the window another couple of inches to admit the cooling breeze from the ocean. A white half-moon illuminates the air in strange, ghostly streaks, drawing my attention first to the sticks of brown furniture, then to the drawings on the wall, which are mostly scenes of war and football, except for a single calm landscape. Why, this room must have belonged to one of the boys, I think, and then, Of course it did, you idiot. When they were all alive, all young and perfect and untouched by peril, full of that irrepressible boyish spirit, fighting every waking second, charging down hallways and across rooms and into surf like bolts of human electricity. Like my own brothers, only better dressed.

I cross the room and examine the photographs atop the battered four-drawer chest against the nearby wall. There are two of them, both laid into intricate silver frames and surrounded by miniature soldiers of painted tin. One is of all three boys in bathing suits, linking arms on the deck of a large, thick-masted sailing boat. They're lined up in order, oldest on the left and Billy small and wiry on the right, maybe eight or nine years old. In the middle stands Anson, not so tall as Tommy but already thick about the shoulders and neck, his hair a shade darker than that of his towheaded brothers. Unlike the other two, who grin broadly for the camera, Anson wears a serious, almost quizzical expression, like he's thinking about something else, like his brain occupies a different world than the present ship upon which he stands. His legs are planted square beneath him, toes curled like hooks into the wooden boards. One hand resting on the mast just behind him. Mouth just parted. I brush my thumb against that mouth, those familiar wide lips, and I wonder where I was at the exact moment this photograph was taken. Whether our meeting was even then written down in some astronomical book, or whether all this, all the million individual acts that led to my standing here in this bedroom, holding this silver-framed photograph in my hands, came about as a matter of chance.

I set down the picture and pick up the next, which depicts a man in a football uniform, about to throw a pigskin from his right hand in a scene that's clearly staged for the purposes of photography. The camera captures his face at an angle, and he's wearing one of those leather helmets, and the strange thing is I can't quite tell which brother this is. I guess all men look alike in uniform. He's got a firm jaw and an expression of what they call steely determination, and by the prehistoric line of that nose he's likely not Billy. But I can't say absolutely that it's Anson, either. This perfect, manufactured image doesn't possess enough humanity to tell, one way or another. I will say this: if it's Tommy, the two of them resembled each other, and I wonder what effect that likeness has on Mrs. Marshall. Whether she sees her dead son in Anson's face, or whether he inhabits his own corner of her memory, like a shrine that cannot be duplicated.

Outside the window, a movement catches my eye. I peer through the glass and see an elegant, black-coated figure standing at the edge of the stone terrace: lit by the moon, shrouded in blue smoke.

I bend over Patsy and kiss her good night.

# 8

When I reach the terrace a few minutes later, Mr. Marshall hasn't moved an inch except to smoke his cigar. He greets me civilly and asks if I mind. I say of course not, and it's the truth. Seems there is something comforting about the smell of a cigar in the evening, when it's washed by a salt breeze and blown into ribbons.

"Billy's looking better, don't you think?" he says.

I don't reply, because I've just been thinking the opposite. That Billy's looking tired and fretful, and hardly ate anything at dinner. Not that he's capable of eating much at all, except for his pureed soup taken in through a straw, but even that remained mostly in its bowl. Just wine. Caught him refilling his own glass twice, with a hand that shook the decanter.

"Still pale, of course," Mr. Marshall continues, "but healing nicely. At least the bruises are fading, thank God."

"Thank God."

"Would you like to sit down, Miss Kelly? Take a walk, perhaps?"

"I'd love to walk, thank you. A dinner like that, you should certainly walk afterward."

He laughs and offers his elbow. I like his voice, which is sonorous and old-fashioned, each word considered. "That's true," he says, "but we rarely do. You shall change us all for the better, Miss Kelly."

"Don't say that. I like you Marshalls well enough the way you are."

"Do you?" We step together off the terrace and into the grass. "I suppose you'll learn better, soon enough. We're a terrible old set of sinners."

"Everyone's a sinner these days. Haven't you heard? Anyway, we're only human, most of us. Weak and vain and liable to self-interest, even when we mean well. Even Anson isn't . . ." I check myself.

"Anson? Do you mean Ollie?"

"Sorry. I do forget to call him that."

"But how do you know Ollie?"

"Didn't Mrs. Marshall tell you?"

His brow furrows in the moonlight. "I don't think she said anything about Ollie. She said you were engaged to Billy. That's why you're here, isn't it?"

The grass is thick and newly clipped, and in the long pauses between the rushes of surf, our feet make faint crunching sounds like the tick of a pulse. Mr. Marshall turns us away from the sand. I suppose he doesn't want to mar the liquid shine of his shoes. His head is bare, and the moonlight turns his tarnished head to silver. In his youth, he must have been wonderfully blond, like Tommy and Billy and their brilliant golden helmets.

"Yes," I say softly. "That's why I'm here."

Mr. Marshall pats my arm with his opposite hand, the one holding the cigar. "We're glad to have you, Miss Kelly."

"Are you really? I may be vain, but not so much as to imagine I'm the daughter-in-law you dreamt of. You don't know my folks, or where I'm from."

"Maryland, isn't that right?"

"Yes."

"Your stepfather was some kind of bootlegger, and your father . . . ?"

I shrug. "Who knows? Except the bastard himself, of course."

"Are you trying to shock me, Miss Kelly?"

"Maybe."

"Well, I won't be shocked. In fact, I believe I'm going to return the favor, and tell you frankly that since I own responsibility for a bastard or two of my own, I'm in no position, morally speaking, to complain about the irregularity of your own paternity. We are all sinners, as you said. Weak and vain and blind, especially to our own faults. One of the few compensations of growing older is an enlarged capacity to forgive those weaknesses in others."

"Not everyone does, in my experience. Only the wise ones."

"Ah, my dear girl. Enough of me. Tell me something about yourself. A much more fruitful line of inquiry, I believe."

"There isn't much to tell."

"Nonsense. Your history intrigues me immensely. Have you any idea at all of your father's true identity?"

"Not really."

"Any clue your mother, perhaps, might have given you?"

My left hand is wrapped around Mr. Marshall's arm. With my right hand, I finger the edge of my cardigan pocket. "Why do you ask?"

"Oh, an old man's curiosity, for one thing. And for another, it seems to me—it has so seemed, ever since I first comprehended your plight—that I might be able to help you. If, of course, you're inclined for the assistance of an ancient and not entirely reformed reprobate, many years past his prime."

"Try me."

He lifts his cigar to his lips and smokes thoughtfully.

"I believe I knew your mother," he says.

# 9

Mama hardly ever spoke of her time in New York. I don't even properly know how I came to learn of my origins; I bear no recollection of her telling me. Maybe I was too young. Maybe I always knew. I was but two years old when she returned to River Junction and married Duke Kelly, and while I can't remember living anywhere else, it's possible this knowledge lies within me, in the same way I know I can't abide mushrooms.

She was a showgirl in a revue. I don't know what kind of revue, but I don't believe it matters. They weren't any of them quite respectable, if you know what I mean. Like most girls, she ran off to the city in hopes of fame and stardom, of Lillie Langtry or something, and ended up on display for the delectation of gentlemen, singing and jiggling in a sequined dress in the days before decent women wore sequins. At some point, her jiggling attracted the fascination of my father, and this fascination grew and transmogrified into me, Geneva Rose, born the third of October 1901, somewhere in the state of New York, if not the city itself.

As for what occurred between my birthday and May of 1904, when Mama and Duke joined together in holy matrimony, I haven't the slightest idea. Nobody ever told me anything, least of all my mama.

I have only those letters she bequeathed me, and a box of curious buttons she kept on her bureau, one of which bears the crest of Harvard University.

And that's about all I know.

# 10

Except now I know something else. I know that Mr. Sylvester Marshall of Fifth Avenue and Southampton, New York—father of my beloved—might have had to do with my mama as well. These showgirls, they do get around, it seems.

I expect he feels the tremor of my pulse. He pats my hand again and stops us both, turning me toward him, though I will not meet his eyes. Stare at his satin lapels instead. The narrow pleats of his shirt.

"I don't mean I knew her," he assures me. "Not in that sense."

"Lord Almighty, I hope not."

He laughs fondly. "But we all knew of her. She had dozens of admirers, your mother, and many of my friends counted themselves among them. For a time, she was the headline act at the old Monarch Theatre, on Thirty-Eighth Street. But of course, you know that already."

"In fact, I didn't. Mama never spoke about it."

"Didn't she? Not at all?"

"As if it never happened."

"Well, perhaps she wanted to forget all that, in her new life. But I believe I can still picture her. Rose of Monarch. Beautiful girl. The toast of old Broadway, for all too short a time."

A sudden weight of disappointment falls into my stomach. "Maybe you have the wrong girl. I don't believe she was ever so famous as that. She was just a showgirl in some revue. Anyway, her name was Elspeth, not Rose."

"My dear, none of these girls used their real names. That was her stage name. Useful things, stage names. Allows one to lead such a life, without the fear of shaming one's family."

"Then how are you so certain she was my mother?"

For some time, Mr. Marshall's been gazing out to some distant point upon the ocean, cigar drooping from his hand, but he now turns back to me with keen eyes. "I knew at once. You don't have the precise look of her, but there's no mistaking you. I'm surprised nobody recognized you before. Perhaps I'm only showing my years."

"Not so many years."

"It seems like an age ago. Before the war, you see. Everything before the war seems like an age ago. Another lifetime." He lifts his cigar at last, but only to rub his temple with his thumb. "I always did wonder what became of her."

"Well, now you know."

"It was such a sudden thing. One day there, the next day gone. It must have been about the time you were conceived. I don't recall exactly, but it was the sensation of the day. She walked away at the height of her fame.

Simply left the theater one night and never came back. I remember some of the press actually speculated that she was kidnapped. There was some kind of brief hullaba-loo with the police. But the theater manager, I believe, came forward and said she had delivered a note. She was leaving to start a new life, that sort of thing."

"But with whom? Somebody must have known who her lover was."

"That was the devil of it. She had admirers, but so far as I knew—so far as anybody knew—she hadn't any lovers. Except your father, it seems. Well, whoever the fellow was, the two of them kept it secret, God knows how." He sucks briefly on the cigar and smiles at me. "Lucky fool."

"My mother was less lucky." I reach into the pocket of my cardigan and hand him the letter I received from Christopher last night. "I don't suppose you recognize the handwriting?"

"What's this?"

"I suspect it's his. My father's. Matches the writing on my mother's letters, anyway."

Mr. Marshall, bent over the folded note, raises his head to peer at me. "You have letters?"

"My mother left them to me after she died."

"I see." He returns his attention to the paper before him. Holds it aloft to the faint illumination of the windows behind us. "I'm afraid I'm going to need more light, to say nothing of my reading glasses. Another of the ravages of age. Do you mind if I take it inside with me?"

"Keep it."

"Don't you want it back?"

"Not especially."

"And yet you want me to discover who he is."

"Not because I'm sentimental," I say. "Only because the devil seems to know who I am, and I don't particularly enjoy the mismatch."

Mr. Marshall's face falls into a thoughtful frown. "You realize, my dear, it's entirely possible the fellow means well. Men make terrible mistakes in their youth. Perhaps he wishes to atone. Perhaps there's some other side to this story."

"If you had seen my mama in her deathbed, Mr. Marshall, you wouldn't say that. All shook with fever, her skin all sunk around her bones. You wouldn't let an animal suffer that way. You would shoot it from mercy."

"Ah, the poor girl." He shakes his head. "Poor, sweet girl."

"Yes. And now there is none left of that poor girl but me and Patsy, for I don't count my wicked brothers left back in River Junction. None left but us, and I don't mean to allow that fellow that sired me to claim anything that belonged to my mama. Seems to me, he's got enough from her already."

Mr. Marshall breaks away to stare at the house. He says hoarsely, "Have you considered the possibility that he loved her?"

Inside the house, a light winks out on the second floor.

"No," I say. "I'm afraid I have not."

# 11

Funny thing. As the next day passes, and the next, I keep expecting Mr. Marshall to take me aside—after breakfast, say, or during some interminable game of backgammon in the library while the rain pours down outside—and tell me something about my father's letter. But he doesn't, and I never do seek to ask him. Our entire exchange on the beach that first evening might never have occurred.

So I remain mostly upstairs with Patsy and Marie, playing at school, or else downstairs with Billy and backgammon, as I am now, listening to the dull crackle of rain on window glass and trying to think of something clever to say. Lift Billy out of this rain-cooped backgammon doldrums, this imprisonment that smells of damp, warm wood and cigarettes, of which I am smoking far too many. But my God, can you blame me? What else is there to do amid this jittery silence, this gloomy, humid atmosphere that makes you feel as if the roof's about to tumble down? You close your eyes and the image of a dark-sided ship floats before you. You open your eyes again and look out the window at the frightful, heaving ocean and you light one cigarette to calm your nerves. You finish that one in no time at all, and your nerves still jump at the sound of creaking floorboards or a closing door, so you light yourself another. Pretty soon the ashtray's full, and you're pouring yourself a drink to get through the next ten minutes, and you look at the clock and it's only been three minutes, and . . . well, you get the idea. I tap my finger on the edge of the table and return my attention to the backgammon set before me. "Billy-boy," I say, ever so gently, "it's your turn."

In fact, it's been Billy's turn for the last twenty minutes or so, and when he lifts his head, his eyes are glassy and exhausted and his skin's the color of paste. Except for his jaw, which is now pink with irritation at the wire cage holding his bones in place, at the chafing of his growing beard that can't be properly shaved, howsoever carefully his nurse performs the task. I reach across the table and squeeze his hand.

"How stupid of me," I say. "I forgot all about your nap before dinner."

He makes this noise of protest, but it's a feeble one. I ring for the nurse and she sees about his pills while I urge him upstairs. There's a chaise longue in his bedroom—he won't submit to the indignity of napping in an actual bed, like an invalid—and I order him to lie in it. Read him the sports page of the New York Post while he falls asleep. On the third floor, the girls will be getting what their English nanny calls tea—I'd say it was supper—before a thorough scrubbing in the claw-foot bathtub and a strict tucking-in at seven o'clock. When Billy's eyes are indubitably shut, I lay aside the newspaper and climb the stairs to the third floor.

## 12

After three days of rain, the girls are as fidgety and anxious as I am, and Nanny's face is red with the effort of maintaining her patience and her sanity.

I hold up my forefinger. "I have an idea!"

The nanny regards me with unamused eyeballs. Marie picks up a sandwich, takes a bite, and places it back on the tray. Patsy jumps from her chair and claps her hands like a pair of cymbals. "What? What?"

"Let's count the ships out to sea."

Patsy runs for the binoculars. Marie runs for the window. Nanny sighs wearily and starts to clear up the tea things. You will perceive we've played this little game before, up here on the third floor of the Marshall house overlooking the ocean.

The rain strikes the window in relentless bursts. Patsy looks first and complains that she can't see anything, there's too much rain. Marie demands her turn and gives up in disgust a few seconds later. I take the binoculars from her fingers and raise them to my eyes. Adjust the focus. The girls are right, of course. You can't see a thing through all that rain. Even the dock is only just visible. The gray sea merges into the gray sky, and though the wind remains calm, still I think of those ships on the horizon, hidden from view by this curtain of water, decks awash and sailors drenched, the smell of brine and misery.

"Come along, girls," the nanny says. "Let's start your baths, nice and hot."

The girls protest. I remain by the window, fruitlessly adjusting the focus of the binoculars. The sound of the rain is like gravel thrown against the glass in rapid handfuls. My damp palms cause the glasses to slip, or maybe it's the way my hands are shaking. The gray field wobbles before me and then clarifies, without warning, on the shape of a trim, dark-sided ship, crisp in every detail, its triangular white sails curved with air against a charcoal background.

I close my eyes and brace my elbow against the window frame, while the world sways and pitches around me, and when the dizziness passes I look again through the binoculars but the vision is gone.

"Is everything all right, miss?" the nanny asks.

"Fine."

I turn from the window just as a figure appears in the doorway in a gust of ozone, his brown hair dripping with rain.

"Hello, Ginger," he says.

# 13

Both girls squeal and run into Anson's arms, which is a good thing, for I'm too stunned with relief to either speak or move. I stare stupidly as he lifts them both, one under each arm, and spins them around until they shriek and Nanny commands him to stop. He sets them back down on the floor and kisses each head, blond and black, and when he straightens his gaze goes straight to mine.

"Everything all right?" he asks.

"You might have telephoned first."

"I did. Spoke to Mother. Didn't she tell you?"

"No."

"How's Billy?"

"Taking a nap before dinner."

The girls are tugging at his hands, begging for more spinning. Nanny detaches them and says it's time for bath, time for bath. "Go with Nanny, now," he says. "Go with Nanny and I'll read your stories when you're all clean."

I don't believe either of us moves, not until the clamor of footsteps disappears down the hallway. I stare at him and he stares at me, faces growing graver and graver, and then comes the sound of the bathroom door shutting, and the faint whoosh of the faucet, and the two of us spring forward at the exact same second. Near enough bust my nose, so hard as I slam into his chest. I taste his wet shirt, the smell of rain and perspiration. His arms bind me so tight, I scarce can breathe; I expect I do the same to him. His hands tug at my hair. "I'm sorry," he says. "I'm sorry."

"Sorry for what?"

"Acted like a bum the other night."

"I guess you had a right."

"No, I didn't. I was just mad. Mad to find you in New York with Billy."

"I would have told you if I could."

"I know. I was a bum, all right? The past three days . . ."

"The past three days, what?"

"Nothing. I'm here, that's all. Told the captain I had some business onshore I couldn't put off any longer. I think he was happy to see me go. You're laughing?"

"Yes." Shoulders shaking, eyes prickling. "I thought you were dead."

"Dead? Why in God's name did you think that?"

"The rain," I gasp out, in between his buttons, and he holds me snug while I laugh in terrible spasms, laugh like Christmas morning, and I know he comprehends me when I feel him chuckling, too.

# 14

Turns out, my mama was right about rain. When it's worst, it's nearly over, she used to tell me, and though I always had the feeling she wasn't necessarily speaking of the rain, there's no denying the crackling eases off as we dress for dinner, progressing from torrent to drizzle to mist in the space of an hour. By the time we finish dessert, nothing remains except the puddles on the terrace, and the slow drip from the boughs of the trees. Anson takes his brother upstairs, and Mrs. Marshall suggests we go for a walk, since the weather's so much improved.

I have dressed with especial care this evening, not that I'm spoiled for choice, and I inspect the black sky anxiously as we step through the French doors to the terrace.

"Don't worry, it's over." Mrs. Marshall lifts her face to the clouds, so we are like a pair of horses sniffing the wind. "Can't you feel that lovely dry breeze?"

"Not quite."

"Ah, when you've lived here long enough, you'll feel it when the weather changes. When I woke up this morning, I knew the rain would lift."

"You're sure it wasn't just rheumatism? My mama's brother could always tell the weather by his joints."

"It's not my joints, I assure you," she says crisply. "About this party tomorrow."

"Oh, now it's a party?"

"It's always a party when people come together. I've heard from Mr. Stone and Mr. Parkinson, who will both attend."

For some reason, this information causes a little shiver at the back of my neck, the way you feel when you've climbed to the top of a mountain waterfall and there is no other way but down. "All right," I say, and then, in a mutter: "Thank you."

"Well, I've done my bit. The rest is up to you. There will be plenty of champagne to loosen them up, and other men there so they're not so suspicious. If there's anything to learn, you ought to be able to learn it."

"And since Anson's already here . . ."

"Yes, it's all working out perfectly, isn't it? As I said it would."

"Though I don't see how he's going to stand by quietly while you're serving up all that contraband liquor."

She laughs and loops her arm through mine. "Ah, but I won't be selling it, will I? Nor transporting. He'll have absolutely no proof at all that anything illegal's taken place."

"And if he did?"

"Then I guess he'd be forced to arrest his own mother." She laughs again, but her heart's not in it.

Glances up at the windows behind us, and I follow her gaze to see that Billy's light is already out.

"Something wrong?" I ask.

"How does Billy look to you?"

I pick through my words. "I guess he seemed a little overtired at dinner."

"More than usual?"

"It's the weather, I'll bet. Three days of solid rain will get to anybody."

She nods. "Just so. Just so. Tomorrow, when the sun's out . . ."

A bird cries out sharp from the darkness. Another one answers. Comes a zephyr out of the west, shaking loose a shower of drops from some nearby tree or another.

"Wind's picking up," I observe.

"He'll perk up tomorrow, I'm sure."

"Yes."

"You'll wear that green dress of yours, won't you? It's so becoming."

"Sure I will, if you want."

"Sets off your hair—"

A deep voice interrupts her. "Conspiring on the terrace, hmm? I thought I might find the two of you out here."

We snap about right quick, Mrs. Marshall clockwise and me counterclockwise, so that we crash shoulders against each other. If you can be said to crash silk upon silk. Mrs. Marshall puts her hand to her chest, almost as if she's got a heartbeat to quell.

"My God! Sneaking up on us like that. You're as silent as a cat."

Anson bends forward to kiss his mother's cheek. "You weren't paying attention, that's all."

"I always pay attention. Are you staying for the party tomorrow?"

He glances at me. "I'm afraid I can't."

"That Bureau of yours. Can't you get a little more time away? It's not as if you're doing anything vital, bobbing about on that Coast Guard ship."

We are beyond the immediate reach of the light from the house, and the moon's still stuck behind the thinning clouds. Still I notice the movement of the tendons in Anson's throat, and the way the muscles of his jaw sort of twitch around his ears. He's wearing a dinner jacket, you see, and his tanned neck is so dark against the white of his shirt collar, I can't seem to pull my eyes away from the contrast. I tuck my hands behind my back to stop myself from touching him. "Seems to me the Coast Guard thinks he's vital enough," I say, "since they want him back so quick."

There passes a strange little pause, in which Mrs. Marshall lifts her chin and gazes at some point above the bridge of Anson's sturdy nose, and he stares back without the hint of a smile, and while the two of them don't exactly speak, the words do volley back and forth between them like tennis balls, silent and violent. Reminds me of some book I once read, where the rich people spoke in French so the servants wouldn't understand. I'm just opening my mouth to interrupt them when Mrs. Marshall beats me to it. Parts her lips and covers them with her hand. Stretches her face into a tremendous yawn.

"My goodness. What a day. I really must go in."

Anson offers her an arm.

"No, no. You stay outside and enjoy the fresh air. You must never waste an evening like this, when you're young. It all passes so quickly."

"What passes?"

She's already walking away. White shoulders swallowed up by the gold-lit house. "The enchantment!" she calls back, lifting her hand, waving her fingers. "Good night, darlings!"

We stand there watching her, or what remains of her, long past the moment she moves beyond reach. Maybe Anson's all out of conversation, after that spirited exchange. I have no such excuse, but still I can't think of anything to say that isn't so commonplace as to be more awkward than saying nothing at all.

When Mrs. Marshall's silhouette flashes against the French doors, Anson turns to me. Offers the same arm he offered his mother. "Shall we walk a little?"

"Where to?"

"Wherever you like."

I slide my arm into the crook of his. "I think I'd like to see this horse of your mother's, the one that's causing such a fuss tomorrow."

# 15

Now, don't tell Anson, but I've already been to see Tiptoe. Made over to the stables on the second day of the monsoon, one part curiosity and nine parts cabin fever. The girls came with me, one from each hand, disregarding the rain in the way of young folk. Marie led me straight to the mare's stall, and I do believe that space measures larger than the entire first floor of Duke Kelly's old house in River Junction, the one he tore down to build his mansion made of moonshine. That was the first thing I noticed. The second thing I noticed was the mare's sweet disposition, for little Marie scrupled not to jump right inside this great, luxurious box stall and play jump rope with Tiptoe's tail.

But I don't imagine her big brother would see the humor in this story, do you?

So I keep my gob shut as we cross the lawn and the drive, finding our way by triangulation from the position of the house, for there isn't much light to speak of. Nor does Anson speak up. Just the crisp beat of our shoes on the gravel. The night birds calling out to one another. The creak of the stable door as Anson opens it, and the click as he shuts it back again. When he flips on the electric light, four astonished heads turn toward us, blinking eight dark eyes. Anson makes for one of them. She whuffles a greeting and sticks her beautiful head into his ribs, and the crooning sound in his throat makes my chest hurt.

"Ever ride her?" I ask.

"Yes."

He smooths her forelock and strokes her long nose. She's looking for treats, though he surely hasn't got any, and yet he sticks his hand in his jacket pocket and produces something, I don't know what, which she sweeps into her mouth with her large, soft lips. The gestures have the flavor of a ritual, and as I lean back against the stall door and breathe in the atmosphere of hay and horse sweat, dust and leather, I begin to wonder if I'm intruding. Ask if the two of them would rather be alone.

Anson laughs. "Jealous, are you?"

"Might be."

He moves to the side and strokes her neck. "I'll miss her, though. Can't believe Mama's selling her. Loves this horse like her own children. You should have seen them in the ring. It was like watching a centaur. Tack room's full of trophies and ribbons."

"Good Lord. Doesn't that take an awful lot of practice? Where did she find the time?"

"You find the time, don't you, when something matters enough. She loved the riding, she loved the competition. She loved the mare. It was something she could throw herself into, something that never let her down."

"What about people? She had a husband, didn't she? You boys."

"People always let you down, Ginger, one way or another. We have all kinds of ways to betray each other. Boys grow up and go to school. Find other people to love. Sometimes husbands do, too."

I consider Mr. Marshall's conversation on the terrace. I wonder if Anson knows anything about this, anything of the particulars of his parents' marriage. Naturally, you can't tell from looking at him. His eyes are soft, staring at Tiptoe's ears or something. "So maybe you're right," I say. "Maybe you can't trust anybody except dogs and horses. Still doesn't explain why your mama's selling this particular horse."

Anson leans his elbow on the stall door, so that Tiptoe's dark, inquisitive head bobs between us. "She took a hard fall, right after Marie was born. Might have scared her a bit. Realized she couldn't take falls the way she used to."

"Ah. So a horse can let you down."

"Wasn't Tiptoe's fault. Was it, old girl? You didn't mean to hurt her."

Tiptoe makes this furious nod and withdraws into her stall, leaving the two of us staring at each other, nothing to obstruct our proximity.

"Nobody ever means to hurt anybody," I say. "It just happens. Things happen. Sometimes you're careless, sometimes you have no choice."

The lightbulb wavers and regains strength, like something has interrupted the flow of electricity. I study the way the incandescence appears on Anson's face, the way it casts shadows beneath his cheekbones and his brow ridges, the way it turns his skin the color of honey. The way it touches the specks of his beard.

"I don't like this, Ginger. I don't like sneaking around with you. I don't like lying to Billy."

"Wasn't my idea, believe me."

"But you're going along with it."

"Your mama's awful persuasive."

"You're stronger than she is, believe me."

I smack my hand against the post, causing Tiptoe to startle. "Damn it, Anson. You were the one racked with guilt over Billy. You were the one who wouldn't admit what lay between us, remember?"

"That was before."

"Before what? Before he got hurt?"

He looks at me with great heat and says softly, "Like I said, back in Florida. I may have been a little drunk that night, Ginger, but not so much I didn't know exactly what I was doing."

"Then why haven't we done it again? Why aren't you kissing me right now? Lord Almighty, Anson, I'm only flesh and blood. I'm standing here waiting, don't you know that? Don't you know what it means when a girl asks you to walk her to a stable and see about a horse?"

Along the side of his neck, his pulse is twitching hard. He goes on staring at me, warmth rising right up his cheeks and into his hair, until Tiptoe, moved to curiosity by these interesting vibrations, sticks her head back out and into his chest. Near enough knocks him over, so little notice does he take of her. He recovers and turns away. Walks down the aisle of the stable to a large, open area that must once have held a carriage of some kind. Ties his hands behind his back and looks up at the rafters. "Do you care to know why I left in such a fury the other day, when I saw you at my parents' apartment?"

I come up behind him and lay my hand on the center of his back. Though we are not far apart in height—me being so tall and long-limbed—still he is dreadful big before me, wide shoulders hung with thick muscle, neck like a tree, and he takes over the whole world when we stand so close. "Because you were upset. Upset about my agreeing to move in and make up with Billy. And you were right to—"

"No. You're wrong. That was part of it, but not the real reason. The truth is, I understood. I knew why you did what you did, and I guess I was more sorry than anything. I certainly didn't need to rush off the way I did. In fact I was planning to stay the night. I wanted to see you. I wanted—I was aching to see you, Gin, aching to see you and touch you and speak to you. But Mama took me aside after dinner, while we were waiting for you, and said something that—she asked me—or maybe told is a better word . . ."

"What did she say?"

He speaks real soft, real bitter. "She had this brilliant idea, you see. She figured that since Billy was so set on having a baby with you, well, that we—the two of us, you and me, Ginger—we should give him one."

My hand falls away, like somebody smacked it. "She said what?"

Anson turns to face me, and if his cheeks betrayed a little warmth before, they are livid now. "You heard me."

"Baloney. She couldn't have."

"She did."

Feel like something's set to boil inside me, like there is something bubbling up from my guts so hot and fierce, it might kill me. Or someone else. I can't speak; my throat's all gummed up. I whip around and commence to bolt back down the aisle toward the door, but I am gone only a step or two before Anson takes my arm. "Hold on, Gin—"

"You let me go! I am not sticking around this place like some breeding mare—"

"I told her no! What do you think I said? I said no!"

"I'm going to kill her."

"No, you're not."

"What kind of mother—"

"The kind that would do anything, Ginger, anything to keep her son alive." He speaks right in my ear now, right through all the steam blowing out. "Because she loves him. Because she's already lost one boy, and she can't lose another."

"Me having a baby ain't going to save that boy. Any kind of baby. Most especially his brother's baby."

"I think—I think what Mama expects—he isn't supposed to ever find out."

And I go quite still, except for the headstrong smack of my heart. I stare at the scrubbed wooden floor and consider all this, consider everything Anson is suggesting as if it were fact, and I whisper, "Why, she means me to marry him."

"Yes."

"While you—you and me—"

"There is, after all," he says bitterly, "ample historical precedent."

"Did she say that, too?"

"She said a lot of things, Ginger." When I start to break away again, he holds me fast. "I told her I wouldn't do it. What did you think I said?"

"I expect you told her to go to hell."

"No, I didn't say that. I told her I would go to hell before I'd sneak around with my brother's wife."

"Well, I'm not Billy's wife. I'm never going to be Billy's wife."

"Are you sure about that? You were going to stay down in Florida, too. You were going to lie low until I could return for you. And Mama convinced you otherwise."

I turn about. "So you are mad."

"I'm only saying . . ." His voice fades, like he has lost all words at the sight of my face. We are so close as to inhale each other's breath, to count each other's eyelashes. "I'm saying I can't do this, Ginger. Can't stick around and watch you pretend to be engaged to Billy. Watch you kiss him before the world and then take me to some stable at night, in the dark—"

"Oh, Anson."

"Because sooner or later, when you pretend long enough, it starts to become real—"

"It's not going to become real. You're real, this is real." And I lift my two good hands, all healed, and place them on his two cheeks, shaping my palms around the ridges of his cheekbones, thereby connecting the electromagnetic circuit that runs along between the two of us, Anson and me, strumming along at a high, fine voltage since the moment of our meeting.

He leans his forehead into mine. I believe his eyes are closed.

"You let Mama drag you up here. Drag you into her damned intrigues."

"Nobody drags me into anything, Anson, not if I don't have my own angle. Do you want to know the real reason I said yes? The real reason I came up north with your mother? Wasn't those letters, not really. Wasn't even for Billy's sake. Billy will be just fine without me; that boy will fall in love a hundred more times before he's done."

"Why, then?"

"Because I had to get near you. If the Lord Almighty meant me to live a thousand miles south of you, He wouldn't have sent your mama down to fetch me."

The horses rustle about. Somewhere outside, a gust of wind starts to whistling along the sides of the building, the pitched roof and the windows, the weather vane up above. Some cock and arrow whirling about in a demented circle, trying to figure out which direction to point. We stand there regarding each other, Anson and Ginger, both of us panting a little.

"I would never leave you," he says.

"Unless by dying. By walking out of here and taking some bullet, taking some knife to your neck. Some ambush, some fistfight, some act of retribution. Dead by the hand of some rumrunner or bootlegger, leaving me and Patsy with nothing to show for you."

He doesn't reply. Just reaches up and rubs my cheek with his thumb, over and over, until some kind of understanding spreads over me and I reach up and I seize that hand of his.

"Why, you're about to leave right now, aren't you? You came to say good-bye."

"Ginger—"

"Where? Where are you headed this time? Nassau? Bimini? Cuba?"

"Saint Pierre," he says.

"Saint Pierre?"

"That island off the coast of Newfoundland, the one Logan was talking about. Got a lead on one of the big Canadian rackets, moving liquor through the port."

"And you're going there? With the Coast Guard?"

He reaches inside his pocket and takes out a piece of folded paper. "The crew's taking in stores tonight. We've wrangled a couple of cutters. Rendezvous tomorrow with the other ship, out of New Bedford. If something happens, if you need help of any kind, telephone that number."

"Whose number?"

"A friend. Promise me."

"I make no promises, Anson. Not when you're lighting off in some Coast Guard cutter to get yourself slaughtered for no good reason. You're not going to stop one single drop of liquor from making its way to a thirsty nation."

"It's the law, Ginger. And I'm sworn to uphold it. I'll be back inside a week, and then—"

"Then what?"

"Then I'll quit. If that's what you want. If that's what you need, you and Patsy. I'll ask for a transfer to some desk job, New York or anyplace. Something safe and quiet, come home every night. Seven days, and I'm back. I swear it, Ginger."

And here is something strange. Just after he says those words, as I'm staring back into his eyes, trying to find the truth inside them, trying to see the future inside them, I hear this echo. Not his voice, exactly. More like someone else's, something accustomed to shrieking, pitching itself deep to sound like his.

Seven days. I swear it, Ginger.

All the blood is falling from my veins. Like someone has poured a bucket of ice water inside me. I step forward against him, or I might fall, and he catches my elbows.

"Then don't leave at all," I say. "Don't go. Don't go, Anson, don't go."

He speaks slowly. "Listen to me. Do you know how long I've spent working on this business? Tracking down this fellow and his distillery shipments?

The names of his ships, the dates of departure? Every day of the past three weeks, Ginger, ever since Luella—"

"Oh, Luella!"

"—ever since she squeezed the tip out of one of her contacts and brought it to me. I'm the one who pushed for this, the mission and the extra ship, against a wall of opposition you wouldn't believe. I can't walk out. Captain's standing off Montauk at dawn to pick me up. But I'll be back, Ginger, I promise you. After this, I'm back for good."

"And I am telling you," I say, each nerve stinging, each hair standing in its pore, "I am telling you not to get on that ship."

"Listen, Ginger, just listen—"

"Listen to me, Anson! Why won't you listen to me?"

"Because it's too late. Because I can't just walk on board and hand in my resignation because of some intuition of yours. Some dream you had about a ship. This isn't about me, Ginger, it's about all those men heading out to sea on my command. If I walk out because I might get killed, where does that leave them?"

I step back and smooth my hair. Run my fingers under my eyes. My hands are shaking, my legs are wobbling. "Then go. Go. If it means that much, you had better just get on going. Go on out to sea and get your guts ripped out, like your destiny calls you to do. I guess we'll just carry on back home without you, drinking and fornicating and going about our wicked ways."

The air turns to glue around us. No movement, not horses nor wind nor untimely ghost. Just the quiet darkness. The white points of Anson's shirt. The smell of panic. I think, This isn't what I wanted to say, this isn't what I meant. I should be kissing him, I should be dragging him into some pile of hay and soldering him to my skin, we should be doing what Mrs. Marshall sent us here to do. Bring to life something between us that might act as a magnet against the terrible allure of danger. But the dust seems to have stuck to my throat.

Anson leans forward and kisses my cheek, just under my eye, and then the other cheek in the same exact quarter of skin, and I realize I must be crying. I lift my hands to his neck. He kisses my lips with wonderful gentleness and says, "The only one with the power to rip my guts out, Ginger, is you."

He sets my hands back down against my sides and walks away, and I don't even try to go after him. Don't try to move again for a long while.

# 16

When at last I step forward, seems I've transformed into some kind of machine, treading sightless past the stalls and horses, the halters and ropes and bridles hanging from their hooks. I remember to switch off the electric light before I pass through the door, and as I do so, I catch sight of a figure standing a few feet off, hands shoved inside the pockets of a long coat.

"Anson?" I whisper.

But when I step forward, I realize that the coat is a dressing gown, and the figure, though about the same height, possesses a set of shoulders maybe half the heft of those I have recently embraced. I cast my mind back to the beginning of that conversation in the stables, the machinations of Mrs. Marshall, the complicated fix I'm in. Realize I am shivering, that the air outside has taken on a chill, and I wear nothing but my dinner dress. I cover my arms with my hands, as best I can.

"How long have you been here, Billy?"

He doesn't answer me. I guess his mouth can't manage so many words, wired shut as it is. Just stands there, wavering a little, poor Billy. My original sin, slipping into temptation with this boy during the bleak midwinter. All his trouble fell from my fateful weakness.

"You all right, Billy-boy?" I ask softly. "You ought to be in bed right now."

Instead of replying, he takes off his dressing gown and lays it about my shoulders, and I am so struck with guilt and shame I can't even thank him. Can't say a single thing as we walk back to the house together, through the tall French doors to the back staircase, helping each other up the steps.

# 17

During the night, I dream I'm riding out a storm on the deck of a vast, creaking, old-fashioned ship, while the wind screams and the rain flies horizontal against my face, and the rat-a-tat-a-tat of a Thompson submachine gun tears apart the air. When I fall to the deck, the wooden boards run not with rain but with blood, Anson's blood, his thick and coppery blood, and I wake up choking to a tranquil, sun-soaked morning. The air is like water, the ocean so blue as my mama's own eyes. I lie there on my bed gathering breath, opening and closing my two fists in spasms. Swallowing hard to banish the taste of metal. Blinking against the radiance that strikes my eyeballs. I guess it figures the sun would turn up just in time for Mrs. Marshall's horse party.

Mrs. Marshall. I would have woken her up last night, but I don't know which room is hers, and I didn't want to rouse up anybody else in case I needed to kill her. Anyway, as I saw Billy to his room and walked down the hallway to my own handsome chamber, all that rage and grief and terror boiled down to a jelly that filled my limbs, I thought I should sleep on it. Should consider the whole thing from top to bottom, sideways and backward and what have you. Lay down my rabid emotion and take up the mantle of logic.

And then kill her.

But sure enough, as I lie in my bed, returning to this clean, sunny world from the nightmare in which I dwelt, I recollect Anson's words, spoken in his own voice in the air of the stable last night. The kind that would do anything, Ginger, anything to keep her son alive.

Because she's already lost one boy, and she can't lose another.

And I think, why, we're not so far apart, Mrs. Marshall and me.

And the truth is, I am bound to Billy, too. I can no more abandon that boy in his present condition than I could abandon Patsy. I am tied to earth by sturdy ropes of conscience, and though I may flail I can't ever break them, not if I mean to remain whole. There is another thing. When you are tied to the earth, you run no risk of crashing. Your folk don't die because of you. No brass knuckles, no brains spilt out upon the floor of a Village speakeasy, no brother's head bent at an unsurvivable angle against the cold, dripping wall of a mountain springhouse. All these nightmares and bloody visions that plague you, they fade and disappear into the plain, monochrome hue of domestic life. You're safe.

# 18

Now, it's strange how you start to remember a thing or two as you get older, things your mama taught you when you was but small, and you paid little mind at the time. But maybe you did. Maybe it sunk inside you and became a part of your character, and it's only now that you're grown that you start to recollect how it got there.

Like truth. I don't like dissembling, and I never did. Starts something to sloshing in my guts, something I figure has lived there all my life. But a memory takes shape as I lie in this Southampton bed, listening to the terrified smack of my heart while the new sun burns my hair: Mama great with child, sitting on the old back stoop inside her own patch of light, telling me gravely that nothing on this earth gets you in trouble so much as a lie. How even one that starts out small and means well—not to hurt somebody's feelings, maybe, or not to get somebody in trouble—contains the potential for catastrophe, like a geyser fixing to blow. I see the gray dress she is wearing, the worn apron tied above her gravid belly. Her bare, blistered feet and her flame hair just a-peeking from the kerchief that covers it. The hungry shadows beneath her cheekbones. She says to me that telling the truth is like lancing a boil. Might hurt at first, but nothing like the harm a boil can do when you leave it to grow and fester, until it commences to infect the surrounding flesh, to putrefy and sometimes even to kill you. That's my advice, Geneva Rose, she finishes gravely, and she closes her blue eyes and holds her belly tight with her two hands, as if to stop her baby from getting any bigger.

# 19

I roll on my side and heave myself out of bed. Wash and dress so fast as I can and head downstairs to the breakfast table. Ask the maid whether Mr. Oliver has yet eaten. She gives me this strange look and says Mr. Oliver left two hours ago, Miss Kelly, had his breakfast and drove away in his automobile before the sun had properly risen. I look at the clock above the mantel and perceive that the hour stands just past seven o'clock.

# 20

I discover Mrs. Marshall before the typewriter in her attic office, eating breakfast from a chipped enamel tray. You might think she is nonplussed, but I catch the flush in her cheeks and know better. She offers me coffee, which I decline. Asks if I had a nice evening.

I plant my bottom on the edge of the desk, not far from the typewriter. Gives me a vantage of advantage, if you know what I mean. "Wouldn't you like to know."

"I'm afraid I don't know what you mean."

"Don't you? Because I understand your eagerness to become a grandmother knows no limits."

Mrs. Marshall settles back in her chair, the better to regard me. She's wearing a loose day dress of striped cotton, head all wrapped up in another one of those turbans, or maybe the same one as before. The skin of her face and neck and arms is quite pale, except for that blush, which is already fading. I expect she's twenty or twenty-five years older than my mama was, sitting on that stoop in my memory, and yet she might be Mama's younger sister, from the look of her. Maybe it's the light, which flattens out the lines around her eyes. Maybe it's her state of expensive preservation, which you can't purchase out in River Junction, everhow rich you might be, but most especially if you're poor like Mama was, and bred back to the likes of Duke Kelly every nine months.

"I suppose Ollie spoke to you."

"He did. I might even take joy in describing how you got bit by your own hound dog, but my heart's not in it. Too broke, I guess." She starts to speak, and I hold up my hand to stop her. "So now I figure I got no choice. These waters are too deep for me, Mrs. Marshall. I'm going to come clean to Billy about this whole—"

She jumps from her chair. "You will not!"

"I surely will. Right after the party, I'm going to tell him the truth. I don't mean to hurt him, but he has to know, Mrs. Marshall, I just can't continue to deceive him like this. I wasn't born to hide the state of my heart, like you were."

"You'll kill him."

"That's not true. Just look at him, the way he is now. My coming to stay with you hasn't helped a bit. And do you want to know why? Because he knows, deep down. He knows I'm not his. I can act and act, but I can't be. And Billy's a damn sight smarter than you give him credit."

The rage just gathers and gathers in her face, until she can't seem to bear the sight of me and whips about to stare at the window. "You're just going to leave, then. Run off with Ollie, after all you've done."

"I didn't say that. What I'm going to do is sit down with Billy and tell him there's no baby after all, no chance of my marrying him, but I will stay right by his side until he's healed again. Not because I'm in love with him, but because I do love him, Mrs. Marshall, I love him like the brother he is to me. And where I'm from, we take care of our own, most especially when we have done them wrong, as I have done to Billy."

Mrs. Marshall places her hand on the side of the window frame. The sun casts her in silhouette. There is a beautiful line to her neck and shoulders, like those belonging to a ballerina. "I suppose I ought to admire you. Such principles."

"They're all I've got."

"That's not true." She turns her head to present me with her profile. "You have my sons. You hold both of them in your palm, you damned bitch, and it seems there's not a thing I can do to rescue either one."

I ought to be mad, I guess, but I'm not. I am assailed instead by the softness of pity.

"For what it's worth, you're wrong. The two of them, they love you to death, if you would but slow down and listen." I slide off the desk and make for the door. "As for your Ollie, happens he's heading out to sea this moment, off to intercept some rumrunner up north. And if you can keep that fellow to shore, let alone in the palm of your hand, why, you're a better man than I am, Gunga Din."

# 21

A horse party. I don't know what else to call it. Seems to me a strange reason to have a party, but the rich never do follow the same logic you and I are expected to uphold. I figure we might see eight or ten guests, mostly men, sipping lemonade and running their hands down Tiptoe's precious legs. Instead, there are fifty at least, and they're not sipping lemonade, believe me.

I stand next to Billy at the edge of the riding ring, soaking up sunshine while Tiptoe goes through her paces. In my hand is a tall glass of gin and tonic. In Billy's, a low glass of whiskey and a paper straw. He seems to have gathered strength since last night. His face has taken on color, and he sucks that straw with considerable might. Maybe Mrs. Marshall's right, maybe he just needs fresh air and sunshine to make him healthy again. My arm's tucked inside his. I haven't spoken to him yet. Going to wait until afterward, when everybody's gone home, so we don't make some kind of scene. "Beautiful day," I say, into his good right ear.

He nods and drains away the last of the whiskey. Raises one finger to signal the maid.

"Maybe you should give it a rest with the sauce," I suggest.

I don't know if he hears me, but certainly he pays me no mind. Returns his attention to the ring while the maid makes off to refill his glass. Mrs. Marshall's in the saddle, wearing a black jacket and a smart black bowler hat, the way they do in horse shows, I guess, and since Tiptoe herself bears a dark bay coat, almost black, the two of them have the look of a single creature. A centaur, as Anson said, describing large, perfect circles at a walk, a trot, a canter. Then soaring over a jump or two, just as easy as whistling. There's a burst of appreciation from the assembled guests, which the mare acknowledges with a swish of her long tail, and Mrs. Marshall by a salute of her leather crop. They come to a stop, and a crowd ambles out to meet them. I turn to Billy.

"How do you feel about selling her?" I ask, but Billy doesn't have the chance to answer me. A hand taps his shoulder, belonging to a blonde of perfect, angular proportions and a fine pale dress that exposes a tremendous amount of peach-colored skin.

"Why, Billy Marshall, you handsome devil," says Julie Schuyler. "Don't say I didn't warn you about that wicked redhead of yours."

# 22

Now, I reckon it goes without saying that Julie and I have some history between us. For one thing,

Julie has history with just about everybody in New York City, and for another thing . . . well, you can just tell, can't you, by the way we greet each other with kisses that don't quite touch, and an exchange of blue-eyed gazes that most certainly do. The truth is, our relationship is strictly business, though we once shared the same lover—namely, the photographer who's responsible for those artful portraits of me, the ones you can buy in sets like baseball cards from behind the counter of your nearest newspaper stand. In which I'm not wearing much in the way of clothing, mind you. Gentleman artists do adore to celebrate the female form.

As for Julie, she was the brains behind the camera, and I expect she cleared a fair fortune from our association, so you might think she would greet me with considerably more appreciation. Ha! You don't know Julie.

Still, we're women, so we enact a decent pantomime of friendship. How are you, darling? and Is that how you're doing your hair? So charming and What an absolutely fascinating dress you're wearing! That kind of thing. I take great pleasure in the smudge of crimson lipstick across Julie's right front tooth, and I expect she takes great pleasure in some flaw of mine I'll discover later in the mirror. When we're done we turn to

Billy, whose face is flushed with either bemusement or whiskey—probably both—and Julie asks him all kinds of questions he doesn't understand. The maid returns with more whiskey. I hand her my empty glass of gin and tonic. You can get used to that, maids fetching you gin and more gin, while the sun heats the crown of your hat.

Julie, exhausted by the chore of making herself understood to Billy and then understanding him in return, returns to me. "I was so delighted by the invitation. I'm stuck out here in East Hampton with my brother Charles and his wife, and I can't tell you how bored I've been." She leans forward and whispers over her glass, which happens to contain the same recipe as mine, judging by the telltale scents of juniper and quinine. "She's a dry!"

"Who's a dry?"

"Why, my sister-in-law! Egad, she's coming right this way. Just as if she heard me, the bitch! Quick."

Julie takes my arm and Billy's arm, but Billy's too slow and we hear ourselves hailed in the kind of lockjaw dialect that reminds me of my first and only year of college, which is not a pleasant recollection, believe me.

"Julie! Could you attend me, please? There's someone I'd like you to meet."

The voice belongs to just the kind of person you
might think. She's about forty years old and wears an
unimpeachable dress of navy blue trimmed in white
grosgrain, and her cloche hat bears a small rosette made
of same. Her hair is dark, not bobbed but gathered back
at the nape of her neck and marcelled within an inch of
its life. Her lips are the color of old blood. Her eyes are
small but perfectly shaped above an elegant nose, and
I think she must have been pretty right up until a few
years ago. If you could sensibly describe a woman as
both fashionable and old-fashioned at the same time,
well, this Mrs. Schuyler would be that woman. Do you
know what I mean?

Anyway, she holds out her upturned palm to Julie,
and it's the kind of small, bejeweled hand you can't
ignore, but Julie ignores it all the same. Just laughs
and says, "Oh, but Harriet, I've got someone even
better for you to meet," and poor Harriet finds herself
stuck right between bad manners and a hard place.
What does she do? Why, she screws up her mouth
and marches on over the hard place, because there is
nothing on earth worse than bad manners, don't you
know.

(In case you're wondering, I'm the hard place.)

# 23

Well, I won't bore you with the scene that follows, except to say that it's brief and stiff, and Mrs. Harriet Schuyler does not like the look of me one iota. Eventually Charles dear comes to join her—that's her husband, a tallish, trim fellow, running to gray maybe a few years earlier than he should, but none the less handsome for it—and I have the feeling he likes the look of me far better than his wife does. Most men do. His eyes linger on my eyes, his hand lingers on my hand. I have the familiar feeling he's trying to place me, which often happens, I'm afraid, when a gentleman's introduced to a lady whose naked, nameless form luxuriates on a popular series of indecent photograph cards. We exchange the usual pleasantries. There are inquiries after health, inquiries after Billy's convalescence. I ask if he's going to buy Mrs. Marshall's favorite mare, and he laughs and says he can't afford her.

"Charles dear," says Harriet, "the van der Wahls have arrived."

He makes this smile that begs my patience. "I'm afraid we'll have to continue this conversation later, Miss Kelly."

I make a little curtsy and say I'm at his service, and as I straighten from this gesture my gaze happens to fall upon a tall, stilted figure like a praying mantis, bent in conversation with Mr. Marshall.

Benjamin Stone, as I live and breathe.

# 24

Now, a word about Mr. Stone, for whom I have the highest professional respect. He is some kind of partner at the investment firm of Sterling Bates & Co. on the corner of Wall and Broad—where, until recently, I had the honor of occupying a desk in the typing pool—and whether he directed the entire municipal bond division or merely its underwriting department, I can't quite recollect. When I first delivered him a fat brown envelope with the compliments of Duke Kelly, he handled the exchange in an honorable, forthright fashion, and I make no doubt that Duke got full value for his money, whatever exactly he was paying for. As for me, I suppose you might say that from that moment until the day I left during my lunch break, never to return, my position at Sterling Bates was unassailable, should anyone in the world have discovered the itch to assail a member of the typing pool.

Now, those are the facts of the case. There's plenty more I don't know. For instance, what did Mr. Stone do in exchange for his filthy bribes? A fellow who underwrites municipal bonds for a living, who makes it his business to make nice with mayors, whose clients might include any or all of the metropolitan officials along the Atlantic coast of the United States, why, he might prove invaluable to a fellow who makes it his regular business to breach the constabulary defenses along said coast. (Or so Anson explained to me one night, when we were discussing the matter.) But I never did understand whether Mr. Stone was just a middleman in the whole affair, or whether he occupied a position of real authority. Whether he was taking the shots or calling them.

Whether Anson has nothing to fear from him, or everything.

And there's another thing I don't know. I don't know whether anybody's bothered to inform him that Miss Kelly turned out to be a rat.

# 25

So you'll understand why, when I first recognize the sticklike figure in the light gray suit across the lawn, I experience a deluge of what you might call second thoughts. I turn away and toss back a gulp from my glass, which that nice maid in her uniform had the goodness to refill, while my guts contract and my eyes kind of sting a little. Life, for all its inconveniences and its heartbreaks, is still worth living. Patsy still needs a sister to care for her. Oliver Anson Marshall can damn well take care of himself.

When I glance back mantis-ward, however, I see that Mr. Stone's body has shifted, revealing Mrs. Marshall in her smart black jacket and mutton-leg breeches, looping her arm through his and turning the both of them to face me. She lifts her hand and waves, just so I know what's coming, and she leads him right across the lawn to where those Schuylers are making their excuses, scowling Harriet and laughing Julie and smiling Charles, while Billy looks on in bemusement. The sun gilds Mrs. Marshall's round hat and sets her polished black boots to gleaming. Mr. Stone leans his ear attentively downward, for while she's nearly as tall as I am, you'll recollect he's a praying mantis. Or is it preying mantis? I never could remember. Now it's too late.

"Darling Geneva," she says, just as the Schuylers poise to make their escape, causing a grimace of bloody frustration to cross Harriet's face. "I wonder if you might know my old friend Benjamin Stone, who's a partner at Sterling Bates. Benjo, our darling Miss Kelly used to be a typist at your firm, before she became engaged to my son Billy. Isn't it the funniest thing?"

For some reason—I can't imagine why—during the entirety of this journey across the lawn, Mr. Stone's confined his attention to a narrow range of vision that encompasses the blond hair and sparse dress of Julie Schuyler. Redheads in modest clothing don't apparently cut his mustard. But the words Miss Kelly (or even perhaps typist, who knows) seem to penetrate this magnetic field. His head bolts upward and his shocked eyes find mine, and the color—such as it is—just falls away from his skin, leaving it the same shade as his hair. Gray as paste.

Not that I'm paying all that much mind to the state of Benjamin Stone's face. I've fastened instead on something Mrs. Marshall said, something she just tossed off in that merry, fragrant voice of hers, and it seems Julie Schuyler noticed it too, because we both open our mouths and exclaim the exact same thing at the exact same instant.

"Engaged!"

"Yes! Isn't it wonderful? We couldn't be happier. Look at the two of them. Won't they make the most beautiful pair?"

There is a barrage of congratulation. Julie's delighted. Harriet's disguising her disapproval. Charles shakes Billy's hand and says he's a very lucky man. As for Mr. Stone, he says nothing at all. Just looks at me while I aim a dagger at Mrs. Marshall's satisfied mug and mutter, "I don't believe you could say we're officially engaged . . ."

"When did all this come about?" Julie demands. "Where's the ring?"

"There isn't any ring. There isn't any—"

Mrs. Marshall inserts herself between me and Billy, takes one arm from each of us, and says, "Oh, the story's too long to tell! But after all they endured together, the way Billy sacrificed himself for her sake, why, I suppose they simply realized they couldn't do without each other. Isn't that right, darling?"

She means Billy. I can't see him, standing there on the other side of his mother, so maybe he's nodding or something. But he doesn't say anything. For a brief interlude, all you can hear in that bright May air is anticipation. The pollen drifts between us. Charles

Schuyler's eyes go a little narrow. Even Mr. Stone turns his gaze to Billy's face and lifts his gray eyebrows to his gray hairline. Billy makes this desperate, stammering noise, and I blurt out, "Billy's the kind of fellow every girl dreams of marrying," which is true enough, isn't it? Makes all the nervous faces relax around us. Except for Charles Schuyler, I guess, whose eyes are still narrow, and of course Mr. Stone, who returns a quick sidelong glance to me, as if testing a puddle to see how deep it goes.

And I am gathering courage to address him with some telling question, or else some suggestion that we take a moment to compare our experience at Sterling Bates, when my gaze strays to that gray hair at his temple and I perceive a certain kinship between us.

Mottled among the silver grow a few tiny, precious strands of ginger.

## 26

"Why, Mr. Stone," I say, "it seems we have something more in common than our place of employment."

"Do we?"

I take the ends of my bobbed hair between my thumb and forefinger and waggle the little wisp of mare's tail. Mr. Stone's expression softens.

"Oh yes," Mrs. Marshall says. "I'd forgot you were a terrible redhead in your salad days, Benjo."

"Benjo," I say. "What a dishy nickname. They call me Ginger, or else just Gin."

"For no reason that anybody can fathom," says Julie.

Mrs. Marshall makes a show of looking at her wristwatch. "Why, it's almost two o'clock! Billy's going to need his medicine. Forgive me, darlings. I'll just take him inside to the nurse."

"No," says Billy. "Gin."

"Oh, it's no bother. I was already going inside to change clothes. Benjo, you'll let me know about the mare, won't you? I've already had two handsome offers!"

She's sailing away, Billy firmly in train, but there's something desperate about the way he glances back at me over his shoulder, as if he's calling for help of some kind. I step forward and stop her. Turn him to face me. The flush has left his face, leaving the skin clammy and wan. Brown eyes unsteady. I take his hand, which is shaking, and ask him how he's feeling.

"Cold," he says.

I look at Mrs. Marshall and say softly, "I think he's starting a fever."

"Nonsense. It's just the heat."

"Then why is he shivering?"

Mrs. Marshall looks at Billy's face and reaches up to touch her knuckles to his temple. "He isn't warm."

"Not yet, he's not. He's working up to it, believe me."

"Billy," she says, "how are you feeling?"

Well, he can't speak very well, not through those wires, though we are used to understanding him by now. Still, these noises aren't what you'd call words. Like he doesn't have the strength to convert his thoughts into language. Stammers through his teeth, stops and draws breath and starts again, but he doesn't make more than a syllable before his eyeballs commence to rolling upward in their sockets.

"Charles!" screams Mrs. Marshall. "Help me!"

And that dear Charles, who was just discreetly beginning to walk away with his wife and his sister Julie, turns on a dime and sprints up the little rise toward us, just in time to receive the toppling Billy in his arms.

# 27

By the time Billy's tucked into bed, damp cloth to his forehead, doctor worrying over his pulse, the party's over. Mrs. Marshall won't leave the bedside, so it's up to yours truly to make my way downstairs and offer regrets to what guests remain. As I pass through the drawing room, a figure unbends its limbs from one of the armchairs in the corner and calls my name, softly.

"Mr. Stone," I say. "I thought you might have left by now."

"I wanted a word with you first."

"Well, then. Here I am. What's your business?"

"Sit down."

"I really ought to be seeing off Mrs. Marshall's guests."

"Sit down, please. I won't be a moment."

So I sit and straighten my dress and try to return my attention to the subject of bootleggers and bribery and the trouble Anson's in, though it seems awful remote to the terrible scene before, Charles Schuyler carrying Billy up to his bedroom while Julie ran for the telephone to find the doctor, only to discover he's actually right here among the guests. General rumpus as everybody passed the word for Doctor Harris, until

Julie herself discovered him in the tack room, three-quarters drunk, in flagrante with somebody's wife. (Julie wouldn't say whose.) He retained enough wits to diagnose Billy with an infection of some kind, nothing to do except make him comfortable and pray he rides it out, a fine, strong boy like that. I stood by the bedside of that fine, strong boy and all I saw was my fine, strong mama, fighting off the childbed fever while a blizzard fell in outside the window, no doctor for her, burning and shivering in turns, fits and delirium and what have you, and while she did prevail by the mercy of the Lord Almighty, she was never the same. Ground her down to dust.

So I arrange my skirt over my knees and see that my fingers are trembling, and I ask Mr. Stone again what business he has with me.

"To be perfectly frank, Miss Kelly, I rather thought you had business to discuss with me," he says.

"Oh?" (Feigning what innocence I can.)

He makes a spreading gesture with his long arm. "I thought it was a little strange, Theresa asking me here today. Selling that mare of hers and having a party about it. And then she brought me over to you."

"You think this was a setup?"

He leans back in his chair. "Let's not waste time. What do you want from me, Miss Kelly?"

"Depends on what you have to give me, I guess."

"Money?"

"Oh heavens, no. Haven't got need nor desire for money, Mr. Stone. I'm just curious."

The fingers of Mr. Stone's right hand commence to tapping on the arm of his chair. He glances to the room's entrance and back again. "Curious? Curious about what?"

"Why, I guess we might start with the subject of what my stepfather was paying you for, Mr. Stone. I believe it's fair to presume you were providing him with some kind of service, in exchange for that kind of kale."

"Your stepfather? He's your stepfather?"

"Indeed he is. Or was."

Mr. Stone's shaking his head. "I don't understand. Surely you know already, if you're—you're making deliveries for him. If Grendel's your stepfather. If he trusts you to—"

"Grendel?"

"Your stepfather."

"I don't—was that some kind of nickname?"

"Oh! I beg your pardon. We called him Grendel at school. Beowulf's monster." Mr. Stone offers me the edge of a smile, kind of rueful. "I don't suppose Mary calls him Grendel, does she?"

I press my damp palms upon my knees. My pulse ticks away at my neck, in my wrists, like I have turned some corner to find myself poised on the edge of an unexpected cliff. Mary. Who the devil was Mary?

"No." I draw out the syllable so long as I possibly can. "No, Mary does not call him Grendel."

He brushes back a bit of hair from his forehead, and I realize he's perspiring. Temples glittering in the brilliant afternoon light. He returns his fingers to the arms of the chair and goes tap-tap-tap. Not cut out for this business at all, our Mr. Stone. No more than I am. Maybe even less.

"I hope I haven't done anything wrong," he says in a low voice.

"Of course you haven't, Mr. Stone."

"Has there been a—an indiscretion of some kind?"

"Yes. An indiscretion. There's been an indiscretion. A leak, as we call it."

"Miss Kelly, I assure you—"

"Nobody means to drop valuable information, Mr. Stone. It's just carelessness. Unless somebody's a rat, of course. That's a different story."

"Oh no! I'm not—I would never betray him. You must know that. We went to school together."

"I'm sure you wouldn't, Mr. Stone, but the leak's there, all the same, just the same as a double cross. You know what a double cross is, don't you?"

"Yes. Of course. And I wouldn't dream of it."

"Good." I pause, because my heart's still rattling, my breath's still a little short. Feel as if I might burst from the weight of the chance just dropped in my lap by dear, unsuspecting Benjo, whose face now bears a blush of eagerness, whose body now pitches a little forward in his chair. And I myself am struggling not to pitch forward, struggling not to jump free of chairs altogether and pace about the room and maybe even dance a step or two. A name. All I need now is a name. The name of a fellow who went to school with Benjamin Stone and did something to earn himself the sobriquet Grendel.

The trouble is, Benjo thinks I already know it.

Benjo bursts out, "But are you really his stepdaughter? I must say, I'm astonished. He never mentioned—I thought that Mary was—oh!" His fingers go still.

"Maybe stepdaughter isn't exactly the right word." I tinkle out a laugh. "I'm sure you understand."

"Yes! Yes, of course. I understand fully."

I put my finger to my lips. "Our little secret."

"Naturally. Naturally." Both hands curl around the ends of the armchair. "Am I free to—that is, if I haven't done anything wrong—is there perhaps something else he wants me to do? Is that what you mean by this?"

"We just want to impress on you, Mr. Stone, the need for discretion. Why, you shouldn't even be talking to me, here in the middle of this room. You never know who might be listening."

"Of course, of course. I just—because I already know you, you see, and Grendel trusts you—"

"Naturally." I smile. "Grendel. Going to rip him up about that, the next time we meet. How the devil did he get a moniker like that?"

Well, Mr. Stone blushes, right up to his hair, and he's just starting to stammer out some reply that, I suspect, bears only a passing resemblance to the truth, when Charles Schuyler's voice comes right out of nowhere.

"Grendel? My God, Benjo, are you still speaking to that scoundrel? There's no accounting for taste, I guess."

"What do you know," I say. "Seems everybody's acquainted with old Grendel."

"The three of us went to school together," says Schuyler, tone of finality, face of grimace, like that's all he's ever got to say on the subject of old Grendel. He then commands me not to rise, please, he just wants to know how poor Billy's doing, before he leaves.

In direct disobedience, I stand and tell him exactly what Mrs. Marshall told me to say, if anyone asked. "I'm afraid he's not well. But we have every hope he'll be back on his feet before long." Then I offer him my hand. "Thank you so much for your kind assistance, Mr. Schuyler."

He clasps the hand and meets my gaze with such strength, I bite back a little gasp of wonder.

"Not at all, Miss Kelly. We're practically neighbors, you see; I've known Billy since he was in short pants." He hesitates, wraps his other palm around our handshake, and applies an intimate squeeze. "I hope I may have the pleasure of seeing you again in happier times."

I'll bet, I think. But my smile, I believe, is everything Mrs. Marshall would want.

"I'm sure we shall."

Behind me, Benjamin Stone has already climbed to his feet, for he is that kind of gentleman. He now clears his throat and holds out his own hand. "If that's all your news, Miss Kelly, I believe I'll take my leave along with Rufus."

"Rufus?" I shake Benjo's thin hand and look at Schuyler, who rolls up his eyes to regard the ceiling. "I'm beginning to wonder what the three of you used to get up to, back at school. Surely seems like more fun than the nuns ever allowed us at my school."

Now, if I'm hoping to learn the name of this fine institution that reared up such upstanding gentlemen, it seems I'm about to be disappointed. The two of them exchange that kind of telling male expression that seals a secret—you know the look I mean—and in that instant, whatever it was they got up to at school gets thrown into the kind of cast-iron safe a mere female never could crack. Nothing so loyal as the old school tie, is there?

Good old Benjo says he'll be off, now. Not to worry about young Billy, Miss Kelly, a lad like that will pull through just fine.

"I'm sure he will, Mr. Stone," I say, and the two of them head off across the drawing room and out the French doors to the empty lawn, where the sun is turning a deep, lazy gold and the clouds have begun to scud across the sky. A scene of great beauty, I guess, all held in place by the great, flat ocean, but I pay it no mind. My head's a-spin, my fingers dance at my sides.

And then I snap them.

Mr. Marshall. Of course! Mr. Marshall will know where Benjo and Grendel went to school.

He may even know who the devil Grendel is.

# 28

Last I saw, Mr. Marshall stood at the door of Billy's bedroom, looking grave, before he treaded back downstairs to attend to his guests. Guests must be attended to, after all, even when the host's son has fallen down with some terrible illness, some infection in his blood for which modern medicine has yet no cure. They must be soothed and sent on their way; orders must be given to servants; valuable horses must be sponged down and put in stables. Heavy are the duties that befall rich folk.

But when I strike off in search of the lord and master, he's not to be found. He's like the Holy Grail, or the Golden Fleece: everybody remembers seeing him, somewhere, but he's never there when you arrive. Not the south lawn, not the west lawn, not the stables, not the hot, sunlit driveway that still reeks of gasoline exhaust. I head back indoors and make for Billy's bedroom. Might as well wait there for him; a father's got to check on his son eventually, hasn't he? A long Oriental carpet runs the length of the upstairs hallway, swallowing the sound of my footsteps, and the air has taken on that intent, brittle quality of a house struck by illness. Even the sunlight—hanging in diagonal shafts from the windows—looks as if it might shatter.

I turn the corner where Billy's room lies. About a foot of triangular space exists between door and frame, and I consider knocking. Mrs. Marshall's still there, no doubt; she certainly didn't look as if she ever meant to leave, when I departed an hour or so ago. For an instant, I hover outside, knuckles primed, lips bitten. Breath held back in my throat.

And in that space of hesitation, to knock or not to knock, I hear a quiet, rhythmic noise that starts the fear in my blood. I push open the door and see Billy on the bed, his chest moving uneasily beneath flat white sheets, his head supported by pillows to keep him from thrashing about and disturbing the wire cage on his jaw.

In the armchair beside him sits Mr. Marshall, holding his wife in his lap as she sobs and sobs into his shirt. He returns my stare with reddened eyes. A piece of long, tarnished hair has fallen into his forehead. Mrs. Marshall still wears her black jacket and tan breeches and riding boots. There is a scuff of dirt or something along one calf, but the dark leather gleams like oil everywhere else.

I step backward out of the room and close the door.

# 29

My legs carry me upward to the third floor, I don't know why. The girls were in the care of the nanny today, wearing white lawn dresses and enormous blue bows in their hair and generally being fawned over by grown-ups susceptible to that kind of thing. Can't remember seeing either of them since Mrs. Marshall put the mare through her paces in the riding ring.

As I reach the landing, however, I begin to perceive the faint, lonesome snuffle of a crying child. I rub my cheeks and follow it next door, Marie's room, and sure enough she lies curled up on her bed sobbing, and Patsy lies curled around her in comfort. Patting her back. Neither one hears me enter, and I hear Patsy say something like, "My brother died too, incept he went to heaven where he lives with Lord Jesus," and Marie asks her something snuffly about Lord Jesus, and Patsy replies solemnly that He is seated at the right hand of the Father, ain't He, and Marie says Nanny says you mustn't say ain't.

"Nanny's right," I say, and both girls bolt up and stare at me. Their white dresses are stained with green, and Marie's lost her blue bow. Her eyes are pink like a rabbit's and her cheeks are wet and swollen. She holds out her wee arms to me and what can I do? I go to the bed and haul her under one arm and Patsy under the other.

"Is Billy really going to die?" asks Patsy.

"I don't know, darling. He's real sick. He's a strong fellow, though, and he's going to fight it every inch."

"But he might die. Like Mama died and Johnnie died."

"Why, what makes you say that? What makes you think Johnnie's passed on?"

"Ginny," she says, so witheringly as only a not-yet-six-year-old girl can speak, "I ain't stupid."

"You aren't stupid."

"Anyways, I see him, don't I? Right next to Mama."

Marie, who is the squirming kind of child, wriggles free of my arm and slides feetfirst to the floor. Sobbing seems to have died away. She toddles to the dollhouse in the corner and begins solemnly to undress the sister doll, the one with the delicate face and large brown eyes. I just sit there watching her, holding Patsy against the side of my chest, feeling the silk of Patsy's hair under my chin. Her little heart beating away next to mine.

"When do you see him, sweetheart?"

"See him all the time. Him and Mama. He was sitting by me when we was driving with Mr. Marshall.

He was holding my hand while I was sleeping. And he tucks me in some nights, just like back home. Then Mama kisses me after. But some nights they just stand there a-watching me."

"Just at night, then? They come just at night?"

"Maybe sometimes in the afternoon, when I play." She pauses and moves her head. "Why, there he be now."

"What? Where?"

"By the window. Mama by the drawer chest." She slips her thumb in her mouth, a habit I have tried to break her of, but I don't admonish her now. Oh no. I turn my head to the side of the room that contains the drawer chest and the window and nothing else, just blank wall painted in lilac, a pretty watercolor in a frame hanging from the picture rail.

Back of my right hand starts to tingle.

"Does Marie see them, too?" I whisper.

"Course not," Patsy says wetly, around her thumb.

Trying to ignore the thrilling in my backbone. Electric buzz gathering around my hair.

"I guess it might just be your imagination, Patsy."

Tingle on the back of my hand sharpens to a sting.

"Is not," she says.

Hurts so bad, I squeeze my eyes shut, and then it's gone. Gone altogether, no sting nor tingle, just my ordinary hand. I rub the skin against the comforter of Marie's bed. "You don't ever see your daddy, though, do you?"

She turns under my arm and sort of scrambles to sit up. Her face is all stricken; her thumb falls out of her mouth. "Is Daddy dead, too? Is Daddy gone to heaven with Johnnie and Mama and Lord Jesus?"

I open my mouth to tell her there's not a chance Daddy's gone to heaven, but the sight of her gathering tears chokes me. Makes my own eyes sting, my own heart sick. I think, I don't know what to say. I don't know what to do. Why can't I just love a thing, without it falls into mortal danger, and me helpless to save it? Why, Mama?

And as I think these things, the crackling along my nerves and my scalp sort of changes, as to a mere vibration, a hand laid upon the skin of my soul. I lift my shaky fingers to smooth back a piece of Patsy's beautiful hair. "I don't know about that, Patsy. I guess there's a lot of things I don't know. I guess we just have to hold each other tight, you and me, hold each other tight and hope that everybody comes home safe."

She nods and lays her head back on my shoulder, watching Marie, who is now commencing to dress the sister doll in some other article of clothing.

"I guess we might could pray, too," she says.

"Pray?"

"Praying helps. Mama said so."

I glance at the empty patch of wall next to the drawer chest. "Just now?" I ask, kind of hoarse, but Patsy's already climbing out of my arms and off the bed. Walking over to Marie and her dollhouse. She takes Marie's hand and says we're going to pray now, come along. Marie rises obediently and goes to the window with Patsy, and the two of them settle on their knees on the wooden floor and fold their tiny hands into pious knots.

Patsy calls softly. "Come here, Ginny. You has to say the words."

So I slide off the bed and join them, just to Patsy's left side, lowering myself to my shaky knees before the window. Haven't prayed like this since I was but small, except at the convent, which doesn't really count, does it, because I had to kneel down for penance and didn't mean a word. I guess the Lord Almighty does wreak His revenge for blasphemy like that. Penitence that was not penitence at all, but the opposite. The sun is truly falling now, sinking into rest, making the ocean glitter like cloth of gold. I fold my hands but I do not close my eyes. I want to scour the sea. Lord Jesus, I say aloud, but real quiet, we do thank Thee for the holy blessings Thou hast showered upon us, we truly do, and now we ask Thee to keep safe Thy servant Billy, who is struck down in innocence, for he was but striving to save another.

"Amen," says Patsy.

And we do commend the souls of Thy servants Dennis and Johnnie to Thy keeping. And I guess we do pray for the salvation of Dennis too, whose soul be Thine alone to judge.

"Who's Dennis?" whispers Patsy, and I whisper back that Dennis was her daddy's real name, except everybody just called him Duke.

Marie pipes Amen! and makes to rise.

"Ginny, come," says Patsy, tugging my shoulder.

But I stay where I am. Curl my fingers into one another until the nail beds burn. Fix my gaze upon the tiny dots on the eastern horizon, illuminated by the sun that faces them. Long line of dots, all the way from Maine to Florida, connecting the tip of the coast to its tail, connecting Bangor to Miami, connecting me, Geneva Rose Kelly, to a thousand schooners and motorboats and steamships and cutters, connecting me to Anson, somewhere along that line of dots, somewhere upon that sea, somewhere under the plentiful sky.

Just keep that damned fool safe, Lord, keep him safe in the hollow of Your two almighty hands. Or if You can't do that, why, send me some kind of sign, some kind of signal, something to let me know if he be alive or dead. Some little cord that leads me to him. That's all. Amen.

(I don't say that prayer aloud. Don't imagine it rises any higher than the base of my throat, the beat of my pulse, the hollow where the tendons of my neck find anchor.)

# 30

Now, I don't know whether the Lord does heed my words at all, so wicked a magdalen as I am. But I do know this. Sometime past midnight, I am woke smack in the middle of a dream I don't remember, by the sound of a voice calling my name.

And there is nobody by my door, nobody by my window, but when I steal outside I am met by Mr. Rubin, who tells me he's no rat, but he thought I should know there's talk going round that the men of the Watchful have been sent straight into an ambush off the coast of Nova Scotia two days hence, that's all.

## East Hampton, New York, April 1998

Somewhere past Jamaica, where the train branched south, the phone vibrated again. Patrick. The car was nearly empty, but not quite. Ella picked up the call and said, in a soft voice, "I can't talk right now. I'm on a train."

"We have to talk! Ella, you're pregnant!"

"I know that. I can't talk right now."

"Ella, I can't think, I'm so—oh my God. Where are you?"

"On a train. Good-bye, Patrick. I'll call you back when I get off."

"Wait—"

"Seriously, not now. I'll call you back. Good-bye."

Ella flipped the phone shut, and a few seconds later it vibrated again. She looked out the window and let it buzz, buzz, buzz until it went to voice mail. Started buzzing again. Then again. He tried twice more before giving up. Left two voice mails. The first one was agitated.

Ella, I'm sorry, I know you don't like talking on the train, but get off or something, I can't wait, this can't wait. A baby. I can't believe it. I'm so—why didn't you say anything this morning? I guess—Jesus, Ella, please don't do anything stupid. Where are you going? Please, I swear to God, please don't do anything without talking to me. I'm begging you. Okay. I'm going to try again. Please pick up. Good-bye. I love you.

The second one was angry.

Come on, Ella. Fuck. You have to pick up. If you are going somewhere to abort this baby, I swear to God—Jesus, Ella, please. Holy shit, I will fucking—I will—this is my baby, Ella, my baby too, I will fucking call up every lawyer in town, I will—shit, please, Ella, don't do this, I'm going crazy here. I'm dying. Don't fucking do this. Don't kill my baby, Ella. You have no idea what—oh my God, I can't even think about it, I will fucking murder somebody, I swear to God. I just—please. No, I didn't mean that. I just—please, please, please, Ella. Please, a thousand times. Whatever I've done, don't take it out on the baby. Begging you. Good-bye. Just don't. Oh my God, don't. Call me. Like now—

Ella flipped the phone shut and quietly gagged into a paper bag. When her stomach settled again, she sipped from a water bottle. She couldn't read, because of the nausea. Hated helplessly that she couldn't do anything except stare out the window, the passing grass, the passing trees, the glimpses of houses and cars and streets, people making their way, people living their messy lives, kids and houses and schools and shopping malls and freeways. Life.

**The phone** vibrated again just as the train was pulling into Patchogue. Ella nearly turned it off before she saw it was Hector.

"Hello, there," she said.

"Ella! Where are you?"

"On the train." (Softly.) "I can't talk."

"Okay. That's okay. The train to where?"

"I'm going to see my Aunt Julie in the Hamptons. I'll be back tonight, don't worry. I just need to talk to her about something."

"Because your dad stopped by. He said to keep an eye out for you, that you might be upset. Is everything okay? Anything I can do?"

"I'm fine. This is unrelated. Sort of."

"Okay. That's cool." He made a deep breath against the phone. "Look, I know there's something bothering you, and I know you don't want to talk with, like, a dozen people listening in a train car. So just let me ramble for a second. Let me just reassure myself that you're okay, that you'll be back tonight, that we can sit down and talk about—whatever it is. That you will let me—allow me—to help you, whatever's got you down. Because there is no happy for me unless you're happy, okay?"

"Okay."

"So I'm going to hang up and play some music, get some work done on this thing of mine—"

"It's going well, right?" she whispered. "Everything went well this week?"

Two rows ahead, a man craned his neck around and gave Ella an angry look. She lifted her middle finger, behind the seat where he couldn't see it. But it was there.

"The best," Hector said. "Can't wait to tell you about it. Can't wait to have you back. Make you some dinner, maybe, talk everything out. Or maybe I should take you out? I feel like we should go on a date or something. We haven't gone on a date, isn't that crazy? I really, really want to take my best girl out on the town.

I'll put on a jacket and tie, you'll put on a little black dress—"

"Hector, you nut—"

"All right, all right. You're tired, we should stay in. The Hamptons, right?"

"Yeah. She's at this place called Maidstone Meadows. It's kind of a hoot."

"Yeah, I'll bet. Just take care of yourself, okay? You didn't look good this morning. You're pale and just—I thought you were going to pass out, for a second."

"I'm fine."

"No, really. Take it easy, please? If something happened to you . . ."

"Nothing's going to happen to me. I'm on a train, visiting my aunt."

"Really?"

"Really."

"Because, to me, you taking off like that, barely saying hello, just jumping on a train and heading out to the far end of Long Island the instant I get home, I don't know. Feels like you're running away."

"I'm not," she said, and thought, I am. I'm running like a rabbit.

"Look. I'm not here to tell you what to do and where to go. I just need you to tell me what's up. Need you to come back home, face-to-face, and tell me where I stand, okay?"

"I will. I'll be back tonight."

"Okay. Good. No pressure. I'll make some dinner, you can rest, get your color back. Take care of you, make you better. Deal?"

"Deal."

"Love you. Bye."

He was gone, the line was dead. She thought of Hector this morning, hammer in hand, hole in T-shirt, sawdust in hair. Building her a new kitchen. Refinishing her floors. Make you better, he said, like she was a ruined apartment, a piece of fine American chestnut, like she was something he could fix with his dexterous hands. Something that could be beautiful again, if you just cared for it enough.

She looked down at the silver phone. Flipped it open. Pressed redial. Hector picked up on the first ring.

"Ella?"

"Hi."

"What's wrong? You sound—"

She looked out the window. They were passing some kind of town now, not a town really, just row after row of strip malls, undulating past the window. "Nothing's wrong. I mean, here's what I mean. You can't fix me."

"Fix you?"

"I mean, there's something I have to tell you. The reason I've been running. Why I couldn't face you. I thought it could wait for a while, but I don't think it can. I don't think it's fair to you." She spoke low and fast; she could feel the ears pricking up on the train around her, the dozen or so pairs of ears. Trying to tap into this interesting new frequency.

"Okay," Hector said. "Okay. I'm listening."

"Not over the phone. I'll tell you tonight, when I get back. I just want you to know that you don't need to worry, I'm not sick or anything. I'll be fine. I'll deal with it. There's nothing you can do."

"What does that mean? Deal with what?"

She was saying it all wrong. She was making it worse, not better. She ground her teeth, she made a fist, she shut her eyes and tried to imagine the right words, what she meant to say, in order to ease his worry and to push him back. But you couldn't do both at once, could you? She shouldn't have called at all. Should have waited until tonight.

"Ella? Something's wrong, isn't it?"

"No! Nothing's wrong. I just mean—it means you're free, Hector. I'll explain tonight. But you're free, okay? You don't need to take care of me. I'll be just fine on my own."

"Ella, stop. Whatever it is, just tell me now. Don't wait until tonight, for God's sake—"

"Please, it's nothing, just go back to your music and everything and don't worry. I'm not at death's door, I'm just—"

"Just what?"

"Just—"

"Ella, tell me!"

"Just pregnant!"

There was a terrible, teeming silence inside the car, atop the clatter of wheels. The whoosh of the air conditioning. A strip mall turned into a parking lot turned into a field, a woods, all in the space of a few seconds.

"Hector? Did you hear me?"

A voice carried back from the front of the train. "Jesus Christ, lady, the whole fucking train heard you!"

The phone made a beeping noise. Ella lifted it away from her ear and saw that the call had disconnected. There were no bars, no service. The battery was almost dead. In the back of the car, somebody started to laugh and turned it into a cough. Laughed at her, at Ella. She was a laughingstock. The day's entertainment on the LIRR.

Ella turned back to the window and pressed her fingers to her wan reflection in the glass. Cradled the phone to her stomach, all the way to the East Hampton station. When she rose to get off the train, a short, kind-faced woman touched her arm and handed her a card.

"Planned Parenthood, honey," she said. "You'll be okay."

**The residents** had already eaten lunch, but Aunt Julie kept food in her apartment and offered Ella a peanut butter sandwich and a vodka. Ella consulted her stomach and said yes to the peanut butter, no to the vodka.

"Are you sure? You look like you could use a drink," Aunt Julie said.

"I can't. I'm pregnant."

"All the better, darling."

"Seriously, Aunt Julie. You haven't read the news? Pregnancy? Alcohol? Let me get that bread for you."

"No, sit down. You've got the morning sickness, haven't you? Dreadful thing. You sit right down. I'll get the bread. You're sure about the vodka? I won't tell. God knows you need it."

"Really, really sure. Water's fine." Ella sat gratefully in the spindle-backed chair before the kitchen table. The apartments at Maidstone Meadows were small, and Aunt Julie had brought in a fleet of carpenters when she moved in, creating shelves upon shelves:

not for books, of which she had few, but all the photographs and knickknacks, the flotsam of china figurines, the silver cups and the vases and the candlesticks. Ella wasn't prone to claustrophobia, but she always felt the walls closing against her skin when she was inside Aunt Julie's apartment. The figurines leering madly. The junk multiplying and dividing.

"In my day," Aunt Julie was saying grandly, moving about the tiny Formica kitchenette, "we drank like men and we didn't complain about it, even when we were pregnant."

"You were pregnant?"

"No. But I had friends who were. Jelly? I have grape and strawberry."

"Ugh. I mean, no thanks. Just peanut butter and bread. And go easy on the peanut butter."

Aunt Julie clattered the plate before her. "There you go. The water here tastes like a swimming pool. How about club soda?"

"You know what, soda sounds good."

Aunt Julie poured her a club soda and opened a bottle of Beefeater. "I only keep vodka for you young people," she said, sitting down carefully in the chair next to Ella. "The trouble is, you can't find good gin anymore. Tanqueray is all right. The English, now, they know their gin. Cheers."

They clinked glasses. Ella sipped her club soda, nibbled her sandwich. "You didn't seem surprised about the news."

"That you were pregnant? Darling girl, I realized last weekend, when you came to visit. Your chest was out to here." Julie gestured. "And I didn't think you were the type for that awful surgery the girls are doing, these days."

"Well, you figured it out before I did. Congratulations."

"Darling, I'm ninety-six years old. I know when a girl's got herself up the stick. I assume That Bastard is the father?"

"If you mean Patrick, yes."

"Who else would I mean?"

"Nobody." Ella fingered her sandwich and set it down. Drank a little soda and said, "So about the Redhead—"

"Christ. I forgot. That's why you're here. Speaking of gin."

"Speaking of gin?"

"The Redhead. Gin. That's what we called her. Gin, short for Ginger. Because of her hair." Julie motioned to her own bouffant mess of pale gold. "Also, and this will interest you not at all, gin—the liquor, I mean—is short for genièvre, which is French or something for juniper, which is what flavors the gin. Genièvre, Geneva. Same thing."

"Really? That's fascinating."

"No, it isn't. You start to get old and your head's crammed with useless information, and you can't remember anything important. Anyway, the Redhead. You were saying?"

Ella swallowed down a sticky bite. "I went to see this dealer."

"I know. The fellow rang me up, so impertinent. That's another thing, darling. There's a trust between us, darling, a family trust. We don't talk to outsiders. You want to know something about anything, you come to me. God knows I have the keys to all the closets."

"What does Geneva Kelly have to do with the family?"

Aunt Julie fiddled with her gin. "As I said, I'm starting to get a little old."

"Um, starting?"

"I am old. I'm dreadfully old, and I ought to have died years ago. God knows I've sinned enough. But you know what they say about sinners. We live forever. It's you angels who die young."

"I'm no angel."

Julie snorted and threw back her gin. "My God, darling, you have no idea what we used to get up to. No idea. Your generation thinks it invented sex. Every generation does, I guess. We certainly did. Threw off that musty old Victorian shroud and lived. Oh, how we lived. But as I said, you start to feel your age a bit, and it occurred to me, you moving into that house, the strangest coincidence . . ." Her voice drifted, her claws grew soft around her empty glass. "Or maybe it's not a coincidence at all."

Ella set aside her sandwich and leaned forward. "Tell me something. What happened to her?"

"Happened to whom, darling?"

"Geneva Kelly! The Redhead. We were just talking about her?"

"What do you mean, what happened to her?"

"The guy at the art dealer said that she disappeared in 1924, and nobody heard of her afterward."

Julie laughed. "Well, that's nonsense. She didn't disappear in 1924."

"She didn't?"

"Of course not. Gin didn't disappear until at least 1928. Or was it 1930? I can't remember. The point is, she was alive and kicking and up to no good. It's the pictures that stopped in 1924. The Redhead photographs."

"But why did they stop?"

"Because she didn't need the money. She had the house by then. She had her father's dough. Of course, she ended up throwing it all away. On a man, of course. They always do. But there was a time—there was a moment—" Aunt Julie pushed back her chair and rose. "Come with me. There's something you need to see."

**There were** twenty-two of them, each one silvery in the light of the closet bulb. "Photographic plates," said Aunt Julie. "I got Anatole to hand them all over to me. Don't ask how."

"Who's Anatole? Oh, wait! The photographer! The one who took all the Redhead pictures! You knew him?"

"Well enough," Aunt Julie said, looking mysterious, and for a moment Ella could almost see her old beauty. Mumma said that Julie was once one of the most glamorous women in New York in her day, the most photographed. She went by the single name JULIE in the society press; everybody knew her. Now she stood in a closet with her great-grandniece, holding a box of old photographic plates in her bony hands, and the only bright thing about her was the magenta lipstick on her mouth, smeared by the gin glass, and the diamond engagement ring left on her hand in 1960 by her last husband.

"Was he one of your lovers, Aunt Julie?" Ella asked daringly.

"Oh, we were lovers, of course, but we were also business partners, which was much more satisfactory, believe me." Aunt Julie held out the box. "For you, my dear. I think it's time you had them."

"Me? But these are priceless!"

"I've got nobody else to leave them to."

"Other than about a hundred and twenty nieces and nephews."

"But you're the one she chose, darling." Aunt Julie stuck a fingernail into Ella's chest. "You're the one she wants."

"Who?"

"Why, Ginger, of course. She got you in that house of hers. I expect she's given you a reason to stay, if I know her. So here you are. Your inheritance. Take them. God knows I can't stand the sight of them."

Ella stared down at the box and back at Aunt Julie. "Why not?"

"Because he loved her better than me. My God, with a pair of headlights like that, who could blame him? Now go. That's all I'm going to say on the matter. You'll have to figure out the rest on your own."

"But wait. You can't just—"

"I can do anything I damned well please, Ella. It's the privilege of age. Now scurry along, before you miss the next train."

"I don't understand. What else is there to figure out? Where am I going to find it? You have to give me some kind of clue."

"My God." Aunt Julie pulled the chain on the bulb and pushed her out of the closet. "Do I have to spell it out for you? It's all in that damned house of hers. She wants you to find it, that's obvious. So start looking. And get the hell out. Antonio's coming by for my back-rub in five minutes, and I need to fix my hair."

**The taxi** took ages to arrive, and it was almost four o'clock by the time Ella reached the train station for the journey back to Manhattan. Her small elation over the Redhead had dulled back into misery. She'd rushed out of Maidstone Meadows without finishing that club soda, and she'd left her water bottle some-where. The apartment, probably. It didn't matter. She was hungry, she was thirsty, but the thought of water revolted her. The thought of anything.

On her lap, the Redhead plates sat in a brown Bloomingdale's bag, wrapped in old tissue from Aunt Julie's closet. Aunt Julie always recycled wrapping from Christmases and birthdays, and she'd grudged the loan of the tissue paper like it was made of gold foil. The weight of the box sank into Ella's thighs. Train wouldn't arrive for another fifteen minutes, and the platform was empty. Who went into the city from East Hampton on a Friday afternoon in April? Just Ella. She opened her pocketbook and took out the plastic bag containing Redhead Beside Herself. Six figures' worth of vintage photograph, and she was carrying it around in her pocketbook. She opened the ziplock and unwrapped the felt. Geneva Kelly. Ginger. Gin. Had known Aunt Julie; wasn't that funny? They'd shared a lover, the photographer Anatole, who had also painted the Redhead. Ella touched her fingertip to the portrait above the sofa, the luxurious, lugubrious Redhead.

It's been a hell of a week, she thought.

Just tell me what to do. Tell me where to go. I'm so mixed up, I don't even know who I am anymore. Somewhere along this chain of events—the one that started a single month ago, at the moment when Patrick stood in the stairwell of a Tribeca apartment building, unbuttoned his shorts, and had sex with a hooker—somewhere along this line of terrible dominos I have lost myself. I have lost everything I thought was real.

Nothing left to me but ghosts.

This ghost.

Gin.

Ella's head swam, her eyes swam, and in the middle of all this sloshing around, the Redhead—the photographic image of her, not the portrait—turned her head and winked one playful eye.

It's me, Ella. It's going to be all right.

Ella's vision telescoped to a single, white point: the Redhead's light-bathed face turned toward her in a wink.

Ella, it's me. I'm here. It's okay.

The point disappeared, and everything went dark.

# ACT V

# We Are Tossed Upon the Sea

## *(the Lord have mercy upon us)*

**North Atlantic Ocean**
**May 1924**

# 1

The moon follows us all the way past Nantucket, where it disappears behind a bank of thick cloud. Mr. Marshall frowns and seeks out one of his instruments. Some round thing like a clock, except the numbers are all different and written small. A barometer, I guess.

I wrap my hands around a mug of black coffee and ask if something's the matter.

"Just weather," he says. "About what you might expect, this time of year."

"I don't happen to expect anything, Mr. Marshall. Never having sailed in these parts. Never having sailed at all, to be perfectly honest."

He turns to me with the same old expression he's worn since I first shook him awake at Billy's bedside, two mornings ago. Two centuries ago. "It's the North Atlantic, Miss Kelly. If you don't like the weather, as they say—wait a few minutes."

I reach out and lay my hand around his upper arm,

and I consider that I am now past redemption, having dragged a father away from the bedside of his dying son in order to chase fruitless after the living one. Having engaged this weary old man in an adventure that might could kill him, and all for probably nothing. Chance in a thousand. A sure voyage to a bad end. And did I not foresee all this? Did I not learn my lesson? Yet here I am again, riding atop the mad Atlantic in some damn vessel, just as that dream of mine did warn me. I try not to think about that, but the vision rises before me with every pitch of every wave, and every moment I expect some dark-sided schooner to sail in view, some Flying Dutchman carrying my precious ghosts beneath its hatches.

And I have brought Anson's father into all this, God forgive me.

"Call me Ginger," I tell him.

# 2

As I said, I am no sailor. I can maybe row a boat in a straight enough line, if pressed and sober, but the arrangement of sheets and spars is mystery to me, and if you're longing for some technical description of our race from the eastern point of Long Island, where the Marshalls keep this fine yacht moored, to Halifax, Nova Scotia, where we are bound—some notion of wind and tack, trim of sail and direction of compass and what have you—why, you've come to the wrong redhead, brother.

Still I do my best. The tick of minutes makes my heart sicken. Urges the terror inside me to greater strength. We are maybe already too late, but maybe not. Maybe, if we strain every timber, we can catch Anson's ship before the rendezvous with the Coast Guard vessel Surprise tomorrow afternoon, off the coast of Nova Scotia. I follow each order that flies my way, until my palms turn raw and my throat bare, until my arms and legs fix to fall from their trunk. Currently I'm nursing a sore head from an unexpected boom by the boom, if you know what I mean, and though Mr. Marshall tells me I can crew for him anytime, I have the feeling he's only being kind.

Julie Schuyler, on the other hand. Can that blonde sail a boat.

# 3

Wasn't my idea that the Schuylers should join us on this adventure, believe me. When I dragged Mr. Marshall from his dying son's bedside and explained to him, in rough terms, the desperate situation before us, I emphasized that discretion was paramount, paramount, on account of the clear presence of some kind of double cross in our midst. And what did Mr. Marshall say, first thing? He scratched his tarnished head and blinked his crusted blue eyes, and he said, "I'm going to need someone to crew the boat."

An hour later, we were roaring east along the highway in Mr. Marshall's Buick Battistini speedster, toward the sheltered cove where fellows like Marshall keep their watercraft safe from harm. I hardly noticed when he swerved off the main road and made a series of swift turns that landed us before a pretty gray-shingled mansion much like the one we just left. Jerked myself to attention and asked where the devil we were. Mr. Marshall said, Schuyler's place. And in that instant I realized I never did ask him about Benjamin Stone and Charles Schuyler, and where the two of them went to school together, and whether he's heard of some third character who also moved in their circle, someone who acquired the nickname Grendel.

I seized his hand and said, "No! We're not taking Charles Schuyler along!"

"Of course not," he said. "Schuyler drove back to Manhattan last night. But his sister won the club sailing championship last year, and God knows we need somebody else on board who knows how to trim a sail."

"His sister?" I asked, kind of stupidly, because it had been a hell of a forty-eight hours, you recollect, when you lined them all up end to end.

"Yes. I believe you've met Julie, haven't you?" He opened up his door and came around the hood to open mine, though I was already taking care of that business myself, believe me. "At the party yesterday, remember?"

Well, you know very well that I didn't just meet Julie Schuyler at the party yesterday, but I wasn't so stupid that I told Mr. Marshall all about our history together. I just said I remembered the encounter very well and I didn't realize she was such a sailor, and off we trudged across the trim gravel drive to pound on the Schuylers' door and drag the lucky dame out of bed.

But it turned out that Charles Schuyler hadn't returned to New York City the evening before, after all. He had changed his plans. He'd driven instead to this gray-shingled estate in East Hampton, where his wife and children were settling in for the summer, and spent the night there. And he wasn't about to let his kid sister go off on an impromptu weeklong yachting expedition in the North Atlantic without a chaperone, oh no. He looked at me and he looked at Mr. Marshall, and he went right off to fetch his sou'wester, and here he is right now, strolling into the deckhouse like he owns the joint. (Trait seems to run in the family.)

"My watch," he says. "Get some sleep, Marshall."

# 4

The deckhouse of the Ambrosia is not a proper deckhouse, you understand. Just a bit of shelter around the wheel, open to the sides and back, so that you don't catch so much rain and spray as you go about the tender business of steering the boat across the ocean. Mr. Schuyler places his hands at ten and two and inspects the compass heading. His sou'wester is buttoned up like he expects a storm of some kind, and his cap lies straight on his forehead. Somehow he has shaved without nicking himself, presenting an aspect of clean and almost boyish enthusiasm, and I have the uncanny feeling that he has done these things—dressed carefully, shaved carefully—for my benefit. Maybe it's his hands, which clench the wheel a little too ferociously.

I rise from the stool and stretch my arms. "Guess I had better turn in for an hour or two."

"If you're going below, I could murder a cup of coffee."

"Maybe if you ask nicely."

He smiles faintly and glances back down at the compass. Or possibly it's the barometer. "Might I trouble you, please, for a cup of hot coffee, Miss Kelly?"

"Cream or sugar?"

"Both."

I turn to leave, and he adds, kind of soft, "Thank you."

# 5

Naturally, the sweet Ambrosia possesses a galley. How are you supposed to enjoy the pleasures of shipboard life without fresh food, prepared for you (in ideal circumstances) by a chef of the first water? Failing a chef on short notice, there's just me, boiling water for coffee the way my step-daddy showed me, when I was but small. The smell of the beans, which I grind myself in an old-fashioned mill, awakens in me the genuine, particular desire for java that cannot be satisfied by anything else. I brew enough for two. When I'm finished, I pour the business into two enamel cups, add sugar to mine and cream plus sugar to Mr. Schuyler's, and I carry them both up top like I am bearing the king's own jewels.

"Ah," says Mr. Schuyler, taking the mug in his left hand, "perfect."

"You haven't even tried it yet."

"The smell's enough." He drinks and I drink, not looking at each other, and I sit back down on the stool and think what I might say to this man. Charles Schuyler. Brother to Julie. Friend to the Marshalls. Schoolfellow of Benjamin Stone and Grendel. He gulps his coffee like a man with no regard for the lining of his throat, and his cheeks, I believe, bear a little more pinkness than the weather demands.

Me, on the other hand. All bundled up in a sou'wester sized for a man, hair blown to pieces, face stiff and chilled by the wind. If I had a mirror handy—which I thankfully do not—I don't suppose I'd be best pleased with my reflection. I never quite look like I imagine myself; I'm always the tiniest bit shocked to see the woman staring back at me. Her eyes are set too far apart; her mouth's too wide; her cheekbones too sharp and her chin too narrow, like that of a witch. Photographs well, I guess, but in real life this mug is just too much. Too pale and ginger-haired and odd-featured. I can't imagine what men seem to like about a face like that. Or maybe it's not my face at all. Maybe it's something else, my shapely chest that defies fashion and has earned me a pretty penny in the indecency racket. My legs, my smart mouth. Maybe these fellows can just tell I'm the kind of girl who runs at a hotter temperature than some, and what fellow doesn't want to warm himself beside a fire like that? Especially now, when the wind's coming on to blow across the cold salt ocean, and the moon's slid silently behind a cloud.

My mother, now. My mother truly was a beautiful woman, at least before Duke Kelly got to her, and for some reason I find myself thinking of her, as I sit on my stool, nursing a cup of hot, sweet coffee between my hands, and watch the blushing Charles Schuyler pilot this elegant craft through the Atlantic night.

"Have you got any children, Mr. Schuyler?" I ask, though I happen to know the answer, because Julie's already told me.

He startles at the sound of my voice. Spills a little coffee on the side of his hand and reaches up to siphon it off. "I have a son. Fourteen years old in August."

"Now, let me guess. Is his name Charles, too?"

Mr. Schuyler makes this apologetic laugh. "His mother insisted."

"I'm sure he's a worthy namesake."

"Yes. He's a good lad." He hesitates, and then adds: "We had another, but I'm afraid he wasn't strong. Died soon after he was born."

"I'm sorry."

"Harriet was crushed, of course. She may seem hard, but—" He kind of catches himself on the but. Drinks more coffee and sets the mug on the ledge so he can grip the wheel with both hands. "She was rude to you yesterday. I apologize."

"No need. Plenty of women don't take to me."

"Yes, but—" Again, the check. He taps his fingers on the wheel. "Well, it's obvious why. You're something of a magnet, you know. You gather attention around you. I don't believe you even try. You're just a force of energy. A very pure, very intense light. It's a rare quality."

"Don't feel especially energetic at the moment, I'm afraid."

"And yet you're sitting there like a small blue star."

"Blue?"

He finishes the coffee in a spasmodic gulp and sets the empty mug back on the ledge, except it topples off. He swears. Leans down, picks it up, sets it right. "Tell me what's going on with Ollie. I thought you were engaged to the other one."

"It's a long story."

"I gather he's in some kind of danger? That's why we're racing across the sea like this?"

I rotate my cup in my hands. "Now, see. Here's what I don't understand. What's your game in this, Mr. Schuyler? Aren't you supposed to be sitting in some nice office someplace? Law or government bonds or something? And we stop by your house and mention how we're heading off into the North Atlantic for a week or two, can we borrow your sister, and you just run off and grab a coat for no reason."

"No reason? Who could resist an adventure like this?"

"Plenty of people could resist. Cold and wet and dangerous. You have no horse in this particular race. What's Oliver Marshall to you?"

"His father's a friend of mine, for one thing."

I rise from the stool and set down my coffee cup on the ledge, right next to his. "Don't imagine I'm a fool, Mr. Schuyler."

"Believe me, I don't."

"Because if something happens to that man, if something untoward happens to Oliver Marshall, why, I don't know what I'd do. I mean if you want to talk about a force of energy, Mr. Schuyler, an intense blue light? The really hottest, angriest kind of flame?"

"Indeed," he says. "Indeed."

I lay my hand along the side of his face, and the skin is warmer than I thought, because at that age—forty or forty-five or whatever he is—a man's face usually suffers from a wind like this one. But not his. Charles Schuyler is fully alive just now. His keen eyes attach to mine.

"So you understand me," I say.

"I understand you perfectly."

"Ollie?"

"Won't come to any harm, so long as I can help it, Miss Kelly."

"Good." I lean forward and kiss his other cheek. "I'm going below."

# 6

When I slide into my bunk, Julie's sleepy voice floats out to find me. "Wind's changed, has it?"

"Depends on what you mean by wind."

"I mean the stuff that blows across the ocean and makes us go."

"Then I wouldn't know."

She makes a noise of frustration, or maybe fatigue. Had a doughty spell on deck this afternoon, our Julie, and while I always considered her something of an orchid, some kind of Manhattan hothouse plant, city bred and precious, she worked like a mule trimming those sails, she surely did. And you can't get higher praise than that from me.

The wood groans softly beside me, the waves slosh. I don't consider myself prone to seasickness, but this experience of rolling and pitching inside a closed cabin, no light nor air nor sense of progress, starts my insides to trouble. I lie on my back and stare at the void—and that's unsettling enough, isn't it, opening your two eyes into exactly nothing—and I concentrate my attention on the map of the North Atlantic I have committed to memory. Currents and sea lanes. The relative positions of Montauk and New Bedford and Halifax, Nova Scotia and Newfoundland. That small stand of rock they call Saint Pierre. By tomorrow noon we must be standing off Halifax, straining our eyes for the Surprise, straining our eyes for a ship out of New Bedford that might or might not have steamed there under flag of the United

States Coast Guard. The wind is picking up. Surely that will help, won't it? Carry this swift, elegant craft in the palm of its hand.

Oh Lord. Blow the wind like a trumpet, oh Lord. Carry this swift, elegant craft in the palm of Thy hand.

"Julie," I say, though she might be fallen asleep again, so drowsy a voice as she gave me, "just where did your brother go to school?"

"Charles? School? Why?"

"Curious."

"Oh, Dalton, wasn't it. Then he prepped at Phillips Andover. Only the best for our little prince."

"I don't guess you recollect if he had a friend called Grendel, do you?"

There is the faintest pause, which might just be the sound of her recollecting. Sifting her sleepy mind through the mesh of memory.

"I don't think so," she says. "Not that he mentioned. But I was only a small thing when he was at school."

"This would be a friend he still keeps today."

"Gin, darling. Don't you ever sleep?"

"Not if I can help it."

"Try it sometime, why don't you."

So I do. I try to sleep. Stare at nothing and think of everything. How we are supposed to intercept Anson's ship at the Halifax rendezvous. Whether we are fast enough to catch up in time. Nautical miles and angles of arc and what have you. Hours left on a diminishing clock. When the numbers start to jumble and slide together, I just think of Anson, the shape of his shoulders against a white pillow. A patch of yellow sand. Standing on one knee and parting Patsy's hair away from her damp face, the better to see her.

# 7

I guess I do fall asleep, in contravention of my own wishes, because I find I am once more bearing down on a dark-sided ship, except this time the sea is not calm but angry. Ship heaves in and out of sight, and now I am desperate, eager as blood to reach that craft, called to it the way you are called to breathe air.

I've just reached the port-side railing when I am jerked awake, a shock so profound that for some minutes I lie but stiff, heart going smack, staring at a beam and wondering where the devil I am. Knowledge returns in cold, reluctant facts. I figure that something's awoken me, some outside disturbance has surely tugged me back into the world. But nothing strikes, the ship continues its rhythms, and I'm left to contemplate a question I never asked before, in all the other nights I've encountered this dream.

Upon what vessel was I myself riding, that I should fly aboard that ship of death?

I slide from the bunk to the carpeted deck beneath—the Ambrosia's fitted with all kinds of such comforts—and perceive that dawn has arrived. A thick gray light fills the cabin I share with Julie. Her bunk is empty, however, so I fit my feet into my shoes and snatch my woolen cardigan and crawl up the stairway to the main deck.

The morning hangs like ash as we dip across the long, shallow waves, for the wind has died during the night. Can't even properly tell where the sun is coming from. A pair of hushed voices disturbs the stillness at the stern, and though my vision is not yet clear, still I discern the two figures through the window of the deckhouse. Man and woman. Talking in hot, terse sentences. Julie, of course. With Schuyler or Marshall?

Schuyler.

So close and heated is their exchange, they don't catch any glimpse of me, slipping along the deck inside my cardigan the color of sheep's wool. My copper hair bound beneath a hat. Wish I could find the shape of a few more words, but the mist seems to hold each vowel and consonant in place so they don't escape. I creep closer. Gaze off at some unseen horizon as if I'm only absorbing the morning fog. Edge past the corner of the deckhouse to the open side, and all at once the syllables become clear.

Schuyler: "—ought to have told me the two of you were friends."

Julie: "We aren't friends, exactly—"

Schuyler: "Close enough to know each other's secrets."

Julie: "She doesn't know a thing, believe me."

I sink to a sitting position on a coil of rope. Make myself small beneath the vantage of the deckhouse.

Schuyler: "Then why? Why seek her out?"

Julie: mumble mumble

Schuyler: "Marshall says you introduced her to Billy."

Julie: mumble "—my idea. That friend of yours asked me to."

Schuyler: "Which friend?"

Julie: "Why, the blonde. Didn't you know? She set the whole thing up."

The deck goes silent. I catch a drift of cigarette smoke, of heavy contemplation. Julie says something else, but she's turned away again, and I can't make out the words. A breeze picks up, laying itself against my cheek, stirring the ends of my hair, and beneath my feet the boat responds with a faint surge of energy. A creak of wood, a rustle of disturbed canvas.

Hand falls on my shoulder. "Good morning, Ginger."

I jump right off my coil of rope and whip about. But it's only Mr. Marshall, looking maybe a hundred years old, skin creased, hair white as the sails.

"Did you sleep at all?" he asks.

"A little. What's happened to the wind?"

"Seems to have died down."

"No kidding."

He narrows his eyes at that place where the horizon ought to be. "Should pick up again soon. The weather around here doesn't stay placid for long."

"How soon? Can't be more than six hours until noon."

Marshall glances at his watch. "Six and a half. I've made some coffee down below."

"Don't think I could swallow it."

"Try," he says.

He gives my shoulder another pat and walks on to the deckhouse. Some kind of subdued, masculine greeting passes between him and Mr. Schuyler. No sound from Julie. I contemplate that horizon, thinking about blondes. One blonde in particular. When I glance back some time later, Mr. Marshall stands alone at the wheel, but in the bow, staring into an obscure distance, Mr. Schuyler smokes a cigarette in short, fierce strokes.

# 8

A word about Luella Kingston, in case you're not acquainted. She was Anson's partner at the New York Prohibition enforcement bureau, in the days before somebody framed him up and got him kicked out of the place in disgrace. But she stood by him. Yes, she did. She kept her ears and eyes open, as they say, working from the inside to help him discover which rat was behind this terrible betrayal. When we drove out to River Junction to rescue Anson and Billy, she took the wheel of the car in her anxious, lovestruck fingers, for she is head over heels amorous toward Oliver Anson Marshall, just plain goofy for him, though for some reason he doesn't return that particular compliment. So far as I can tell, she gets nothing but loyalty out of him, which must annoy the dickens out of a dame like that.

I should mention she's beautiful. Have I mentioned that already? Of course she's beautiful. She has the kind of thin, elegant, bosomless figure you see in magazine advertisements, except it's real; she is made of ice and porcelain, perfectly drawn, head of platinum, skin of cream, eyes of silver. Altogether colorless, if you ask me, but nobody asks a funny-faced redhead anything when Luella's in the room, drawing out her vowels like she has all the time in the world. I have never really gotten to the bottom of her, even during that harrowing drive to Maryland; like ice or porcelain or silver, she keeps her skin intact no matter how you try to chip something away. I've always thought her voice sounds a little too high-bred for a working girl, but maybe that's just part of her racket. Maybe she's got her mask on so long, there's nothing left behind it.

# 9

Well, enough about her. If she's the one who asked Julie to introduce me to Billy, why, it just figures. You don't sit back and witness the man you adore fall in love with someone else—some audacious Appalachia bootlegger's daughter he's trailing about—

without wanting to do something about it, do you? So you have this brilliant idea to keep him safe. You fix up the redhead with his brother. Decent, honorable fellow like Anson isn't going to move in on his brother's doll, is he? Of course not.

So there's nothing more to it.

Except one thing, I guess. How does a dame like Luella get acquainted with Charles Schuyler?

# 10

The wind does pick up again, but not enough. The fog lifts to a dull haze, exposing the position of the sun as it climbs the eastern half of the sky. I find a place near the bow to grip the rail and strain the muscles of my abdomen, urging some kind of additional speed to the wood beneath me. Scour the water for some sign of anything. Afraid to blink. I don't watch the clock, just that vague spot of brightness behind the clouds, making its way to the top of the world. When it stands overhead, I'll know we've lost. No possible way to catch up in time. No possible means to warn Anson, whose ship ought to be standing off Halifax this instant, waiting for the arrival of the Surprise out of New Bedford in order to proceed into the sea lanes between Newfoundland and Boston, that he sits directly inside a neat, steel-toothed trap.

From time to time, I'm called to assist with some kind of nautical maneuver. I pull on whatever rope I'm told; I even take the wheel once, while the others untangle some difficulty in the rigging. Each time I return to my position on the rail, I look to the sun. Track its excruciating progress. Hold up my hand as if I might block it from view. Might stop it entirely. Hold back the sun, oh Lord, hold back the sun until we are borne to Anson's side.

But the sun don't stop. Tick tock. The sun don't stop.

Noon.

# 11

Wind's blowing steady now. Sails full. Salt water spitting up from below. My heart goes jump at the sight of a craft on the horizon, until I perceive it's some kind of passenger steamship, great big ocean liner of three funnels, bit in her teeth for the last stretch to New York Harbor.

Pair of arms comes to rest on the rail beside me. I recognize the slender yellow sleeves of Julie Schuyler's sou'wester. Seems all the rich folk have them, in case of weather.

"Charles says we're making up speed," she offers.

"Every bit helps, I guess."

"You're taking this awfully hard. Does it matter so much?"

"Guess you wouldn't know."

She leans on her elbows. "Oh, I know a little bit about love, darling. You might think I haven't got a heart, but I do, all right. Cracked and chipped in all the best places. Yours, on the other hand. Who knew Ginger Kelly was harboring such a passion for my old friend Ollie?"

"Who says I am?"

"Oh, sure. We're just racing out to sea like this for our own health. Just because you care so much for your future in-laws. Well, I guess it's a sensible plan, to keep one brother in reserve in case the first one doesn't make it."

I say nothing. Takes all my strength just to stand here without breaking down; I don't have any words to spare for a barb like that.

"Or maybe you just have it bad for the wrong fellow," she says, a little more softly. "I've heard it can happen to anyone."

"All right, then. You've got me figured out. What about you, Miss Julie Schuyler?" I turn to face her. "Why are you and your brother so eager to rescue Oliver Marshall? Don't tell me you're in love with him, too."

"Me? Ollie? Not on your life. Not my type at all. I require my fellows much naughtier than that. Where's the fun in going out with a saint?"

"So maybe you've got some other interest in this business, then."

Julie knits her fingers and presses the pads of her thumbs together. The right nail is chipped and ragged, like she caught it on something. "Now, why do you ask that?"

"Maybe because I have a nose on my face, and it smells something funny. And if I discover somebody's done something to put Oliver Marshall in danger, if he's killed out there on that water because somebody stands to make a dime or two from his absence—"

"Oh, go find yourself a place to cool down, Ginger. You're barking up the wrong tree."

"Am I? So why'd you get me stuck in this business to begin with? Take Luella Kingston's advice and invite me to a party with Billy Marshall?"

"Listen." She straightens up to face me. "I just did a friend a favor, that's all. I didn't see any harm. I thought the two of you might hit it off. Which you did, as I recall. Any business you got into, any trouble you found with the wrong brother, you jumped into it yourself."

"And you're just helping me get out of it? From the goodness of your own heart? Because you can't bear to see your old friend Marshall lose both his sons at once?"

Julie flicks her gaze to the deckhouse, where her brother holds the wheel of the Ambrosia. Directly above our heads, the sun breaks free to cast a brief, lurid shadow along the deck.

"Doesn't matter, though, does it?" she says. "We're too late."

# 12

More ships appear on the gray ocean before us, fishing boats mostly, going about the business of making a living. I examine each one through the pair of binoculars Mr. Marshall keeps in the deckhouse.

Shape and color and crew. Heart smacking hard in my throat, even though I know it can't be Anson, I know this or that small, battered, ramshackle craft cannot possibly bear the agents and officers of the United States Coast Guard, or the Prohibition enforcement bureau. Sometime past two o'clock, the headlands of Halifax Harbor pop into view. Mr. Marshall comes to stand beside me and asks if I've seen anything interesting.

I hand him the binoculars. "That depends on your opinion of cod, I guess."

He brings the binoculars to his eyes and makes a careful sweep of the water ahead, but I have the feeling it's just for show. "Julie's got the wheel," he says. "We're going to tack back and forth. They might be farther out to sea, east or west. One or the other of them might have been held up."

"Of course."

Marshall lowers the binoculars. We're standing remarkably close, so I can feel all the tiny adjustments of his legs and arms as the yacht ducks and soars through the waves. His left sleeve brushes my right sleeve. He toys with the object in his hands while his face points toward the horizon, taking the draft without flinching. "You know," he says, after a bit, "I only watched him play once."

So abrupt is the change in subject, I take a moment to consider his meaning. "Football?" I venture.

"Yes, football. He played for Princeton."

"I hear he was something."

"I couldn't stand it. Brutal sport. Every damned game, I expected a ring on the telephone to tell me he'd been hurt, he'd been killed. I couldn't imagine how he survived all that violence." A line of foam springs from the water, and we both jump back. He puts his hand out to steady me. Continues in a firm voice, because the air is full of noise, wind and sails and water. "But he was captain his senior year, and toward the end of the season I thought I really should watch a game, just once. Didn't want to regret later that I hadn't done it."

"How much Scotch did you need?"

"None. Forgot to bring any. Even if I had, I'd have forgotten to drink it."

"Because you were too afraid?"

"No, because he was mesmerizing. He didn't just run, you see. He charged. He was so damned strong, so invincible. They might tackle him, but he jumped straight back up, and near the end I could see he was tired, they sent him running just about every play, he was blowing like a racehorse, but he kept going. There was no finish to him. Every time you thought he was down, you thought he was done, why, he rose up again, and I thought, how was it possible that this—this extraordinary man was my son? How had I not seen this in him? He was tough, of course, he was always such a serious, determined boy, you couldn't ever budge him, but this. I wept, watching him. I don't know why. Whether it was the beauty of it, or because I had come to that moment—every father does, I suppose—when you realize this tiny child you once conceived, this infant you once held in your arms, has become a man. And you never—pardon me—you never—" There are sobs in his chest, which he tries to subdue. "You never saw it was happening, until it was too late. Until it had all passed you by, and was gone."

"Until what had passed you by?"

"His youth." He hands me back the binoculars. "Keep looking, Ginger. You'll find him."

# 13

The sun climbs back down. The hours lengthen. We make a zigzag pattern, combing the miles of water while Nova Scotia slips in and out of view to the north.

It's May, and the latitude is high, and the sun describes a long, steady, interminable arc toward the horizon, but that's only an illusion, isn't it? The day will end, the night will coat the sky. What will I do, if night falls with no sign of Anson?

Around six o'clock, Schuyler offers to take the tender into Halifax and ask for news.

I answer with a bit of scorn. "Who's going to have news of a pair of ships meeting off the coast?"

"Why, the fishermen, of course. Terrible gossips, fishermen, and most of them should already be back in port. If there was any"—he glances at Marshall—"anything unusual out there, they will no doubt be discussing the incident in the usual sorts of places."

"Now, that sounds like my kind of fun," says Julie. "I'll come with you."

"No. I'll go."

Everyone turns to me, the way you turn to somebody who's dropped a glass full of liquor bang smash in the middle of a party. I fold my arms and fix my gaze right between Charles Schuyler's thick, grave eyebrows.

"Miss Kelly," he says, "these are rough men."

I start to laugh. "Rough men. Oh, that's rich. Rough men. Believe me, Mr. Schuyler, they don't come any rougher than the devil who raised me."

Schuyler makes this little jerk, like I've hit him. Marshall says, Oh, Ginger, in such a way that conveys a heart full of grief.

I turn to Julie, who stands quietly by, leaning one shoulder on the corner of the deckhouse. I point to her sleeve and say, "I'm afraid I'm going to need that jacket of yours, if you don't mind."

# 14

The tender has a motor, which Schuyler starts once we're lowered in the water. Well, I guess he couldn't do otherwise, could he? We crawl toward the mouth of the harbor while the late sun parts the clouds to the west. Don't say much. Too much weight in the air, too much dread. Remember what I told you, Mr. Marshall said, as he helped me into the boat. There's no finish to him.

Fine words, I remember thinking, but they're not true. Everyone has a finish to him. We are all but mortal, waiting our turn to die.

The harbor grows large and full of crawling detail. Atop the hills to the west, there is a fort of some kind, a lighthouse. The tender skips across the waves, aiming for a series of docks beneath the citadel, and I turn to examine Schuyler's face as we approach our landfall. Some hint of what he intends to do. Inside the pocket of Julie's sou'wester lies the pistol Anson gave me, loaded with bullets; it has journeyed with me by train and automobile and now by ship, like a loyal friend, and its weight comforts me as I regard those narrowed eyes, that grim jaw, that graying hair disguised by a trim officer's cap.

Study the eyes. Who told me that? Duke? I can just about hear his voice. Man's eyes will always tell you where he's headed next.

We slow into the harbor mouth and putter to an empty dock. I jump out first and catch the rope Schuyler tosses me. An edgy silence persists between us, as if distrust were some kind of sticky substance that has closed our throats, until Schuyler knots the rope and straightens, adjusting his cap, and I say, "Where to?"

"The first saloon we can find." He nods toward the street that fronts the harbor. "They won't be too far from the docks, trust me."

Now, here's the funny thing. You walk into an establishment, any establishment, and you discover a long wooden bar, polished or dull, clean or dirty, along which several men are drinking what is obviously some kind of intoxicating liquor, beer or whiskey or what have you, right there in the open air. In the open! No thick, plain, unmarked door; no atmosphere of secrecy and furtive debauchery. Just a bartender polishing a glass with a white cloth, a line of customers pulled up on stools, arms moving up and down, perfectly ordinary, perfectly legal.

Only thing missing is women.

So these customers pulled up on their stools, these fellows standing around flapping their gums, these bartenders polishing glasses and drawing beer, they just stop and stare at us, me and Mr. Schuyler, but mostly me. Because why? Because here in civilized climes, where the drinking of alcohol remains legal and even decent, a decent woman wouldn't dream of entering a drinking establishment.

Nor, for that matter, would the indecent kind. And in my windblown, redheaded state, wearing an oilcloth jacket and a salt-stained skirt, I guess I positively reek of indecency.

Under the onslaught of those masculine eyes—shocked at first, and then affronted—I falter a step or two, but Schuyler puts his hand gently to my back, urging me forward. I fill out my chest and press on directly for the empty corner of the bar, where the bartender looks straight past the top of my head to address Charles Schuyler. Asks him what he'll have, in the kind of voice that suggests he doesn't appreciate the intrusion.

"Miss Kelly?" Schuyler says. "Something for you?"

"Scotch whiskey, if you don't mind."

"Two of your best Scotch whiskey, sir. Neat."

The words ring out into the room, which has naturally gone as still as a church. If disapproval were something you could leak out from your pores into the air, like some kind of noxious gas as crippled the soldiers in the late war, why, I am surely choking on it now. The bartender continues to stare at Mr. Schuyler behind me, and I have the idea they are communicating with each other at a masculine pitch beyond my hearing. Will against will. Stone face against stone face.

"Aw, come on, then, Smitty. She's all right," says the man to my right, a young fellow whose raw, chapped hands sit around a pint glass of dark ale. "American," he adds, with significance.

"Maybe I am and maybe I'm not," I say.

The fellow laughs, while the bartender turns grudgingly away. "Can aboot smell it on you, miss. What brings you to Halifax? Business or pleasure?"

Schuyler says the word business, about as solid and sharp as a thrown rock.

"And what line of business is that?"

"Looking for somebody."

"Lucky fellow."

"Not so lucky. He's got some trouble after him."

"What kind of trouble?"

"Well, you see—"

Schuyler breaks in, kind of thunderous. "Look, all we need to know is whether you've heard of a ship getting taken, a United States Coast Guard vessel—"

"Now, see here, mister," the young fellow says calmly, caressing his glass, "it seems to me the lady and I were having a conversation."

"The lady's with me."

"I don't know. Maybe we should ask the lady her opinion."

The bartender returns with a pair of glasses, one of them full and the other one containing about a half measure. He sets that one down before me, scowling, and the full one before Schuyler. I raise mine and throw the whiskey right down the back of my throat. Beside me, the fellow whistles.

"Schuyler," I say, "why don't you go see what you can discover at the other end of the room."

# 15

Now some of you drys out there—and I don't blame you, for there are a thousand reasons to mistrust the demon rum, and maybe I'm one of them— you drys may not believe this, but that whiskey is just bang exactly what I need, even so small a tot as that bartender allowed me. Flowers in the center of my belly, rendering me just enough reckless, lending me just enough wit. Schuyler slams down his glass and slumps off down the bar, and the Young Fellow chuckles at us both. I don't dare look him square in the face. Might be pushing my luck if I do. But I tilt my cheek and place the pad of my thumb on the rim of my empty glass, and when he asks if he can buy me another I say sure, why not?

He makes a signal to the bartender, who's down at the other end, being summoned by Schuyler, and while we're waiting for this signal to take effect, he says, "What's this talk about the Coast Guard? Don't say you're in trouble with the authorities, now."

"I might be."

"Shame. A nice girl like you—"

"Who says I'm such a nice girl?"

"Why, it's written all over your face like a lead pencil, Miss . . . Ah, now. You never did say your name."

"That's true."

Bartender turns up, face maybe a degree less stormy than before. Young Fellow orders a pair of whiskeys— And measure them fair, now, Smitty, the girl can take it—and as he's doing so, I snatch a glance down the bar, where Schuyler huddles over a drink or something, shoulders canted at such an angle that I can't quite tell what he's imbibing.

"So what is it?" the Young Fellow asks.

"What?"

"Your name."

"They call me Gin," I say, "short for Ginger."

"Pleased to meet you, Gin. They call me Dick." He holds out a rough hand. "Short for Dickens."

"Dickens. Enchanted. How's the herring catch today?"

"What makes you think I'm in the herring business?"

"Aside from those hands of yours, you mean?"

He holds them up, palms toward his face, and laughs. "And the smell, I guess."

"I've smelled worse."

"Well, it ain't such a bad business, these days. But maybe you know that already."

"Now why would I know a thing like that?"

Bartender arrives, slams a wee dram of whiskey directly in front of me, in such a way that an arc of precious liquid slings over the edge, to be wiped away by an angry dishcloth. I lift the glass and salute my benefactor. "Cheers."

"Cheers," he agrees. "This fellow of yours, the one the guardsmen are after—"

"Actually, it's the other way around. He's with the guardsmen."

"Snitch, is he?"

"No, he's straight. Straight as an arrow. It's the Bureau that's crooked."

"You mean the Prohibition bureau?"

"I mean all of it. The Bureau, the Coast Guard, every man and woman who rows a dinghy out to a mother ship or sips a gin and tonic on American soil. You and your so-called herring. We're all crooked, aren't we? Except him."

"So you're hooked, is that it? Nice girl like you. Hooked on this one fellow who ain't on the take."

Lift my glass. "That about sums up the entire business."

Dickens sits and chews on that. Washes it down with a sip or two from his mug of dark ale. His knuckles are enormous, swollen, scarred like they have been split open more than once, and yet his fingers, operating the mug's handle, caressing the rim and that kind of thing, move gently. Puts me in mind of the way my big brother Johnnie used to tickle fish from the water. Wiggle his thick fingers in a slow, delicate dance, so as to draw them near, and then he strikes.

Well, I guess I can be patient too, though a clock ticks loud inside my head, in time with the crash of my pulse. The beat of my terrified blood. In my fear, I imagine that time itself slips presently through my veins and spills out through some hole in my wrist, leaving me desiccated, a husk of myself. I lift my head and stare at the back of the bar, at the bottles lined up in rows and columns of ragtag soldiers, each uniform different, and then the shelves of glassware on either side. An enormous, high-polished mirror reflects our heads and shoulders back to us, and I am startled by the size of my eyes, by the color of my hair, by the paleness of my skin, all of them somehow magnified, the way I myself have magnified in sensation and intensity, four times more Ginger than the Ginger who lived yesterday, a dozen times more than the one the day before. Next to me, Dickens stares too, and our eyes meet inside the glass like a pair of strangers. He is smoother than I expect, more groomed. I hold him for a moment or two, just to show I'm no coward, and then I slide down the bar, one man after another, most of them returned to the important business at hand, until I fix at last upon Charles Schuyler, who is not drinking something as I thought, not nursing his defeat over another glass or two of Scotch whiskey, but instead speaking fiercely into the mouthpiece of a telephone.

"Excuse me," I say, rising to my feet.

But Dickens takes my hand and stills me. "Maybe I got something for you."

# 16

Now, this is not the first time I have gone in desperate search of Oliver Anson Marshall, on account of some trouble he's gotten himself into while seeking to defend the United States Constitution from one scoundrel or another. Just two months back he led me deep into that heart of darkness River Junction, where I was bred up, except in that instance Luella Kingston drove by my side. Platinum Luella, smoking her cigarettes and pretending not to care. Pretending her pores didn't seep the scent of unrequited love.

We mostly kept quiet. What do the two of you say to each other, when you're both in love with the same man? But I expect we thought all kinds of things. I know I did. Speculated what Anson thought of her, what he said to her. How often they had met, how often they had touched. Whether they had—in the heat of some moment, saving each other's lives, or else in the slow pulse of boredom—ever kissed. Whether any other impulse than friendship, than loyalty, than camaraderie had ignited Anson's breast when he gazed upon that shining wealth of hair, those elegant legs, that fashionable bosom.

I would rather have died than ask, of course. And though I had myself taken Anson's virginity the night before, still I seethed beside this woman, who had known him longer and better than I had. Had maybe even loved him more, for in the middle of March that passion I felt for Anson was still a revelation to me, a hand newly laid upon my heart. I recollect how the hours passed, mile after mile beneath the wheels of a Franklin two-seater borrowed from the Marshalls' own Southampton garage, too proud even to ask for a cigarette. Maybe she knew this; I don't know. I do recall how, sometime after we had passed through the Philadelphia suburbs, while the afternoon settled upon the rambling gray ribbon of the Lincoln Highway, she leaned her elbow on the doorframe and maneuvered the wheel with the first three fingers of her right hand, and into this slight lapse I asked her about how Anson got canned from the Bureau.

She wanted to know why I wanted to know.

Just curious, I told her.

She rubbed the side of her forehead with the thumb holding the cigarette and said something about how she saw it coming, how nobody as naïve as Marshall stood a chance in that place.

Naïve? I said.

"Naïve," she said. Nodding and smoking at the same time. "What's that saying about the innocent? How when you're innocent—or pure, that's it. To the pure, something like that—"

"You mean the Bible verse," I said. "Unto the pure, all things are pure."

"That's it," she said. Nodding her head.

I continued, "Unto the pure all things are pure, but unto them that are defiled and unbelieving is nothing pure, but even their mind and conscience is defiled."

"Exactly," she said.

"That's Titus," I told her. "Book one, verse fifteen."

She stubbed out her cigarette and tossed it through

the crack in the window. Asked how a girl like me got to know her Bible by heart.

So I told her about the nuns. How my mama sent me away to the convent for my education when I was but eight years old, and there I learned just about every verse in the Good Book, for one penance or another. Usually forgot them afterward, but for some reason, this particular number always stuck in my head. Told her I didn't know why. Just stuck, that's all.

I remember how Luella lit up another cigarette, striking the match with her right paw while she held the wheel in her left, and how her fingers shook a little as she performed this maneuver. Took her a couple tries to get the match to properly flame.

Once the cigarette was lit, she sucked on it for some time before she asked whether I realized this Titus fellow was talking about Jews. By defiled and un-believing, he meant Jews.

Lord Almighty, I said. I never thought of that. Maybe I was too young. Didn't meet a single Jew until I moved to New York.

Anyway, she said, collecting herself, Jews or no Jews, that was how those bastards got Marshall. Because he never saw it coming. Never believed that a fellow he trusted might betray him.

# 17

Well, maybe Luella's right. Maybe Anson's too virtuous for this line of work. Maybe he can't see a double cross coming, maybe he doesn't spot a snitch until she saunters across the street and socks him in the kisser.

Whereas I—defiled and unbelieving as I am—never did trust the bitch.

Because you know what that nice young fellow Dickens tells me, don't you?

He tells me some tall, skinny dame with hair the color of moonshine hung about the fishing fleet just this morning, break of dawn, quizzing the whereabouts of a United States Coast Guard vessel. Last he heard, she'd hired the fastest speedboat in Halifax Harbor and roared off by herself to the east-southeast.

# 18

Charles Schuyler catches up with me as I'm running down the dock toward the Ambrosia's tender. Just how I intend to get the boat running without his help, I don't know. Guess I might find a way, like I always do. Anyway, he grabs my arm and demands—in that upwind high society voice of his—what the devil's going on.

I wriggle free and tell him it's none of his beeswax, that's what.

"Not my business that you go bolting out the door without a word?"

I work my fingers at the knot holding our mooring in place. "You had plenty of business of your own, I thought."

"What's that supposed to mean?"

"Saw you gabbing on the telephone. Were you trying to reach Luella? Figure out how to get to Anson before I did?"

"Of course not! My God!"

"Or maybe someone else, someone I don't know about." The knot won't give. Some kind of maritime configuration, like they teach to fishermen and yachtsmen but not to us no-good floozies from the mountains. I start to swear at the rope, at my fingers that can't budge it.

"Look, I don't know what you're accusing me of, but—oh, for God's sake. Let me." He nudges me aside and digs his fingers into the knot, which commences immediately to part. "I was on the telephone to a friend of mine, a Navy fellow. Thought he might be able to help us."

"Sure you were. And I'm the Queen of Sheba." I climb in the boat, lurching my way up to the wheel. Look for the ignition switch to start the motor.

"If you think for one minute—"

"I don't have a minute to think about it! All I got is my gut, Schuyler, and it's screaming at me."

"Screaming what?"

The rope falls free, and still no motor. I start to press buttons, any buttons. Boat makes a lurch as Schuyler climbs aboard, and I cry out something foul, something to shock him. And maybe he's shocked, maybe he flinches, but he keeps on coming, moving his sea legs like a man who was practically breeched on board some boat or another. He reaches me. Sticks one hand on my shoulder. Offers something in his palm, which turns out to be a key.

"Even so," he says, "you'll need this."

# 19

Under way, I clam up. No point letting him know what I know; all I have left is surprise. Not even that. Already knows I'm onto him, doesn't he? I let the engine do all the speaking, the engine and the loud salt wind, the spitting sea. Just stand there, clenching the edge of the wooden side with one hand.

Fingering the butt end of my pistol with the other.

Inside my head, I form plans and discard them at a manic pace. Fly back across the water to the Ambrosia, I think, and then what? Luella went off to the east-southeast in her motorboat. Must have known where she was going, right? Must have known what she was going to find there. Dickens said she was pointed toward the sea lanes between Saint Pierre and Boston, a route well-known to the Halifax fleet: thick with rum smugglers and rum pirates and United States Coast Guard vessels seeking to catch them both. No, Dickens hadn't heard of any particular Coast Guard vessel on patrol during the last day or two, but the sight was too common to remark on anymore, wasn't it?

Still, a motorboat. You can't go too far from shore in a regular motorboat, not unless you mean to hitch your wagon to a star of some kind, a nice big ship belonging to somebody else, Coast Guard or pirate or smuggler.

Moreover. If she left sometime this morning—Dickens didn't know exactly when—and flew toward her destination inside Halifax's fastest speedboat, she must have arrived there some time ago, wherever it was. So maybe I shouldn't be wondering where Luella had gone in her motorboat.

Should be wondering where she'd gone once she got there.

East toward Newfoundland? Or west toward home?

I turn to the man beside me and speak loud, above the engine and the wind. "How do you know Luella Kingston?"

"Who?"

"Luella Kingston!"

"Kingston? Don't know her."

"Sure you do. Tall good-looking dame, bleaches her hair, legs all the way to China. Used to work with Anson—with Marshall—in the Bureau, before he got canned that first time. You know the broad I mean."

Schuyler's lost his cap somewhere, maybe chasing me down the Halifax wharves, and the wind kicks up his hair. Looks like he was a blond himself before he got hit by a bucket of silver, only much darker than Luella. Golden or strawberry, hard to tell. Still thick, though. Thick and straight, tufts beautifully in the draft, like a photo of a yachtsman on the cover of one of those high-society magazines. Why, for all I know, he was that yachtsman.

"You must mean Bronfman," he says. "Luella Bronfman."

"Oh, is that what she calls herself? Woman's got more names than the king of England."

"Is that what this is about? Luella Bronfman?"

"You tell me!"

The motorboat hits some chop, and I grab hold of the seat behind me, an instant before the boat's movements send me crashing into it. Schuyler keeps his legs beneath him, of course. He's used to this.

"She's acquainted with a friend of mine, that's all," he says.

"Which friend? You have to tell me!"

"Doesn't matter!"

The boat settles back to its rhythm. I lever up from the seat and help myself to a handful of Schuyler's shirt. "Doesn't matter? The hell it doesn't! She's out there right now, you bastard, she ran out of Halifax Harbor this morning in a speedboat headed east, and you say it doesn't matter whose side she's on?"

"Christ," he says.

I pull Anson's pistol out of the pocket of my jacket. "I think you better tell me right now—right now— what's going on, Schuyler. Because if that man dies, if a single hair on his head gets clipped a single fraction of an inch, I swear to God I will spend the rest of my born days hunting down each and every—"

"Put that gun down," he says coldly, and I realize

he's not even looking at me. One hand still on the wheel, face turned to the left, skin pale beneath the ruddiness of ocean travel.

I follow his gaze, and at first I don't see anything. Just a strange shape between us and the horizon, an irregular, unexpected object that can't be a ship. I squint. Drop the shirt. Scrabble for the binoculars, and as the object comes into focus, I realize it's two ships. A slim, thoroughbred yacht, sailing so near to a dark-sided schooner they might as well be attached.

"The Ambrosia?" I gasp.

Schuyler tightens up on the wheel and reaches for the throttle.

"Listen to me," he says, while the engine roars into frenzy and the tender tilts its nose to the sky. "If you want to know whose side I'm on, it's yours."

"Mine?"

"Yours. That's all."

# 20

He doesn't say another word, and neither do I. Maybe it's the last word I ever hear from him;

who knows? We send out a long, agitated wake behind us, curving toward the two silent ships. The spray coats my sou'wester and finds the cracks at my collar and sleeves, my everywhere, until I'm as wet inside as out, and I hardly notice, I never care. The sting of salt on my skin might be nerves. The numbness of my face and fingers might be terror.

The ships grow larger. Dark sides grow blacker against the water. Late afternoon sun catches the sails, which are mostly furled tight against the yardarms, turning them gold instead of white.

I lift the binoculars and examine the decks, first of the Ambrosia and then the schooner, and I think maybe I see some small movement near the schooner's stern. Or maybe not. Maybe it's just my hand, shaking a little under the weight of the glass. And I think, this isn't real. This feels less real than a dream, like I have already done this thing, lived this scene, and now I'm just remembering it.

The Ambrosia seems to be fixed to the schooner by ropes, two or three of them, hooked to the railing of the larger ship. Schuyler swings the tender alongside the yacht. I grip the pistol and launch myself toward the Ambrosia's deck. Behind me, Schuyler shouts something, some note of caution I reckon, but I just scramble upward without paying him any heed, using my legs and my free hand to lever myself aboard, and when I have accomplished this I scream Marshall's name, scream Julie's name, run across the deck to the other side where the ropes stretch upward to the schooner's railing.

There is no answering shout, no reply of any kind. Maybe I can't hear anything, maybe this strange buzz in my ears prevents all noise from penetrating. I reach the ropes and start to climb. Ambrosia's a large yacht, I guess, large enough to possess a motor tender, and there's maybe five feet of vertical distance between her main deck and the main deck of the schooner. Still I feel I am climbing the air itself, near enough soaring up and over those dark sides, until I land oomph on the wooden boards of the schooner's deck, not like my dream at all, not tidy and well-tended and empty but crammed tight with dead men and overturned crates, wet with blood.

I scream and crawl to the nearest one and turn him over. His face has been peeled away as if by a paring knife, except sized for men instead of potatoes, and his bleeding eye sockets stare sightless back at me.

I don't hear myself scream, but I guess I must. I start to crawl from man to man, and each one is the same, unrecognizable, might be anybody, flesh still warm. Maybe ten men. Maybe a dozen. I don't count.

Near the stern I come to a woman. Lies face down on the wood, golden hair spread about her head. I dare to touch her. Turn her over, and her face is immaculate, except for a bruise rising beneath one eye. Julie's face. She opens her mouth a little and lets out this tiny groan, as if to say I'm alive, you damn fool, and I turn my head and shout something over my shoulder, something like I've found your sister, get your sister, and I set Julie's head carefully down and keep crawling. I don't know why. You don't think logical at a moment like this. You just crawl and crawl until you find what you're looking for, and then you find it. A face you know, still intact, hair and skin all covered with blood. You reach out and touch its hand. Somewhere distant, you hear somebody shouting, but you don't care about that anymore, you don't care about anything. You mutter something over and over, and you hardly notice when somebody takes you by the shoulder, whisks a knife in the direction of your throat, some fellow with dark hair and a bloodied face. You reach for the pistol in your pocket and start to lift it, but before you can stick your thumb on the safety catch, a boom fills your ears, more like a cannon than a gun, and the man sags away.

You stagger. You turn to find the noise, and there is a ghost, can't be Anson, can't be actually Anson, blazing in the late afternoon sun, gun to his hand. Next to him stands a dirty, long-legged dame, hair almost white, face stretched in horror. Staring not at your face, but your arm.

You follow her gaze to a waterfall of your own red blood.

You start to fall, and somebody catches you. Familiar saltpeter smell of gunsmoke.

## Southampton, New York, April 1998

She woke up in a bed of some kind. The room around her was white and harsh and warm, and she couldn't move anything except her eyelids. Maybe her lips. She started to gag.

"Nurse! Quick! She's waking up, she's choking!"

I'm not choking, she thought. I'm just barfing. She tried to say this out loud, but her throat was too sore.

There was a steel bowl underneath her chin, and she barfed obediently, though nothing much came out. Just her throat burned. Someone was saying her name in a soothing, male voice, and she recognized this voice as Patrick's.

She moved her head so fast, she caught her hair in the IV line. "What the hell are you doing here?"

"Hold on, Ella! Hold still."

His fingers picked at her hair, untangling the line. She stared at the small puddle of yellow bile in the stainless steel bowl and raged. You should be Hector, she thought. You should be Mumma or Daddy or Granny or Stefan or Joanie or Charlie or Aunt Viv or anybody, anybody but you.

"There you go," Patrick said. He set her tenderly back in the pillows. He was wearing the same thing as he had the last time she saw him—same cashmere sweater, same button-down shirt beneath, same bruises underneath his eyes—and his hair stuck in several different directions. He smiled at her. "You're looking better already."

"Where am I?"

"Southampton Hospital. You passed out on the train platform. Dehydration, the doc says, brought on by a possible case of hyperemesis gravidarum."

"By what?"

"It's an extreme form of morning sickness. The good news is, it means the pregnancy's going well." He beamed. "Before you ask, the baby's fine. They did an ultrasound. I listened to the heartbeat, honey, it was amazing. It was magic. I was shaking like a leaf. Our baby."

"Heartbeat? What—I'm, like, barely even six weeks along."

"Well, guess what? There's a heartbeat." Patrick squeezed her hand; she hadn't realized he was holding it. "I wish you'd heard. They gave you a sedative in the ambulance. You were thrashing around and they couldn't get an IV line in."

"Oh my God." Ella closed her eyes. "I don't remember anything."

"They were afraid you'd hit your head or something on the train platform, but nothing showed up on the MRI, so—"

"The MRI? How long have I been out?"

Patrick looked at his watch. "It's almost midnight. I jumped in the car as soon as I got the call."

"But—an ambulance? I was in an ambulance?"

"Some Samaritan called 911. You were lucky, babe, really lucky. You need to take it easy. They've given you some doxylamine—don't worry, it's not like the stuff they used to give, back in the day, the one that caused all the birth defects—"

"Thalidomide," Ella whispered.

"Is it helping?"

"Sort of. Not really." She blinked her eyes. "A little, maybe."

"Well, they want to keep you here another twenty-four hours for observation, fill you up with fluids and nutrients, and then I'm taking you home."

"Home?"

Patrick leaned his elbows on the bed rail and bent to kiss her forehead. "Home, honey. You need someone to take care of you for the next six weeks or so—"

"Six weeks?"

"Until this thing passes. Since I am currently unemployed and have an awesome, well-equipped apartment at my disposal, I nominated myself. You know, the father of the baby?" Patrick grinned. "Now hold on. I'm going to get your mom and dad and let them know you're awake."

"Mumma's here?"

"In the waiting room." He braced himself on the bed rail and rose. Smoothed back her hair and kissed her forehead again. "You look beautiful, you know that? Even inside an ass-ugly hospital gown."

**Mumma was** affronted. "I don't understand," she said. "I never had morning sickness."

"Because you're perfect, Mumma."

"That's not quite true, Pepper," Daddy said. "There was that business with the toothpaste."

"It made me queasy, but I didn't vomit," she said, as if vomiting were a sign of weakness. She looked at Ella, and her face softened. "But everyone's different, I suppose. Poor Vivian felt awful, remember? She was very brave to have four, I think. Anyway, your uncle Paul's driving down as soon as he's done with some surgery he's on. He'll set these doctors straight, I'm sure."

"Mumma, he's a pediatric surgeon. I don't think he's going to be that knowledgeable about pregnancy."

"Why not? He went through three of them with Vivian, including the twins, and God knows . . ." Mumma shook her head, which sent a shiver down her lustrous blond ponytail and made her blue eyes catch white from the fluorescent light. Only Mumma could look that good in the middle of the night, having caught the last flight out from National airport, because only Mumma had the kind of bones and skin that deserved a special display in the Smithsonian or someplace, the Museum of Natural History, some diorama of the siege of Troy with Helen glowing in the middle. Here is Beauty. Ella used to gaze at her own face in the mirror and wonder where it had all gone wrong, why she didn't have those cheekbones and that shining hair, why you could see the resemblance but the chemistry, the finish wasn't right, and Ella had ended up just kind of pretty, not bad. Patrick called her beautiful, but Patrick probably told his hookers they were beautiful. "God knows," Mumma was saying, with her lips that needed no lipstick, "any man would be an expert, after spending nine months with Vivian when she's got a bat in her cave. God, remember those mackerel sandwiches she used to have him make her?"

Ella groaned.

"Enough of that," said Daddy. "Ella needs her rest, more than anything. Let's head back to the hotel. Patrick?"

Patrick was standing out this exchange at the side of the room, arms crossed, looking respectful and faintly bored. He raised his head at the sound of his name. "Yes, sir?"

"Let's give Ella a little peace and quiet, all right?"

"If you don't mind, sir, I was just going to sleep in the chair over there."

"As a matter of fact, I do mind. Ella's too polite to say it, but I have the feeling you're the last person in the world she wants inside this room with her."

"Sir—"

"He's right," Ella said. She stared at her parents, one on each side of Patrick, and she thought, I don't know these people. Patrick who is not my husband. Daddy who is not my father. Mumma who was in love with another man, who made me with someone else. The three of them, looking at me with the same eyes, the same faces, and I don't know who they are. She said again, "Daddy's right. I need some peace and quiet. I've got a lot to think over."

"Like what?" Patrick said. "What have you got to think over?"

Mumma walked over to Patrick and put her arm around his shoulders. "Come along, Patrick. We'll give you a ride to the hotel."

"But—"

"Patrick, darling." Mumma gave him a squeeze and spoke sweetly. "Now."

**Uncle Paul** showed up in his scrubs at half past six o'clock, bearing a shadow of stubble over his chin and Aunt Viv at his side. He was impossibly cheerful. He studied Ella's charts and said her urine was looking great, she should be going home soon.

"Wow," Ella said. "Doctors give the best compliments. Your pee is awesome, honey."

Aunt Viv rolled her eyes and kissed Ella's forehead, right where Patrick had kissed her earlier. "He was exactly the same when I was crouched over the toilet with the twins. Not an ounce of sympathy."

"Did the surgery go well tonight?" Ella asked. She always hated to think of all the children who came under Uncle Paul's scalpel, all those anxious parents desperate for him to save some precious life. When she was little, she used to stare at his hands and imagine what they had done that day, what miracles they'd performed. Or failed to perform. Ella had spent a week in their apartment after leaving Patrick, so she knew that his cheerfulness was sometimes absent. Only Aunt Viv knew how to deal with him then. He'd walk in the door, and she'd know everything in an instant, just by the way he looked at her. Put down whatever she was doing, whatever conversation, even midsentence, and take him into the study or the bedroom, and sometimes Ella heard them talking and sometimes not.

"Very well," Uncle Paul said now, smiling, and Ella wanted to take this as an auspicious omen, but she was too deflated, and anyway there was a forced quality to his smile, to Aunt Viv's smile, and she knew what they were thinking. Uh-oh. Ella's up the stick without a husband. "And this little fellow looks like he's doing all right," added Uncle Paul, flipping a few more pages.

"Who?"

He pointed his pen to her belly. "That one in there."

"It's a he? You can tell?"

Paul laughed. "Not yet. He or she. The heart rate's normal, looks about six weeks' gestation by the size. Am I right?"

"I guess so. I wasn't exactly counting."

"Of course not." He sat on the edge of the bed. "Anything you want to talk about? I am a medical professional, you know."

Ella glanced at Aunt Viv, who looked like Mumma only not quite so perfectly beautiful, just merrier. Not today, though. Her face was heavy, her eyes narrow with concern. So much love inside Aunt Viv, so much loyalty. "Not really," she said. "Still trying to get my head around it. Maybe we could talk later?"

He patted her leg. "Whenever you like. What I really want to do right now is track down that Samaritan who found you at the train station and shake his hand."

"Yes," said Aunt Viv, "thank God for that."

**Ella tried** to sleep, but people kept coming into the room. The doctor, the nurses, the orderly with the breakfast tray. She was on a special bland diet, and she managed to swallow some plain oatmeal and white toast. A slice of pear. The electrolyte water in the plastic bottle. When she didn't throw it right back up, the nurse unhooked the IV and said they would see about her discharge papers.

Then Patrick and her parents came in, and Ella knew at once that some discussion had passed between them. Patrick's face glowed with some kind of victory, while Daddy and Mumma looked wan and weary. Patrick always could close a deal. Not even a pair of lawyers could withstand him.

"Look," Mumma said, cool fingers against her cheek, "if you want to come with us back to Virginia, or else we could get a rental in the city. I hate to ask Vivian—"

"No, don't. They've done enough already. It's okay. I'll figure something out."

"You're really going back to him?"

"I'm not going back to him. I'll spend the night there, maybe, just because I can't go back to my apartment like this . . ."

"Well, what about Hector?" said Daddy. "Can't Hector give you a hand?"

Patrick was in the back of the room, speaking with the nurse. He looked up. "Hector? Who's Hector?"

There was an electric pause. Mumma's eyes widened. Daddy looked like he had just bitten off his own tongue. Patrick . . . Ella couldn't look at Patrick.

"What the hell?" Patrick said. "Who's Hector?"

Ella stared at her father. "He's the handyman at my new apartment. He's a friend of mine."

"A friend, huh? Is this the guy you were bragging about last week? The one who wanted to get in your pants? Hector?" He snapped his fingers. "Wait a minute. Yesterday morning, over coffee. Hector, right?"

"Yes," Ella said.

Patrick turned to Daddy. "What the hell is going on here? Is she sleeping with this guy?"

"Either way, young man, I don't think that's any of your business," Daddy said quietly, in his lawyer's voice. "Not anymore."

"Well, I can tell you, she's not going home to him. That's for sure. She's sick. She's not going back to some shitty apartment and some horny asshole who—"

"That's enough." The nurse spoke sharply. "I won't have that kind of talk in here."

"She can't go home with him!"

"She's not going home with him."

"I'm her husband. She's pregnant. She's carrying my baby, she comes home with me."

Ella said, "I don't need to go home with anybody. I'm a grown woman."

"Oh yes, you do," said Patrick. "They can't discharge you without a caretaker, a family member, and that's me. I'm your next of kin."

"Wait, seriously?"

"That's not quite—" began Daddy.

"Everybody leave," said the nurse. "Now."

---

**The nurse** was from Jamaica—the Caribbean island, not the neighborhood in Queens—and she wasn't taking any guff, not even Patrick's. Especially not Patrick's. Earlier, when she was changing Ella's IV, she told her she'd moved to Long Island with her parents and her brothers and aunties when she was thirteen, and her island accent was so faint it was more of a lilt. She had beautiful cheekbones and light brown eyes, and her name was Campbell. Nurse Campbell.

"That is some family you have there, Mrs. Gilbert," she said, shaking her head, stretching out the word some to its most expressive length.

"Yeah, you should see them at Christmas. So what's the story? Am I free to go?"

"Not so fast, young lady. The doctor's going to be coming through after lunch. He'll be the one signing your discharge papers, so you had better behave yourself."

"And then? If I pass?"

"Then you'll be on your way home with a bottle of pills and a lot of pages telling you how to take care of yourself. I don't want to see you coming through my ward again."

"I won't."

"You rest and take your pills and keep yourself hydrated. Find somebody to take some care of you. It's okay, you know, to let someone else take care of you, when you're having a baby and as sick as you are. Young ladies these days, they want to be so independent. You let someone else do the caring for now, okay?"

"I'll try."

"Now, to answer your question," Nurse Campbell continued, wrapping the blood pressure thing around Ella's arm, "it is yes. Given your condition, you must be discharged into the care of a responsible family member."

"My husband?"

"That's your choice," said Nurse Campbell, in a tone that made Ella think that Patrick wouldn't be her choice, for sure.

Ella hated having her blood pressure taken, absolutely hated anyone measuring her pulse or anything like that. She looked the other way while the nurse pumped away and the vise tightened around her upper arm, until she could feel the queer, hard blip of her heartbeat in her artery, a sensation that always made her nervous. What if something was wrong with that blip? On the ledge she saw her personal effects: her pocketbook, the Bloomingdale's bag with the photographic plates inside. Thank God. She'd forgotten all about those; at least someone remembered to gather them up and put them in the ambulance with her, while she was out.

"Hmm," said Nurse Campbell, unwrapping the band.

"Everything okay?"

"Everything okay."

"Can I ask you a favor? Can you pass me my pocketbook from the ledge over there?"

The nurse handed her the pocketbook, and Ella hunted inside for her cell phone. The battery was dead, of course. The charger was back in Hector's apartment.

"You better not be thinking of turning that thing on in here," said Nurse Campbell.

Ella looked up. The nurse hummed to herself, looking wise. "Of course not." She held up the phone. "Battery's dead."

"They are the instruments of the devil. People gabbing away all the time now, while the world goes by." Nurse Campbell made a movement with her hand, like a wave. "People need to slow down. They need to sit down and talk to each other, you know? Face-to-face."

Ella slipped her phone back into her pocketbook and snapped the fastening shut. "Can you tell me something? Has anyone left a message for me or any-thing?"

"You mean like this Hector fellow?"

Ella blushed. "Anyone."

"Ah, I see that color on your cheeks. Mmm-mmm." Nurse Campbell shook her head, but not in a way that signified disapproval. More like sympathy. "You got yourself in a bit of a fix, haven't you, Mrs. Gilbert? Out of the frying pan . . ."

"A fix. That's what my grandmother called it."

"I see his kind before." Nurse Campbell nodded at the door, where Patrick had left a few minutes ago, casting Ella the kind of look that said he'd be back. Her accent was picking up a little strength. "I always feel a little sorry for the wives, you know? A man like that, he like to have his own way. Sweet as molasses when he get what he want, but when he don't? Mmm-mmm," she said again, shaking her head. "Now, that man who brought you in—"

"What? Who?"

"That nice man who came in the ambulance, hold-ing your hand."

"What man? Oh my God. What man?"

"All the nurses in the ER, they were talking about him, oh my. A handsome devil. Thick, dark hair, nice figure. Skin like he just step off the beach. He was the one who found you on the train platform, called the ambulance for you. Rode all the way to the hospital. Called your daddy."

"Where did he go?"

"Why, he left, madam. As soon as your daddy came, and your husband. He slip away in the dark." Nurse Campbell made another motion of her hand, a flutter of her long, capable fingers.

"What was his name?" Ella whispered. "You have to tell me his name."

"Ah, now. I don't think I can tell you his name, madam. But I might just have a little something in my pocket right here, something he give the nurse for you." Nurse Campbell reached into the pocket of her smock and drew out a piece of folded paper. "Now remember. If anybody ask, I don't know anything about it. Not a thing."

**After lunch,** the doctor came. Examined Ella, asked her questions—how was she feeling, any vomiting—and exchanged a few words with Uncle Paul, who was on his way back to the city with Aunt Viv. Conferred with the nurse, who said that Ella had been drinking her electrolyte water and hadn't vomited since the morning. Ella sat upright in the bed while they talked in their low voices. Her nerves drummed. In the pocketbook tucked beside her, the folded paper seemed to leech heat into her leg.

"All right," said the doctor, and he signed her discharge papers and handed them back to the nurse with a prescription for pyridoxine, which he told Ella to fill at the hospital pharmacy before she left.

"Okay, now," said Nurse Campbell. "I'm going to get your paperwork ready. You get yourself dressed, okay? And maybe I will tell that husband of yours to fill this prescription for you, down at the hospital pharmacy. Mind you, Mrs. Gilbert, they are sometimes pretty slow down there. And if I call down and say to them that a certain order is not urgent, they will maybe take their time, you know?"

Ella got up and went to the bathroom. Changed back into yesterday's clothes; nobody had thought to bring her any fresh ones. Brushed her teeth and her hair with the toiletries Aunt Viv had brought her from the gift shop. Gathered her things and picked up the telephone receiver on the bedside table.

"Daddy?" she said, when her father picked up. "I need a favor."

# Finale
## (alive, alive oh)

**Halifax, Nova Scotia**
**May 1924**

# 1

I am no good invalid.

Anson does his best to spoon broth into my mouth and that kind of thing, but after seven days in bed, I don't care who you are, you commence to become frisky, as I call it. (I'm sure Anson has another word, but he's too polite to say so.)

Anyway, when he's gone seeing about the steamship tickets, I rise and walk across the little room, as I do whenever he leaves it. Stride back and forth from one wall to another, a distance of maybe four steps. At first, I could only manage a few of them, but now that seven days have passed since that pirate—that's what he was, it turns out, a pirate left behind for dead during the hijacking of the schooner Perseus, laden with Canadian whiskey on its way to Rum Row—since that pirate, as I say, slashed for my throat and got the tender inside of my arm instead, I seem to have recovered enough blood to keep going for all of eleven and a half minutes before my head starts to get a little dizzy.

So I sit on the end of the bed, clad in a virtuous white nightgown and robe, staring out the window at Halifax Harbor, and I try not to think about anything. Try not to see anything except the delicate play of sailboats on the water, the tiny patches of white curling upon the surface, the gray steamship laboring into harbor's shelter. The skift of clouds before the noon sun. The sturdy brown wood of the window frame making a rectangle around it all.

# 2

Mr. Marshall is dead. I feel I should tell you that, before Anson walks in that door wearing his face of desolation and tells me to eat, to drink, to rest. Anson sleeps atop that cot in the corner. Hangs his feet over the edge. Makes the bed up again in flat, precise planes of sheet and blanket as soon as he rises, which is generally before the sun does. Goes out for a walk in the damp streets and returns an hour later to bring me breakfast. I imagine he thinks I don't know all this, but I do. As soon as he eases the door shut, I crawl out of bed and look out the window. Watch him step out of the house and pass beneath a streetlamp, hands in pockets, staring directly ahead. Wait there leaning upon the sill until he saunters back, and then I crawl back into bed and pretend I was sleeping all along.

According to Julie, they were tacking east about an hour after we parted company when they spotted the schooner. The pirates had grappled on the port side and were loading crates of booze, barrels of it, hundreds of thousands of liquid dollars. There was a call of distress. Julie said to wait; Marshall insisted on boarding because he was certain Anson was aboard. Well, Anson wasn't aboard, but the pirates made short work of Marshall anyway, not having the time to tenderly strip away his face like they had the crew, and he lay dead on the deck until I found him.

Julie fared better. She always does. Only a bump on the noggin for our Julie, because she did as Marshall told her and hid inside the Ambrosia until somebody found her and drug her upside and . . . well, that's just details, isn't it? Don't worry, Julie's just fine. Not violated, if that's what you're wondering. I guess they didn't have time to mix pleasure with business. She returned to Long Island in the Ambrosia with her brother and awful news, just as soon as the city of Halifax released the body to them.

So it's just the two of us left here in Canada, me and Anson, waiting for my depleted veins to gather strength enough to sail home. In fact, I can hear his quick, heavy footsteps on the stairs right now. Went to purchase tickets on a New York steamer, because the good doctor from the hospital—the one who stitched me up when they carried me in a week ago, a thing I don't properly remember, you understand, as I fainted for good soon after Anson had tied his shirt around my arm—anyway, that same doctor inspected me just this morning and pronounced me fit to travel. Coming along right strong, according to my mountain breeding.

Anson, however. Anson is not coming along strong, though he puts up a front for my sake. Anson knocks briefly and opens the door, and this time I don't bother to scramble back into bed. I rise and stand before him in my virtuous white nightgown, and he just stares at me with those anguished eyes of his and doesn't say a word. He's holding a tray. Tray contains tea and broth and egg and bread and some apple, cut in small pieces the way you cut food for invalids and small children.

"At last," I say, so cheerfully as I'm able. "I'm famished."

# 3

We eat. Anson reads aloud from the newspaper. Tells me he's booked us passage on the L'Oiseau two days hence. A single cabin, he says, looking away, blushing a little. The ship was nearly full. Summer season coming on.

I shake my head. "Then I guess we'll have to get married first," I say, tone of resignation, and that's the first time I've laughed since God knows, just looking at his face when I tell him this.

"You'll bust your stitches," he says.

"No, I won't."

"I can bunk in steerage. I'm sure there's room."

"The hell you're going to leave me alone in second class."

"First."

"Well, la-de-da."

He regards me as you regard someone who might be drunk. I regard him right back, until a muscle contracts at the leftmost corner of his mouth and breaks open a dam of joy inside my chest. I lift my hand and touch that merry corner with my thumb, and then the remainder of his mouth, sliding across the top lip and then the bottom lip like a typewriter carriage.

"I'm sorry," he says. "You were right. You were always right. I should have stayed with you in Florida."

"I was stupid. Can't beg you to become someone you're not."

"I spoke to Mama on the telephone. Terrible connection. She's moved the funeral to Thursday."

"So you can attend after all. That's good. How's Billy?"

He looks stricken. "I forgot to ask."

"Don't worry. If there was any news, she'd surely tell you."

Anson steps away and starts to clean up the tray.

"It wasn't for nothing," I say. "You caught those pirates. Luella—well, she came up trumps, I'm bound to admit, she found you in time. You caught the schooner, you have its papers. And now we know this was an inside job, we know we're just a step away from finding out—"

"No." He stacks the teacups on the tray. "You were right. I shouldn't have taken the bait and gone back to the Bureau. You were right about pretty much everything."

"Anson—"

He lifts the tray and heads for the door. "You should call me Ollie. Everyone else does."

# 4

When I lift my head sometime in the middle of the night, he sits naked on the end of the bed, facing the window, resting his elbows on his knees and his head in his hands.

I crawl from the blankets into the cool air. Slip my arms around his waist and rest my cheek on the nook where his neck meets his shoulder. Heat of his body shocks me.

Go back to sleep, he says.

I am so slight and small, resting against his coal-hot skin. Maybe half his weight. Maybe a little more, I don't know. Bastard redheaded child, bred up hard-scrabble, no family nor friends nor treasure to speak of. Mountain water runs through my veins. I have got just about nothing to give this man, no gift at all, no light nor hope, not the slightest glue to hold him together. Save one small promise.

No, I say.

He sighs beneath me. I ride it out like you ride upon a wave, floating atop the ocean by some Florida beach in another universe.

I slide my hands down his waist and place them upon his thighs, palms down. In his ear, I whisper something. I won't tell you what.

# 5

You might think he would resist, but he doesn't. Maybe there's no fight left in him; maybe the state of his soul is even worse than I thought. Maybe he was sitting naked on my bed for just this reason. He pauses only to ask me if I can stand this kind of thing, am I strong enough. I tell him I believe I am, so long as he takes on most of the labor.

Though he has not much experience in these matters, still Nature guides him well. Nature and his own imagination, maybe, for I reckon a fellow like him— quiet, vigorous, disciplined—might ponder much on the act of love, though he lies but alone in his bed, night after night. He kisses me for some time before he reaches for the hem of my nightgown. Then he kisses me more, not on my lips, while I indulge the luxury of lying passive for once, lying nearly still while Anson's mouth touches my throat, my arms, my breast, my stomach. Back upward to the tenderness behind each ear. He rises on his elbows. Slides right into me, and for a moment we rest there, not even breathing. In the lamplight, his eyes might be green. I tell him he smells like the ocean, the smell of brine and fresh air. He dips to kiss my mouth.

Commences to ride me vigorous, until we are both flushed red, each one desperate as the other. At last, the sweet burst of incandescence, leaving me warm and woozy. We remain joined as a single, strange beast while I drift to sleep, listening to the slow draft of his breath in my ear.

# 6

The steamship tickets are made out to a Mr. and Mrs. Oliver Marshall of New York City. I poke Mr. Oliver in the ribs. "So we're married after all."

He hardly stirs. Poor fellow, during the course of the past day and night he has fucked himself near enough into oblivion, the way some men discover oblivion in liquor. Seeking to atone for all those years of abstinence, I guess, while I lie back and reap the abundant fruit of his penitence. He summons just enough strength to open his eyes halfway and mutter, Married?

I wave the tickets across the bridge of his nose. "Mr. and Mrs. Oliver Marshall, it says."

Closes his eyes again and asks do I mind. So I settle myself down along the naked length of him, belly to belly, and draw the blankets close, for there remain but a few hours before we must rise.

I think not of that photograph of Mama and Duke, on the day of their wedding, but of something else. Some other world entirely. Warm sunlit house, man and woman smiling some secret at each other. The smell of the ocean.

"We'll go away," I tell him. "For good, this time. You and me and Patsy. Your mama and Marie, too, if they need. Find some corner of the world and never come back."

He doesn't reply, but in the hour before rising, when the window turns gray with the promise of dawn, he turns me over and pins me to earth, drawing my body back into rapture as quickly and easily as you might draw elixir from a bottle. When I cry out, he stops and asks me if I'm hurt, reopened the wound or something. No, dear fellow, nothing like that. Reassured, he finishes in a hurry, rolls us together on our sides, cradles me close, still buried deep, as if he does not mean ever to leave. His left arm crosses my chest, as heavy as an ingot, while his right palm rests against my belly. There is a looseness to his limbs that suggests he might be falling back asleep, but he isn't. His breath is too wakeful. The hour's too late.

Time to rise, I think. Time to rise and dress and face what remains. Grief and nightmare and mortal sickness. The innocent needfulness of kid sisters, who are left alone in this wicked world, their menfolk sacrificed to a constitutional amendment.

On the empty pillow before me lies the steamship ticket, curling at one end. Mr. and Mrs. Oliver Marshall of 11 Christopher Street, New York City. Stateroom 22.

## Greenwich Village, New York City, April 1998

He was playing the piano. Of course he was. Actually, he was composing something, probably something for the film he was scoring: the reason he spent last week in Los Angeles. Played a few bars, stopped, played them again. Stopped, played another few bars. There was no other sound in the building; it was only five o'clock in the afternoon. Hours yet before Hector could expect any accompaniment.

Ella walked up the steps on Daddy's arm. He insisted, even though she said she was feeling much better. That wasn't quite true; she was feeling better, but not much. Enough to climb stairs. Enough to keep down a little electrolyte water. Enough to swallow her pill and hold down the nausea. She let Daddy carry the

Bloomingdale's bag, but the pocketbook she slung over her arm. She had a little pride left.

"Are you sure?" Daddy said, as they passed her door at 4D.

"Yes. For one thing, I don't even know if the water's back on. The plumber was supposed to come . . ." She didn't finish the sentence. She didn't care about the plumber, and she didn't have enough energy to talk about things that didn't interest her. The familiar smell of the building filled her nose, the old wood and the new paint, the indefinable essence of home. Her spine began to tingle.

At the top of the stairs, she turned right and headed for the door. Apartment 5, no letter because there was no other apartment on this floor. Just Hector. The music stopped; the door opened before they reached it. Nellie shot through the gap between Hector's legs and flung herself at Ella, yipping and barking and whining. Ella bent and gathered up the soft, wriggling body. Buried her nose in the doggy smell of her. "Missed you, pup," she whispered, stroking Nellie's long, slippery ears.

"She missed you, too."

Hector's voice was rougher than she expected, pitched extraordinarily low. She set down Nellie and straightened on Daddy's arm. "How are you feeling?" Hector asked.

"Much better," she said, and this time she meant it. Sort of.

**Daddy kept** his coat on and stayed near the door. Just kind of cast his eyes around the apartment, the way the modern father awkwardly assesses the apartment of the man who is sleeping with his daughter. Hector helped Ella to a counter stool, even though she didn't really need help, and asked if he could get her something.

"Saltines," she said. "There's a box in the bottom cabinet, with the rice and stuff."

Daddy cleared his throat. "When you're finished, Hector, I'd like to have a word."

"Of course, Mr. Dommerich."

Hector found the saltines and put them out for Ella. Ran her a glass of water from the faucet. Kissed the top of her head as he passed her by, on the way to Daddy, who had stepped just outside the door. Ella could hear them talking on the landing, in low, quiet voices. Mostly Daddy. A few words from Hector. A short chuckle; she couldn't tell from whom. Nellie sat at the bottom of the stool and looked up with her face of anxiety. Ella dropped a casual cracker crumb and ate the rest. The pills were helping; she still felt unsettled, a little dizzy, but not as bad as before.

She took the note out of her pocketbook and read the words again.

*No more running. Please come home. H.*

The men walked back through the door, Hector stepping aside politely to let Daddy through first, and Daddy went up to her and kissed her cheek.

"We'll talk more later, all right? You let me know if you need anything. Mumma says you hired Willig, Williams & White to handle the divorce."

"Yep. Getting the petition ready as we speak."

"Good." He kissed her again, on the forehead. "You should talk to Mumma, when you're ready."

She took his hand and squeezed it. "Love you, Daddy."

Hector was still standing by the door. Daddy stopped and shook his hand. "That was some good music you were playing there, son. Keep it up."

"I will, sir." (Ella smiled at the sir.)

"And remember what I said. You have my number? Yes, of course you do. Good night. Take care of her. Make sure she keeps those fluids down."

Hector said something Ella couldn't hear, because he was turned to the door. Ella wondered how Hector had Daddy's number, and then she remembered what Nurse Campbell had said, about how Hector had been the one to call Daddy from the ER. Maybe they'd exchanged numbers, when Daddy came back from the diner without her. Made a pact of some kind. Daddy was an idealist, but he also knew when to cut a deal.

The door closed. Hector turned, and together they listened to Daddy's firm footfalls, down the landing and the stairs, until they disappeared into the ordinary voice of a Manhattan apartment building in late afternoon. The weather was warming, and Hector had opened the windows fronting the street. You could hear the cars whirring past, the faint shouts and laughter and sirens and horns that made up the city's everyday street music. The smell of fresh air and food, cooking in some restaurant nearby, prepping for the Saturday evening date trade.

"I guess I should thank you," Ella said.

"Thank me for what?"

"For peeling me off the train platform."

"I didn't peel you off. You were staring at that photograph and you started to fall over, and I caught you, just in time."

"Wait, you were there? Before I passed out?"

"Didn't you hear me?"

Ella thought back. She couldn't remember the scene clearly. Looking at the photograph and then—a voice of some kind—Ella, it's me, I'm here, it's okay.

"Maybe I did," she said.

Hector's hands were shoved in his pockets, his face uncertain. "Anyway, no need for thanks. I'm just glad—that's a dumb word—grateful, thankful, whatever. On my knees before God, I guess, that I got there in time to help. What were you thinking, Ella?"

"I didn't realize it was so bad. The dehydration—"

"No, I mean going out to the Hamptons. Running away."

"I wasn't running away. Aunt Julie called. She wanted to talk to me about something. And when your ninety-six-year-old aunt calls you up and says she has something important to give you . . ." Ella tried to smile.

"Was it something to do with that photograph you were holding?" Hector nodded at her pocketbook. "The Redhead?"

"You've heard of her?"

"Yes." He pulled his right hand out of his pocket and rubbed his forehead. "I know her pretty well."

"Really? You know she lived here and everything?"

Hector pushed himself off the door and walked toward her. Pulled up the stool next to her and swung onto it. Took her hands, the way he had on Saturday night, just before he made love to her for the first time. An age ago. When it was all so simple. Just a matter of falling in love and falling into bed. "Yes," he said. "I know all that."

"Seriously? You know? Why didn't you tell me Saturday night? When I asked you about the building and everything?"

"You didn't ask me about her. I didn't know you knew."

"And you weren't going to volunteer the information?"

"Ella, I can't read your mind. If I knew you had an interest in Gin Kelly . . ."

"Of course I do! Didn't she live in this building?"

"She did," Hector said. "In fact, she owned the building. She was the one who deeded it to my grandfather."

"Bruno? The musician?"

"Yep."

"And what else?"

"What else? I don't know. He had stories about her. She was a real spark plug, my dad said. Pretty much as you might guess from the Redhead photographs."

"But what happened to her?"

Hector frowned. "What do you mean?"

"I mean, she apparently sort of disappeared, around 1930 or something. Do you know where she went?"

"I don't know. Maybe Dad said something. I can't remember. Why do you care?"

"I don't know," she said. "I just do. When I look at her, I feel this weird connection, like she's trying to tell me something. Like today, at the train station . . ."

The sentence trailed away, because that hadn't been the Redhead's voice, speaking to her in that moment, had it? It had been Hector's.

"Hey," he said. "Everything okay?"

"Yeah. Just tired."

"Okay. Hold tight a second, all right? I have something for you."

He kissed her hands and dropped them and went over to the piano, where he picked up a small, black enamel box that was resting on the case.

"My buttons!" Ella rose from the stool and hurried after him.

"Found them when I was ripping up the rest of your kitchen today. Box was wedged behind one of the cabinets."

"That's so weird. I left it on the kitchen counter."

"Maybe the plumber knocked it back?"

Ella took the box from his hand and lifted the lid. The buttons nestled inside, the ones she'd found underneath a loose floorboard in her apartment, when she and Hector were taking out the soiled carpeting. She touched one, and a slight buzz communicated through the skin of her fingertip. Not painful or anything. More like hello. She looked up at Hector, whose face was soft in the early April light that coursed through the nearby windows. "Thank you," she said.

"Any time."

"When I'm feeling better . . ." she began, and stopped. A breeze crept in under the window sash and swirled around her arms and neck. Hector stood about a foot away, one hand resting on the piano, the other hanging by his side. He wore his usual uniform, the one he wore when he was making music: soft gray T-shirt, soft blue jeans. Barefoot. She always thought of him like an animal, some kind of wolfhound, not fully domesticated, but maybe she was wrong. Maybe he was just a guy, a musician who also built cabinets, pretty good in the sack, and all the rest was her imagination. Was just Ella getting away from Patrick and crowning some guy in her apartment building with all kinds of virtues he didn't really possess.

And she was pregnant. Needing a mate. That clouded your judgment, for sure.

"It's not fair," she said. "It's not fair, what I'm doing to you."

"What do you mean, what you're doing to me?"

"This. You deserve better than this. It's so complicated."

"Jesus, Gilbert. I'm a musician. Complicated is what I do. How boring would it be, if you were just some girl who showed up with no baggage?"

Ella started to laugh. "Oh, I've got baggage, all right. I've given you more baggage in one week—"

"Come here," he said, but in one word: C'mere. He sat down on the piano bench, straddling it sideways, and pulled her down before him, so her back was nestled against his chest. He bent down and kissed her neck. Put his warm hands around her waist to rest against her complicated middle. "So. What are you going to do, Gilbert? What's the plan?"

"The plan. I don't know the plan. The plan seems to have veered off course. You were the rebound who might be the real thing. Now there's two of me, and I have a big decision to make."

"So what are your thoughts?"

"My thoughts. Well. I was thinking about something, during the drive today. Something my dad said to me. And my grandfather. There was all this drama, apparently, stuff I never knew about, and they just dealt with it, and maybe I should just deal with it, too. Deal with the messiness. Life is never perfect, right? And what if . . ."

"What if what?"

Ella allowed her hands to fall on Hector's legs, just above the knees, and leaned back against his chest. "So then, there's another thing. We were trying for a baby for a while, Patrick and I. We tried for a year, actually, and nothing happened. Like, every month, disappointment. So what if this pregnancy is a total fluke? What if this is the only chance I ever get? What if—you know—what if this baby is the only baby I ever have?"

"Or maybe it was him," Hector said. "Patrick. Maybe he was the one who got lucky here."

"Well, we don't know for sure, do we? Either way. I mean, a baby's forever, but so is termination. By definition. You can't take it back. You can't say, ten years later, I want that baby back, can I have it back, please? And what if I'm aborting Einstein?"

"Probably not," he said. "But you never know."

"Not that it matters, I guess. All equal in the eyes of God and all that. But okay. Those are my thoughts, in summary. So enough about me. What do you think?"

"Ella." He lifted one hand and stroked the hair at her temple. "Don't listen to me. You need to make this decision without giving a damn what I think."

"Okay. If I were your girlfriend, what would you want me to do?"

"Ella, maybe I'm getting ahead of myself here, but I sort of do consider you my girlfriend. For lack of a better word."

"You know what I mean. If this were your baby, I mean."

"Well," he said, very slowly, "here's the deal, Ella. See, I'm in love with you. The way I see it, if you're having a baby, I'm having a baby. The sperm donation aspect of the case is not material to me at all. I'm with you. We do this together. With a side helping of your ex-husband that makes my head hurt to think about, but that's—what did you call it? The messiness of life. File under Stuff You Have to Suck Up and Deal With. So, yes. It's your call. And I'm not saying that you're the kind of girl who would end a pregnancy just because her new boyfriend isn't up for fatherhood. But if you were, which you're not, you'd be wrong to think that. I'm up for this if you are. I'm ready to—I'm ready to—" His voice went rough. His right hand returned to her waist, joining his left, and his head bent back down to her neck. "Ready for whatever you want to throw at me."

"Okay," she said. "Okay."

"I was awake all last night, thinking about all the fucking bourbon I fed you, the wine. I swear, Ella, if anything's wrong—"

"The doctor said not to stress about it. It wasn't actually that much. I mean, it happens. I just never in the world imagined . . ."

"I poured it all out. Every bottle, every drop. I was cussing like a sailor. You should have heard me."

"You didn't! All of it?"

"Every drop. I was so pissed at myself, I kind of lost it."

"Hector, you fool. That was some seriously expensive booze."

His arms went tight around her. She gripped his forearms, his elbows, the tendons of him, so taut and anxious. Nellie padded over and sat in front of her, looking puzzled.

"I am a fool for you, Ella," he said. "That's all."

"Yes, you are. You are such a fool."

The faint note of a clarinet wound its way through the window. Hector's arms went stiff. His lips stilled against the soft skin beneath her ear. "Wow. Kind of early for that stuff, isn't it?"

A trumpet joined the clarinet, and then a double bass. Hector said, Whoa, and loosened his grip around Ella, reached with his left hand for the piano keyboard while his right arm remained around her waist. He started to pick out a tune, matching the music that came through the window, through the floorboards, the walls, from no particular source. Just there. In the room around them. "Grandpa approves, I guess," he said.

"That's not Bruno? The bass player?"

"Dunno for sure. But he did play bass down there."

Ella was too tired to play along. Too tired and too woozy. She leaned her head against the hollow of his shoulder, closed her eyes, and listened. Could hear his heartbeat through the thin cotton of the T-shirt, like some kind of percussion underneath the music itself.

"What did my father say to you? In the hallway?"

"Dad stuff. Along the usual lines of, Hurt one hair on her head and I'll slice your balls off."

Ella opened her eyes and started to laugh. "Oh God. I'm so sorry. What did you tell him?"

"Me? I said that if I ever hurt you, I'd hand him the knife myself."

"Oh."

"He also warned me that the ex–Mr. Ella might be a problem. Apparently he's the jealous type, which I find kind of ironic, under the circumstances."

"I am such a pain in the neck. The complications never end."

"Eh, don't worry about him. I used to fence in college." He paused his left hand on the piano to make a few Zorro moves. "I got your back."

She giggled and drew her hand back again, leaving Hector to play by himself. The wooziness was lifting with the laughter. Or was it the music? The ghosts in the speakeasy next door, playing their tunes. Next to the music stand sat the black enamel box with its delicate gold trim, the lid still open. She wound her fingers around his, where they lay at her waist.

"You never let me say it back," she said.

"What's that?"

"On the phone. You never gave me the chance to say it back."

"Ah." He chuckled. "Was that evil of me?"

"No. It was evil of me not to call you right back and make you hear it."

"Didn't need to hear it, Gilbert. I just needed to know that you heard it."

Ella stared at the fingers of Hector's left hand, still moving nimbly around the keyboard. Her head was full of his woolen smell, of the sound of his piano. "Remember how we sat right here a week ago?" she said. "You poured me a drink and sat me down with you, because I was so nervous."

"I admit, that was some case of nerves. I was so afraid you'd back out."

"I hadn't slept with anyone but Patrick in five years. I felt like such a slut."

"But you came around."

"It was the music," she said. "The music reminded me I was home. That it was okay to be a slut with you. And you were amazing. You were so patient."

He laughed again. "Mind over matter, Gilbert. If you knew how horny I was right then, you'd have run screaming."

"I always knew you were a perv, deep down."

"Yeah, I figured the same about you."

It was strange, how quickly the dizziness dissolved from her head. The music from downstairs or the laughter or the buzz along her spine, who knew? Maybe the pills or the water. She was not exactly herself, but she could glimpse Ella. Could just about touch her.

"Aunt Viv used to get morning sickness," she said.

"Did she? How do you know?"

"She came to visit at the hospital this morning. Pulled up a chair next to the bed, when the others weren't looking, and gave me a list of things that made her better. Some of them were pretty interesting."

"Oh? Like what?"

She turned her head and whispered in his ear.

Hector's hand paused on the keys, midnote. In the absence of the piano, the other instruments faded almost to nothing. But not quite. The clarinet remained, just barely, like a fine, reedy thread winding them together.

"Wow," Hector said, not moving. "That sounds like a pretty unconventional treatment, to me."

"She's a pretty unconventional aunt. But she says it works, every time."

Hector lifted his hand from the piano keys and gently closed the keyboard.

"Whatever it takes," he said.

# Acknowledgments

When I first set out to write a series set around Prohibition (beginning with The Wicked City in 2016) I didn't quite realize how challenging a task it would prove, since these books, about which I feel so passionately, would have to fit around the yearly publication of my stand-alone novels. Many thanks to my publisher, William Morrow, and especially my editor, Rachel Kahan, for standing by Gin Kelly and her unique voice as she continues through the tumultuous twenties, when our modern world was taking shape. My gratitude is also due to the wonderful team of editorial assistants, copyeditors, and marketing and publicity professionals, who turn my words into books and bring them to readers around the world.

I am forever indebted to my formidable literary agent, Alexandra Machinist at ICM, who advocates so tirelessly for my books, and to her assistant, Ruth Landry, who keeps everything (including your author) in perfect order.

To my family, who give me such love and support, my thanks are unending.

And to you, my readers, who kept asking when Gin's story would continue—and who demanded to know about "that redhead" who turned up in the epilogue of Cocoa Beach—I want you to know that your support means the world to me.

# HARPER LUXE

## THE NEW LUXURY IN READING

We hope you enjoyed reading
our new, comfortable print size and found it
an experience you would like to repeat.

**Well – you're in luck!**

HarperLuxe offers the finest in fiction and
nonfiction books in this same larger print size and
paperback format. Light and easy to read, HarperLuxe
paperbacks are for book lovers who want to see
what they are reading without the strain.

For a full listing of titles and
new releases to come, please visit our website:
**www.HarperLuxe.com**